Dear Reader,

Looking back over the years, I find it hard to realise that twenty-six of them have gone by since I wrote my first book—*Sister Peters in Amsterdam*. It wasn't until I started writing about her that I found that once I had started writing, nothing was going to make me stop—and at that time I had no intention of sending it to a publisher. It was my daughter who urged me to try my luck.

I shall never forget the thrill of having my first book accepted. A thrill I still get each time a new story is accepted. Writing to me is such a pleasure, and seeing a story unfolding on my old typewriter is like watching a film and wondering how it will end. Happily of course.

To have so many of my books re-published is such a delightful thing to happen and I can only hope that those who read them will share my pleasure in seeing them on the bookshelves again...and enjoy reading them.

Back by Popular Demand

A collector's edition of favourite titles from one of the world's best-loved romance authors. Mills & Boon® are proud to bring back these sought after titles and present them as one cherished collection.

BETTY NEELS: COLLECTOR'S EDITION

101 A SUITABLE MATCH
102 THE MOST MARVELLOUS SUMMER
103 WEDDING BELLS FOR BEATRICE
104 DEAREST MARY JANE
105 ONLY BY CHANCE
106 DEAREST LOVE
107 THE BACHELOR'S WEDDING
108 FATE TAKES A HAND
109 THE RIGHT KIND OF GIRL
110 MARRYING MARY
111 A CHRISTMAS WISH
112 THE MISTLETOE KISS
113 A WINTER LOVE STORY
114 THE DAUGHTER OF THE MANOR
115 LOVE CAN WAIT
116 A KISS FOR JULIE
117 THE FORTUNES OF FRANCESCA
118 AN IDEAL WIFE
119 NANNY BY CHANCE
120 THE VICAR'S DAUGHTER

DEAREST LOVE

BY
BETTY NEELS

MILLS & BOON®

DID YOU PURCHASE THIS BOOK WITHOUT A COVER?
If you did, you should be aware it is **stolen property** as it was reported *unsold and destroyed* by a retailer. Neither the author nor the publisher has received any payment for this book.

All the characters in this book have no existence outside the imagination of the author, and have no relation whatsoever to anyone bearing the same name or names. They are not even distantly inspired by any individual known or unknown to the author, and all the incidents are pure invention.

All Rights Reserved including the right of reproduction in whole or in part in any form. This edition is published by arrangement with Harlequin Enterprises II B.V. The text of this publication or any part thereof may not be reproduced or transmitted in any form or by any means, electronic or mechanical, including photocopying, recording, storage in an information retrieval system, or otherwise, without the written permission of the publisher.

This book is sold subject to the condition that it shall not, by way of trade or otherwise, be lent, resold, hired out or otherwise circulated without the prior consent of the publisher in any form of binding or cover other than that in which it is published and without a similar condition including this condition being imposed on the subsequent purchaser.

MILLS & BOON and MILLS & BOON with the Rose Device are registered trademarks of the publisher.

First published in Great Britain 1995 by Mills & Boon Limited,
This edition 2000
Harlequin Mills & Boon Limited,
Eton House, 18-24 Paradise Road, Richmond, Surrey TW9 1SR

© Betty Neels 1995

ISBN 0 263 82453 5

73-0900

Printed and bound in Spain
by Litografia Rosés S.A., Barcelona

CHAPTER ONE

DEAR Sir,

With reference to your advertisement in this week's *Lady* magazine, I wish to apply for the post of Caretaker/Housekeeper.

I am twenty-seven years of age, single with no dependants, and have several years' experience in household management including washing, ironing, cleaning and cooking. I am a cordon bleu cook. I have a working knowledge of minor electrical and plumbing faults. I am able to take messages and answer the telephone.

I would wish to bring my cat with me.

Yours faithfully,

Arabella Lorimer

IT WAS the last letter to be read by the elderly man sitting at his desk in his consulting-room, a large apartment on the ground floor of a Regency house, one of a terrace, in Wigmore Street, London. He read it for a second time, gave a rumble of laughter, and added it to the pile before him. There were twelve applicants in all and Arabella Lorimer was the only one to enclose references—the only one to write legibly, too, neatly setting down all the relevant facts. It was a pity that she wasn't a man…

He began to read the letters again and was interrupted halfway through by the entry of his partner. Dr Titus Tavener came unhurriedly into the room, a very tall man with broad shoulders and a massive person. He was handsome with a high-bridged nose, a firm mouth and rather cold blue eyes. His hair, once fair, was pepper and salt, despite which he looked younger than his forty years.

Dr James Marshall, short and stout and almost bald, greeted him with pleasure. 'Just the man I want. The applications for the caretaker's post—I have them here; I've spent the last hour reading them. I've decided which one I shall accept. Do read them, Titus, and give me your opinion. Not that it will make any difference to my choice.' He chortled as Dr Tavener sat himself down and picked up the little pile of letters. He read them through, one after the other, and then gathered them neatly together.

'There are one or two possibles: the ex-bus

driver—although he admits to asthma attacks—then this Mrs Butler.' He glanced at the letter in his hand. 'But is she quite the type to open the door? Of course the joker in the pack is Miss Arabella Lorimer and her cat. Most unsuitable.'

'Why?'

'Obviously a maiden lady down on her luck. I don't think I believe her skills are quite what she claims them to be. I'd hesitate to leave a stopped-up drainpipe or a blown fuse to her ladylike hands.'

His partner laughed. 'Titus, I can only hope that one day before it's too late you will meet a woman who will turn you sides to middle and then tramp all over you.'

Dr Tavener smiled. 'Unlikely. Perhaps I have been rather hard on the lady. There is always the possibility that she is an Amazon with a tool-kit.'

'Well, you will soon know. I've decided that she might do.'

Dr Tavener got up and strolled to the window and stood looking out on to the quiet street. 'And why not? Mrs Lane will be glad to leave. Her arthritis isn't getting any better and she's probably longing to go and live with her daughter. She'll take her furniture with her, I suppose? Do we furnish the place?'

'It depends—Miss Lorimer may have her own stuff.' Dr Marshall pushed back his chair. 'We've a busy day tomorrow; I'll see if your Amazon can come for an interview at five o'clock. Will you be back by then?'

'Unlikely—the clinic is overbooked as it is. In any case, I'm dining out.' He turned to look at his partner. 'I dare say you've made a good choice, James.' He strolled to the door. 'I've some paperwork to deal with. Shall I send Miss Baird home? You're going yourself? I shall be here for another hour yet—see you in the morning.'

He went to his own consulting-room, going through the elegant waiting-room with a smile and a nod for their shared receptionist Miss Baird, before going down the passage, past the stairs to the basement and his separate suite. This comprised a small waiting-room, a treatment-room where his nurse worked and his own room facing the garden at the back of the house. A small, narrow garden but well-tended and bright with early autumn flowers. He gave it a brief look before drawing the first of the patients' notes waiting for his attention towards him.

Dr Marshall read Miss Arabella Lorimer's letter once more and rang for Miss Baird. 'Send a note by special messenger, will you? To this address. Tell the lady to come here at five o'clock tomorrow afternoon. A pity she hasn't a telephone.' He got up and switched off his desk light. 'I'm going home, Miss Baird. Dr Tavener will be working for some time yet, but check that he's still here before you leave.' He nodded and smiled at her. 'Go as soon as you've got that message seen to.'

He went home himself then, to his wife and family, and much later Dr Tavener got into his Rolls-Royce and drove himself home to his charming house overlooking the canal in Little Venice.

Arabella read Dr Marshall's somewhat arbitrary note sitting in the kitchen. It was a small, damp room, overlooking a weary-looking patch of grass and some broken fencing, but she preferred it to the front room where her landlady sat of a Sunday afternoon. It housed the lady's prized possessions and Arabella hadn't been invited in there because of her cat Percy, who would ruin the furniture. She hadn't minded; she had been grateful that Billy Westlake, the village postman, had persuaded his aunt, Miss Pimm, to take her in for a few days while she found a job and somewhere to live.

It hadn't been easy leaving Colpin-cum-Witham, but it had been necessary. Her parents had died together in a car accident and only then had she discovered that her home wasn't to be hers any longer; it had been mortgaged to the hilt and she had to leave. There was almost no money. She sold all but the basic furniture that she might need and, since there was no hope of working in or near the village and distant aunts and uncles, while full of good advice, made no offer to help her, she took herself and

Percy to London. She had no wish to live there but, as the postman had said, it was a vast city and somewhere there must be work. She had soon realised that the only work she was capable of was domestic. She had no skills other than cordon bleu cooking and, since she had never needed to work in any capacity, she had no experience—something which employers demanded.

Now she read the brief letter again; she had applied almost in desperation, anxious to get away from Miss Pimm's scarcely veiled impatience to get rid of her and Percy. She had agreed to take them in for a few days but it was already a week and, as she had said to Arabella, she was glad of the money but she was one who kept herself to herself and didn't fancy strangers in her home.

Arabella sat quietly, not allowing herself to be too hopeful but all the same allowing herself to picture the basement room which went with the job. She would furnish it with her own bits and pieces and with any luck there would be some kind of a garden behind the house where Percy could take the air. She went up to her little bedroom with Percy at her heels and inspected her small stock of clothes. To be suitably dressed was important.

She arrived at Wigmore Street with two minutes to spare—the clocks were striking the hour as Miss Baird ushered her into Dr Marshall's consulting-room. He was sitting behind his desk as she went in and put down his pen to peer at her over his glasses. Just for a moment he was silent, then he said, 'Miss Lorimer? Please sit down. I must confess I was expecting someone more—more robust…'

Arabella seated herself without fuss—a small, nicely plump girl with mousy hair pinned on top of her head, an ordinary face and a pair of large grey eyes, thickly fringed. Anyone less like a caretaker it would be hard to find, reflected Dr Marshall with an inward chuckle, and just wait until Titus saw her.

He said pleasantly, 'I read your letter with interest, Miss Lorimer. Will you tell me about your last job?'

'I haven't had one. I've always lived at home—my mother was delicate and my father was away a good deal; he had his own business. I always did the housekeeping and dealt with minor repairs around the house.'

He nodded. 'Why do you want this job?'

She was sitting very quietly—no fidgeting, he noticed thankfully.

'My parents were killed recently in a car accident and now my home is no longer mine. We lived at Colpin-cum-Witham in southern Wiltshire; there is no work there for someone with no qualifications.' She paused. 'I need somewhere to live and domestic work seems to be the answer. I have applied for several jobs but they won't allow me to have Percy.'

'Percy?'

'My cat.'

'Well, I see no objection to a cat as long as he stays in your room—he can have the use of the garden, of course. But do you suppose that you are up to the work? You are expected to clean these rooms—mine, the reception and waiting-room, the passage and the stairs, my partner's rooms—and polish all the furniture and brass, and the front door, then answer the bell during our working hours, empty the bins, lock up and unlock in the mornings… Are you of a nervous disposition?'

'No, I don't think so.'

'Good. Oh, and if there is no one about you will answer the telephone, run errands and take messages.' He gave her a shrewd glance. 'A bit too much for you, eh?'

'Certainly not, Dr Marshall. I dare say I should call you sir? I would be glad to come and work for you.'

'Shall we give it a month's trial? Mrs Lane who is retiring should be in her room now. If you will go with Miss Baird she will introduce you. Come back here, if you please, so that we can make final arrangements.'

The basement wasn't quite what Arabella had imagined but it had possibilities. It was a large room; its front windows gave a view of passing feet and were heavily barred but the windows at the other end of the room, although small, could be opened. There was a door loaded down with bolts and locks and chains beside them, leading out to a small paved area with the garden beyond. At one side there was a door opening into a narrow passage with a staircase leading to the floor above and ending in another heavy door and, beside the staircase, a very small kitchen and an even smaller shower-room. Mrs Lane trotted ahead of her, pointing out the amenities. 'Of course I shall 'ave ter take me things with me, ducks—going up ter me daughter, yer see; she's got a room for me.'

'I have some furniture, Mrs Lane,' said Arabella politely. 'I only hope to be able to make it as cosy as you have done.'

Mrs Lane preened. 'Well, I've me pride, love. A bit small and young, aint yer?'

'Well, I'm very strong and used to housework. When did you want to leave, Mrs Lane?'

'Just as soon as yer can get 'ere. Bin 'appy 'ere, I 'ave, but I'm getting on a bit—the stairs is a bit much. 'Is nibs 'as always 'ad a girl come in ter answer the door, which save me feet.' She chuckled. ''E won't need 'er now!'

Back with Dr Marshall, Arabella, bidden to sit, sat.

'Well, want to come here and work?'

'Yes, I do and I will do my best to satisfy you, sir.'

'Good. Fix up dates and so on with Mrs Lane and let me know when you're going to come.' He added sharply, 'There must be no gap between Mrs Lane going and you coming, understand.'

Outside in the street she went looking for a telephone box to ring the warehouse in Sherborne and arrange for her furniture to be brought to London. It was a matter of urgency and for once good fortune was on her side. There was a load leaving for London in three days' time and her few things could be sent with it and at a much smaller cost than she had expected. She went back to Mrs Lane, going down the few steps to the narrow door by the barred window and explaining carefully, 'If I might come here some time during the morning and you leave in the afternoon, could we manage to change over without upsetting your routine here?'

'Don't see why not, ducks. Me son-in-law's coming with a van so I'll clear off as soon as yer 'ere.'

'Then I'll let Dr Marshall know.'

'Do that. I'll 'ave ter see 'im for me wages—I'll tell 'im likewise.'

Back at Miss Pimm's, Arabella told her that she would be leaving in three days and ate her supper—fish and chips from the shop on the corner—and went to bed, explaining to Percy as she undressed that he would soon have a home of his own again. He was a docile cat but he hadn't been happy at Miss Pimm's; it was a far cry from the roomy house and garden that he had always lived in. Now he curled up on the end of her narrow bed and went to sleep, instinct telling him that better times were in store.

Dr Marshall sat at his desk for some time doing nothing after Arabella had gone. Presently he gave a rich chuckle and when Miss Baird came in he asked her, 'Well, what do you think of our new caretaker?'

Miss Baird gave him a thoughtful look. 'A very nice young lady, sir. I only hope she's up to all that hard housework.'

'She assures me that she is a most capable worker. She will start in three days' time and I must be sure and be here when Dr Tavener sees her for the first time.'

It wasn't until the next morning, discussing a difficult case with his partner, that Dr Marshall had the chance to mention that he had engaged a new caretaker. 'She will start in two days' time—with her cat.'

Dr Tavener laughed. 'So she turned out to be suitable for the job? Let us hope that she is quicker at answering the doorbell and emptying the wastepaper baskets.'

'Oh, I imagine she will be.' Dr Marshall added slyly, 'After all, she is young.'

'As long as she does her work properly.' Dr Tavener was already engrossed in the notes in his hand and spoke without interest.

* * *

Despite misgivings that her furniture wouldn't arrive, that Percy would disappear at the last minute or that Dr Marshall would have second thoughts about employing her, Arabella moved herself, her cat and her few possessions into the basement of Wigmore Street without mishap. True, empty it looked pretty grim and rather dirty, but once the floor had been cleaned and the windows washed, the cobwebs removed from the darker corners, she could see possibilities. With the help of the removal men she put her bed in a corner of the room, put a small table and chair under the back window and stacked everything else tidily against a wall. Her duties were to commence in the morning and she conned Mrs Lane's laboriously written list of duties before she made up the bed, settled Percy in his cardboard box and rolled up her sleeves.

There was plenty of hot water and Mrs Lane had left a variety of mops and brushes in the cupboard by the stairs. Arabella set to with a will; this was to be her home—hers and Percy's—and she intended to make it as comfortable as possible. Cleanliness came before comfort. She scrubbed and swept and polished and by evening was satisfied with her work.

She cooked her supper on the newly cleaned stove—beans on toast and an egg—gave Percy his meal and sat at the table, well pleased with her efforts, while she drank her tea and then made a list of the things she still needed. It was not a long list but she would have to buy a little at a time each pay-day. Her rather muddled calculations showed her that it would be Christmas before she had all she wanted but that didn't worry her—after the last awful months this was all that she could wish for.

She washed her dishes and opened the back door with Percy tucked under one arm. The garden was surrounded by a high brick wall and ringed by flowerbeds but there was a good-sized strip of lawn as well. She set Percy down and watched him explore, at first with caution and then with pleasure. After Miss Pimm's little yard this was bliss...

She perched on a small rustic seat, tired now but happy. It had been a fine day but it was getting chilly now and dusk had dimmed the colourful garden. She scooped up Percy and went back indoors and then, mindful of Mrs Lane's instructions, went up the stairs and inspected each room in turn, making sure that the windows were closed and locked, the doors bolted and all the lights turned out. The two floors above her were lived in, Mrs Lane had told her, by a neurologist and his wife. They had a side entrance, a small door at the front of the house, and although he was retired he still saw the occasional patient. 'But nothing ter do with us,' Mrs Lane had said. 'Yer won't ever see them.'

All the same it was nice to think that the house wasn't quite empty. She took her time in locking up, looking at everything so that she would know where things were in the morning and, being of a practical turn of mind, she searched until she found the stop-cock, the fire-extinguisher and the gas and electricity meters. She also searched for and eventually found a box containing such useful things as a hammer, nails, spare light-bulbs, a wrench and adhesive tape. They were hidden away in a small dark cupboard and she felt sure that no one had been near it for a very long time. She put everything back carefully and reminded herself to ask for a plunger. Blocked sinks could be a nuisance, especially where people would be constantly washing their hands. Satisfied at last, she went back to her room, had a shower and got into bed, and Percy, uninvited but very welcome, climbed on too and settled on her feet.

She was up early, tidied the room and made the bed, fed Percy and escorted him into the garden, ate a sketchy breakfast and took herself off upstairs, wearing her new nylon overall.

There was everything she might need—a vacuum cleaner, polish and dusters. She emptied the waste-paper baskets, set the chairs to rights, arranged the magazines just so, polished the front door-knocker and opened the windows. It looked very nice when she had finished but a little austere. She went back downstairs and out into the garden; she cut Michaelmas daisies, dahlias and one or two late roses. She bore them back, found three vases, arranged the flowers in them and put one in each of the consulting-rooms and the last one in the waiting-room. They made all the difference, she considered, and realised that she had overlooked the second waiting-room. Back in the garden, she cut asters this time, arranged them in a deep bowl and put them on the table flanked by the magazines.

She hadn't met Dr Marshall's partner; she hoped he was as nice as that gentleman.

She went back to the basement then, tidied herself, made sure that her hair was neat and when the doorbell rang went to answer it. It was Dr Marshall's nurse, who had introduced herself as Joyce Pierce and then exclaimed, 'You're the new caretaker? Well, I must say you're a bit of a surprise. Do you think you'll like it?'

'Well, yes. I can live here, you see, and I don't mind housework.'

She was shutting the door when the second nurse arrived, small and dark and pretty. 'The caretaker?' she asked and raised her eyebrows. 'Whatever's come over Dr Marshall?' She nodded at Arabella. 'I'm Madge Simmons. I work for Dr Tavener.' She spoke rather frostily. 'Come on, Joyce, we've time for a cup of tea.'

The first patient wouldn't arrive until nine o'clock so Arabella sped downstairs. There was still a tea-chest of bed-linen, table-linen and curtains to unpack. As soon as she could she would get some net and hang it in the front window, shutting off all those feet…

At a quarter to nine she went upstairs again. There was no sign of the two nurses, although she could hear voices, and she stood uncertainly in the hall—to turn and face the door as it was opened. The man who entered seemed to her to be enormous. The partner, she thought, eyeing his elegance and his good looks and was very startled when he observed, 'Good lord, the caretaker!' and laughed.

The laugh annoyed her. She wished him good morning in a small frosty voice and went down to her room, closing the door very quietly behind her. 'He's what one would call a magnificent figure of a man,' she told Percy, 'and also a very rude one!'

The front doorbell rang then, and she went upstairs to admit the first patient. For the next hour or so she trotted up and down the stairs a dozen times until finally she shut the door on the last patient and Miss Baird came to tell her that Dr Marshall wanted to see her.

He eyed her over his specs. 'Morning, Miss Lorimer. Where did you get the flowers?'

The question surprised her. 'From the garden—only the ones at the back of the beds…'

'Nice idea. Finding your feet?'

'Yes, thank you, sir.'

'Miss Baird will tell you what to do when we've gone. We'll be back this afternoon, one or other of us, but not until three o'clock. You're free once you've tidied up and had your lunch, but be back here by quarter to. We sometimes work in the evening, but not often. Did Mrs Lane tell you where the nearest shops were?'

'No, but I can find them.'

He nodded and looked up as the door opened and Dr Tavener came in. 'Ah, here is my partner, Dr Tavener. This is our new caretaker.'

'We have already met,' said Arabella in a chilly voice. 'If that is all, sir?'

'Not quite all,' said Dr Tavener. 'I owe you an apology, Miss...'

'Lorimer, sir.'

'Miss Lorimer. I was most discourteous but I can assure you that my laughter was not at you as a person.'

'It was of no consequence, sir.' She gave him a fierce look from her lovely eyes which belied the sober reply and looked at Dr Marshall.

'Yes. Yes, go along, Miss Lorimer. If you need anything, don't hesitate to ask.'

A practical girl, Arabella paused at the door. 'I should like a plunger, sir.' She saw that he was puzzled. 'It is used for unstopping sinks and drains. They're not expensive.'

Not a muscle of Dr Tavener's handsome features moved; he asked gravely, 'Have we a blocked sink, Miss Lorimer?'

'No, but it's something which usually happens at an awkward time—it would be nice to have one handy.'

Dr Marshall spoke. 'Yes, yes, of course. Very wise. We have always called in a plumber, I believe.'

'It isn't always necessary,' she told him kindly.

'Ask Miss Baird to deal with it as you go, will you?'

Dr Tavener closed the door behind her and sat down. 'A paragon,' he observed mildly. 'With a plunger too! Do we know anything about her, James?'

'She comes from a place called Colpin-cum-Witham in Wiltshire. Parents killed in a car crash and—for some reason not specified—she had to leave her home. Presumably no money. Excellent references from the local parson and doctor. She's on a month's trial.' He smiled. 'Have you got flowers in your room too?'

'Yes, indeed.' He added, 'Don't let us forget that new brooms sweep clean.'

'You don't like her?'

'My dear James, I don't know her and it is most unlikely that I shall see enough of her to form an opinion.' He got up and went to look out of the window. 'I thought I'd drive up to Leeds—the consultation isn't until the afternoon. I'll go on to Birmingham from there and come back on the following day. Miss Baird has fixed my appointments so that I have a couple of days free.'

Dr Marshall nodded. 'That's fine. I'm not too keen on going to that seminar in Oslo. Will you go?'

'Certainly. It's two weeks ahead, isn't it? If I fly over it will only take three days.' He glanced at his watch. 'I'd better do some work; I've that article to finish for the *Lancet*.' He went to the door. 'I've two patients for this evening, by the way.'

As for Arabella, she went back to her room, had lunch, fed Percy and, after a cautious look round, went into the garden with him, unaware that Dr Tavener was at his desk at the window. He watched her idly, admired Percy's handsome grey fur, and then forgot her.

Miss Baird had been very helpful. There were, she had told Arabella, one or two small shops not five minutes' walk away down a small side-street. Arabella put on her jacket and, armed with a shopping-basket, set off to discover them. They were tucked away from the quiet prosperous streets with their large houses—a newsagents, a greengrocer and a small general store. Sufficient for her needs. She stocked up with enough food for a couple of days, bought herself a newspaper and then went back to Wigmore Street. On Saturday, she promised herself, she would spend her free afternoon shopping for some of the things on her list. She was to be paid each week, Miss Baird had told her and, although she should save for an uncertain future, there were some small comforts she would need. She would have all Sunday to work without interruption.

After that first day the week went quickly; by the end of it Arabella had found her feet. She saw little of the nurses and still less of Dr Marshall, and nothing at all of his partner. It was only when she went to Miss Baird to collect her wages that she overheard one of the nurses remark that Dr Tavener would be back on Monday. 'And a good thing too,' she had added, 'for his appointments book is full. He's away again in a couple of weeks for that seminar in Oslo.'

'He doesn't get much time for his love-life, does he?' laughed the other nurse.

Arabella, with her pay-packet a delightful weight in her pocket, even felt vague relief that he would be going away again. She had been careful to keep out of his way, although she wasn't sure why, and the last two days while he had been away she had felt much more comfortable. 'It's because he's so large,' she told Percy, and fell to counting the contents of her pay-packet.

While her parents had been alive she had lived a comfortable enough life. There had always seemed to be money; she had never been spoilt but she had never gone without anything she had needed or asked for. Now she held in her hand what was, for her, quite a large sum of money and she must plan to spend it carefully. New clothes were for the moment out of the question. True, those she had were of good quality and although her wardrobe was small it was more than adequate for her needs. She got paper and pen and checked her list…

It took her until one o'clock to clear up after the Saturday morning appointments and then there was the closing and the locking up to do, the answering machine to set, the few cups and saucers to wash and dry, the gas and electricity to check. She ate a hasty lunch, saw to Percy's needs then changed into her brown jersey skirt and the checked blouson jacket which went with it, stuck her rather tired feet into the Italian loafers she had bought with her mother in the happy times she tried not to remember too often, and, with her shoulder-bag swinging, caught a bus to Tottenham Court Road.

The tea-chests had yielded several treasures: curtains which could be cut to fit the basement windows and make cushion covers, odds and ends of china and kitchenware, a clock—she remembered it from the kitchen; a small radio—still working; some books and, right at the bottom, a small thin mat which would look nice before the gas fire.

She needed to buy needles and sewing cottons, net curtains, scissors and more towels, shampoo and some soap and, having purchased these, she poked around the cheaper shops until she found what she wanted: a roll of thin matting for the floor—it would be awkward to carry but it would be worth the effort. So, for that matter, would the tin of paint in a pleasing shade of pale apricot. She added a brush and, laden down with her awkward shopping, took a bus back to Wigmore Street.

Back in the basement again, she changed into an elderly skirt and jumper and went into the garden with Percy. It was dusk already and there were no lights on in the rooms above. The house seemed very silent and empty and there was a chilly wind. Percy disliked wind; he hurried back indoors and she locked and bolted the door before getting her supper and feeding him. Her meal over, she washed up and went upstairs to check carefully that everything was just as it should be before going back to lay the matting.

It certainly made a difference to the dim little room; the matting almost covered the mud-coloured flooring, and when she had spread an old-fashioned chenille tablecloth over the round table its cheerful crimson brightened the place further. It had been at the bottom of one of the tea-chests, wrapped around some of the china, and the curtains were of the same crimson. It was too late to start them that evening but she could at least sew the net curtains she had bought. It was bedtime by the time she had done that, run a wire through their tops, banged in some small nails and hung them across the bars of the windows. She went to bed then, pleased with her efforts.

She woke in the middle of the night, for the moment forgetful of where she was and then, suddenly overcome with grief and loneliness, cried herself to sleep again. She woke in the morning to find Percy sitting on her chest, peering down at her face—part of her old life—and she at once sat up in bed, dismissing self-pity. The walls had to be painted and if there was time she would begin on the curtains...

'We have a home,' she told Percy as she dressed, 'and money in our pockets and work to keep us busy. It's a lovely morning; we'll go into the garden.'

There was a faint chill in the air and there was a Sunday morning quiet. She thought of all the things she would do, the places she would visit in the coming weeks, and feeling quite cheerful got their breakfasts.

She had covered the drab, discoloured wallpaper by the late afternoon and the room looked quite different. The pale apricot gave the place light and warmth and she ate her combined tea and supper in great content.

The smell was rather overpowering; she opened the door to the garden despite the chilly evening and cut up the curtains ready to sew, fired with enthusiasm. As she wielded the scissors she planned what to buy with her next pay-packet: a bedspread, a table-lamp, a picture or two—the list was neverending!

CHAPTER TWO

DR TAVERNER, arriving the next morning, saw the net curtains and grinned. Unlike Mrs Lane, the new caretaker disliked the view from her window. Mrs Lane, on the other hand, had once told him that she found the sight of passing feet very soothing.

There were fresh flowers on his desk and there wasn't a speck of dust to be seen; the wastepaper basket was empty and the elegant gas fire had been lighted. He sat down to study the notes of his first patient and hoped that such a satisfactory state of affairs would continue. She was quite unsuitable, of course; either she would find the work too much for her or she would find something more suitable.

Arabella, fortunately unaware of these conjectures, went about her duties with brisk efficiency. Miss Baird had wished her a cheerful good morning when she had arrived, even the two nurses had smiled as she opened the door to them, and after that for some time she was opening and closing the door for patients, ignored for the most part—a small, rather colourless creature, not worth a second glance.

She had no need to go to the shops at lunchtime—the milkman had left milk and she had everything she needed for making bread. She made the dough, kneaded it and set it to rise before the gas fire while she started on the curtains. She was as handy with her needle as she was with her cooking and she had them ready by the time she had to go back upstairs to let in the first of the afternoon patients. She would hang them as soon as everyone had gone later on.

By half-past five the place was quiet. The last patient had been seen on his way, the nurses followed soon afterwards and lastly Miss Baird. Dr Marshall had already gone and she supposed that Dr Tavener had gone too. It would take her an hour to tidy up and make everything secure for the night but she would hang the curtains first…

They looked nice. Cut from the crimson curtains which had hung in the dining-room of her old home they were of heavy dull brocade, lined too, so that she had had very little sewing to do. She admired them drawn across the hated bars, and went upstairs to begin the business of clearing up.

She had a plastic bag with her and emptied the wastepaper baskets first—a job Miss Baird had impressed upon her as never to be forgotten. She went around putting things in their proper places, shaking the cushions in the waiting-room chairs, turning off lights, picking up magazines and putting them back on the table. She went along to Dr Tavener's rooms presently and was surprised to find the light on in his consulting-room.

He was at his desk and didn't look up. 'Be good enough to come back later, Miss Lorimer. I shall be here for another hour.'

She went away without saying anything and went back to the basement and began to get her supper. Percy, comfortably full, sat before the fire and the bread was in the oven. She whipped up a cheese soufflé, set the table with a cloth and put a small vase of flowers she had taken from the garden in its centre. She had been allowed to take essential things when she left her home—knives and spoons and forks and a plate or two. She had taken the silver and her mother's Coalport china plates and cups and saucers; she had taken the silver pepperpot and salt cellar too, and a valuable teapot—Worcester. She would have liked to have taken the silver one but she hadn't quite dared—though she had taken the Waterford crystal jug and two wine-glasses.

She ate her soufflé presently, bit into an apple and made coffee before taking the bread from the oven. By then almost two hours had elapsed. She put her overall on once again and went upstairs to meet Dr Tavener as he left his rooms.

He stopped short when he saw her. 'Something smells delicious…'

'I have been making bread,' said Arabella, cool and polite and wishing that he would hurry up and go so that she could get her work done.

'Have you, indeed? And do I detect the smell of

paint? Oh, do not look alarmed. It is very faint; I doubt if anyone noticed it.' He stared down at her. 'You are not afraid to be here alone?'

'No, sir.'

He wished her goodnight then, and she closed the door after him, bolting it and locking it securely. He paused on the pavement and looked down at the basement window. She had drawn the curtains and there was only a faint line of light showing. He frowned; he had no interest in the girl but living in that poky basement didn't seem right... He shrugged his shoulders; after all, she had chosen the job.

A week went by and Arabella had settled into a routine which ensured that she was seldom seen during working hours. Tidying Miss Baird's desk one evening, she had seen the list of patients for the following day, which gave her a good idea as to the times of their arrival. Now she checked each evening's list, for not all the patients came early in the day—once or twice there was no one until after ten o'clock, which gave her time to sweep and dust her own room and have a cup of coffee in peace. Nicely organised, she found life bearable if not exciting and, now that her room was very nearly as she wished it, she planned to spend part of her Sundays in the London parks. She missed the country. Indeed, come what may, she had promised herself that one day she would leave London but first she had to save some money before finding a job near her old home.

'We will go back,' she assured Percy, 'I promise you. Only we must stay here for a while—a year, perhaps two—just until we have enough money to feel safe.'

Only Dr Marshall came in on the Monday morning. Dr Tavener would be in directly after lunch, Miss Baird told her. He was taking a clinic at one of the nearby hospitals that morning. 'He's got a lot of patients too,' she warned Arabella. 'He probably won't be finished until early evening—he doesn't mind if he works late; he's not married and hasn't any ties.' She added kindly, 'If you want to run round to the shops I'll see to the phone and the door.'

'Thank you. If I could just get some vegetables? I can be back in fifteen minutes.'

'Don't hurry. You do cook proper meals for yourself?'

'Oh, yes. I have plenty of time in the evening.'

It was a cheerless morning, not quite October and already chilly. Arabella nipped smartly to the row of little shops, chose onions and turnips and carrots with care, bought meat from the butcher next door and hurried back. A casserole would be easy, she could leave it to cook gently and it wouldn't spoil however late she might have her supper. A few dumplings, she reflected and a bouquet garni. It would do for the following day too.

She prepared it during the lunch hour, gave Percy

his share of the meat and tidied herself ready to open the door for the first of Dr Tavener's patients.

The last patient went just before six o'clock and Arabella, having already tidied Dr Marshall's rooms, started to close the windows and lock up. There was still no sign of Dr Tavener when she had done this so she went down to the basement, set the table for her supper and checked the casserole in the oven. It was almost ready; she turned off the gas and set the dish on top of the stove, lifted the lid and gently stirred the contents—they smelled delicious.

Dr Tavener, on the point of leaving, paused in the hall, his splendid nose flaring as he sniffed the air. He opened the door to the basement and sniffed again and then went down the stairs and knocked at the door.

There was silence for a moment before he was bidden to enter—to discover Arabella standing facing the door, looking uncertain.

Neither of them spoke for a moment. Arabella was surprised to see him—she hadn't known who it was and had secretly been a little frightened—and as for Dr Tavener, he stood looking around him before remarking, 'Dear me, you have been busy and to very good effect.' He glanced at the table, nicely laid with a white cloth, the silver, one of the Coalport plates, a Waterford glass and a small vase of flowers. Their new caretaker was, indeed, a little out of the common. 'I hope I didn't startle you; something smelled so delicious that I had to see what it was. Your supper?'

She nodded.

He said with amusement, 'Are you a cordon bleu cook as well as a plumber?'

'Yes.'

'Surely if that is the case you could have found a more congenial post?'

'No one would have Percy.'

Dr Tavener studied the cat sitting before the little fire staring at him. 'A handsome beast.' And then, since their conversation was making no progress at all, 'Goodnight, Miss Lorimer.' As he turned away he added, 'You will lock up?'

'I have been waiting to do so, sir.' Her voice was tart.

His smile dismissed that. 'As long as you carry out your duties, Miss Lorimer.'

He had gone then, as quietly as he had come.

'He isn't just rude,' Arabella told Percy. 'He's very rude!'

When she heard the front door close she put the casserole in the oven again and went upstairs to clear up his rooms, close the windows and turn the key in the door before the lengthy business of locking and bolting the front door. Only then did she go back to her delayed supper.

Sitting by the gas fire later, sewing at the cushion covers, she allowed her thoughts to dwell upon Dr

Tavener. He didn't like her, that was obvious, and yet he had come down to her room—something Dr Marshall would never think of doing. Perhaps she should have been more friendly, but were caretakers supposed to be friendly with their employers? She doubted that. He unsettled her. While her parents had been alive she had had friends, cheerful young men and women of her own age, but none of the young men had fallen in love with her, nor had she been particularly attracted to any of them. Dr Tavener wasn't like any of them. It wasn't only his good looks—perhaps it was because he was older. She gave up thinking about him and turned her attention to her work.

She had only brief glimpses of him for the rest of that week and beyond a terse greeting he didn't speak to her. On the other hand, Dr Marshall, while evincing no interest at all in her private life, was always friendly if they chanced to encounter each other.

Then Dr Tavener went to Oslo, his nurse took a holiday and Arabella found herself with less to do. True, she checked his rooms night and morning, but there was no need to Hoover and polish now he was away. There were fewer doorbells to answer too, so she had time to spare in which to make apple chutney from the windfalls dropping from the small old tree at the bottom of the garden. She had, of course, asked Dr Marshall first if she might have them and he had said yes, adding that he had had no idea that they could be used. So for several evenings there was a pleasant smell of cooking apples coming from the basement. She made bread too, and a batch of scones; and buns with currents—nicely iced; and a sponge cake, feather-light. The tiny old-fashioned pantry, its shelves empty for so long for Mrs Lane had only fancied food out of tins, began to fill nicely.

Dr Tavener was due back on the following day, Miss Baird told her. Not until the late afternoon, though, so there would be no patients for him. 'And I daresay he'll go straight home and come in the next morning.'

So Arabella gave his rooms a final dusting. There were still some Doris pinks in the garden; she arranged some in a glass vase and added some sprigs of lavender and some veronica. The room was cool so they would stay fresh overnight—she must remember to turn the central heating on in the morning and light the gas fire. She put everything ready for the nurse too, so that she could make herself a cup of tea when she arrived, then she went round checking the windows and the doors, and went downstairs again.

Dr Marshall had a great number of patients the next morning; she was kept busy answering the door and Dr Tavener's nurse, short-tempered for some reason, found fault with her because the central heating hadn't been turned on sooner. In the afternoon it began to rain—a steady downpour—so the patients left wet footprints over the parquet flooring and dropped their dripping umbrellas unheeding on to the two chairs which flanked the side-table. Arabella had taken a lot of trouble to clean them and polish them and now they were covered in damp spots. She would have liked to bang the door behind them as they left…

The house was quiet at last and she fetched her plastic bag, her dusters and polish, and lugged the Hoover from its place under the stairs. There had been no sign of Dr Tavener; he would have gone straight home as Miss Baird had suggested. Arabella bustled around, intent on getting back to her own room. Tea had been out of the question and she thought with pleasure of the supper she intended to cook—a Spanish omelette with a small salad. She had made soup yesterday, with bones and root vegetables, and she would have an apple or two and a handful of raisins. Bread and butter and a large pot of tea instead of coffee—what more could anyone want?

The weather had turned nasty, with a cold wind and heavy rain. It was a lonely sound beating on the windows; she wondered why it sounded so different from the rain on the windows of her home at Colpin-cum-Witham. There the wind used to sough through the trees—a sound she had loved. She had finished her tidying up when she remembered that the nurse had complained about the light in the waiting-room.

The bulb wasn't strong enough, she had been told, and another one must replace it. She fetched it and then went to haul the step-ladder up from the basement so that she might reach the elaborate shade hanging from the ceiling.

She was on the top step when she heard the front door being opened, and a moment later Dr Tavener came into the room. He was bareheaded and carried his case in his hand. He put it down, lifted her down from the steps, took the bulb from her hand and changed it with the one already in the socket. Only then did he get down and bid her good evening.

Arabella, taken by surprise, hadn't uttered a sound. Now she found her voice and uttered a stiff thank you.

He stood looking at her. 'It's a filthy night,' he observed. 'You wouldn't be kind and make me a cup of tea or coffee—whichever is easiest?'

She started for the little kitchenette leading from his rooms but he put out a hand. 'No, no. No need here—may I not come downstairs with you?'

She eyed him uncertainly. 'Well, if you want to,' she said matter-of-factly. 'I was going to make tea.'

She went down to the basement, very conscious of him just behind her. The room looked surprisingly cosy; she had left one of the little table-lamps lit and the gas fire was on. She went to turn it up and said rather shyly, 'Please sit down, the tea won't take long.'

He sat down in the small shabby armchair and Percy got on to his knees. 'Have you had your supper? Do I smell soup?'

'Are you hungry?' She warmed the teapot and spooned in the tea.

'Ravenous. My housekeeper doesn't expect me back until the morning.' He watched her as she made the tea. 'I could go out for a meal, I suppose. Would you come with me?'

She looked up in surprise. 'Well, thank you for asking me but I've supper all ready.' She paused to think. 'You can share it if you would like to, though I'm not sure if it's quite the thing. I mean, I'm the caretaker!'

He smiled and said easily, 'You are also a splendid cook, are you not?' He got up out of his chair. 'And I don't believe there is a law against caretakers asking a guest for a meal.'

'Well, of course, put like that it seems quite...' She paused, at a loss for a word.

'Quite,' said Dr Tavener. 'What comes after the soup?'

She laid another place at the table. 'Well, a Spanish omelette with a salad. I haven't a pudding, but there is bread and butter and cheese...'

'Home-made bread?' And when she nodded he said, 'I can think of nothing nicer. While you are cooking the omelette I shall go and get a bottle of wine. Five minutes?'

He had gone. She heard the door close behind him and the car start up. She broke three eggs into a bowl and then a fourth—he was a very large man.

The omelette was ready to cook when he got back, put a bottle on the table and asked if she had a corkscrew. It was a good wine—a red burgundy of a good vintage, its cost almost as much as half of Arabella's pay-packet. He opened it to let it breathe.

Arabella was ladling soup into the large old-fashioned soup plates which had belonged to her grandmother. Dr Tavener, sampling it, acknowledged that it was worthy of the Coalport china in which it was served.

He fetched the wine and poured it as she dished up the omelette and, warmed by its delicious fruitiness, Arabella forgot to be a caretaker and was once again a well brought-up young lady with a pleasant social life. Dr Tavener, leading her on with quiet cunning, discovered a good deal more about her than she realised. Not that he asked questions but merely put in a word here and there, egging her on gently.

They finished the omelette and sat talking over coffee and slices of bread and butter and a piece of cheese. If he found the meal a trifle out of the ordinary way of things he gave no sign. Bread and butter, he discovered, when the bread had been baked by his hostess, was exactly the right way to finish his supper. Being a giant of a man, he ate most of the loaf and a good deal of the butter. She would have to go to the shops the next day…

It was almost ten o'clock when he went, taking her with him so that she could lock up after him. He stood on the pavement, thinking of her polite good-night and listening to the bolts being shot home and the key turned in the lock. He had never worried about Mrs Lane being alone in the house for the simple reason that she frequently had had various members of her family spending a few days with her, but Arabella had no one. The idea of Arabella being alone at night nagged at him all the way to his home.

It was on the following Saturday afternoon that Arabella added another member to her household. She was returning from the shops, laden with a week's supply of basic food, taking shortcuts through the narrow streets which would bring her into Wigmore Street. It had been a dull, chilly day and bid fair to lapse into early dusk bringing a fine drizzle of rain. Head bowed against the damp wind, weighed down with her shopping, she turned down a short alleyway which would take her close to Dr Marshall's rooms.

She was almost at its end when a faint movement in the gutter caused her to stop. A puppy lay there, rolled up and moving to and fro, its yelps so faint that she could hardly hear them. She put down her plastic bags and bent to take a closer look. It was a pitiful sight, thin and very wet, and someone had tied its back legs together. Arabella let out a snort of rage and knelt down the better to deal with it. The cord was tight but roughly tied; it took only a moment to untie it and scoop up the small creature, pop him on top of her shopping and carry him back to her basement.

He was a very young puppy and, even if well fed and cared for, would have had no good looks. As it was he was a sorry sight, with tiny ribs showing through his dirty coat and sores on his flanks. Notwithstanding, he lay passive on the table while she gently examined him, and even waved a very long and rat-like tail. She dumped her shopping, fetched warm water and some old cloths, and cleaned him gently, wrapped him in an old curtain and set him before the gas fire where he lay too tired to move when Percy went to examine him in his turn.

'Bread and warm milk,' said Arabella who, living alone with only a cat for company, frequently uttered her thoughts out loud, and suited the action to the words. It was received thankfully and scoffed with pathetic speed so she gave him more warm milk with some vague idea about dehydration and then, aware of Percy's indignant stare, offered him his supper too, before taking off her jacket and putting away her shopping. She got her own tea presently, pausing frequently to look at the puppy. He was sleeping, uttering small yelps as he slept, and presently Percy stretched out beside him, with the air of someone doing a good deed, and curved himself round the small skinny creature.

'That's right, Percy,' encouraged Arabella. 'He could do with a good cuddle. He'll be a handsome dog if we look after him.'

He woke presently and she gave him some of Percy's food and took him into the dark garden, and when she went off to bed she lifted him on to its foot beside Percy. He looked better already. She woke in the night and found him still sleeping, but Percy had crept up the bed and was lying beside her.

It was then that she began to wonder what Dr Marshall was going to say when he discovered that she had a dog as well as a cat. Why should she tell him? The puppy was very young—his bark would be small and until he was much stronger he might not bark at all. Indeed, he would be no trouble for some time; he was far too weak to behave as a normal puppy would. Things settled to her satisfaction, she went back to sleep until Percy's nudges woke her once more.

Being Sunday, she had the place to herself and nothing could have been more convenient. The puppy, shivering with terror, was borne out into the garden again and then given his breakfast while Percy ate his, afterwards curling up before the fire and allowing the puppy to crouch beside him. Presently Percy stretched his length before the warmth and the puppy crept even closer and went to sleep.

He slept and ate all day and by the evening he cringed only occasionally, waving his ridiculous tail in an effort to show his gratitude.

'I shall keep you,' said Arabella. 'Percy likes you and so do I! And you're more than welcome.'

The puppy, unused to a kind voice, gave a very small squeaky bark, ate a second supper and went to sleep—this time with his ugly little head on Percy's portly stomach.

Monday came and with it a nasty nervous feeling on Arabella's part, but she went about her duties as usual and by the end of the day was lulled into a sense of security by the exemplary behaviour of the puppy who, doubtless because he was still very much under the weather, did nothing other than eat the food she offered him and sleep, keeping as close to a tolerant Percy as possible.

By the end of the week he had filled out considerably although he was still quite content to curl up and sleep. He went willingly enough into the garden before anyone was about and, although the dark evenings scared him, provided Percy was nearby he ventured on to the grass and even scampered around for a few minutes.

It was carelessness due to her overconfidence that was Arabella's undoing. On the Friday evening everyone left as usual and, after a quick reconnoitre upstairs to make sure that that really was the case, she went into the garden before she tidied the rooms. It was a fine clear evening and not quite dark and she took her torch and walked down the path while the animals pottered on the grass.

Dr Tavener, returning to fetch a forgotten paper, trod quietly through the empty rooms and, since there was still some light left, didn't bother to turn on his desk lamp. He knew where the paper was and he had picked it up and turned to go again when he glanced out of his window.

Arabella stood below, her torch shining on the animals.

'Well, I'm damned,' said Dr Tavener softly and watched her shepherd them indoors before going silently and very quickly back to the front door and then letting himself out into the street. He got into his car and drove himself home, laughing softly.

As for Arabella, blissfully unaware that she had been discovered, she gave her companions their suppers and went upstairs to clean and tidy up, then cooked her own meal before getting on with another cushion cover.

Saturday morning was busy. Dr Tavener, Miss Baird told her, had only two patients but he was going to the hospital and would probably not be back until after midday. 'So I'm afraid you won't be able to do your cleaning until he's gone again.'

Arabella, who turned the place upside-down on a

Saturday, changed the flowers and polished everything possible, said she didn't mind. Secretly she was annoyed. She would have to do her weekly shopping and she didn't like to go out and leave him in his rooms—supposing the puppy were to bark? The shops closed at five o'clock—surely he wouldn't stay as late as that?

It was a relief when he came back just before everyone else went home, shut himself in his room for a while and then prepared to leave. Arabella was polishing the chairs in the waiting-room since Hoovering might disturb him and she heard him coming along the passage.

She had expected him to go straight to the door and let himself out but instead he stopped in the doorway, so she turned round to wish him good afternoon and found him staring at her. Her heart sank; he looked severe—surely he hadn't discovered about the puppy?

It seemed that he had. 'Since when have we had a dog in the house, Miss Lorimer?' His voice was silky and she didn't much care for it.

She put down her duster and faced him. 'He isn't a dog—he's a very small puppy.'

'Indeed? And have you Dr Marshall's permission to keep him here?'

'No. How did you know?'

'I saw him—and you—the other evening in the

garden. I trust that he isn't rooting up the flower-beds.'

She was suddenly fierce. 'If you'd been thrown in a gutter with your legs tied together and left to die you'd know what heaven it is to sniff the flowers.'

His mouth twitched. 'And you found him and of course brought him back with you?'

'Well, of course—and I cannot believe that, however ill-natured you are, you would have left him lying there.'

'You are quite right; I wouldn't. Perhaps if you could bear with my ill nature, I might take a look at him? He's probably in rather poor shape.'

'Oh, would you?' She paused on her way to the door. 'But you won't take him away and send him to a dogs' home? He's so very small.'

'No, I won't do that.'

She went ahead of him down the stairs and opened the basement door. Percy, asleep on the end of the bed, opened an eye and dozed off again but the puppy tumbled on to the floor and trotted towards them, waving his ridiculous tail.

Dr Tavener bent and scooped him up and tucked him under an arm.

'Very small,' he observed, 'and badly used too.' He was gently examining the little beast. 'One or two nasty sores on his flank…' He felt the small legs. 'How long have you had him?'

'Since last Saturday. I thought he was going to die.'

'You have undoubtedly saved his life. He needs a vet, though.' He looked at Arabella and smiled—a quite different man from the austere doctor who strode in and out of his consulting-room with barely a glance if they should meet—and she blinked with surprise. 'If I return at about four o'clock would you bring him to a vet with me? He is a friend of mine and will know if there is anything the little chap needs.'

Arabella goggled at him. 'Me? Go to the vet with you?'

'I don't bite,' said Dr Tavener mildly.

She went pink. 'I beg your pardon. I was only surprised. It's very kind of you. Only, please don't come before four o'clock because I've the week's shopping to do. It won't take long, will it? Percy likes his supper...'

'I don't imagine it will take too much time but you could leave—er—Percy's supper for him, couldn't you?'

'Well, yes.' She took the puppy from him. 'You're very kind.'

'In between bouts of ill nature,' he reminded her gently. Then watched the pretty colour in her cheeks. He went to the door. 'I will be back at four o'clock.'

Arabella crammed a lot into the next few hours. There was still the rubbish to take out to the dustbins outside and the brass on the front door to polish; she would see to those later, she told herself, changing into her decent suit and good shoes and doing her face and her hair. It was important to look as little like a caretaker as possible—she wouldn't want Dr Tavener to be ashamed of her. She took all the money she had with her, remembering the vet's bills for the dogs when her parents had been alive and, the picture of unassuming neatness, she went to the front door punctually at four o'clock.

He came in as she put her hand on the doorknob. He didn't waste time in civilities. 'Well? Where is the little beast?'

'In the basement. He's not allowed up here. I'll fetch him and bring him out to the car from my front door.'

'Do that. I'll be with you in a moment.' He went along to his rooms and she heard him phone as she went downstairs.

He was waiting by the car as she went through the door and up the steps with the puppy tucked under an arm and ushered her into the front seat, got in beside her and drove off.

The puppy was frightened and Arabella, concerned with keeping him quiet, hardly noticed where they were going. She looked up once and said, 'Oh, isn't that the Zoo?' and Dr Tavener grunted what she supposed to be yes. When he stopped finally and helped her out she looked around her with interest. She didn't know London very well—in happier days she and her mother had come up to shop or go to a theatre, and birthdays had been celebrated by her father taking them out to dine.

'Where is this?' she asked now.

'Little Venice. The vet lives in this house. His surgery is in the Marylebone Road but he agreed to see the puppy here.'

'That's very kind of him.' She went with him up the steps of the solid town house and, when the door was opened by a sober-looking woman in an apron, followed the doctor inside.

'He's expecting us, Mrs Wise,' said Dr Tavener easily. 'Are we to go up?'

'Yes, sir, you're expected.'

They were met at the head of the stairs by a man of the doctor's age, tall and thin, already almost bald. 'Come on in,' he greeted them. 'Where's this puppy, Titus?'

Dr Tavener stood aside so that Arabella came into view. 'This is Miss Arabella Lorimer—John Clarke, a wizard with animals.' He waited while they shook hands. 'Hand over the puppy, Miss Lorimer.'

They all went into a pleasant room, crowded with books and papers. There were two cats asleep on a chair and a black Labrador stretched out before a cheerful fire. 'Sit down,' invited Mr Clarke. 'I'll take a quick look.' He glanced at Arabella. 'Titus has told me about his rescue. At first glance I should imagine that good food and affection will soon put him on his feet.'

He bent over the little beast, examining him carefully and very gently. 'Nothing much wrong. I'll give you some stuff to put on those sores and I'll give him his injections while he's here. There's nothing broken or damaged, I'm glad to say. What's his name?'

'He hasn't got one yet.' She smiled at Mr Clarke, who smiled back.

'You can decide on that as you go home.' He handed the puppy back and she thanked him.

'Would you send the bill or shall I...?'

'Oh, I don't charge for emergencies or accidents,' said Mr Clarke cheerfully. 'Bring him for a check-up in a month or so—or earlier if you're worried. There will be a fee for that. Titus knows where the surgery is.'

'Thank you very much. I hope we haven't disturbed your Saturday afternoon.'

He flicked a glance at Dr Tavener's bland face. 'Not in the least. Nice to meet you and don't hesitate to get in touch if you are worried.'

Getting into the car again Arabella said, 'It was very kind of you, Dr Tavener, to bring us to the vet. Mr Clarke is a very nice man, isn't he? We've taken up a lot of your time. If you would drop us off at a bus stop we can go home...'

'Have you any idea which bus to catch?'

'Well, no, but I can ask.'

'I have a better idea. We will have tea and I will drive you back afterwards.'

'Have tea? Where? And really there is no need.'

'I said, ''have tea'', did I not? I live in the next street and my housekeeper will be waiting to make it. And don't fuss about Percy—we have been away for rather less than an hour and tea will take a fraction of that time.'

'The puppy?'

'Is entitled to his tea as well.' He had turned into a pleasant street bordering the canal and stopped before his house. 'Let us have no more questions!'

CHAPTER THREE

CLUTCHING the puppy, Arabella was swept into his house, one of several similar houses with their backs overlooking the canal and their fronts restrainedly Georgian. The hall was square with a curved staircase to one side and several doors leading from it. Out of one of these emerged a large, bony woman with a severe hairstyle and a long thin face.

'Ah, Alice. Miss Lorimer—this is my housekeeper, Mrs Turner. Alice, I've brought Miss Lorimer back for tea; could we have it presently?'

Arabella offered a hand and Mrs Turner shook it and said, 'How do you do?' in a severe manner and cast a look at the puppy. 'In five minutes, sir. And perhaps the young lady would like to leave her jacket.'

'No need,' he said cheerfully. 'She won't be staying long—it can stay on a chair.' He took the puppy as he spoke and Arabella took off her jacket and laid it tidily on a rather nice Regency elbow chair and went with him into the drawing-room.

It was large, running from front to back of the house, the back French windows opening on to a small wrought-iron balcony which overlooked the canal. She crossed the room, dimly aware of its beauty but intent on looking out of the window. 'It isn't like London at all,' she declared, 'and there's a garden…'

As indeed there was, below the balcony—small, high-walled, screened from the houses on either side by ornamental trees and shrubs, with the end wall built over the water.

Dr Tavener stood watching her and saying nothing and presently, aware of his silence, she turned to look at him. 'I'm sorry, I've been rude, but it was such a lovely surprise.'

He smiled then. 'Yes, isn't it? I've lived here for some years and it still surprises me. Come and sit down and we'll have tea.'

She looked around her then, at the comfortable chairs and the wide sofa before the fire; the Chippendale giltwood mirror over the fireplace and the rosewood table behind the sofa; the mahogany tripod tables with their lamps and the Dutch marquetry display cabinets each side of the fireplace. It was a beautiful room, furnished beautifully. There was a rosewood writing-table under the windows, its surface covered by silver-framed photos. She would have liked to have examined them but good manners forbade that so she sat down composedly in one of the armchairs as Mrs Turner came in with the tea tray.

Cucumber sandwiches, muffins in a silver dish and a rich fruit cake. She sighed silently and swallowed the lump in her throat; it was a long time since she had seen such a tea, eaten and drunk from fine china with the tea poured from a silver pot.

'Be mother,' invited the doctor, and sat down opposite her. He still had the puppy in his arms.

'Shall I have him?'

'No. No, he is no trouble. It is a pity that my own dog isn't here. She's a gentle creature—a golden Labrador—she would have mothered him.'

Arabella opened her mouth to ask him where she was and stopped just in time. Perhaps he would tell her. He didn't, but asked if he shouldn't be given a name.

She bit into a sandwich. 'Well, yes. Something rather grand, I thought, to make up for the beastly time he's had.'

'What a good idea. Have some of this cake—Mrs Turner is a good cook.' He smiled a little. 'But I'm talking to one, aren't I?'

She wasn't sure about the smile—perhaps he was being a bit sarcastic.

'What kind of a dog is he?'

'Rather mixed, I fancy; the ears are very like a spaniel's and I imagine he will grow to some considerable size—look at his paws. I'm not sure about that tail. As to the name…how about Bassett?'

She gave him a thoughtful look and then laughed. 'Of course—how clever you are. Bassett's Allsorts!'

When she laughed she looked almost pretty, he

decided. It would be interesting to find out more about her; when she forgot to be the caretaker she was someone quite different.

However, she hadn't forgotten. She put down her cup and got to her feet. 'I've stayed longer than I intended. I hope I haven't spoilt your afternoon, sir.'

He didn't try to keep her but fetched her jacket and settled her with Bassett in the car, making pleasant conversation as he did so. He went with her into the rooms at Wigmore Street when they arrived, checking that everything was as it should be, before bidding her a coolly friendly good evening and opening the door. He was closing it behind him when she cried, 'Stop, oh, do stop. Must I tell Dr Marshall about Bassett?'

'Of course. On Monday morning before his patients come.' He stared down at her troubled face. 'I will have a word with him first—he is a very kind man and besides, you are a very good caretaker.'

'Oh, will you? You promise? You won't forget?'

His eyes were cold. 'I keep my promises, Miss Lorimer, and I have an excellent memory.'

'Oh dear, I've annoyed you.'

'No, you don't annoy me; you surprise me, vex me and intrigue me, but that is all.' He nodded and this time the door closed firmly behind him, leaving her in the hall, her thoughts in a fine muddle.

She had forgotten to thank him for her tea too. She went down to her room and attended to the animals' wants and then went back to finish her cleaning. Tomorrow, if it was fine enough, she would take Bassett for a walk—Regent's Park wasn't too far away. She would have to carry him, of course, for she had no lead and he had no collar. She dismissed Dr Tavener from her thoughts. He had been kind and helpful but he didn't like her—worse, she doubted if he had formed any opinion of her at all. She was of no interest to him whatsoever, although he was prepared to help her if necessary—just as he would help a stranger who had stumbled in the street, or an old lady to cross a road. It was mortifying but it made sense.

She enjoyed her Sunday, walking briskly in the park with Bassett tucked under her arm and going back to her dinner—lamp chop, potato purée, sprouts and carrots cooked with sugar and butter. The three of them ate their meal and settled down for the afternoon before tea by the fire. Really a very pleasant day, decided Arabella, getting ready for bed later, and she was so lucky to have a home of her own and a job. She had managed all day to forget about seeing Dr Marshall in the morning but she woke in the night and worried about it, dropping off again at last with the thought that Dr Tavener had said he would have a word. 'I dare say,' she said, addressing the sleeping animals, 'he is a very nice man under that distant manner. If I knew him better I might even like him.'

* * *

Dr Tavener, driving himself home in the early hours of the morning after an urgent summons to a patient's bedside, was thinking about her too. He had telephoned Dr Marshall and told him about Bassett, and James Marshall, good-natured and amused, had agreed to allow the puppy to stay.

They had laughed about it together but now, driving through the silent streets, his thoughts were more serious. Arabella was a nice girl; she shouldn't be a caretaker in the first place. She might have no qualifications but she came from a good background; he remembered the nicely laid table when he had had his supper with her and her unselfconscious assurance at his house that afternoon. This wasn't her kind of life at all but he could see no way of bettering it. Finding something more suited to her would be difficult because of the cat and puppy and he knew enough about her to realise that she would never give them up.

He let himself into his house and Beauty, whom he had fetched that afternoon, came to meet him and went with him to the kitchen while he made himself a cup of coffee.

He sat, a tired man, drinking it with her at his feet. 'The answer is to find her a husband,' he told her. Beauty thumped her tail and he rubbed her ears gently, saw her into her basket and went back upstairs to his bed—there were still two or three hours before he needed to get up. His last thought before he slept was that finding exactly the right man for Arabella would be a difficult task.

Arabella, very neat in her overall, presented herself at Dr Marshall's desk as soon as he was sitting at it. His good morning was kindly. 'Problems?' he wanted to know.

She didn't beat about the bush, but she didn't mention Dr Tavener either. He might have forgotten to speak to Dr Marshall and that might be awkward. He hadn't forgotten. Dr Marshall smiled at her. 'Ah, yes, Titus tells me that we have acquired a dog. Splendid, I have no objection just as long as you don't let him loose on our patients. Quite comfortable, are you? Settled in now?'

She could have flung her arms round his neck. 'Yes, thank you, sir.'

'Run along, then, the doorbell will be ringing at any moment now.'

As she was leaving he stopped her. 'I think it would be more suitable if we called you Arabella. You have no objection?'

'No, sir.' They could call her anything they liked; Bassett was hers.

She was admitting a patient when Dr Tavener arrived, nodded a good morning and went straight to his room. The next patient to arrive was for him—a tall, good-looking girl, dressed expensively and skilfully made-up.

No one bothered to give Arabella more than a fleeting glance and sometimes a vague smile of thanks and she was about to do the same but stopped short. 'Arabella—whatever are you doing here? Good gracious—that frightful overall and your hair all screwed up.'

Arabella closed the door. 'Hello, Daphne. I work here. You're here to see Dr Tavener? He's down the hall…'

Daphne laughed. 'Oh, my dear, I know where he is—we're old friends. But what do you do exactly?'

'I'm the caretaker.'

Daphne pealed with laughter. 'My goodness, what a marvellous joke.' She would have said more but the doorbell was rung again and Arabella went to answer it. When she turned round Daphne was gone.

Presently, ushered into Dr Tavener's room, Daphne sat down opposite his desk. 'Hello, Titus. It's ages since we saw you—Mother was asking what had happened to you. I'm not ill but I do wish you'd give me something for my headaches.' She crossed an elegant leg. 'I've had such a surprise—Arabella, a girl I know, opened the door. She said she was the caretaker, of all things! A caretaker—I ask you. I expect you know she was left penniless when her parents were killed some months ago. A bit of a come-down from living in comfort. Not a great friend, of course,' she laughed. 'We lived some miles away from each other but we had mutual friends...' She smiled charmingly. 'Now, what about my headaches...?'

He had sat quietly while she talked, now he said blandly, 'You tell me where the pain is exactly. Perhaps you are worried about something or doing too much?'

'Parties, you mean? Well, I do enjoy life—why not? We're only young once and besides, it helps one from getting bored.'

'The boredom probably accounts for the headaches. I suggest that you miss a few late nights and take a long walk every day. Cut down on the drinks and go to bed at a reasonable time.'

She pouted prettily. 'Oh, Titus, you stuffy old thing! And I was going to invite you to come home for the weekend but now I shan't.'

'I'm not free in any case,' he told her blandly. He stood up and handed her the prescription he had written. 'Take these for a week and see how you get on. If you're no better we'll delve deeper. I'm sure it's nothing for you to worry about.'

He held the door open for her and she smiled up at him as she went past. A lovely face, he reflected, but nothing behind it. If he was to marry it would have to be a woman of intelligence, who would listen to him without twiddling her earrings or examining her nails. She had no need to be beautiful or even pretty—the right clothes would take care of that... It was only recently that he had wished for a companion. He was, he considered, past the age of falling in love and besides, a marriage founded on liking and compatibility was more likely to succeed than one plunged into in the heat of the moment.

He sat down at his desk, dismissing the matter from his mind, and picked up the next patient's notes.

His day's work done, his thoughts reverted to Arabella. It was unthinkable that she should remain as a caretaker—polishing and Hoovering and cleaning windows and doors, dragging out the rubbish to be collected, polishing the brass and, above all, being alone at night with no protection save that of a very small puppy and a cat. The matter needed urgent consideration.

As for Arabella, she avoided him as much as possible while at the same time wishing that she knew more about him. The small glimpse she had had of his life had intrigued her. She had supposed him to be a dyed-in-the-wool bachelor but, listening from time to time to the nurses gossiping, she had formed the opinion that he was much sought-after socially—a matrimonial prize several women were after. Hadn't she seen with her own eyes how her erstwhile friend Daphne had smiled up at him? She thought that it might be rather nice to be married to someone like him, to live in a lovely house and meet people again. To have clothes—new clothes, bought without having to look at the price-ticket first. That, she told herself, was no reason for marrying. She finished tidying the rooms and went downstairs to get her supper and take the animals for their evening stroll in the garden.

Saturday came round once more. Arabella did her shopping, gave the rooms their usual turn-out and went into the garden to pick some fresh flowers. Bassett had filled out and lost most of his timidity and followed Percy's dignified progress from one flowerbed to the other. Tomorrow, she promised him, he would wear his new collar and walk beside her on his lead in the park.

The evenings were getting colder; they all went indoors presently and had their suppers and then shared the warmth of the gas fire. The cushion covers were finished so she had brought some of the magazines down from the waiting-room and curled up to read them.

Before going to bed she went back upstairs once more to check that everything was closed and locked. The upstairs flat was empty again but she had grown used to being on her own.

She enjoyed every minute of Sunday. The walk in the park had been a great success; Bassett had behaved well, trotting along on his lead, chasing the fallen leaves and barking his small treble bark. They had gone back to Percy's welcome and had their tea and afterwards she sat down and did her sums for the week.

Even with three mouths to feed she was saving a little money each week. The future was uncertain; even if she stayed with the doctors for the rest of her working life, she would still need money when she retired. It seemed a long way ahead, but she might be ill, lose her job, need a home while she found something else. In a month or two, when she felt more secure, she would start looking for a post as a cook. Surely there was somewhere and someone who wouldn't object to a cat and a dog? It was going to be difficult and she was happy enough in her basement but she was aware that both the doctors felt an uneasiness about her working for them. She suspected that Dr Marshall had given her her job on a sudden whim and while he might not be regretting it he could be having second thoughts…

She finished the sums, gave Percy and Bassett their suppers and went into the garden with them and, once indoors again, bolted the door before beginning to get her own supper. That eaten, she decided to check the rooms upstairs and go to bed early. Life, she decided, though dull, was at least secure.

Before she slept she allowed herself to daydream a little. Being a practical girl, she didn't allow her thoughts to dwell on the prospect of some young man falling head over heels in love with her and marrying her out of hand, but on the miraculous offer of a job as cook—a highly paid job in some stately home—with a cottage in the grounds and no objection to pets…

The partners had arrived early on the Monday morning and Dr Marshall had wandered along to Dr Tavener's rooms. 'Nice morning,' he observed affably. 'The garden looks pretty good too.' He glanced at the small chrysanths arranged on the desk. 'Keeps the place looking nice, does our Arabella.'

Dr Tavener had been writing; now he put down his pen. 'James, we shall have to do something about her. We ought never to have given her the job in the first place. I had a patient the other morning—she had been at school with Arabella, known her for years, saw a lot of her before the parents were killed.'

'And this friend, was she shocked at Arabella working in such a lowly capacity?'

Dr Tavener frowned. 'I believe she was rather amused…'

'Hardly a friend. I imagine Arabella is very proud, not wishing to be an embarrassment to her friends, going it alone.'

Dr Tavener said deliberately, 'I don't like the idea of her being alone here at night.'

His partner peered at him through his specs. 'No? Perhaps you are right; she's rather small although not at all nervous, she told me.'

'She would have said anything to get a roof over her head.'

'So what are we to do about it? Other than finding her a husband…'

'She is a cordon bleu cook. If we could find someone who would accept those animals she would be safe and secure and living in surroundings more suited to her.'

'Until she finds a husband. She would make a good wife and a handy one too—no need to call out the plumber or the electrician. Come to think of it, Titus, she would suit you very well and it's time you had a wife—patients like a married man!'

Titus didn't answer and Dr Marshall said hastily, 'Only joking. Time I went back, I suppose. Are you fully booked this morning?'

'Yes, and this afternoon. I've a clinic this evening.'

'You must come to dinner soon—I'll get Angie to phone you.'

'I'd like that, thanks.'

Dr Tavener opened the case sheets before him but made no effort to read them. That was the solution, he decided: to find a job for Arabella. In the country—because she was a country girl at heart. The place would be very empty without her, though.

Arabella, unaware of the future being planned for her, went about her chores, bought some wool going cheap because of the colour—a serviceable brown which wasn't selling well—and started on a sweater, keeping a loving eye on Percy and Bassett.

Dr Tavener, a man of considerable wealth, owned a pleasant small manor house in Wiltshire which had been in the family for more than two hundred years. Whenever his work permitted he drove himself back there, taking Beauty with him, spending his days gardening and walking. His parents were dead but his grandmother lived there with a meek companion, looked after by Butter and his wife who had also looked after his mother and father and probably, if they lived long enough, would look after him in his old age. He couldn't imagine the place without them.

He went there the following weekend, on a blustery autumn day. Twenty miles or so beyond Swindon he turned off the motorway to take a minor road towards Tetbury. Then, turning off again, took a narrow lane which brought him eventually to a small village and, beyond it, to his home.

There were lights in the windows and smoke coming from several of its elaborate brick chimney-pots, and as he stopped before the door it opened to allow a dog to rush out and race to the car, barking happily. Beauty's brother, Duke. He circled the car, delighted to see its occupants, and the three of them went indoors to where Butter was waiting.

'Good to see you again, Master Titus,' said Butter.

'Mrs Butter has tea all ready and waiting. I'll take the dogs along to the kitchen for their meal. Mrs Tavener is in the drawing room.'

Dr Tavener crossed the polished wood floor of the hall and went into the room—long and low-ceilinged, its strapwork still perfect, with windows at either end of it—lattice windows set in square bays—and the heavy velvet curtains blending with the dark green and russet of the vast carpet.

It was furnished with a clever mixture of Jacobean and early Georgian chairs and tables and the fireplace was of the Queen Anne period—ornate and heavily ornamented with a vast mirror above it. On either side of it there were comfortable armchairs and a great sofa but the two ladies in the room were sitting in upright Regency armchairs with a small table between them upon which lay playing cards.

Dr Tavener crossed the room and bent to kiss his grandmother—a handsome old lady, sitting very upright, her features severe. She smiled as he greeted her. 'Titus, my dear, how pleasant to see you again. You don't come home enough.'

'My home is in London,' he pointed out mildly. 'At least while I'm working.'

'Yes, yes and I'm sure it is a very handsome house, but this is the family home.' She paused. 'It is time you had a family, Titus.'

He only smiled and went to shake her companion's hand. Miss Welling was a thin lady of uncertain age with a sharp nose, myopic brown eyes and an anxious expression. There was no need for the anxiety—she received nothing but kindness and consideration from her employer—but meekness and anxiety seemed to be her nature and old Mrs Tavener might look severe but she would never tax her with questions and over the years had come to accept Miss Welling's cautious approach to life.

Miss Welling greeted Dr Tavener in a pleased voice, for she liked him, then excused herself with the plea that she would see if the tea tray was ready and slid out of the room.

'The dear creature,' said Mrs Tavener, 'anyone would think that I beat her. Come and sit down and tell me what you have been doing lately.'

He drew up a chair and embarked on a brief account of his days. The tea was brought in presently and afterwards he took the dogs for a walk in the deepening twilight. When he returned it was to find his grandmother alone. 'Miss Welling has gone to tidy herself, my dear. We have half an hour to ourselves—time in which to tell me what is on your mind.'

When he gave her a half-smiling look she said, 'You are very like your father—the bigger the problem, the more bland the face. Fallen in love at last?'

'No. No, I believe that I shall never do that seriously enough to marry. But I do have a problem…' He told her about Arabella, his voice placid and disinterested, and when he had finished he asked, 'Have you any ideas, Grandmother?'

'The young woman seems to be in most unsuitable work. On the other hand, Titus, she has a home of sorts, independence and is able to keep her pets with her. A sense of security must be very important to her—to be pitched out without warning into poverty and loneliness must have been such a shock. To subject her to an unknown future seems unkind, even if the work was more congenial, and who knows if she would be happy? Besides, you would lose touch with her. You like her?'

'Yes, I do. Surprisingly we have a good deal in common; she is undemanding as a companion and not above treating me with a tart tongue.'

Mrs Tavener hid a smile. 'She sounds as though she is very well able to look after herself, although I do agree with you that being in that place alone at night isn't quite the thing.' She glanced at him. 'But I will ask around, my dear, and if I hear of anything at all suitable I will let you know at once. The girl's presentable?'

'Yes—good clothes but out of date, nice manners, no looks to speak of but nice eyes—beautiful eyes—and a pleasant voice.'

Mrs Tavener considered this reply and decided not to comment upon it. Instead she said, 'I shall be coming up to town next week to shop. Will you give us beds for the night? Miss Welling will come with me, of course, but I promise you we will be no trouble to you.'

'That will be delightful. Would you like to go to the theatre? There are some good plays on. I'm afraid I shall be away from home all day but I can make sure I'm free in the evenings.'

'A play would be most enjoyable. Something romantic with music if possible. Will three days be too much for you?'

'Make it longer if you wish, Grandmother. You know you're always more than welcome.'

'Yes, my dear, I do know. We will come up on the Tuesday and return here on Thursday evening. Butter shall drive us up and fetch us again.' She paused. 'There's no reason why Mrs Butter shouldn't come up with him, then they could drive up early in the morning and she could go to the shops for an hour or two before he picks us up.'

'A good idea. Make any arrangements you like with Mrs Turner.'

'Thank you. Would it bother you to take a look at Miss Welling while we're there? She can go along to your rooms—I'll put her in a taxi. She won't admit it but I don't think she sleeps very well.'

'Yes, of course. I'll get Miss Baird to make an appointment and phone you.'

Miss Welling came into the room and they talked of other things.

He took the old lady to church on Sunday morning

and after lunch spent the rest of the day reading the Sunday papers, taking the dogs for a walk, having his tea and then driving himself back to his house in Little Venice. He made a detour when he reached town so that he could drive along Wigmore Street. The basement curtains were closed but there was a fringe of light showing round them and he stifled the urge to knock at the door and spend an hour with Arabella, telling her about his weekend. 'Ridiculous,' he told himself sharply so that Beauty, sitting beside him half-asleep, gave a sleepy bark.

Mrs Tavener was driven up to London on Tuesday and by the time Dr Tavener got home that evening she was settled in, sitting in his drawing-room playing Racing Demon with Miss Welling. They spent a pleasant evening together and he told her that he had got tickets for a long-running musical which he hoped that she would like. He had seen it himself in the company of an old friend's daughter who had been visiting in London. He hadn't liked the show particularly but perhaps that was because he had found his companion a singularly vapid girl with no conversation who was everlastingly fidgeting with her hair or her lipstick.

As for Miss Welling, she was to see him the next morning despite her timid objections that he was a busy man and she was perfectly well. 'Well, of course you are,' he had told her kindly, 'but since you are here it is a splendid opportunity to have a check-up. It won't take too long and I'll put you in a taxi afterwards so that you can come straight back here.'

Arabella, checking Miss Baird's list of patients, noticed that Dr Tavener had added a name at the end of Miss Baird's list. A Miss Welling—and not until eleven o'clock. Usually on Wednesday he left soon after ten o'clock to take an outpatients clinic at one of the hospitals. She had seen him only briefly on Monday and Tuesday and he had acknowledged her good morning with a brisk nod; she would try to avoid him in future since he seemed to dislike her so much. She puzzled over that, for he had been kind about Bassett and when she had had tea with him he had been so friendly that she had quite forgotten that she was his caretaker...

Wednesday morning was dark and cold and drizzling with rain, and those patients she admitted were short-tempered as a result. To her pleasant good morning they either grunted or let loose a string of complaints while they shook umbrellas over her pleasingly polished floor or hung their damp raincoats over her arms. It was a bit depressing, so when the bell rang once again and she opened the door it was a pleasant surprise to be greeted cheerfully by the elderly lady wishing to enter. She was accompanied by a lady considerably younger with a woebegone face who none the less answered Arabella's cheerful greeting with a smile.

'Miss Welling? If you would see the receptionist and then go down the passage to Dr Tavener's waiting-room. Shall I take your coat?'

The elderly lady gave her companion a poke in the ribs. 'Yes, go along, do. I'll be in the waiting-room.'

She turned to Arabella. 'A wretched day, is it not? London can be horrid in this weather. You live here, I expect?'

'Oh, yes. I'm the caretaker. Would you like me to have your coat too?'

'No. No, thank you. You don't look very much like a caretaker.'

Arabella blushed but the lady was old and perhaps she was just being inquisitive. 'I'm very content; it's a good job. Shall I show you to Dr Tavener's waiting-room?'

'By all means, and here is Miss Welling back again. Good day to you.'

Mrs Tavener swept away with Miss Welling at her heels and Arabella went downstairs. Miss Welling was the last patient; she would have a quick cup of coffee before seeing her out presently.

Miss Welling, emerging from Dr Tavener's consulting-room some twenty minutes later, was accompanied by him to the door. 'I'll arrange a taxi—' He broke off at the sight of his grandmother sitting very erect in the waiting-room. Her 'Good morning, Titus,' was graciously said but she smiled as she spoke.

He said nothing for the moment but smiled a little in his turn before crossing the room and taking her hand. 'What do you think of her?' he asked. 'For that is why you are here, is it not?'

'Of course, you are quite right, Titus, she is most unsuitable. You will have to think of something else. As you said, she is quite without good looks. Although, of course, good looks don't matter if one is a good cook.' She stood up. 'Did you find Miss Welling in good health?'

'On the whole, yes. May we discuss that this evening? I'm late for my clinic.'

His nurse was in the examination room so he saw the two ladies to the door and a few minutes later left himself, so that when Arabella came upstairs again there was only his nurse there, grumbling because he intended to come back that afternoon and she had hoped to be free to go home early.

Arabella, nipping through the rain to the shops, reflected that Dr Tavener probably worked too hard. She hoped that he had time to eat proper meals and had enough sleep. It was difficult to tell because he was always beautifully turned out and he had the kind of face which gave away nothing of his feelings.

Choosing carrots and turnips with a careful eye, she reminded herself to stop thinking about him—it was such a waste of time.

CHAPTER FOUR

DR TAVENER did not know when the preposterous idea first entered his head. Perhaps at a dinner party as he sat with a charming woman on either side of him, both looking for a husband and both divorced. Not a conceited man, he was aware all the same that he had good looks, a splendid physique and more than enough money to satisfy the greediest of women. Or it might have been one early morning, when he had gone to his manor for a weekend and taken the dogs out into the garden before breakfast. It had been a cold night and the frost had iced every blade of grass and twig and he had wanted Arabella there beside him to enjoy it too. 'Not that I am in love with her,' he had told Beauty. 'It is merely that she is a good companion.' She would stand between him and the tiresome women who were introduced to him by his friends in the mistaken idea that he might like to make one of them his wife. She would be restful to come home to…

Because the idea was so preposterous, he avoided her as much as possible. Arabella wondered what she had done to annoy him, for if they did meet the look he cast at her was thunderous. It made her unhappy, for he had been kind, and from time to time had smoothed her path. She did her best to forget it.

It was in the middle of the week, in the morning while she was still getting the rooms ready for the day, that the electricity failed. A fuse probably, she thought, and since it was still dark groped her way to the hall where she had had the forethought to put a torch in the table drawer.

The electrics were in a cupboard at the back of the hall. She peered inside, saw what had to be done and, since the fuses were in a box tucked away behind everything else, she got down on her knees the better to get at them.

Dr Tavener, arriving early, had come in silently and stopped short at the sight of Arabella's shapely person sticking out of the cupboard but before he could speak she had crawled out backwards and got to her feet, clutching the new fuse. She spoke tartly. 'Well, you might have rung the bell or something—I might have known it would be you.'

She wiped a dirty hand over a cheek and left a smudge.

'How did you know that it was I?'

'Your feet…'

'My feet?' He had put down the bag and taken the fuse from her.

She went a little pink. 'Well, I get to know the sound of people's feet.'

He nodded and went past her, fixed the fuse, and came back to where she had resumed Hoovering. She switched off to thank him and when she would have switched on again he put out a hand and stopped her. 'A moment, Arabella. There is something I wish to say to you. Unfortunately there is not time to explain fully but I should like to make you a proposal.'

At her look of astonishment he added kindly. 'Don't look so surprised. I should like you to consider marrying me. If you will think about it we can discuss it sensibly at a later date.'

He smiled then. 'Don't let me keep you from your work.' He had gone into his room and shut the door quietly behind him, leaving her with her mouth open, a white face and a rapid pulse.

As for Dr Tavener, he sat down at his desk and wondered if he had gone mad.

Arabella had no doubts about it—he had been overworking and had had a brainstorm, whatever that was, and hadn't known what he was saying. She would ignore the whole thing, let him see that she hadn't taken him seriously.

The last patient had gone by five o'clock that afternoon and everyone else followed him within half an hour. Arabella collected her cleaning things and went upstairs to tidy up. She had finished and was tying up the plastic bag of rubbish when Dr Tavener returned.

He had a bottle under one arm and a box with a

Harrods label in his hand. 'May I come to supper? You can't leave the place, otherwise I would have given you dinner at home.'

She put the sack down. 'Look, I do understand. I expect you've been working too hard and thought you were talking to someone else. It doesn't matter a bit…'

He took the sack from her. 'No, you don't understand and I'm perfectly sound in my head. Shall we have supper and talk?' He smiled suddenly and she found herself smiling back. 'I have a great deal to explain.'

'Very well.' She led the way downstairs and he took the sack outside to the refuse bins, giving her the bottle and the box to hold. He hadn't been mad at all, he reflected, washing his hands at the sink—this was going to be one of the sanest things he had ever done.

Arabella peered into her small pantry. She had decided to have an egg and a baked potato for her supper but that wouldn't do for her guest. She measured macaroni and put it on to cook, grated cheese and beat an egg, scrubbed two more potatoes and put them in the oven and all the while he sat with Percy on his knee and Bassett curled up on his shoes, saying nothing. It was unnerving. She thought of several things to say but none of them seemed suitable. She held her tongue and laid the table.

He had brought a bottle of claret with him this

time. He uncorked it and left it to breathe and presently he poured it and gave her a glass.

She sipped. 'Delicious,' she said. 'What's in the box?'

'Fruit pies. Can you sit down for a while or must you stay by the stove?'

She had put the macaroni cheese in the oven—it and the potatoes would be another half-hour and there was only a lettuce to dress.

She sat in the armchair and he took a chair from beside the table and sat opposite her. 'I appreciate the fact that I must have taken you by surprise but I do assure you that I was serious.' When she would have spoken he went on, 'No, please, let me explain. I am forty years old, Arabella—not a young man. I have been in and out of love on numerous occasions but I have never found the right woman and so I preferred to stay single. Lately, however, I have wished for a wife, someone to come home to each day, a companion for my leisure and someone who would put an end to my well-meaning friends vying with each other to marry me off to a succession of suitable young women. You see that I wish to marry for the wrong reasons, although perhaps they are no worse than many others. However, those are my reasons. I like you too much to pretend there are others. I am not in love with you and yet I enjoy your company so much that I have begun to miss you when you are not here. It worries me that you are living here alone, doing menial work, and having no friends or fun. We could get along very well together, I think, Arabella, to our mutual advantage.'

Arabella said quietly, 'This isn't...? That is, you are not suggesting this out of pity? Because if you are I shall probably throw something at you.'

She had, she reflected, had several proposals in happier times, but never one as forthright and unsentimental as this one.

Dr Tavener gave her an austere look. 'I do not pity you—never have pitied you. You interest me, frequently annoy me, amuse me, agree with me over the things which matter.'

'You're very outspoken...'

'Would you have me otherwise? Would you have believed me if I had told you that I was in love with you?'

'Of course not! The idea's absurd.' Her nose twitched. 'Supper's ready.'

She liked him for getting up at once to pour more wine and carry the plates to the table, talking now of a variety of matters and never once speaking of themselves. It gave her time to get over the shock.

They ate the macaroni cheese and potatoes and salad, and the fruit pies, all the while carrying on an unforced conversation—arguing about books, disagreeing amicably over the right cultivation of roses, agreeing about the pleasures of having animals to look after. 'I had a pony,' said Arabella wistfully, 'and a donkey.' She paused.

'And?' said Dr Tavener quietly.

'They wanted to sell them, but I took them to an animal sanctuary. They are still there, I hope. I simply hated leaving them.'

'Somewhere near your home?'

'Oh, yes. You must have heard of it.'

When she told him the name he nodded. 'I have heard of it. They have a fine reputation.'

She made coffee presently, while he washed up. He made a good job of it so she asked him if he looked after himself. 'Although you have a housekeeper, haven't you?'

'Mrs Turner took me in hand when my parents died. I admit that I seldom need to do household chores but I'm perfectly able to do so if need be.'

They took their coffee to drink by the fire and the animals pushed and shoved each other as near its warmth as possible.

Arabella took a sip of coffee. She had drunk too much wine and it had gone to her head. It had given her a pretty colour too. She was aware of Dr Tavener's eyes searching her face and buried her nose in her mug.

'Well—' he sounded brisk '—how long to you need to make up your mind?'

'I think,' said Arabella carefully, 'that I won't be able to make it up until I'm alone. You see, while you are here, you distract me.' She added hastily, 'That sounds rude but I don't mean to be; it's just that I have to think about it from a distance, if you see what I mean.'

'Yes, I see. You may have a week, Arabella, and then I shall ask you again. During that week I shall take no notice of you at all—not because I wish to avoid you but so that you can decide for yourself.'

He got up and drew her to her feet, holding her hands between his. They felt cool and comforting and undemanding. 'Thank you for my supper.' He bent and kissed her cheek. 'Goodnight, Arabella.'

She stared up into his faintly smiling face. 'But you might have second thoughts…'

'No, I can promise that I won't.' He went to the door. 'No need to come up, I'll lock the door after me—but remember to bolt it after me later, won't you?'

She sat for a long time doing nothing, her head in a turmoil, but it was no good thinking about it any more. In the morning she would be able to reflect upon her surprising evening with her usual good sense.

She went upstairs and bolted the door and checked the place as she always did and then went back to shower and go to her bed. 'I shan't sleep,' she told Percy, already perched on the end of the bed and giving Bassett a thorough wash. And she slept as soon as her head was on the pillow.

In the half light of a dull November morning the whole thing seemed like an impossible dream. By the end of a busy day peopled by ill-tempered patients, a crusty Dr Marshall and only glimpses of Dr Tavener's broad back it didn't seem quite as impossible.

She was unable to make up her mind. She had argued, with Percy and Bassett as a more or less attentive audience, each evening, weighing up the pros and cons. But however matter-of-factly she put her problems it wasn't the same as talking to someone. With the end of the week looming she decided that something would have to be done. As Dr Tavener, last as usual, left that evening she stopped him as he went to the door.

'Could you spare five minutes? I need someone to talk to and ask advice, only I don't know anyone except you. I wondered if you would mind. It's about us, but if we could pretend that we're discussing two other people, if you see what I mean…'

'A sensible suggestion. Come into my room and we will see what can be done.'

She was relieved to hear nothing but a pleasantly detached voice and accompanied him back to his consulting-room, where he threw his overcoat on to a chair, offered her a seat and went to sit at his desk once more. Arabella, momentarily diverted by the thought that the overcoat—a splendid one of cashmere—should have been hung up properly and not cast in a heap, gathered her wandering thoughts and faced him.

'It's like this,' she explained. 'I—that is, the girl I'm asking you about isn't sure that she would be doing the right thing if she married this man. She doesn't know what will be expected of her. Does he go out a great deal? Would his friends like her? Perhaps she wouldn't like them. She wouldn't want to shame him; she's not clever or witty or anything like that. She might make a mess of the whole thing, and the thing is she's out of date about getting divorced and all that—' She eyed him with a severe look across the desk. 'If you're married, you do your best to make a success of it.'

She was watching his face and seeing nothing but placid interest there.

His voice was quiet. 'The girl is worrying needlessly. She has, if I might say so, too small an opinion of herself. She is perfectly able to fulfil the duties of a professional man's wife. She would be surprised how tiring clever and witty women are after a hard day's work and a marriage undertaken in mutual liking and respect is unlikely to come to grief. Indeed, the fact that there are no strong feelings involved should ensure its success.' He smiled at her. 'Does that help?'

She nodded. 'Yes. I think so. There's one other thing, though. You're rich.'

He said apologetically, 'I'm afraid I am, rather, but

I have never let it bother me, nor would I allow it to bother you.'

'No—well, you see, I wouldn't marry you for your money.'

'No, no, I'm sure you wouldn't.' He spoke gravely; she didn't see the gleam of amusement in his eyes.

She got up. 'Thank you for letting me talk and for giving me advice. I hope I haven't made you late for anything.'

He assured her that she hadn't, bade her a cheerful goodnight and took himself off home where Mrs Turner met him with the warning that he would be late for his dinner engagement with the Marshalls. 'Forgot the time, I suppose,' she observed. 'Head buried in your books as like as not.' She went back to her kitchen saying over her shoulder, 'Time you were married, Doctor. And if I've said that once, I've said it a hundred times!'

He laughed as he went up the stairs two at a time. 'One day I'll surprise you,' he promised her.

'I told you to come early, Titus,' complained Angie Marshall as he offered apologies and an armful of roses.

'Got held up?' asked Dr Marshall easily. 'Come in and have a drink. There's no one else coming so we can talk shop if we want to. You'll come to Angie's dinner party at Christmas, won't you? She's rooting round for a suitable young woman to capture your attention.' He didn't wait for a reply. 'We had a busy day. Stayed behind to catch up on the paper-work?'

'No.' Titus had sat down opposite his host and hostess in the comfortable drawing-room. 'I had a talk with Arabella.'

'Nice little thing. Worried about something, is she?' He glanced at his wife. 'You'd like her, Angie. A pity you can't find her a good husband.'

'No need. She's going to marry me,' said Dr Tavener.

'Bless my soul! She's exactly right for you, Titus. You should have brought her along with you this evening.'

'I left her Hoovering and muttering about dripping taps.'

Mrs Marshall laughed. 'Titus, she sounds a dear and just your sort. Not in the least sentimental, and practical as well. Is she very in love with you?'

He answered calmly. 'Not in the least. Nor I with her, but we like each other and agree about everything which we consider important. I have every expectation that our marriage will be an enduring success.'

'We've known you for a long time—years and years,' said Mrs Marshall, 'and I was beginning to think that you would never marry. We're so happy for you both, Titus.' She added, 'She will be nice to come home to, my dear.'

He smiled. 'Angie, what an understanding woman you are. A good thing James appreciates you.'

'We've been married for sixteen years.' Dr Marshall sounded smug. 'Bring Arabella here for dinner and let her see how successful marriage can be.' He added, 'Oh, lord, we'll have to find another caretaker.'

'How about the ex-bus driver?'

'A good idea. I'll get Miss Baird on to it first thing in the morning.'

The three of them spent the rest of the evening in undemanding talk and later the two men went to Dr Marshall's study to discuss their various patients. It was late when Dr Tavener arrived back at his house; Mrs Turner had gone to bed. He put the car away in the mews garage and took Beauty for a walk through the quiet streets, feeling content.

Arabella was content too. Her mind was made up and she had no intention of altering it. She had seen enough sad results from friends who had married in a blaze of romance and come to grief within a few years to know that liking the same things—books, music, a way of living—as well as pleasure in each other's company were more likely to last even if they lacked excitement. Of course, she admitted to herself, being in love would be marvellous too, but it was obvious to her that Dr Tavener wasn't a man to waste time over romance and, since both of them had nothing but liking for each other, she could see no reason why their marriage shouldn't succeed.

True to his word, Dr Tavener made no attempt to speak to her, the weekend came and went, and suddenly the week was up.

Everyone but the two doctors had gone home. They stood in the hall talking; Arabella could hear them as she collected her cleaning things from under the stairs. Perhaps he wouldn't come—perhaps he expected her to go upstairs… She heard Dr Marshall laugh and the front door bang shut and a moment later Dr Tavener came down the stairs. He took her broom and dusters from her and ushered her back into the room. 'Never mind that now,' she was told briskly. 'Will you marry me, Arabella?'

He could have been asking her to post a letter for all the emotion in his voice. But what else had she expected? She sat down and waved him to a chair. She said, 'Yes,' and, since that sounded a bit terse, added, 'Yes, thank you. I will.'

'Splendid. We can go ahead with our plans. You can leave here at the end of this week—there's a caretaker lined up to start on Sunday. I'll get a special license—James Marshall will give you away—we can be married quietly…'

She said tartly, 'You said our plans—you seem to

have taken it for granted that I would agree to everything you have arranged.'

'I'm sorry—oh, I'm sorry! That was unforgivable of me. All this week I have been planning and plotting. Say what you wish to do, Arabella, and you shall have your way.'

She said seriously, 'Well, actually, it all sounds very sensible. Where am I to go?'

'I have a house in the country—in a village midway between Tetbury and Malmsbury. My grandmother lives there—would you go and stay with her for a few days while I arrange things? Would you object to being married in the village church?'

'No. I'd like that very much, but perhaps your grandmother...I'm a stranger...'

'Not quite, you have met her—she brought her companion to see me.'

'Oh, so she knows who I am?' She sighed. 'That I'm the caretaker?'

He nodded. 'Oh, yes. She also knows that you're a very nice girl who will make me a good wife.'

'I shall do my best.'

He leaned forward and took her hands in his. 'We are agreed that there will be no false sentiment between us? Friends, companions, willing to allow each other to enjoy privacy without rancour, enjoying each other's company, spending our leisure together if we so wish.'

'If that is what you want,' she said steadily. 'You

will help me, won't you? You have friends—perhaps you entertain sometimes?'

'Fairly frequently.' He smiled suddenly. 'And now I shall be able to enjoy that...'

'No more marriage-minded ladies to vex you!' She gave a chortle of laughter. 'They will think that you have gone mad when they see me.'

'In that case they will no longer be our friends. Tell me, Arabella, have you enough money? You will want to buy some clothes perhaps?'

'I've enough to start with. I expect I shall want more clothes after we're married if I'm to look like a consultant's wife. You want me to go and stay with your grandmother—but I must do some shopping.'

'Of course you must. Let me see. If I can get the new caretaker to take over on Saturday instead of Sunday would a couple of hours on Saturday morning be enough? I'll drive you down in the afternoon. When you're there you could get to Bath—Butter could drive you there.'

'Who is Butter?' It was like turning the leaves of a book, discovering something fresh on every page.

'Oh, he and Mrs Butter run the house.'

'Then if you don't mind I'd rather shop there and spend Saturday morning packing up here. What about Percy and Bassett?'

'They will go with you, of course. You have some things you would like to keep from here?' His cool eyes swept the room. 'The china and silver and so on? I'll have the tea-chest delivered and it can be taken round to Little Venice. The furniture?'

'There's nothing I want to keep, only Mother's work table.' A dainty mahogany stand with a faded silk bag. 'When—when do you think we should marry?'

'A week—ten days' time? But only if you agree to that... If you have no objection we might marry on a Saturday morning and come back here on the Sunday.'

'So that you can see your patients on Monday? That seems a sensible idea.' She saw the look of relief on his face and reminded herself that their marriage was to be a friendly arrangement which mustn't interfere with his work.

He went presently. At the door he said, 'I very much dislike leaving you here, Arabella. Must you dust and clean?'

'Well, yes, it's my job, which I must do while I'm here...'

He threw an arm round her shoulders. 'When we are married you need never touch a duster or a dish-mop for the rest of your days.'

'A prospect no girl could resist. Will you let me know when the new caretaker is coming so that I can be ready for him?'

'Tomorrow. Take care, my dear.'

She bustled through her chores—there were only two days to Saturday and there were things to be done. Her clothes would pass muster until she could go shopping; they weren't in the forefront of fashion but Titus wouldn't need to feel ashamed of her. There were her precious bits and pieces to pack carefully and the place to set to rights so that the new caretaker would get a good impression. She told the animals about it while she got their suppers and then she started to wrap up her china and silver with the exception of necessities for the next day or two. She went to bed much later than usual, happily planning what was still to be done.

Dr Marshall sent for her the next morning. 'Well, well,' he said jovially, 'so you are to leave us, although I hope that we shall see a great deal more of you in the future. Of course I never thought that you would be with us for long, Arabella, and may I say that I am truly delighted for you and Titus. I'm sure you will be very happy together. Titus has arranged for the new man to call this morning so that you can show him round and explain things. You can let Titus know when it is convenient for you to be fetched on Saturday. You must come to dinner and meet my wife, although I'm hoping you will ask me to give you away at your wedding in which case perhaps she might accompany me?'

'Of course,' said Arabella warmly. 'And thank you for saying you'll give me away. I—I haven't any family living nearby and in any case I don't think they would be interested.'

* * *

The new caretaker was a middle-aged man, a cheerful cockney who had been made redundant from the buses and was delighted to have a job and a home again. He was a widower, living in a room near the Elephant and Castle and only too happy to move away from there.

He inspected the basement and pronounced it first-rate. 'I'll 'ave ter get some bits and pieces of furniture,' he told her. 'I suppose you wouldn't leave the curtains and the matting? I'll pay yer, of course.'

'You can have them for nothing,' said Arabella, liking the man, 'and I'd be glad to leave the furniture and the saucepans and so on. You see, I'm going to marry and don't need any of them.'

'Cor, bless my soul—yer really mean it?'

'Yes, of course I do. I'm going to make us a cup of coffee and explain the job to you and presently, when the last morning patient has gone, I'll take you round and show you everything.'

'That's a nice little dog you've got there—and a cat. I've got a cat meself. No objection to 'aving 'er 'ere, I suppose?'

'Well, I was allowed to have Percy. Bassett isn't really allowed, only I found him and he hadn't anywhere to go. A cat's company though, isn't it?'

'That she is.' He looked around him. 'This is a bit of all right, I can tell you.'

'It's a good job and everyone's very kind. If you've finished your coffee we'll go upstairs. Could you come on Saturday morning about eleven o'clock? I'll leave the bed made up with clean sheets and there'll be milk and bread and some food in the pantry. After you've cleaned up you are free on Saturday. I went shopping then—there are all the shops you'll need five minutes' walk away. The narrow road on the left as you leave the house. The doctors like the doors to be shut and locked and bolted when they are not here and I check each evening before I go to bed. I expect Dr Marshall told you about answering the door? You'll find the receptionist, Miss Baird, very kind and helpful.'

He went away presently and she gobbled a sandwich and had more coffee before going upstairs to answer the door to the afternoon patients.

There had been no sign of Dr Tavener. It was Miss Baird who told her that he had gone to Birmingham and would not be back until Friday.

'I haven't had the chance to congratulate you, Arabella,' she said kindly, 'and wish you happy. Dr Tavener is a splendid man. I'm sure you will deal excellently with each other.'

Arabella thanked her. 'I don't quite know when we are to be married.'

'We shall miss you—all of us...'

'Thank you. I have been very happy here, you know. The new caretaker seems to be a very nice man, and so delighted to have work again.'

She was up very early on the Saturday morning,

dusting and Hoovering and putting fresh flowers in their vases, and after a quick breakfast she changed into her suit, tied her overall over it and checked that everything was ready for Mr Flinn, before going upstairs ready to open the door.

He came punctually and since there was a lull in the stream of patients she took him downstairs to show him the pantry, explain about the milkman, and point out the list of usual directions she had left on the table.

Dr Tavener hadn't been in and despite her good sense she felt a prickle of apprehension that he had forgotten all about her or, even worse, had second thoughts about marrying her. The idea was absurd, she admitted to herself, and it was only because she was excited and uncertain—a fact borne out by his quiet arrival just before noon.

His hello was friendly and the placid enquiry as to whether she was ready ruffled her feelings. Anyone would think, she reflected crossly, that getting married was a fairly regular event in his life.

He was in no hurry to go either, but stood talking to Mr Flinn before remarking that he would send Butter round for the tea-chest some time that afternoon, scooping Bassett up under one arm and picking up Percy's basket with the other hand. 'Said goodbye to everyone?' he wanted to know.

'Yes,' said Arabella and shook Mr Flinn's hand

and wished him well. In the car she said, 'I thought you said that Butter lived in your other house?'

'Quite right, he does. He's coming up today so that he can drive you down this evening. I've an appointment I must keep this afternoon but I'll come down later tonight. My grandmother is expecting you and Butter will take good care of you.'

If I were beautiful and charming and well-dressed, thought Arabella crossly, I would throw a tantrum, make a scene and have him grovelling for treating me like a parcel.

She went red when he said, 'I'm sorry I can't drive you down—this is something which cropped up this morning and it really must be dealt with.'

He glanced at her pink cheeks and smiled a little. 'Would you agree to the wedding next Saturday? Will that give you enough time to do your shopping?'

'Yes, thank you. Are Percy and Bassett to come with me to your other house?'

'Of course, and we'll bring them back with us on the Sunday. Bassett is turning into a very well-mannered dog and Percy is happy wherever you are, isn't he?'

'Yes. You don't think they'll run away?'

'At the manor? No. There's a high brick wall around the grounds and Beauty's brother, Duke, will keep an eye on them.'

Mrs Turner met them at the door and Arabella,

who had been secretly nervous of her reception, was relieved at the warmth of her welcome.

'I've been telling the doctor he should take a wife these years past,' said Mrs Turner, leading her away to tidy herself. 'And with respect, Miss Lorimer, I think he's chosen well. I'll be glad to serve you.'

'Why, thank you, Mrs Turner.' Arabella stopped and held out a hand. 'Shall we shake on that? I'm sure you know exactly how the doctor likes things done.'

'Indeed I do. Easygoing he may be, but he likes things just so, as you might say. When will you be marrying, Miss Lorimer?'

'Next Saturday. I hope you'll come to the wedding; it's to be very quiet.'

'Nothing would keep me away, miss.'

Arabella was left to pat her already neat head to even more tidiness and add a little lipstick, and since she was feeling a little nervous she didn't hurry over it. Presently she went back into the hall and was instantly hailed by the doctor from a door at the end of it.

'In here, Arabella. We'll have a drink before lunch.' He held the door open for her as she went into the room. It was small and cosy with a bright fire and easy-chairs and rows of bookshelves. The window overlooked the garden and the canal and there was a round table under it with two mahogany dining chairs on either side of it.

'I have my breakfast here and you must use this room as your sitting-room—your mother's work table will look exactly right here, won't it?'

He pulled up a chair for her to one side of the fireplace and nodded to the three animals sitting in a tidy row before the fire—Bassett in the middle. 'I dare say Beauty will adopt him if Percy allows her to.'

He handed her a glass. 'Champagne—for we have something to celebrate, do we not, Arabella? Here's to us and our happy future together.'

Arabella drank. 'Oh, I do hope so,' she said fervently.

CHAPTER FIVE

IT WAS mid-afternoon when Arabella left with Butter in the dark blue Jaguar car which he had driven up. He had greeted her with obvious pleasure and gone away to the kitchen to have a quick lunch before taking her back and now she sat beside him, with the animals on the back seat, conscious that she should be feeling happy and content and aware of a faint prickle of unease. Titus had been kind and thoughtful of her comfort, putting her at ease in what might have been an awkward situation, but all the same she had sensed that he was relieved to see her go. Whatever it was—or whoever it was—he had to deal with that afternoon must have been important. A girl-friend? she wondered uneasily. After all, he had told her that he had fallen in and out of love many times. Perhaps whoever it was was unable to marry him? Married already, or just not wanting to be his wife. He would be going to say goodbye… She brooded over this sad fact of her imagination until it seemed to be true and, being a romantic girl at heart, she could have wept for him. Indeed, if she had been by herself she would have done so but Butter, after a lengthy silence, took it upon himself to tell her about the house they were going to.

'The house in Little Venice is nice enough,' he conceded, 'but the manor's a real home, as you might say. Not all that big but plenty of ground around it and a garden to be proud of, miss. Me and Mrs Butter, we've lived there for years. Served the doctor's father, we did. Very well-liked in the village he is, too. Old Mrs Tavener lives there too—got a companion and has rooms to herself. Under one roof, as it were, but independent, like.' He overtook a huge transporter and kept on in the fast lane.

He was a good driver; she had been surprised at that. He looked to be a very ordinary middle-aged man who would drive a family car at a steady forty miles an hour, and here he was whizzing along at almost twice that speed.

'Not going too fast for you, miss?'

'No, no, I like speed.'

'Now the doctor—he's one for speeding in that Rolls of his. Do you drive, miss?'

'I used to. A Rover.'

'Nice little car. There's a Mini in the garage at the manor, just right for getting around on your own.'

She supposed that she would be on her own for a good deal of her days. She tried to visualise her future and couldn't.

They were almost there and she longed for a cup of tea and at the same time wished that they could drive on for a long while yet because she was nervous of meeting Titus's grandmother. That they had already met wasn't any help for then she had been the caretaker, answering the door and hanging up coats and taking umbrellas. The old lady might hate the idea of her grandson marrying a working girl, never mind what he had said.

The village came in sight, small and red-roofed and stone-built, tucked away in a narrow valley between the hills, the church—much too big for its size— standing in the centre, the one road running past it, uphill a little and turning sharply at the top.

She caught her first glimpse of the manor then, and sighed with delight. It made a lovely picture in the winter twilight, its windows lighted, and as Butter came to a stop before the door it was thrown open and a small, stout woman, oblivious of the cold, stood on the steps.

Arabella, helped from the car by Butter, clasped Bassett to her and crossed the sweep with him, carrying a muttering Percy in his basket.

'There now.' The little woman took Arabella's free hand and shook it. 'I'm Mrs Butter, miss, and very happy to welcome you. Come on in out of the cold—you'll be wanting a cup of tea, I'll be bound. Mrs Tavener and Miss Welling have had theirs this hour past but I'm to see that you have a cup before you do anything else, so let me have your coat and I'll fetch the tea tray. Butter, take the little dog and the cat into the garden and then they can be with Miss Lorimer before they have their suppers.'

'There's a lead tied on to Bassett's basket,' said Arabella, 'and Percy's harness. Shall I do it?'

'Leave it to me, miss,' said Butter comfortably. 'Just you go and have that tea and then Mrs Butter'll take you to Mrs Tavener's rooms.'

So Arabella found herself in no time at all in a small panelled room, softly lighted by wall sconces and table lamps, furnished in great comfort with easy-chairs and with a brisk fire burning in the old-fashioned grate.

'The master uses this room a great deal,' Mrs Butter told her as she arranged the tea tray on one of the tables. 'Comes in from walking the dogs, he does, ''Mrs Butter,'' he says, ''I'm famished.'' And he sits down in his chair and he and the dogs between them eat enough for a giant. Well, I mean to say he is a giant, isn't he, miss? And a good man, never better!'

She paused on her way out. 'We're that pleased that he's getting married. This house needs a mistress and a pack of children.'

Arabella, slightly overwhelmed, smiled and nodded and murmured and, left alone, drank her tea and then ate the scones and jam. She was beginning to worry about Bassett and Percy when the door opened and Butter came in with Bassett prancing at his heels and Percy under his arm. A black Labrador came in too, nudging Bassett gently and going to Arabella to stare at her with a mild eye. She scratched his head and he sighed heavily with pleasure and then sat down before the fire, and presently the puppy settled beside him. Then, much to Arabella's surprise, Percy, after a few tentative advances, sat down too.

'Now, if you are ready, miss,' said Butter, 'I'll take you along to see Mrs Tavener. We can close the door and leave these three to make friends.'

He noticed her hesitation. 'Never fear, miss, Duke's as mild as milk and he loves cats too.'

The house, she discovered, was larger than she had thought, with a great many passages and steps and unexpected staircases. Mrs Tavener's apartments were on the first floor, at the end of a passage at the back of the house. Butter knocked on a door at its end and Miss Welling answered it, greeting Arabella with a smile and invited her in. 'Mrs Tavener is so looking forward to seeing you again, Miss Lorimer. May I wish you every happiness? We are all so delighted that the doctor is to marry.'

She led the way along a small passage with several doors and opened the end one. The room beyond was large with a bay window at one end and rather overfull of furniture. It was also very warm for there was a great fire burning in the elegant fireplace. Mrs Tavener was sitting upright in a tall-backed chair, a book on her lap.

'Ah, Titus's bride. My dear, I am so happy to welcome you to our family—come here and kiss me.'

Arabella weaved her way carefully through the tables, chairs and display cabinets and kissed the elderly cheek and, bidden to sit down, sat.

'Titus telephoned not half an hour ago. Wanted to know if you had arrived. He was on the point of leaving—such a nuisance that he couldn't drive you down himself. But I believe this was a matter which he wished to deal with personally. It will be delightful to have you here for a few days, my dear. You must treat this house as your home, for that is what it will be. I live here with Miss Welling, but I promise you that I don't interfere or intrude into Titus's life—nor will I with you.' She smiled. 'I hope that if you want advice or just someone to talk to you won't hesitate to come and see me.'

Arabella liked the old lady. 'I expect I shall need a great deal of advice. You see, I know very little about Titus's private life.'

Mrs Tavener gave her a thoughtful look. 'Well, dear, I'm sure that he will tell you anything you want to know. I don't suppose you have had much opportunity to talk together.'

Which was true enough, reflected Arabella.

Presently Mrs Butter came to fetch her. 'I'll show you your room, miss, for the doctor will be here within the hour and you'll want to be ready for him. I've taken the liberty of unpacking your things.'

Her room was charming, furnished with yew and applewood, its curtains pastel chintz, echoing the pale colours of the carpet and the bedcover. She bathed, resisting the wish to lie for ages in the warm water and allow her thoughts to wander, and then, wearing her only dress—needlecord in teal-blue, several years out of date but still elegant—her face nicely made-up and her hair neatly coiled, she went downstairs to the small room again to find the animals still sitting, apparently on the best of terms and very content. The carriage clock on the mantelpiece chimed the hour—seven o'clock, she saw with something of shock—and she wondered how much longer Titus would be.

He came in a few minutes later, Beauty with him. 'I'm sorry I wasn't here when you came down,' he said cheerfully. 'I got here half an hour ago and I've been in my study. You're quite comfortable? You've seen Grandmother? Good. Butter and Mrs Butter are looking after you, I hope?'

He sat down opposite her and Beauty edged her way past him to sit beside Percy.

'They seem to have settled down very well—I hope you will do the same, Arabella.'

She took care to sound pleasantly satisfied as well as friendly. 'Oh, I'm sure I shall. This is a very beautiful house, isn't it?'

'Yes. Tomorrow I'll take you over it and show you the grounds. Will you come to church with me in the morning?'

'Yes, I'd like that. Did you have a good drive down?'

'Excellent. We must try and come here as often as possible and it would be very pleasant for me if you will come with me when I have to keep appointments out of town. I must go over to Leiden at the end of the month—just for a couple of days. I have friends there whom I think you will like.'

'They're Dutch?'

'He is—his wife is English. We'll come here for Christmas, of course.'

Her head on the pillow and half asleep, several hours later Arabella decided that even if she had had doubts she had them no longer. Being with Titus was like being with an old friend. He had been quite right—without deep feelings for each other they were able to behave towards each other like old and tried companions.

She woke in the night and just for one moment thought that she was in her basement room. She sat up in bed, worried because she couldn't feel the animals on her feet, and then remembered that they had settled to sleep quite happily with Titus's two dogs in the kitchen and that she was in a quite different room.

The rector came back with them after church the next morning and his wife came too, frankly curious about Arabella and full of questions about the wedding. Over sherry Titus parried her artfully put questions and when they had gone told Arabella that she was a splendid rector's wife but eager to know everyone's business. 'She'll be at the wedding, of course. You won't find ten o'clock in the morning too early? We will have lunch here with Grandmother afterwards and drive up to town in the afternoon.'

He crossed the room and took her arm. 'Come and look round the house before lunch.'

It was a roomy old place. Besides the vast drawing-room there was a dining-room, his study, the little room the animals seemed to consider was theirs, and a room overlooking the garden at the back and opening on to a conservatory. They stood at its open door for a few moments, surveying the wintry gardens. 'There's a swimming-pool at the end behind those rhododendrons and the kitchen garden is through that small doorway at the end of the wall.' He turned away. 'Come upstairs—we'll leave the kitchen for the moment or we shall get under Mrs Butter's feet.'

At the top of the staircase he crossed the circular landing and opened double doors. 'This will be your room.'

It was large, with windows opening on to a small balcony, and carpeted in the colour of clotted cream. The curtains were rose-patterned and silk, as was the bedspread. The bed was a four-poster with a cream canopy highlighting the sheen of its mahogany. There was a vast dressing-table in the same wood, bedside tables bearing pink-shaded lamps and a chaise longue and small comfortable chairs in misty blue. It would be an enchanting place in which to wake up each morning. 'Oh, it's beautiful,' said Arabella, rotating slowly. 'What's through those doors?'

'Bathroom and beyond that a dressing-room. The other door is a clothes closet.'

Beyond the bathroom and dressing-room there was another bedroom, smaller and rather austere. 'My room,' said Titus briefly, and led her through another door back to the landing.

She lost count of the bedrooms she was shown and followed him up a smaller staircase to the floor above. The rooms here were smaller but well-furnished and at one end of the passage there was a baize door.

'The Butters have a flat,' he explained. 'There are two housemaids but they come each day.'

He glanced at his watch. 'We had better go down to lunch. This afternoon if you would like to we will go round the grounds.'

On their way downstairs he stopped. 'I entirely forgot,' he told her gravely, and took a small box from his pocket. 'Your ring…'

She took it slowly and opened its velvet lid. The ring was a half-hoop of splendid diamonds in an old-fashioned setting. 'It's been in the family for a long time—gets handed down from one bride to the next. I hope it fits.'

He made no move to put it on her finger. Arabella told herself that would have been sentimental nonsense anyway. It fitted well and she held up her hand to admire it. 'It's very beautiful.'

However unsentimental the giving had been, she mustn't sound ungrateful. She added warmly, 'Thank you very much, Titus. I shall wear it with pride.'

She smiled up at him and surprised a look on his face which puzzled her, but even as she looked it had gone and been replaced with his habitual bland expression. She must have fancied it.

At lunch old Mrs Tavener said, 'Ah—you're wearing the ring. You have pretty hands, Arabella. What do you think of your future home?'

They talked about the house and its history, the village and the people who lived there, and when the meal was finished the old lady went away to her room. 'Miss Welling goes down to the rectory for lunch on Sundays,' she explained, 'and Mrs Butter settles me for a nap. I dare say I shall see you at tea.'

After she had gone they sat for a little while over their coffee in the drawing-room, the animals stretched out before the fire, until Titus said, 'Fetch a coat and I'll take you round the gardens before the light goes.'

Even in the wintry weather the gardens were a great delight, and when he opened the door into the kitchen garden she said delightedly, 'Oh, it is—it reminds me…' and fell silent.

'Of your garden at home? I suppose that most of the country houses in these parts have these walled gardens. Come and see the greenhouses. I inherited the gardener with the house; he's old and crotchety and grows everything under the sun. I took on his grandson this summer—he will be just as good in time.'

'Only an old man and a boy for all this?' She waved an arm around her at the orderly rows, the bare fruit trees and the fruit bushes.

'A couple of men come in several times a week to give a hand with the heavy work. Come this way.'

She stayed where she was. 'Titus, I'm not sure…that is, I'm not sure if I can live up to you and all this.'

He took her arm and began to walk along the path bordering the rows of cabbages and leeks. 'Ah, now you can understand why I need a wife—someone to help me live up to it as well.'

'But it's your home.'

'And will be yours too…'

'You have an answer for everything.'

'No, no. The last thing I wish to do is coerce you. You have only to say, my dear, and you will be as free as air again.'

That brought her up short once more. 'You really

want me to marry you?' she asked. 'You're quite sure?'

'Quite sure.' He bent and kissed her cheek and took her arm again. 'Come with me, I've something to show you.'

He flung an arm around her shoulders and her doubts melted away. Surely being his wife wouldn't be as difficult as caretaking. 'Not another garden?' she asked as he went through a second arched doorway. 'Oh, stables.' She peered around her in the afternoon gloom. 'Do you ride?'

'Yes, as often as possible.' He opened the first stable door and said, 'Come inside.'

There was a pony there, and there was a small donkey too, and both raised their heads as she went in. The pony whinnied and came to meet her, followed by the donkey.

'Why,' said Arabella, 'it's Bess—and Jerry too!' She went between them, hugging them, murmuring into their ears and stroking them.

'A wedding present,' said Titus quietly. 'Here—sugar for Bess and a carrot for Jerry.'

She ignored that. 'Titus, oh, Titus, how can I ever thank you? It's the most marvellous thing to happen to me since I left home.' She didn't see the lift of his eyebrows and his faint smile. She left the animals and stretched up to kiss his cheek. 'You have no idea...' she began, and burst into tears.

He put an arm around her and let her weep into

his shoulder. Presently she gave a great sniff and muttered in a sodden voice, 'Oh, I'm so sorry, what a way to behave. Only, I'm so happy.'

He offered a large snowy handkerchief. 'It's nice to meet old friends again,' he observed in a comfortable voice. 'They're in good shape—you don't ride Bess any more, I imagine?'

'No, not since I was about fifteen. She's very old—so is Jerry.'

'Yes, I suppose so. Well, they can enjoy the rest of their lives here. There's a paddock beyond the yard here—we've had them out for a few hours each day. Old Spooner's grandson—Dicky—is splendid with animals. You can safely leave them in his care.'

She gave him a wide watery smile. 'I can't keep saying thank you,' she began.

'No need. I am delighted to have pleased you. Shall we go back to the house? I have to go directly after tea.'

She gave the animals a final hug, assured them that she would see them the following day, and walked back to the house, happily unaware that her unremarkable face wasn't improved by tearstains and a very pink nose.

Back at the house she went to her room and was horrified at the sight of her face in the looking-glass. At least it had been almost dark outside; Titus would have noticed nothing. She repaired the damage, smoothed her hair and went down for tea—a meal taken in Mrs Tavener's company with Miss Welling sitting like a shadow beside her. She still looked apologetic but Arabella noticed that she ate a hearty tea. She thought that probably Miss Welling was perfectly happy despite her downtrodden expression—she was certainly treated as an old friend by the Taveners and she had beamed her delight when she had wished Arabella happy. It was a pleasant meal but soon Titus got to his feet. 'I must go, Grandmother. I'll be down next Saturday morning, early. I'll see Butter about that.'

He stooped to kiss the old lady's cheek, shook Miss Welling's hand and whistled to Beauty. From the look he gave her, Arabella guessed quite rightly that she was to see him out of the house. She followed him into the hall where Butter was waiting.

Dr Tavener's directions took only a minute or so before Butter tactfully withdrew, leaving Arabella and Titus facing each other at the door. If she had hoped for anything of even a slightly romantic nature, she wasn't going to get it.

'Take Duke for a run each day, will you? Butter usually takes him but I dare say you'll go at a pace to suit Duke better. Let Butter know what day you want to go shopping. Don't bother to buy too much; you can shop all you want to when we get back to London. Take care of that puppy of yours and Percy—they seem to have settled down very nicely.'

He didn't ask if *she* had settled down nicely. A

flicker of resentment flamed inside her and died when she remembered Bess and Jerry.

'Drive carefully,' she said, and bent to pat Beauty's head.

He said, surprising her, 'You are happy, Arabella?'

'Thank you, yes, I am, Titus.'

He opened the door, kissed her briefly on a cheek, ushered Beauty into the car, got in himself and drove away with a casual wave as he went.

'After all, what did I expect?' Arabella asked herself, and went back to discuss a wedding outfit with Mrs Tavener.

Everyone was very kind; she was surrounded by warmth and comfort and people anxious that she should feel at home and happy. Although she had her meals with Mrs Tavener and Miss Welling she had the rest of the days to herself and despite the wintry weather she took Duke for long walks, getting to know the surrounding countryside. She had coffee with the rector and his wife too. The rector's wife was a dear little woman who took it for granted that Arabella and Titus were deeply in love. 'So very nice to have you at the manor,' she confided to Arabella. 'Titus has been single for too long. I look forward to you living there—it's a lovely old place, isn't it? Marvellous for children too.'

She misinterpreted Arabella's pink cheeks and smiled cosily.

Halfway through the week Butter drove Arabella to Bath, arranged to pick her up again in the late afternoon and drove off, leaving her to the exciting business of buying clothes. Every penny she possessed was in her purse—not a great deal of money but enough for what she intended to buy.

It was lunchtime before she had found what she wanted: a jacket and skirt in a fine wool in the blue of a winter sky. There was a matching silk top to go with them and, after a bit of poking around, she found a velvet hat with a high crown and a tiny brim. Pulled well down over her eyes, she fancied, it improved her looks…

It had been an expensive outfit so she went in search of the high street stores and found a pleated checked skirt with a three-quarter-length jacket to go with it, a couple of sweaters, some undies and a simple dress in stone-coloured cotton jersey—and she was almost penniless. She had pretty shoes and several pairs of good gloves salvaged from earlier days. She would have liked a handbag but that must wait. She ate a very overdue lunch in a small and cheap café and walked to where Butter was to pick her up.

Back in her room at the manor, she spread her purchases out on the bed. They were all right as far as they went but she would need to go shopping once she was married. Her wardrobe was woefully inadequate for the wife of an eminent physician. She tried on the hat and decided that it had been worth every penny of its price.

At dinner that evening she assured Mrs Tavener that she had had a most successful day shopping. 'I won't tell you what I've bought—I'd like it to be a surprise.'

Titus had telephoned once during the week. He would drive down with his best man—a friend of long-standing—and arrive for breakfast. Dr Marshall and his wife would arrive on the Friday evening—Butter had his instructions; they would stay the night at the manor. He would see her on Saturday morning at the church.

He had rung off with the kind of goodbye she might have expected from an older brother.

Mrs Butter, a great one for tradition, brought her breakfast up to her room on Saturday morning. 'The doctor's here, miss,' she said breathlessly. 'Dr and Mrs Marshall are having breakfast with him now. Do eat up—I'll be back in half an hour or so to run your bath. You mustn't be late at the church.'

Arabella ate her breakfast, for she had the good sense to know that she would be too excited to eat anything else for the rest of the day. She dressed carefully, wishing to make the best of herself; it was after all her wedding-day. She didn't look too bad, she considered, inspecting herself in the pier glass. It would have been nice if she had been pretty but since Titus wasn't in love with her she supposed that

that didn't matter very much, and the right clothes, the right make-up and a visit to a good hairdresser would certainly improve her looks.

It was time to go. Mrs Butter came to fetch her, wearing an overpowering hat and a buttonhole in her winter coat.

'You look lovely,' she said. 'Just like a bride should. The master's gone to the church and Dr Marshall's waiting for you.'

Dr Marshall kissed her. 'You look beautiful—that's a pretty thing you're wearing and I do like the hat. Let's go.'

It was to have been a very quiet wedding but half the village had crammed into the church. Arabella hesitated at the door but Dr Marshall nipped her arm. 'Titus wants you to have these,' he whispered, and handed her a little bouquet of roses and miniature lilies, pale pink, and mixed in with them were lily-of-the-valley, miniature daffodils and small sprigs of rosemary. She buried her nose in its fragrance and then took Dr Marshall's arm and walked serenely down the aisle, her eyes on Titus's broad back. When they were almost by him he turned to look at her and smile and she smiled back. Two old friends meeting, she thought in a muddled way. Everything was going to be all right.

She made her vows in a small firm voice, meaning to keep every word of them. The future was unpredictable but she intended to do her best to be the kind of wife he wanted. She didn't hear a word of the rector's short homily, so busy was she with her own thoughts.

The rest of the day passed in a dream; she smiled and talked and shook hands and was kissed, drank a little too much champagne, cut the cake with Titus's firm hand upon hers and at length found herself in the Rolls with the animals crowded in the back and all of them covered in confetti.

Once they were clear of the village Titus pulled into a lay-by.

'We should have brought a dustpan and brush with us,' he observed. 'Come here and be brushed down.'

They laughed about it together while she did the same for him and then the more difficult task of getting the confetti out of whiskery faces and furry coats commenced.

'That's better,' said Titus. 'Now I can see you. I like the hat!'

'Thank you, and thank you too for the beautiful flowers. It was a very successful wedding, wasn't it?'

'Indeed, yes. Now we will embark upon a successful marriage. Quite a different thing but one to which I look forward.'

'Me too,' said Arabella.

Mrs Turner had been at the wedding and Butter had left with her an hour or so before they had. She would be at Little Venice by the time they got there, ready to welcome them, and Butter would have started the drive back to the manor, anxious not to miss the party to be held in the village pub to celebrate the wedding.

Dr Tavener made good speed; there was very little traffic and although dusk was falling the road was clear but it was almost dark when he drew up before his house. All the lights were on and Mrs Turner flung open the door with a flourish.

'That's the best wedding I've ever been to,' she assured them as they went indoors. 'All the lovely flowers and the organ, and you, madam, looked a fair treat.'

Titus went to let the animals out and she said, 'Tea's all ready in the drawing-room. I'll see to the animals—you must both be needing a cup.'

'You're a jewel, Mrs Turner. Will you take Mrs Tavener up to her room first? I'll take the dogs and Percy into the garden—perhaps you would feed them presently?'

Arabella followed Mrs Turner up the staircase to a room at the back of the house, overlooking the canal. It was very large with doors opening on to a wrought-iron balcony and furnished in much the same style as her room at the manor—soft pastel colours, a wide four-poster bed and a dressing-table of applewood. There were a couple of comfortable chairs and pretty lamps on the tables, and delicate water-colours on the cream satin-striped walls.

'The bathroom's through that door and the dressing-room's on the other side, madam, and you've only to ask for anything you would like.'

'Mrs Turner, I'm sure everything is just perfect. I hope you will give me your advice…'

'That I will, with pleasure. Not lived in London before you went to the doctor's rooms?'

'No, my home was in the country, near Sherborne. Not anywhere as large as the manor but a nice rambling sort of house. This house is beautiful, though. It isn't like living in London at all and it's so quiet.' She turned from the window. 'You do have help in the house, Mrs Turner?'

'That I do. Maisie comes in each morning—a good girl, does her work as it should be done and always cheerful. I'll be going down to make the tea, madam, you must be fair parched.'

Later, sitting opposite Titus in the drawing-room, talking in a desultory manner while he went through his letters, Arabella had the strange feeling that they had been married for years, sitting in each other's company like an elderly married couple, easy with each other, comfortably silent if they wished. It was reassuring and what she supposed she had expected, only there was a vague doubt at the back of her head that Titus might discover one day that there was still a lot of life left before they reached the cosy stage. Supposing he met someone—some beautiful woman—and fell in love? He wouldn't be content to sit by the fire then, would he? She wasn't sure but she thought that he had never really looked at her, only as one would look at some familiar friend or a member of the family. He was comfortable with her, she was sure of that, and he liked her, but wouldn't he find that insufficient after a time? Would he miss his dinner parties and the divorced ladies bent on amusing him?

She frowned a little; she mustn't start thinking such thoughts on her wedding-day. She would make plans to improve her looks, buy clothes, meet people, give smart little dinner parties…

Dr Tavener, watching her, wondered what she was thinking. He said, 'It's been a long day. I dare say you are tired?'

'Well, yes, I am.' She uttered the fib with composure. 'You won't mind if I go up to bed?'

The alacrity with which he went to open the door was hardly flattering. She wasn't sure what she had expected; it certainly wasn't his pleasant goodnight. 'Sleep well, Will breakfast at eight-thirty suit you?'

'Yes, thank you. Do we go to church in the morning?'

'If you would come with me I should be very glad.'

'Well, of course I will. Goodnight, Titus.'

He kissed her cheek. 'No regrets?'

'Not a single one. I'd like to go to the kitchen and say goodnight to Percy and Bassett.'

'Of course. Have them in your room if you would like that.'

'No, no. I'm sure they are happy with Beauty.'

She slipped past him on her way to the kitchen and she didn't look back.

CHAPTER SIX

ARABELLA wasn't in the least tired. Curled up in the vast bed, she reviewed the day. It had gone without a hitch but then she had known it would; Titus wouldn't have stood for less than perfection. She had enjoyed the wedding and she felt at home here in this comfortable house by the canal although the manor house had her heart—besides, Bessy and Jerry were there. They would go there very often, Titus had said, and she knew him well enough to know that she could rely on him not to go back on his word. She wondered how she would fill her days, and went to sleep while she was still pondering that.

They breakfasted together, the two dogs and Percy lined up between them before the fire, discussing when they would go to the manor again, which day Arabella would like to go shopping, the best walks for the dogs—a pleasant, undemanding conversation. Arabella, notwithstanding her doubts of the previous night, felt very much at her ease.

'We'll take these two into the park this afternoon?' he suggested. 'Bassett needs a good run and Beauty will keep an eye on him.' He glanced at his watch. 'We can walk to church—it's only ten minutes or so. I've some telephoning—can we meet in an hour?'

She wandered round the house, getting to know her way around it, and then she went into the garden with the animals. It was a chilly morning and she was wearing her suit; her winter coat had seen better days and she hesitated to wear it to church. Probably Titus was known there and people might think her a very shabby sort of wife. It was fortunate that she still had a felt hat which would go very well with the suit—a dateless hat, plain and elegant and made by a well-known hatter.

He was waiting for her when she went downstairs. She was conscious of his eyes raking her person and went pink. 'Very nice,' he told her, 'but shouldn't you be wearing a thicker coat?'

She said simply, 'My winter coat is too old—you'd be ashamed of me.'

'Never. But you will be happier without it. Tomorrow you shall go to the shops and start to buy whatever you need, Arabella. I don't mean any shops—I've an account at Harrods; you'll go there, please, and buy anything and everything which may take your fancy.'

'That's a risky remark to make to a woman.'

'Not to you! As soon as I have time I'll get you settled with an allowance; in the meantime use Harrods.'

'It's a very expensive shop. I haven't been there for years.'

They were walking to church along the quiet

streets. 'Well, now you can have a browse round and see if it still suits your taste. I'll give them a ring in the morning and let you have my account number.'

'Thank you, but you must let me know how much I can spend—I haven't the least idea.'

He mentioned a sum which brought her to a halt. 'You can't mean that—why, it's a small fortune!'

He took her arm and walked her along. 'My dear Arabella, you are now my wife and I am proud of you, therefore, like all husbands, I want you to have all the pretty things you would like. Besides, now that I am a safely married man we shall have to entertain and I warn you that before you know where you are you will find yourself sitting on committees, drinking coffee and organising bazaars. For all these occasions you will need clothes. You like clothes, presumably?'

'Like them? Of course I do. I shall run mad at Harrods—it will take more than one day's shopping, too.'

'Take as many days as you like. I've a busy week ahead of me. We will go down to the manor at the weekend, though, and the following week I have to go to Leiden and I would like you to go with me.'

'I'd like that very much. My passport's out of date, though.'

'We'll see about that in the morning.'

They had reached the church and sure enough a number of people there greeted Titus as they took their places in one of the pews. She enjoyed the service even if once or twice her thoughts strayed to the shopping delights ahead of her.

Mrs Turner was a splendid cook—the roast beef was done to a turn, the vegetables were just right and the queen of puddings which followed was deliciously light. They had their coffee and since the winter days were getting short took the dogs into the park, walking until it was dusk, and Bassett was so tired that Arabella tucked him under one arm while Beauty raced to and fro, apparently inexhaustible.

They had tea round the fire and spent a pleasant evening discussing the week ahead. He would take her out to dinner during the week, he told her, adding with a twinkle, 'So that you will have a chance to air one of your new dresses.'

She sparkled. 'Oh, how lovely. Where?'

'Claridge's—we can dance.' He watched the colour come into her cheeks. 'I should be home early on Wednesday—shall we go then?'

'Oh, yes, please.' For a moment she was lost in a pleasant dream—transformed into a beauty overnight, wearing a gorgeous dress, making the kind of conversation which would set him smiling. She could at least have a try. Suddenly she wanted him to notice her, not just as a friend and companion but as an attractive woman…

'What plan are you hatching in that neat head of yours?' he wanted to know. 'We'll go down to the manor at the weekend and lay our plans for the trip to Leiden.'

Presently they dined, well pleased with each other's company so that later, Arabella, getting ready for bed, reflected that living with Titus was going to be a success. Of course it was early days yet but they had made a good beginning. They might even, she thought wistfully, become fond of each other in time. She had no illusions about his falling in love with her—if he hadn't lost his heart to all the charming females he must have known he wasn't likely to lose it to her. She chuckled about that and then went to sleep on a sigh.

They breakfasted together quite early and Arabella, aware that Titus wished to sift through his post, checking the various reports on his patients, did no more than wish him a cheerful good morning. Later, she thought hopefully, she would have post of her own. She had plenty to think about. She had wakened early and made a list of the clothes she would buy; now she reviewed it mentally, adding a few articles she had overlooked, trying to guess what everything would cost. She gave a guilty start when Titus said suddenly, 'Remember, Arabella, if you go shopping today, buy what suits you and don't look at the price labels.'

'Don't you want to know how much I've spent?'

'No. I'll pay the bills when they arrive and if they're too wildly extravagant I shall tell you so.' He smiled across the table. 'I gave you some idea of how much you might spend but I shan't cavil at a few hundred more.'

He left the house presently and she took the dogs and Percy into the garden. Beauty had already had an early morning run with Titus and Bassett was happy enough running around, teasing the patient Beauty and chasing an indignant Percy. They all went back indoors presently and Arabella went to the kitchen to talk to Mrs Turner.

'Will you take me round the house one day?' she asked. 'And tell me what the doctor likes and doesn't like—and I'd love to do the shopping sometimes if you would tell me what to buy.'

'Lor' bless you, madam, it'll be a pleasure to take you round the cupboards and pantry. There's china and linen and silver you must inspect and the tradesmen's bills. If you would come each morning we could discuss the meals for the day and make a list of the shopping if it's needed.'

'I'm going out now, Mrs Turner; I expect I'll be gone for quite a while. Would you please look after Beauty, Bassett and Percy?' She couldn't resist saying, 'I'm going to buy clothes.'

Mrs Turner looked positively motherly. 'And what could be nicer?' she wanted to know and added, 'But mind and have lunch, madam—shopping's tiring.'

Arabella wore the suit and felt hat; they were hardly high fashion but her shoes and gloves would pass muster anywhere. Mindful of Titus's request that she should take a taxi, she did so, feeling extravagant but it was a nice build-up to her day. She went through Harrods' elegant doors and began the delightful task of spending money.

By mid-morning she had acquired a winter coat—tobacco-brown cashmere—a brown and cream knitted three-piece, a jersey dress in copper, a beech-brown wool skirt, a cashmere cardigan and several blouses. She had a cup of coffee then, got her second wind, and went to look at dresses.

The choice was endless but she had a very good idea of what she wanted. By lunchtime she had tried on and bought a deep rose-pink dress in crêpe de Chine with a tucked bodice and a gored skirt which floated round her as she walked, a silk velvet dress in forest-green—very simple with a narrow skirt, long tight sleeves and a square neckline and, since she couldn't resist them, a wide midnight-blue skirt and an evening blouse with long full sleeves and a ruffled neck.

She went to the restaurant and had an omelette and coffee and decided that she had bought enough for one day. She had kept a rough check of the prices and although everything had cost a good deal there was still plenty over. Undies, shoes and a suit, she decided, as she was being taken back to her new home in a taxi loaded down with dress-boxes. It had begun to rain and she prudently added a raincoat to her list.

She had lunched late and Mrs Turner offered her tea as soon as she had got indoors. 'Well, just a quick cup,' said Arabella, 'before I take everything upstairs.'

'I'll see they go to your room, madam. Just you sit down and have that tea. Shopping can be tiring.'

So Arabella had her tea and presently, with the animals trailing stealthily behind her, went to her room. Here they arranged themselves tidily in a corner and watched her while she undid her packages and inspected what she had bought. She couldn't resist trying some of them on; she was twirling round in the pink crêpe de Chine when there was a knock on the door. It would be Mrs Turner, come to remind her that it had gone six o'clock and the doctor would be home presently. Arabella turned a guilty face to the door. 'Mrs Turner—do come in…'

Only it was Titus. She stopped in mid-twirl. 'Titus—I forgot the time—I thought it was Mrs Turner, come to tell me to come downstairs. I'm sorry—I did mean to be there, waiting for you…'

'Sitting with your knitting and the drinks poured?' He laughed then. 'My dear girl, you in that pink dress do me much more good than a soberly occupied wife.'

He cast his eyes round the room, strewn with clothes and tissue paper. 'You've made a start,' he commented drily. 'Will you wear this on Wednesday?'

She felt shy. 'If you would like me to. There are other dresses—I've bought an awful lot.'

'Splendid. I wondered where Beauty had got to. One of an admiring audience, I see.'

'Do you mind? I mean that they came upstairs with me? They were glad to see me.'

He crossed the room and took her hand. 'I'm glad to see you too, Arabella.' He kissed her briefly. 'Come down and have a drink before dinner. I'll take these three into the garden for a few minutes.'

He went away, whistling to the animals, who trooped after him, leaving her to get out of the pink dress and into the jersey dress, do her hair and do things to her face in a perfunctory way.

Dressed and ready on the Wednesday evening, she took stock of her person in the pier glass. The pink dress certainly gave an illusion of prettiness and between bouts of shopping on the previous day she had found time to buy the very best of face creams and powders and have her hair shampooed and cut. Indeed, fired by enthusiasm, she had tried out various new hairstyles but none of them seemed right. She ended up pinning her mousy locks on top of her head as she had done for years.

Perhaps it was the pink dress which made the evening such a success, although hardly a romantic one. Titus had had a busy day and she was a good listener.

A good deal of their dinner was taken up with his comments and observations on treatments, medicines and the art of the physician as opposed to that of the surgeon. Arabella listened with interest, filing away some of the longer words she had never heard before so that she could look them up later and know what he was talking about next time.

The waiter had come to offer them coffee when Titus asked, 'Would you like to dance? It seems a pity not to display that pretty dress.'

She got up at once, making some cheerful remark about the band while under the pink bodice she seethed with a sudden ill-temper. He might have made some pleasant remark about her person, never mind if it wasn't true. She was no beauty but she was aware that she looked attractive against the luxurious surroundings. Never mind the lack of looks, she told herself, you know how to dance…

She certainly did. She was light on her feet, as pliant as a reed and a graceful dancer. Titus, a good dancer himself, after the first few moments bent his head to say quietly in her ear, 'It's like dancing with a moonbeam! What a treasure I have married—not only a first-rate plumber but a delightful dancer. We must do this more often before I get too middle-aged!'

She looked up at that. 'Middle-aged? Of course you're not. Aren't you supposed to be in your prime?'

'Why, thank you, Arabella, you encourage me to fend off the encroaching years.' He smiled down at her. 'Do you know you're attracting a great many admiring glances?'

'Oh, no, I didn't.' She had gone pink. 'I expect its the dress...'

He stared down at the top of her neat head, smiling a little. He found her company delightful; she was so very natural, so unassuming, so ready to fall in with his plans and wishes. She made no effort to attract him either, and that, after the scheming young ladies he had from time to time considered himself in love with, was something that he was already appreciating.

They went down to the manor at the weekend and, since it was cold clear weather, they walked for miles with Beauty and Duke bounding ahead and Bassett doing his small best to keep up with them. Arabella, scooping him up, said, 'Perhaps we should have left him with Percy—he's still so very small.'

'He has the heart of a lion. Let me have him; he can sit inside my jacket.' He slowed his stride so that she could keep up. 'We go to Holland on Thursday. I think it might be a good idea if we brought this lot down before we go. Butter can look after them and Mrs Butter dotes on Percy. Are you looking forward to going?'

'Yes, I am. Will you be away all day?'

'Most of it, but I'm sure you'll get on with

Cressida. I've known Aldrik since we were students. Leiden isn't a large place but there are some good shops and plenty to see. You will be invited to the dinner which marks the end of the seminar—black ties and long dresses.'

'But everyone will be Dutch...'

'Well, I'm not, for a start. Besides, everyone there will speak English.'

'I think it might be fun.'

Titus, looking at her glowing face, found rather to his surprise that he agreed with her.

They had tea with Mrs Tavener before they went back to London. The old lady, with Miss Welling in close attendance, wanted a blow-by-blow account of their life there. 'It is a great deal more healthy here than in your London house,' she declared. 'Arabella's looks have improved a great deal since you arrived yesterday.' She broke off to take stock of Arabella, who blushed and looked into her teacup and thus missed Titus's long thoughtful stare. 'Of course,' went on the old lady, 'once the children come along, you will have to spend more time here; they'll thrive in the country air.'

Arabella went on looking into her teacup, while wishing it could give her a suitable answer. It was Titus who said easily, 'You are quite right, Grandmother, small children are happiest in the country. I hated leaving here when I was first sent to boarding-school.' A successful red herring which led the old lady to reminisce until it was time for them to leave.

If he even mentions it, thought Arabella, sitting silently beside him in the car, I'll throw something at him.

He never mentioned it, but talked easily of this and that so that by the time they were back at Little Venice she had managed to forget about it. All the same, she wished that they could have said something about it, laughed over it together, made a joke of it. It was the first time, she reflected, that they had avoided talking about something and she felt awkward about it. It was a good thing that Titus appeared to have forgotten about it, but perhaps he hadn't felt anything other than an amused interest in his grandmother's remarks.

They left early in the morning on Thursday to take the dogs and Percy to the manor, had a quick lunch there and then, after Arabella had raced down to the stables to make sure that the pony and the donkey were safe and well, they drove to catch the night ferry from Harwich. It was a long journey but Arabella, snug in her winter coat, her feet encased in fashionable boots, enjoyed it. They sped smoothly along the motorway until they reached the turning and circled round London to Watford, and then on to Hatfield, where they stopped for a late tea. It was a small café cosily lit and chintzy with very ladylike waitresses in flowered aprons; the tea was hot and plentiful and the buttered crumpets were delicious. Arabella sank her splendid teeth into them with a contented sigh.

'This is fun,' she said.

Titus found himself agreeing with her, reflecting that when he was with her he felt ten years younger.

They drove on presently and went on board the ferry. After dinner Arabella went to her cabin and despite the rough crossing slept soundly. Titus, watching her enjoying an early breakfast of rolls and coffee, smiled to himself. Their marriage was going to be a success; she was not only a good companion, she was sensible—accepting situations without fuss, undemanding of his attention and time and, he had to admit, really quite pretty now that she had new clothes. He studied her from lowered lids as she buttered a roll. What was more, she was dressed exactly as he would like to see her…

Leiden was less than half an hour's drive away. Arabella got glimpses of it as Titus drove through the town and presently turned into a narrow street lined with gabled houses, old and beautifully maintained. He helped her out, took her arm and urged her across the narrow cobbled pavement and pulled the wrought-iron bellpull beside an elegant front door. It was opened by an elderly rather bony-faced woman and a very large St Bernard dog, accompanied by a small insignificant beast. The woman smiled and the doctor said, 'Mies, how nice to see you again.' He patted the dogs' heads and added, 'Arabella, this is Mies—Cressida's housekeeper.'

She shook hands and was ushered inside as a small young woman came racing down the staircase. 'Titus—I should have been on the doorstep!' She lifted her face for his kiss and turned to Arabella. 'I'm Cressida—I'm so glad to meet you, Arabella.' She beamed happily, her lovely eyes sparkling from a very ordinary face. 'Aldrik has had to go to the hospital but he'll be back before lunch. Come on in and have some coffee. Titus, do go into the drawing-room—I'm going to take Arabella upstairs.'

Arabella followed her hostess upstairs, relieved at finding her so friendly. She had been a little worried that Cressida could have been a statuesque blonde and talked down to her. Instead here was this nice girl the same size as herself and certainly no beauty, although she looked so happy that she could have passed as beautiful.

'Titus said he would be late back each evening—seminars and things,' Cressida said vaguely, 'so I've put you in here and there's a dressing-room next door so that he needn't disturb you if it's the small hours.'

She sat down on the bed. 'This was my room—I mean when Aldrik brought me back here—just for a night, then he took me to Friesland to a friend's house to look after some children.' She smiled gently. 'He's nice—I do hope you'll like him. We think Titus is a dear too.'

Arabella had been poking at her hair and was sitting at the dressing-table, not saying much.

'Come and see the twins before we go downstairs. They're two months old—one of each. We are lucky, aren't we? A splendid start to the family.'

They were asleep—the little girl with mousy hair like her mother, the boy very fair. 'They're very good,' said their proud mother, 'and we've a wonderful nanny—my old housekeeper's niece.'

She led the way downstairs and into the drawing-room. 'Forgive me for talking so much, but I'm so glad to meet you. I've English friends, of course, but most of them live in Friesland—we've another house there...'

The room was warm and bright, with a brisk open fire and furnished with a nice mixture of antique furniture and comfortable chairs.

Titus got up as they came in, and the two dogs with him, staying politely on their feet until the three of them were seated and then collapsing into contented furry heaps before the fire. They talked over their coffee. It seemed that Titus knew many of the van der Linuses' friends and there was cheerful talk about St Nicolaas. 'I wish you could be here for that,' said Cressida. 'It's such fun for the children.' She jumped to her feet. 'Here's Aldrik...'

Arabella took to him at once. He was a year or

two younger than Titus and his hair was already flecked with grey, but he was a handsome man—very tall and broad. He kissed his wife, then shook Titus's hand and smiled down at Arabella. 'I'm only sorry this is to be such a short visit,' he told her. 'Titus must bring you over for a week or two and come up to Friesland. That is our real home.'

Arabella thought privately that the one they were in now would do very nicely. 'Don't you work here?' she asked.

'Yes, but not all the time. Have you seen the twins?'

'Yes, they're adorable.'

He gave his wife a loving glance. 'We think so.' He went to sit down by Titus. 'There's a paper being read on asthma this afternoon. Do you care to come?'

They didn't linger over lunch and the men went away as soon as it was finished so, since it was a fine cold afternoon, the babies were wrapped up warmly, tucked into their pram and taken for a walk. They had been fed and played with and now they slept while the two girls gossiped. It struck Arabella that she had missed that during the last few months—cheerful chatter about clothes and husbands and babies, all of it light-hearted. They went back to tea and then to the nursery to help Nanny bath the twins, feed them once more and tuck them up in their cots. The men came home then, to pay a visit to the babies, which meant lifting them out of their cots while

Nanny clucked her disapproval. Not that they minded—they made small contented noises into their father's broad shoulder and had no objection when they were passed to Titus.

Arabella, changing for dinner, hummed a little tune as she dressed. This was a happy household and the babies were delightful. It would be nice... She wasn't going to think about that, she told herself resolutely, and went downstairs to drink her sherry and enjoy the roast pheasant and red cabbage, game chips and roasted parsnips. It was beautfully cooked and served in the splendour of starched linen and silver, delicate china and crystal glasses.

The seminar started at eight o'clock in the morning and although they all breakfasted together the two men wasted no time over it. Aldrik gave his wife a lingering kiss and Titus pecked Arabella's cheek with a cheerful, 'See you later, Arabella.'

Cressida noticed that out of the corner of her eye and checked a small doubt. It was obvious that Titus and Arabella got on well together, were at ease with each other, but there was something missing...

'After I've fed the babies at ten o'clock would you like to come into the town and see the shops? They are not bad at all although I go to den Haag for my clothes. I do like that suit...'

It was as they were having their lunch that Aldrik phoned to say that he was bringing Dr Tulsma to dinner. 'She met Titus last time he was over here, darling, and shares his interest in long-term medication. I'm sorry—I know you don't like her but she more or less invited herself and Titus seemed quite enthusiastic. It's a subject dear to him, you know.'

'Well, there's nothing to do about it, is there, darling? Only don't let her stay to all hours.'

'We'll be back around six o'clock. Are you having a pleasant day with Arabella? Are the babies all right?'

'I'm enjoying myself very much; she's a dear and the babies are fine.'

'Darling,' said Aldrik, and rang off.

'There's someone coming to dinner,' said Cressida. 'A doctor—she's frightfully clever and she'll talk about enzymes and antibodies and things. She's invited herself and I'm sorry—I was looking forward to a chatty evening. If she suggests coming again I'll say we're going out for the evening.'

They spent a lazy afternoon and after tea bathed the babies and put them to bed since it was Nanny's evening off, and then they changed. Arabella, going through the clothes she had brought with her, decided on the jersey dress. Simple, beautiful material and worth every penny she had paid for it. Doing her hair, she decided that when she got back home she would go to a good hairdresser and have a perm, even have it all cut off—anything as long as it was different from the mousy topknot she was now arranging so neatly.

She and Cressida were in the drawing-room when the men got back.

Aldrik opened the door with a cheerful hello and stood back to allow a young woman to walk past him. Cressida hadn't said what she was like—arrestingly handsome, with large blue eyes and corn-coloured hair in little curls all over her head, and her dress, of some flowing silky stuff, was cut low over an opulent bosom. She didn't look in the least like a doctor but vaguely romantic and mysterious. Arabella, being introduced, smiled and held out a hand. The enemy, she thought silently, and wondered why she had thought that.

Titus had smiled at her as he came into the room but that was all. She felt resentment bubbling up and suppressed it; later she would give it full rein... 'How delightful to meet you,' said Arabella mendaciously. 'What interesting work you do, and you and Titus share a common interest, don't you?' She sat down on a small sofa and patted the place beside her. 'Do sit down and tell me something about it. Have you known Titus a very long time?'

Geraldine Tulsma eyed her carefully. 'On and off for several years. You and Titus haven't been married long, have you?'

'No—but of course we've been friends for some time.' Arabella spoke airily. 'You're not married? Titus says you're very clever.'

Aldrik had given them their drinks and Arabella

settled against the cushions, aware that the dress was falling in very satisfactory folds around her person. After all, that was what she had paid for...

'No, I'm not married. I have refused offers of marriage many times; my work is very important to me.' She spoke sharply. Here was this plain girl asking her patronising questions. 'Has Titus never spoken of me to you?'

'Well, no. What I mean is, I dare say he might have mentioned you—just to remark on your cleverness, you know. We have so many shared interests—nothing to do with his work or hospital.'

'I have come this evening so that I may continue to exchange views with Titus.'

'What a good idea. It's a pity you don't see more of each other.' She looked up as Cressida joined them.

'Getting to know each other?' she wanted to know. 'I'm sorry we haven't got a man for you, Geraldine, but it was such short notice.'

'I do not mind. It is Titus I wish to talk to.'

'Very well, why not? But shall we dine first?'

Arabella ate asparagus, coq au vin and chocolate and orange mousse piled high with whipped cream, and it all tasted the same—of nothing. Her keen dislike of Geraldine had taken away her appetite although she talked and laughed as everyone else did. Geraldine tended to carry on in a tedious fashion about herself, her aims and her ambitions and theories. They went back to the drawing-room for coffee and presently Geraldine suggested that she and Titus should have a quiet talk.

Arabella overheard her. 'I'm sure Titus is anxious to hear your views.' She gave him a smile as bright as a dagger's edge and he blinked at it before saying smoothly,

'Indeed I am, if you don't mind, Cressida? We don't want to inflict medical matters upon you.'

'Use my study,' said Aldrik. 'There'll be more coffee presently.'

When they had gone Cressida went up to the nursery to make sure that the twins were sleeping. 'I'm sorry that Geraldine invited herself here this evening,' said Aldrik, 'she's heavy-going.' He glanced at his watch. 'I'll suggest driving her back as soon as we've had some more coffee.'

'It's very nice,' said Arabella carefully, 'that Titus has met someone he enjoys talking to. I mean, I don't know anything about hospitals and medicine...'

'Nor does Cressida—you have no idea what a blessing and a joy it is to come home each evening to someone who doesn't know ichthyosis from nettle-rash...'

'I do know what nettle-rash is!' said Arabella. They were laughing about that as Titus and Geraldine came back into the room and Aldrik rang for more coffee.

Cressida came back and they sat around drinking

it, chatting idly until Aldrik said, 'Isn't it time you saw to the twins, my love? I'll run Geraldine back home while you're doing that.'

'Don't bother,' said Geraldine. 'I've already asked Titus to drive me back. We can finish our discussion—there hasn't been enough time...'

Titus put down his cup. 'Then, shall we go?' he enquired mildly. 'We start early tomorrow morning, do we not?'

'Such a pity that you are only here for such a short time,' declared Geraldine in her rather loud voice. 'We really should meet more often...'

A little imp of mischief took over from Arabella. 'Then why don't you come and visit us?' she asked, and smiled at Titus. 'Wouldn't that be a good idea, Titus?'

His face was inscrutable; she had no idea if he was pleased or not. 'Oh, splendid,' he said. 'Shall we be going, then?'

Geraldine pecked the air above Cressida's cheek, offered a hand to Arabella and said, '*Tot ziens*,' to the room at large.

'See you all later,' said Titus as he followed her out.

Cressida and Aldrik went to the door with them and Arabella went to the window. The light from the hall streamed out into the street and she could see Titus and Geraldine standing by the car, holding a conversation in which she took no part, laughing at some joke which she couldn't hear.

The enemy, thought Arabella. Geraldine was modern to her fingertips, attractive and determined—divorce would mean nothing to her and Titus was a prize worth having. I'm exaggerating, thought Arabella, and why do I feel like this about her? It isn't as if I love Titus. She caught her breath, because of course that wasn't true. She did love him; she was in love with him. She closed her eyes for a moment and when she opened them the car had gone. A good thing too, she reflected, for I might have gone outside and thumped Geraldine and flung myself at Titus.

She wanted to cry at the hopelessness of it all. Instead she stitched a smile on to her face and turned to make some cheerful remark to Cressida, unaware that she was as white as a sheet and trembling.

CHAPTER SEVEN

CRESSIDA was on the point of asking Arabella if she felt ill but Aldrik touched her arm and said cheerfully, 'Come over to the fire, Arabella. We're going to have another cup of coffee—do have one too.'

He began to talk about the evening and then the various lectures and the seminar he and Titus were to attend. 'Next year it will be held in London and so we shall see something of you there.'

'You must come and stay.' Arabella had pulled herself together. 'We shall love to have you and the babies, of course.'

They sat for half an hour or so and since there was no sign of Titus Arabella went to bed, to lie awake until she heard Titus's tread long after midnight. This is a pretty kettle of fish, she told herself. Of course, now she thought about it, she had been falling in love with Titus for weeks only she hadn't realised it. Would it have helped if she had known that before he had asked her to marry him? she wondered. She would have refused; being married to someone who didn't love you when you loved them would be an unbearable state in which to live. One in which she now found herself. But there is no reason, she reflected, why I shouldn't have a try at getting him to fall in love with me. The right make-up, a good hairdresser, attractive clothes, sparkling conversation and her feelings disguised under a friendly manner—but not too friendly. He must never think that she was trying to attract his attention or that she had no other interest in life but him.

A few tears escaped and trickled down her cheeks and she wiped them away impatiently. If she was to get the better of Geraldine and her like tears would be of no use. Suddenly full of determination to get the better of the enemy, Arabella went to sleep.

The men had already breakfasted and gone when she went down to breakfast with Cressida. 'I've been awake for hours,' said Cressida pouring their coffee. 'Aldrik read his paper to me—he always does, not that I understand any of it. He says it will bring him luck, not that he needs it. Did Titus wake you up to listen to his paper?' She didn't wait for an answer. 'We're a captive audience, aren't we?'

'I expect he's breaking me in gently,' said Arabella lightly. 'Do the twins let you sleep all night?'

'Oh, yes. Once or twice I've had to feed them in the small hours but now they're bigger they usually sleep right through until six o'clock. Aldrik's awfully good—we don't disturb Nanny and by the time they've settled the morning tea arrives.' She poured more coffee. 'Tell me, what did you think of

Geraldine?' She grinned. 'You don't need to be polite.'

Arabella buttered some toast. 'I didn't like her. Far too handsome for one thing and so pleased with herself. All that bosom too…'

Cressida laughed. 'Frightful, isn't she? She's brilliantly clever, though. Aldrik can't stand her but even he admits that he admires her brain.' She glanced at Arabella. 'Did Titus give you his opinion? She kept him long enough—we heard him come in last night.'

'Yes, he was very late—I do hope he didn't disturb you.' She added for good measure, 'He was far too tired to talk about her.'

'You'll get the lot—chapter and verse. That's what's so nice about being married, telling each other things you would never dream of telling anyone else.'

Arabella agreed so quietly that Cressida made haste to talk about something else. 'If you would like to go sightseeing Nanny will have the twins until lunchtime. We might take a look round the town—there's the university and the Pieterskerk and the Rapenburg Canal. We can see the hospital from there too. There's Breestraat and the Town Hall and the St Anna Almshouses…'

'All in one morning?'

'Well, it will be a quick peek here and there but better than nothing. We must find time for coffee at Rotisserie Oude Leyden too…'

The morning was passed pleasantly and rather to their surprise the men came home for lunch.

'We didn't expect you,' said Cressida, lifting her face for a kiss. 'But now you're here we're very pleased.'

'We decided that the whole day without seeing either of you would be too long. What have you done with yourselves?'

They came home again soon after six o'clock that evening, and without Geraldine. Arabella, curling up in bed that night, thought with pleasure of the cosy evening—a delightful dinner and then sitting round the fire in the drawing-room talking about everything under the sun. Titus had kissed her with a sudden and unexpected warmth when she had gone upstairs with Cressida. Of course it might have been because the others were there watching them but she didn't think that he would pretend to something he didn't feel. They were going out on the following evening, she remembered sleepily. She would wear one of her new dresses…

She was glad that she had chosen to wear the pink dress for they drove to den Haag where they dined at the Bistroquet—small and exclusive and, she guessed, wildly expensive. Afterwards they went to Scheveningen, to the Steigenberger Kurhaus, to dance and visit the casino. Titus had bought her some chips and she had tried her luck and won, and so had

Cressida. She would have liked to put her winnings back on the table but the men had swept them back to dance. It had been a lovely evening and she had spent a good deal of it in Titus's arms dancing and, just for the moment, happy.

The next day was their last, with a formal banquet in the evening, and Arabella was glad that she had packed the green velvet. Inspecting her person before she went downstairs to join the others, she decided that she looked like a consultant's wife. She wished that Titus had given her a necklace as she fastened the double row of pearls her father had given to her on her eighteenth birthday. They were good ones and of course her engagement ring was everything a girl could wish for...

'Oh, very nice,' said Cressida as she went into the drawing-room. She looked quite delightful herself in a smoky grey taffeta dress. She wore a diamond necklace and an exquisite bracelet—Arabella caught a glimpse of them as Aldrik wrapped her lovingly in an angora wrap.

Titus held her evening cloak with the impersonal courtesy which he might have afforded an elderly aunt... Arabella, suddenly angry, thanked him politely, her cheeks pink. He might at least pretend.

Titus, watching her from under his heavy lids, thought what a very pretty girl she had become in the few weeks of their marriage. It was the clothes, he supposed. When they got back to England he would look around for some jewellery for her. He felt a surge of delight at the sight of her and bent to kiss her cheek, an action which pleased Cressida, who, in the privacy of their bedroom, had informed Aldrik that their guests didn't behave in the least like a newly married couple.

'My dear love,' her husband had observed, 'you cannot judge others by our own experience. Probably they—er—let themselves go when they are alone, just as we do.'

The banquet was a grand affair and very formal. Arabella had never seen so many large elderly gentlemen in black ties, smoking cigars and tossing off tiny glasses of *genever*, nor had she seen so many dignified ladies with severe hairstyles and large bosoms encased in black satin. There were younger people there, of course, but they were swamped by the senior members of the university and the hospital. They were nice, she discovered, these self-assured dignitaries, and Titus seemed to know all of them. She was handed round and smiled at and patted and told how glad they were to see dear Dr Tavener married to such a charming little wife.

She sat next to a younger man at dinner, with an older man on her other side, both of whom made much of her so that her lovely eyes sparkled and her face glowed—not entirely with pleasure, though. Titus, she noted, had Geraldine on his right on the opposite side of the long table. Geraldine, she had to admit, looked strikingly handsome in peacock-blue chiffon. A pity there was to be no dancing, she reflected. As it was, they sat for a long time over dinner and then listened for even longer to a succession of speeches—some in English but most of them in Dutch. It was hard to maintain a look of interest. When they rose at last little groups were formed while, coffee-cups or glasses in hand, people wandered from one to the other. The men were for the most part serious—swapping diagnoses, she supposed, listening with an air of great interest to an elderly professor detailing the history of the university to her.

It was as they were preparing to leave that she came face to face with Geraldine. 'Oh, there you are.' Her voice was patronising. 'I have hardly spoken to you all evening, have I?' She smiled in a self-satisfied manner and swirled the chiffon to show it to its best advantage. 'Titus and I have had a delightful evening—you don't mind, do you? We have known each other…'

Arabella interrupted her. 'Any friend of Titus's is a friend of mine,' she said sweetly, 'and do remember that we shall be delighted to see you if ever you come to England. Perhaps your work keeps you here, though?'

'No, no. I am well-known both in England and the States, as well as in Europe.' She gave a satisfied little laugh. 'I am free to take a holiday when I wish.'

'How nice,' said Arabella. 'It's been pleasant meeting you. We're going home tomorrow but of course Titus will have told you… So I'll say good-bye.'

Geraldine offered a hand. 'Shall we not say, *tot ziens*? That means—'

'Yes, I know what it means. I must go—I can see Cressida waiting for me.'

There was no sign of Titus. 'A good thing he came in his own car,' said Cressida. 'He's driving Geraldine back. Why that woman can't drive her own car beats me—anyone would think that she had already asked—' She stopped as Aldrik squeezed her arm.

'The trouble with Geraldine is that given an inch she takes an ell.' He took Arabella's arm. 'Did you enjoy your evening? It was all a bit serious, I'm afraid.'

'I enjoyed myself,' said Arabella, her eyes sparkling with temper. 'What a handsome lot of professors and medical people you've got living here.'

'Indeed, yes. I have to keep a tight rein on Cressy when we come to these gatherings; she's inclined to fall for bearded professors!'

'If you ever grow a beard I shall leave you,' declared Cressida as they went out to the car. 'When we get home I shall make a big pot of tea and we can drink it in the kitchen while we tear the women's dresses to pieces. There was one—you must have seen it, Arabella—purple crushed velvet, very tight in the wrong places…'

On this light-hearted note the evening ended, but although she sat for some time, drinking tea out of mugs and discussing the evening, there was no sign of Titus.

Arabella, with the excuse that she must do some packing if they were to leave in time for the ferry in the morning, went to bed, declaring that she hadn't enjoyed herself so much for years. 'You must all come and stay soon,' she said. 'I shall miss you so.'

After she had gone Cressida collected up their mugs. 'Darling,' she began, 'there's something not quite right…'

'My love, Arabella and Titus are grown people.' He smiled. 'Somehow I don't think we need to worry. Arabella is no fool, Cressy.'

'Does that mean that Titus is?'

'No, no—we men are notoriously blind, love, as you well know.'

She skipped across the kitchen into his arms. 'I'd like them to be as happy as we are.'

Titus was at breakfast looking well rested and impeccably turned out. He and Aldrik had been out with the dogs and were in some deep discussion while Arabella and Cressida talked of Christmas and what they planned to do. Presently they went upstairs to see the babies and then it was time to go. The men had joined them in the nursery but time was running out. They made their final goodbyes, got into the car and drove to the Hoek, boarded the ferry and, in due course, landed at Harwich.

They were home that evening to be greeted by Mrs Turner, a great pile of letters for Titus and a number of messages on the answering machine. Titus, coming from his study just before they were to sit down to dinner, came into the drawing-room.

'I have to go to the hospital—it's a matter of some urgency. I'm sorry, Arabella. Please don't wait up if I'm not back. Tell Mrs Turner to lock up; I'll let myself in.'

'We'll leave something for you in the kitchen; it'll keep hot on the Aga. I hope it's nothing too serious and that you can put it right.'

He came across the room and bent to kiss her. 'What a perfect wife you are, Arabella. This does happen from time to time.'

'Well, it's bound to, isn't it?' she said in a matter of fact voice. 'Be sure and have something when you get back if we are all in bed.'

She listened to the street door closing and went to tell Mrs Turner, reflecting that a doctor's wife could expect this—and not just once but over and over again.

She ate her solitary dinner, thinking about him. He was everything a girl could wish for and she loved him—two reasons to strengthen her resolve to make him love her. He liked her and perhaps he felt affection for her—but that wouldn't do. She would have to do something to make him see her with different eyes—not just as a quiet companion, ready at hand to listen when he wanted to talk or walk, but as a girl to take him by surprise so that he really saw her.

He hadn't returned by eleven o'clock; Mrs Turner had already locked up so Arabella went to bed.

'Was it all right?' Arabella asked at breakfast. Titus was already at the table but he got up to pull out her chair. He looked as though he had had a good night's sleep but her loving eyes could see that he was tired. 'Were you up all night?'

'Until just after four o'clock this morning. He'll pull through.'

'I'm glad. It must make you feel good.'

He smiled. 'Yes, it does. I'll be at my rooms until this afternoon, then the hospital. I expect to be home soon after five o'clock.'

'Oh, good. Shall we have tea together?'

'That would be delightful. What are you going to do today?'

'Well—I thought I'd go to the hairdresser. I wondered if I had my hair cut short and permed—'

He said with surprising sharpness, 'No, Arabella, I like your hair just as it is—don't let anyone touch it. Have it washed as often as you like but not an inch of it must be cut off.'

She stared at him round-eyed. 'All right, Titus,

then I won't. Only I thought it would improve my looks.'

'Your looks are very nice as they are.'

'Thank you. I thought you liked short curly hair and I wanted to please you.'

'Well, I don't and that reminds me—why in heaven's name did you ask Geraldine Tulsma to come and see us?'

She looked meek. 'Titus, I thought you liked her, and she told me that you were old friends. You spent a lot of time together…'

She spoke so artlessly that he sat back and looked at her thoughtfully. He smiled then. 'So we did. She's very attractive, isn't she? Apart from her brilliant brain.'

'She's almost beautiful and it must be nice to be able to talk about things and know the person you're talking to understands exactly what you're saying.' She took a breath. 'She would have made you a splendid wife, Titus—if I'd known about her…'

'An interesting thought, my dear.' He got up, patted her on the shoulder in what she felt was an avuncular fashion and said, 'I must be off. See you this evening.'

She telephoned the manor when he had gone and talked for a long time to old Mrs Tavener and then spoke to Butter, who assured her that the dogs and Percy were fine and that Bess and Jerry were full of spirit. 'Looking forward to seeing you, ma'am—coming for the weekend, I hope?'

'I do hope so, but I don't know if the doctor will be free. I want to talk about Christmas with Mrs Butter...'

'We'll hope to see you, ma'am.'

It would be nice to be at the manor again, she thought, and went to put on her outdoor things. She hadn't thought about Christmas presents—it might be a good idea to look round the shops and decide on what to buy. It would have been fun to have had Titus with her.

When he got home he asked her what she had been doing.

'Looking at the shop windows, trying to decide what to buy for Christmas presents,' she told him.

'I'll give myself a half-day tomorrow—in fact I had arranged it some time ago. We'll go shopping together.'

'Oh, Titus, how lovely. I've made a list...'

She didn't think she would ever forget their afternoon together. He parked the car in the forecourt of a hospital near the Brompton Road and walked her to Harrods to embark on the kind of shopping spree every woman would dream of. There were gloves for Miss Baird, a crimson dressing-gown for Mrs Turner, a charming tea-service for the Butters, a fine woollen stole for Miss Welling in rose-pink—to give her some colour, as Arabella said—the latest novels for Cressida, teething-rings for the twins, a hamper for Mr Flinn and a beautiful vase for the Marshalls.

'That takes care of the bulk,' said Titus. 'We give the nurses a bottle of wine and a cheque and the same for the maids and the gardener at the manor.'

'And the boy who helps in the garden?'

He smiled down at her. 'I happen to know that he wants football boots—he's in the village team. The men who come up to help had better have cash. Now we have to find something for Grandmother.'

The jeweller's shop was like an Aladdin's cave. 'What do you suppose she would like?' asked Titus.

'Something she can put on easily,' said Arabella very sensibly. 'And something she can wear each day if she wants to. A chain perhaps?'

They had looked at chains of all types and chosen a fairly long one of gold links with a gold tassel. It was a beautiful thing and just right for the old lady. While it was being wrapped up Arabella went from showcase to showcase, admiring their contents, but only to herself. Titus was a generous man—if she evinced a desire for a diamond necklace she had no doubt that he would buy it for her. That wasn't what she wanted, though. She would rather have a bag of apples he had bought for her without any hint on her part.

They went home presently and piled the parcels on the sitting-room table. 'I'll leave you to wrap them up,' said Titus easily. 'I'm sure you'll do it beautifully. They will keep you occupied tomorrow—I'm going to Birmingham to a consultation; I may stay the night.'

He looked at her as he spoke and she quickly arranged her features to an expression of interested concern. 'Would you like me to pack a bag for you? You'll drive there?'

'Yes—you won't be lonely?'

'Good gracious, no.' She had spoken too quickly and added, 'Not with all those presents to wrap up. Besides, I've still a few more presents to buy and what about the Christmas cards?'

They had chosen them and ordered them to be printed but she had no idea to whom they should be sent when they arrived.

'There is a list in the top right drawer of my desk in the study; you can safely send a card to each address on it. I usually get Miss Baird to do them but it would be much nicer if you were to sign them yourself for us both.'

'Very well. You will be free to go to the manor for Christmas?'

'Yes, unless something very urgent crops up. We'll go down next Saturday too, shall we?'

'Yes, please. It will be nice to see the animals again. Butter says they're all very well and happy and I talked to your grandmother—she was hoping you'd be free next weekend.'

He nodded. 'I've some work to do now—could dinner be put back for half an hour or so?'

'Of course. I'll go along and see Mrs Turner.' As they crossed the hall she said, 'It was a lovely afternoon, Titus, thank you for taking me.'

'I enjoyed it too.' He sounded remote.

In his study he didn't pick up the telephone immediately. It was quite true, he had enjoyed himself—perhaps because Arabella had been so obviously delighted with everything she saw. Her ordinary face under her charming hat had glowed with pleasure. She was, he decided, really a pretty girl and her new clothes had made no difference to her; she was still forthright and sensible and undemanding. A most agreeable person to live with and one he would miss—the very thought of that made him frown. Really he was getting quite fond of her.

His work forgotten, he allowed his thoughts to wander.

Arabella's thoughts were wandering too as she changed into one of her new dresses, but they wandered to some good purpose. Sternly suppressing her more loving thoughts of Titus, she concentrated them on the best way in which to encourage him to fall in love with her. Perhaps she was too much the taken-for-granted friend, rather like a favourite pair of comfortable shoes—hardly noticed but always there. A little coolness perhaps, a slight show of independence—although she had no idea how to set about that. Beyond his remarks that she looked nice from time to time, her beautiful new clothes hadn't had much effect upon him. It was a pity she couldn't alter her face. In the privacy of her room she had tried out various make-ups and decided that all of them made her look peculiar, and he had sounded annoyed when she had suggested that she should have her hair cut off.

'Oh, well,' said Arabella. 'I must leave Fate to take a hand.' She gave her hair a final pat and went down to the drawing-room.

Titus was still in his study but he joined her for dinner presently and spent the evening with her, talking idly about their plans for Christmas. There was an annual party for the children in the village, he explained, and they should attend. The carol singers would come early on Christmas Eve and be invited into the manor—a long-held custom.

Arabella nodded. 'Mince pies and hot drinks. Shall we have a Christmas tree?'

'Of course—Butter sees to that. There will be one or two of the family there.' When she looked up in surprise, for he had told her that his parents had been dead for some years, he said, 'An aunt or so—and a couple of cousins and their children. And a great-uncle to keep Grandmother amused…' He added gently, 'I didn't tell you before—I didn't want you to worry about meeting a number of strangers, but they are family; we meet seldom, but Christmas is a long-standing custom I don't care to break.'

'A house full of guests is lovely for Christmas,' said Arabella. 'It will be delightful to meet your family. If you'll give me a list of their names I'll look for presents…'

'Will you? I'm afraid I shan't have the time. We're not doing anything for the rest of the weekend, are we?'

'Just Dr and Mrs Marshall coming to dinner the day after tomorrow.'

'Ah, yes, of course.' He stretched out his long legs and picked up the newspaper.

'The week after next,' said Arabella in a no-nonsense voice, 'we are invited to a party at Mrs Lamb's. You told me to accept.'

'Oh, lord, I'd forgotten.' He looked at her over the paper. 'An indefatigable matchmaker on my behalf—she knew my mother well and seemed to think that it was her duty to find me a wife.'

'Oh, dear. Need I go? I could have a headache…'

'My dear girl, my main purpose in marrying you was to put a stop to Mrs Lamb's efforts to introduce me to those ladies whom she considered suitable.'

If that was meant as a compliment, thought Arabella, it had been rather ineptly put. She sighed. Not only had she to contend with Geraldine, the enemy, now there was Mrs Lamb too. She said merely, 'Is it a dress-up party?'

'Very much so. Black tie and long frocks. Buy something for it—you always look very nice.'

Who wants to look nice? thought Arabella and smiled sweetly at him.

She would find something to make him open his eyes—black velvet perhaps, with a tight skirt slit all the way up and a plunging neckline. She couldn't hope to compete with Geraldine but she had some nice curves.

Of course she didn't buy the black velvet, but a lengthy prowl at Harrods the next day brought to light the very dress she knew would be right for the occasion. Silver-grey chiffon over a satin slip, cunningly fashioned to emphasise and make the most of the curves. She studied herself in the long mirror in the fitting-room and nodded with satisfaction. It concealed what it revealed—or should that be the other way round? Anyway, it was a masterpiece and never mind the price.

Leaving the shop, the dress box in her hand, she felt guilty at spending money—so much money—when there were so many people who needed it so badly. She opened her purse and gave an elderly man selling cheap cigarettes and lighters its entire contents. She had to walk all the way home after that but at least she had made someone happy.

The cards had come and she went to Titus's study to look for the list he had told her to use. There was another list there too—charities, a dozen or more. She read it and felt a surge of love for him. He might have wealth but he was generous too. She sat down at his desk, in his big chair, and began on the Christmas cards.

The Marshalls came on Sunday evening. She and Mrs Turner had planned a special menu and she had set the table with lace mats and the silver and crystal and arranged a low bowl of holly and Christmas roses with silver candelabra on either side. They were to have watercress soup, rack of lamb and a mince tart with syllabub to follow. Arabella had itched to do the cooking but Mrs Turner's feelings would have been hurt. Besides, she was an excellent cook. Arabella went upstairs to shower and get into the silk jersey dress, well pleased with her preparations. Before she went downstairs she opened the closet door and took another look at the grey dress. It gave her a thrill just to look at it; she hoped that Titus would get a thrill too.

The evening was very successful; the Marshalls were good company and dinner was as good as she had hoped it would be. They had their coffee, idly gossiping in the drawing-room until the men went away to Titus's study to discuss a case, leaving Arabella and Mrs Marshall by the fire.

Mrs Marshall had known Titus for some years and had frequently urged him to marry. Now, sitting opposite his wife, she felt satisfied that Arabella was the right girl for him. No looks, of course, but charm and a pretty voice, a good figure and lovely eyes. They were easy in each other's company too, almost like very old friends. There were none of those side-long loving glances she would have expected from newlyweds, although of course Titus wasn't a man to show his feelings and she didn't think Arabella would either. She began to talk about Mrs Lamb's party, an annual event which was always a success. 'You'll enjoy every minute of it,' she assured Arabella, happily unaware how wildly awry this statement would prove to be.

Arabella and Titus drove down to the manor on the following Saturday morning. It was a cold grey day but the house looked welcoming and as he stopped the car the door was opened by Butter and all three dogs came pelting out to greet them. Percy, more prudent and disliking the cold weather, had stationed himself in the hall and Arabella, making much of all four of them, turned a beaming face to Titus.

'Oh, it is nice to be home.' She paused. 'What I mean is, London's home too, but this is different, isn't it?'

'I know what you mean. Let Butter have your things, we'll go and see Grandmother, shall we?'

Mrs Tavener was in her room, sitting very upright beside the fire while Miss Welling read to her. She looked round as they came in, Percy in Arabella's arms, the dogs at their heels.

'My dears—how delightful to see you. Miss Welling, fetch the sherry—we must all drink to this happy meeting.'

Which they did, while they told her about Leiden—Arabella doing most of the talking while Titus sat, watching her, putting in a word here and there. The day went too fast after that and so did Sunday. They got into the car after tea, this time with Beauty and Bassett—Percy was to stay at the manor since he and Duke had become firm friends.

'We will be down again next weekend,' said Titus, eyeing her downcast face. 'If you would like to do so, there is no reason why you shouldn't stay for a week or two after Christmas.'

She spoke without thinking. 'And leave you alone in London? I couldn't do that.'

He turned to look at her but she was gazing out of the window.

He was away very early on Monday morning to take a teaching round, leaving her to finish the cards and buy the rest of the presents. When he got home in the evening she saw that he was tired. She gave him a second look—not tired perhaps, but worried about something. And when he wanted to know how she had spent her day she told him in her quiet voice.

His eyes were on her face. 'How restful you are,

Arabella,' he observed, and when she looked up, surprised, he asked, 'Have the dogs been good?'

The party was the next day. Anxious to look her best, she creamed her face, did her nails, washed her hair and took another look at the dress.

When the day arrived she bade him goodbye after they had had breakfast and assured him that she would have a late tea ready for him before they needed to dress, and then she went off to the kitchen to talk to Mrs Turner and take the dogs for their romp in the garden. Glowing from the cold air, back indoors, she went upstairs to Titus's room to lay out his clothes for the evening only to be interrupted by a peal on the doorbell. She was at the head of the staircase when Mrs Turner opened the door and after a moment stood aside to admit someone. Geraldine Tulsma.

Arabella, hurrying down to the hall, saw that she had a suitcase with her and her heart sank.

Geraldine was in complete command of the situation. 'Here I am, Arabella. I have a day or two free and I know Titus will be delighted to see me.' She shook hands. 'We have known each other too long to stand on ceremony.'

'He's at the hospital,' said Arabella and added belatedly, 'How nice to see you, Geraldine.'

'He'll be home for lunch?'

Arabella led the way into the drawing room. 'Well,

no, he won't be back until about five o'clock—we're going to a party this evening…'

'I'll come with you. We're bound to get a chance to talk there—you know what parties are, all noise and chatter, ideal for a quiet discussion. There's a theory I intend to tell him about…'

'How nice,' said Arabella, and felt foolish. 'Do sit down and have some coffee. I'll tell Mrs Turner to get a room ready for you.'

It was like being in a bad dream. Geraldine might despise her as a woman but Arabella was an audience; her ears were ringing by the end of the afternoon. Geraldine had a splendid opinion of herself and liked people to know it.

I don't think Titus will be pleased, thought Arabella as she heard the front door being opened.

CHAPTER EIGHT

ARABELLA got up and went into the hall, anxious to tell Titus that Geraldine was there, but Geraldine came with her, hurrying past her and taking Titus's hand in hers.

'I've surprised you,' she exclaimed in her vibrant tones. 'I have a few days off and I came at once, knowing that you would be delighted to talk to someone with a mind compatible with your own.'

The doctor shook the hand on his arm and handed it back. Looking at him, there was no knowing what his feelings might be. He said pleasantly, 'This is indeed a surprise, Geraldine.'

'I knew that you would be delighted.' She waited impatiently as he crossed the hall to kiss Arabella's cheek. 'I hear there's a party tonight. I'm sure no one will mind if I come along too.'

Arabella found her voice and was pleased to hear how pleasant it sounded. 'I'll phone, shall I, Titus? I'm sure Geraldine will be welcome. After all, there will be so many people there that one more won't be noticed.'

He hid a smile. 'Yes, by all means do that, my dear. Now, if you will forgive me I have some phoning to do. I'll be in my study if you should want me, Arabella.'

Geraldine looked disappointed. 'I suppose it is necessary for him to go away,' she observed to Arabella. 'I will go to my room and unpack and rest until he has finished what he has to do.'

Arabella, the epitome of the perfect hostess, led the way upstairs, offered refreshment, an extra blanket and the assurance that she would be waiting to let Geraldine know the moment that Titus was free.

'I hope those dogs will be quiet,' said Geraldine. 'I do not care for them. And you have a cat...'

'Yes,' said Arabella equably, 'we both like animals.'

She went downstairs, her eyes sparkling with rage. It wouldn't have mattered so much if Titus had looked annoyed, even taken aback at Geraldine's appearance. There had been no expression on his face— She paused. Yes, there had. Faint amusement. She couldn't think why.

She went to the phone then, to explain about their unexpected guest, and was assured that their hostess would be delighted to see any friend of Titus's. 'Friend,' muttered Arabella through her teeth, and turned to find Titus in the doorway, watching her.

'Geraldine's very welcome,' she told him airily. 'I'll just go and talk to Mrs Turner.'

That lady's feathers were ruffled—the nice little dinner for two would have to be stretched to three.

'Coming unexpected like that,' she grumbled to Arabella. 'How long will she be stopping, ma'am?'

'Well, not long, I think. She said something about a few days...'

Mrs Turner gave the sauce she was stirring a look which should have curdled it.

Titus was in the drawing-room when she went back there, stretched out in his armchair with Percy on his knee and the dogs drowsing by the fire. Arabella eyed him peevishly. 'I'll go and tell Geraldine that you're out of the study—she asked me to let her know. I'm sure you won't want to miss any time with her!'

She flounced to the door to be halted by his quiet voice. 'Am I mistaken in thinking that you are making it as easy as possible for Geraldine and me to be together, Arabella?'

'Well, that's what you want, isn't it? I hadn't noticed you discouraging her.' She swept out of the room and went to tap on their guest's door.

Dressing for the party, Arabella reflected that if Titus and Geraldine had wanted to be together she had given them every opportunity. After a token appearance with their guest she had excused herself on some household pretext and left them alone. 'And I hope they enjoy each other's society,' she observed to Percy, sitting on the end of her bed, watching her as she dressed.

Contrary to the normal desires of a woman in love,

Arabella ignored the silver-grey dress and picked out a dress which hadn't been designed to catch a man's eye at all—an elegant mouse-brown silk crêpe, guaranteed to be eclipsed by the other gowns worn at the party. She had overlooked the fact that it fitted her quite delightfully and by its very quiet elegance would stand out in a crowd.

Her hair in a french pleat, her face nicely made up, she went down to the drawing-room to find Titus already there. He got up when she went in and took stock of her. 'Charming.' He took a box from his pocket. 'I would like you to wear this, Arabella...'

He had gently unclasped the pearls around her neck and fastened a diamond necklace in its place. He didn't say anything and after a moment she crossed to the great mirror over the fireplace and took a look. It was a delicate affair, the diamonds set in small flower-like sprays in gold, the necklace a series of fine gold loops between each spray. It looked like a spangled spider's web. She touched it gently. 'It's old...'

'Yes. It has been in the family for a great many years and is handed down from one bride to the next.'

She looked at his reflection in the mirror. 'So of course it is right and proper that your wife should wear it this evening.' She turned on him, her cheeks very pink. 'We have to keep up appearances, do we not?'

He had gone rather white. 'If that is how you choose to look at it...'

The door opened and Geraldine came in, wearing another floating chiffon creation in vivid pink.

'What a charming dress,' said Arabella. 'So—so colourful, don't you agree, Titus?'

'Extremely so.'

Geraldine viewed her opulent person with satisfaction. 'One doesn't want to look drab...' She smiled at Arabella. 'Time enough to dress in brown and black and grey when one is old. Are we likely to meet anyone interesting this evening?'

'I'm sure you will meet someone to interest you,' said Titus smoothly.

Arabella added sweetly, 'You can always fall back on Titus.'

A remark which earned her a cold stare from her husband.

The party was in full swing when they arrived. Arabella, Titus's firm hand steering her from group to group, smiled and shook hands and murmured party talk, all the while aware that breathing down her neck was Geraldine, intent on keeping as close to Titus as possible. If he minded this, there was no sign of it and presently, after the dancing had started and he had had the first dance with Arabella, he handed her over to an eager young man and as she danced away she saw him bending his head to hear what Geraldine was saying.

She saw them dancing together presently and then lost sight of them as she went from one partner to the other—a small graceful girl, the brown dress a splendid foil for the diamonds around her neck.

There was a buffet supper and briefly she found Titus with her again but, since there were half a dozen other people clustered around the table, talking was out of the question—besides, what did she have to say?

She danced for the rest of the evening while she laughed and talked and wondered if Titus would ever fall in love with her. Several of the men there had expressed their pleasure in her company, which was more, she reflected unfairly, than Titus had ever done. Memory could be a very convenient thing to lose when one was angry and unhappy and, she had to admit, jealous of the tiresome Geraldine.

Back at the house in the very early hours of the morning, that lady showed an alarming tendency to sit about discussing the evening. Arabella wondered what she should do. Urge the lady to go to bed? Go to bed herself and leave her with Titus? Make some graceful remark and sweep Geraldine upstairs with her? She might not go…

It was Titus who said presently, 'Well, I've some work to finish. I'll say goodnight, Geraldine.' He kissed Arabella very deliberately. 'I won't disturb you, my dear.'

Arabella saw Geraldine's instantly alert face. 'Oh,

I'm a light sleeper, Titus—I dare say I'll still be awake,' she uttered in a voice dripping with sweetness while she glared at him.

Percy was at the top of the stairs, waiting for her.

'I believe cats to be dirty animals,' said Geraldine, sweeping past him.

'Have you ever watched a cat washing itself? A pity some humans aren't as thorough.' Arabella saw her guest to her bedroom door, wished her goodnight and, gathering up Percy, went to her own room.

The house was very quiet. She undressed, put on her dressing-gown and, bidding Percy stay where he was on the bed, tiptoed downstairs again. Bassett and Beauty would be in the kitchen; she always went to see them before she went to bed.

They were snoozing in their baskets but they woke as she went into the warm room. She bade them goodnight, sitting on the floor between them, an arm round Bassett's small body and the other around Beauty's massive neck. The day had been horrid and she was glad it was all over.

'Though mind you,' said Arabella, 'tomorrow may be a great deal worse.'

Presently she crept back through the house and up the stairs, unaware that Titus had opened his study door and was watching her.

Titus was getting ready to leave the house when she went down to breakfast. 'Geraldine not with you?'

he wanted to know.

'She fancied breakfast in bed,' said Arabella, matter-of-factly. 'Did you want to see her? Shall I give her a message?'

His look made her feel uncomfortable. Was it amusement? What had he to be amused about?

'Would you tell her that I have arranged a visit to the Royal College of Physicians? Eleven o'clock—the main door. I'll be home some time after five o'clock, Arabella.' He turned at the door. 'Did I tell you how charming you looked last night?'

He had gone before she could think of a reply to that, which was as well for she was fuming at the thought of him and Geraldine strolling round the Royal College of Physicians. She was vague as to what functions were held there or for what purpose one would visit it—sufficient that the pair of them were going to spend the morning there and probably have lunch together afterwards…

She went upstairs to give Geraldine the message, noting with satisfaction that while her guest when fully clothed gave the appearance of a magnificent figure, in bed she was plain fat. She probably wore a strongly built foundation with bones…

'I shall be out to lunch,' said Geraldine, without bothering to thank Arabella for the message. She took a bite of toast. 'Titus enjoys my company.' She slid a sly glance in Arabella's direction. 'But of course you know about that.'

Arabella sat down in a pretty little armchair by the window. 'No, I don't—at least, not your version. Do tell?'

'Many men have loved me,' declared Geraldine smugly, 'but there is only one whom I wish to marry and that is Titus—he must have told you that he wanted to marry me?' She didn't wait for an answer, which was just as well. 'But I was a silly girl. I wished to make my mark in the medical world and so I continued to refuse him—each time he came to Leiden I would say no. I was wrong, of course—two brilliant minds such as ours are meant to become one. I cannot blame him for marrying you—there is nothing about you which could come between us. You are of no account; you are not clever, nor are you pretty. A very nice person, I am sure,' she added graciously, 'therefore I have no feelings of jealousy about you. You are Titus's wife but of course he has no love for you, that is obvious to my eyes—the eyes of a woman who loves him.'

Arabella found her voice. She could stand no more. 'How very interesting—but I mustn't keep you talking or you will be late. Have you finished your breakfast? I'll take the tray. Mrs Turner is busy and I'm going downstairs anyway.' She added politely, 'Do you know how to get to this place.'

'No.'

'No, nor do I. I should take a taxi or ask a policeman.'

She was in the garden with Percy and the dogs when Geraldine called to say, 'I am going now,' and added, 'I shall be back during the afternoon.'

Arabella went to the front door with her, wished her a delightful day and closed the door after her. She would feel better if she had a nice quiet cry. She leaned against the door and sniffed and snivelled and sobbed, and then went and washed her face, powdered her pink nose and drank the coffee Mrs Turner brought her, carefully avoiding looking at her swollen eyes and ill-disguised nose.

'That woman,' said Mrs Turner viciously to Betty, one of the girls who came in daily to help. 'I'd like to get my hands on her. The doctor must be out of his mind. And don't you remember what I've just said, or breathe a word, or I'll take my rolling pin to you!'

Arabella took the dogs into the park and came back for lunch, which she pushed around her plate and didn't eat. There was no sign of Geraldine but she hadn't expected there to be. She got into her outdoor things again, told Mrs Turner that she was going shopping and would be back for tea, and let herself out of the house.

She had no idea where she wanted to go. A cruising taxi came along and she hailed it and said, 'Oxford Street,' because it was the first place she thought of. There were lights there and the pavements were thronged with people doing their Christmas shopping. She walked slowly, stopping to look at the gaily dressed windows, buying several things she neither needed nor liked particularly—a scarf which was of a colour she never wore, socks with Father Christmas and his reindeer embroidered on them, which Titus would receive with outward pleasure and never wear and a pair of outsize earrings, glittering with imitation jewels, dangling almost to her shoulders. When she got home she put them all carefully in a drawer in her bedroom. The scarf at least would be just right for Betty, who loved bright colours. The socks she buried under a pile of undies but the earrings she put on. They looked absurd and she turned her head to and fro watching them swing and glitter. She kept them on and went downstairs to have her tea in the animals' company.

Mrs Turner brought the tea tray. 'That Dr Tulsma came back an hour ago. Said she needed to rest. Shall I tell her the tea's ready?'

'Please, Mrs Turner.'

Geraldine joined her five minutes later and Arabella handed her her tea, offered the cakes and enquired as to her day.

'A splendid day,' said Geraldine loudly. 'I have never enjoyed myself so much—so much to talk about and a delicious lunch. I do not know how I am going to tear myself away from you…'

'Oh, do you have to go back shortly?' Arabella did her best not to sound delighted.

'My dear Arabella, duty calls and someone in my position cannot ignore that. I go on an evening flight. I rang for a taxi just before you returned home.'

'Rang for a taxi?' repeated Arabella. 'You mean you're on the point of leaving now?'

'Indeed I am.' She glanced at the clock. 'In ten minutes or so.'

'Can't you wait for Titus? He'll be so disappointed and I'm sure he would drive you to Heathrow.'

Geraldine put her hand on her ample bosom. 'We have said goodbye. We have to be satisfied with these brief glimpses of each other—there will be other meetings.'

She went away to fetch her things and Arabella, rather dazed with the suddenness of it all, wished her goodbye and a safe journey.

'You are quite a nice little thing,' said Geraldine. 'I can understand that Titus finds you exactly the kind of wife he needs—undemanding and allowing him to lead his own life and lacking in childish romantic notions. Goodbye, Arabella.'

She went out to the waiting taxi and Arabella shut the door on her for the second time that day. Mrs Turner, coming into the hall, took a look at her face. 'I'll make a nice pot of tea, ma'am, and you just sit down and enjoy it. It's not my place to say so, but it's nice to have the house quiet once more.'

'She's very beautiful,' said Arabella in a small voice.

'Beauty is but skin-deep,' quoth Mrs Turner. 'Just you go back and sit by the fire and there'll be a fresh pot of tea in a brace of shakes.'

Arabella drank the tea and then sat back in her chair, Percy on her knee, the two dogs sprawled at her feet. The day's happenings had been strange and they had sounded the death knell over any hopes she might have had about Titus's feelings towards her. Geraldine had made it clear that she and Titus would have married save for her reluctance to give up her career, and although Arabella hated her she couldn't believe that she would tell a pack of deliberate lies about it. Titus had made it plain before they married that although she and he were friends there was no question of love.

She was still sitting there, the tea forgotten, when Titus came in. It was unfortunate that the first thing he said was, 'Hello, where's Geraldine?'

Arabella sat up straight; the dogs had run to meet him and Percy set indignant claws in her skirt at being disturbed. 'She left for Heathrow half an hour ago.'

He sat down opposite her. 'Rather unexpected—did she get a phone call to return, I wonder?'

Arabella said carefully, 'You don't need to pretend, Titus. She told me about you and her. You said goodbye this afternoon after you'd had lunch together, didn't you? You knew she was going back.' She swallowed the lump of tears in her throat. 'I'm only sorry that you must both be so unhappy. Of course it can all be put right, can't it? It's easy these days and it isn't as if...'

'Before you go on with this rigmarole, Arabella, let us put it into plain language.'

He had spoken quietly but his voice was cold and his eyes, when she looked at him, were hard and cold. 'Not to mince matters, you are telling me that Geraldine and I are in love, that we are unhappy and you are kindly planning to divorce me.'

'Well, that's what I said, didn't I? It was plain enough for an idiot to understand. I can quite see that you need a wife—I suppose all professional men do—but why pick on me?' She answered herself. 'I'm undemanding and allow you to lead your own life and I don't have any childish romantic notions—she told me that.'

'Did she, indeed? Geraldine seems to have told you a great deal. And you believed her?'

'I didn't want to, really I didn't, but someone like her—I mean, an important well-known doctor wouldn't tell lies, would she? Besides, you said that you wished to marry for the wrong reasons—for someone to come home to each day, a companion, someone to put an end to your friends trying to marry you off. I accepted all that but only because I didn't know about Geraldine, did I?'

'You don't want to hear my side of the story?'

'I wouldn't be human if I didn't, would I? But I don't want to—I'm sure talking about it would make you feel unhappy.'

'Not unhappy, my dear Arabella, but blind with rage, and if you persist in sitting there filled with sweetness and forgiveness I shall wring your little neck.'

'In that case,' said Arabella, 'I shall go and sit somewhere else.'

She whisked out of the room, clutching Percy, and went to the kitchen to say that she had a headache and would go to bed.

'A morsel of supper?' asked Mrs Turner.

'No—no, thank you. The doctor will dine at the usual time, please.'

The doctor had poured himself a drink and gone back to his chair. He sat for a long time deep in thought, but presently he laughed. 'What a pair of fools we are,' he observed to the dogs, who mumbled an understanding and went to sleep again.

'Madam's gone to her bed,' said Mrs Turner severely, serving him his soup. 'Got a headache and I'm not surprised. I may be speaking out of turn, sir, but that ladyfriend of yours fair upset madam.'

The doctor tasted his soup. 'Delicious. Dr Tulsma and Mrs Tavener don't have much in common, Mrs Turner, and her visit was unexpected.' He glanced up at his faithful housekeeper. 'I think it unlikely that she will visit us again.'

'That's a good thing, sir, for I don't like to see madam upset—such a sweet little lady she is, as you well know, no doubt.'

'No doubt at all. Will you take a nice little supper upstairs presently? A little food often helps a headache.'

'One of my omelettes,' breathed Mrs Turner, and went back to the kitchen with his soup plate.

Arabella, fortified by a delicious light supper, slept soundly and went down to breakfast. She had no wish to apologise and indeed she couldn't see why she should—he had wanted to wring her neck, hadn't he? He was the one to apologise. She sat down opposite him at the breakfast table and poured herself a cup of coffee, accepted the plate of scrambled eggs he fetched from the sideboard and wished him good morning in a polite voice.

'Feeling better?' he enquired in a breezy manner which annoyed her at once. 'There's nothing like a good night's sleep to help one regain a normal view of things.'

She buttered toast and ate a mouthful of egg. 'My view of things is exactly the same as it was yesterday evening,' she told him frostily. 'I see no point in discussing it any more.'

'Not at the moment, perhaps. You still persist in your absurd accusations, Arabella?' His voice was smooth but it had a nasty edge to it. She reflected with a tiny shiver that he must have a nasty temper beneath that calm visage. Not that he could frighten her, she told herself silently.

She said clearly, 'Yes—and they are not absurd. You told me yourself in Holland that Geraldine was one of the most honest and dependable doctors you had ever met. You're not going to accuse her of lying, are you?'

He glanced at his watch and didn't answer her. 'I must go, I've a good deal to get through today. I'll be home by six o'clock, barring accidents. We are to dine with the Marshalls, aren't we?'

'Yes.'

'Good. In a day or two, when you've calmed down, we can have a quiet talk.'

'I do not want a quiet talk,' said Arabella pettishly. 'I can think of nothing more to say.'

'That astonishes me. I, on the other hand, have a great deal to say. Time enough to say it when we are at the manor.'

He put a hand on her shoulder as he went to the door and the touch of it sent sudden tears to her eyes. She loved him so, and she was behaving in all the wrong ways. She wasn't sure quite *how* to behave; he hadn't been very nice about her being sweet and forgiving…

Christmas was very near now; she wrapped some more presents, arranged Christmas cards all over the drawing-room—for they had been sent any number—and spent a long time making a centrepiece for the table with holly and Christmas roses and trails of ivy and sweet-scented hyacinths. It looked pretty when she had finished it and so did the small Christmas tree standing in front of the window, with its twinkling lights and glass baubles.

Tomorrow, she remembered, several of the doctors' wives were coming for coffee; she had met them at the Marshalls' and at the party and they had offered to tell her about the various festivities which would take place at the hospital after Christmas—to have them in for coffee had seemed a good idea. She was aware that they were curious about her but too polite to show it, and it would be nice if she could become one of their circle.

She took the dogs for a walk then, and presently set out for the last of her shopping. A present for Titus. She had left it until last, hoping to gain some inspiration as to what he would like. He seemed to have everything; the only thing was to go and look in shop windows and hope to see something.

She might be angry with him and unhappy too, but she loved him despite that. It would have to be something very special. She went from one end of Bond Street to the other and down the arcades, peering in windows—what did one give a man who had everything?

She found it at last in a small bookshop, crammed

to the ceiling with rare editions, old maps and prints. An early edition of Chaucer's *Canterbury Tales* in its original text; she remembered that he had mentioned his interest in the book and as far as she knew he had only a modern version of it. She bore it home, reflecting sadly that perhaps this would be the last and only present she would give him. She had an unpleasant feeling that the quiet talk he had suggested might disclose a future she had no wish to contemplate.

In the meanwhile there was the Marshalls' dinner-party that evening. She dressed with extra care—dark green velvet this time, long-sleeved and high-necked, and since she had the time she arranged her hair in a complicated topknot which was well worth the time it took to do.

Titus was home when she went downstairs to the drawing-room. He was sitting with the dogs, reading the afternoon's post, but he got up when she went in.

'I'll go and change. Have the dogs been out?'

She put Percy down by the fire. 'Yes, they've had their walk.'

'Good. Can I get you a drink?'

'No, thank you.'

She sat down and Percy got on to her lap and Bassett danced around her chair.

'You have enjoyed your day?' he asked.

'Yes, thank you. Several people are coming in for coffee tomorrow morning...'

'I shall be away all day, probably until late in the evening. Don't wait up for me tomorrow.'

'I expect you're busy,' she said politely.

'Yes, I have to go over to Leiden in the morning but I shall be back in good time to drive to the manor.'

He went out of the room, leaving her suddenly ice-cold with panic. He was going to see Geraldine, of course, and tell her what had happened, and when he came back they would have their talk and her heart would be broken.

The dinner party at the Marshalls' house was fairly small and she had met everyone there already. The house was decorated with holly and mistletoe and paper chains and an enormous Christmas tree and the atmosphere was decidedly festive. Dinner was leisurely and the talk was light-hearted and afterwards everyone gathered in the drawing-room, still talking. It was late when finally everyone went home, calling the season's greetings to each other as they went.

Back in the house Arabella said, 'That was a lovely evening; I enjoyed it.' She stood in the hall, looking at him. 'I'll go to bed. Will you be leaving early in the morning?'

'Yes. Shall I give your love to Cressida?'

'Oh, will you be seeing her?'

'Yes. Who did you suppose I'd be seeing, Arabella?'

'Well, Geraldine, of course.'

'Ah, yes, of course.' He turned away to go to his study. 'Goodnight, Arabella.'

There he sat, doing nothing behind his great desk. A brilliantly clever man, he hadn't been clever enough to know when he had fallen in love with Arabella. He supposed, since she had never been out of his mind for long since the moment they had first met, that he had loved her at first sight, unaware of it even when he had asked her to be his wife, knowing only that it was something which he wanted.

He gently pulled Bassett's small ears, for the little dog had climbed on to his knee, and then reached down to rest a hand on Beauty's head.

'When I get back,' he told them, 'we must talk, Arabella and I. Perhaps once we have cleared up this misunderstanding she could learn to love me.'

Arabella went down to her solitary breakfast, determined to fill her day so that there would be no time to sit and brood. There were the last of the presents to wrap and plans to make with Mrs Turner, who would stay in the house over Christmas. Not alone, however. Her married sister and her husband would stay with her and Arabella, prompted by Titus, had seen to it that there was an abundance of Christmas fare for them. Titus had several appointments for the day after Boxing Day and they had planned to return to Little Venice very late on Boxing Day. She wondered now, as she listened with half an ear to Mrs Turner's plans for a meal for them on their return, if it would be a good idea if she were to stay at the manor for a while. It would seem a natural thing to do and, in the light of the present situation, sensible too.

The day seemed long despite her efforts to keep busy. She had just got back from walking the dogs when the phone rang. Titus's cool voice sounded very close. He would be unable to get back home that evening—he hoped to be back some time the following afternoon. He would go straight to the hospital where he had a clinic and see her later. 'You are all right?' he wanted to know.

'Yes, thank you,' said Arabella. Even if she could have thought of something to say he didn't give her the chance. His goodbye was brief.

She spent the evening deciding what to take with her to the manor, although her mood was such that packing a couple of sacks would have done very nicely. The day was neverending; the coffee morning had taken up part of it, of course and she had laughed and talked and rather liked her guests and squirmed inwardly at their smiling remarks about brides and a rosy future. Medical men made rather good fathers, one of them had observed, amid laughter. She remembered that now.

Titus got home early the next afternoon, coming in unexpectedly on his way to the hospital. Arabella, tying an artistic bow on the parcel in which she had wrapped Mrs Turner's Christmas present—a handsome dressing-gown—looked up in surprise as he came in.

'I need something from the study,' he explained. 'I'll be home just after five o'clock. Will you be ready to leave shortly after that?'

'Yes. Would you like something before we go? Sandwiches and coffee? Tea?'

'I'll get tea at the hospital—we can have a meal when we get home. Phone Butter, will you? Tell him we'll be there about eight o'clock and will need supper.'

He had spoken pleasantly but she could see that he was impatient to be gone. Her, 'Very well,' was uttered in a matter-of-fact voice although her hands were shaking under the bunch of ribbons.

They left well before six o'clock after giving Mrs Turner her present, loading the boot with things for the manor and stowing the dogs and Percy on the back seat. The streets were crowded with Christmas traffic and it took some time to reach the motorway, and all the while Titus had nothing to say.

Arabella had tried once or twice to start up a conversation but since she received only pleasant monosyllables in reply she had lapsed into silence. Christmas, she thought bitterly. Last Christmas had been a terrible one, with her parents recently dead and the future bleak, but this one was even worse; the future was just as bleak. How could it be otherwise, loving a man who loved someone else?

CHAPTER NINE

THERE was a Christmas tree ablaze with lights just inside the gates of the manor when they reached it, and lights streamed from the many windows of the house. As they stopped before the door Arabella could hear Duke's deep bark and then was almost deafened by the happy barks of Beauty and Bassett. Titus got out, opened her door and let the animals out of the back of the car, picking up Percy's basket at the same time. Just for a moment Arabella stood looking around her; the door had been opened and Duke had come pelting out to greet them and then tear round the garden with the other two. Butter stood at the door and beyond him she could glimpse another Christmas tree in the hall. She heaved a sigh and Titus gave her a quick look which she didn't see.

Butter stood with a beaming face. 'Welcome home, ma'am—and you, sir. There's a nice little supper waiting for you when you're ready and Mrs Tavener Senior hopes that she and Miss Welling may share it with you.'

'Why, of course,' cried Arabella. 'Nothing would be nicer. I'll just take off my things and say hello to Mrs Butter.'

Titus had been taking Percy out of his basket; she took the cat in her arms and went off to the kitchen, glad to get away from Titus's blue stare.

They all had supper together shortly after and even Miss Welling looked cheerful and drank two glasses of wine. Old Mrs Tavener was full of questions which the doctor answered readily enough, referring often to Arabella to bear him out; whatever their differences were in private, they were to be kept that way.

The old lady went to bed presently with the faithful Miss Welling, very slightly tipsy, in attendance.

'I should like to talk,' observed Titus, 'but I think you have no wish to listen for the moment.'

'Well, no.' She sat down near the fire in the drawing-room with Percy curled up on her lap. 'I think I am still angry and hurt—if you wouldn't mind waiting a few days, until I feel all right again, I'll listen…'

'But you will agree with me that the hatchet should be buried over Christmas. I would not like Grandmother to be made unhappy nor would I like the painstaking preparations taken by the staff to be overshadowed; they have been here for so long that they are quick to sense when anything has gone wrong.'

She said quietly, 'Of course I agree with you. I'll do everything to make it as you wish.' She paused. 'Titus, may I stay here for a few days after

Christmas? Just until you come on the following weekend. I think it might be a good idea, don't you?'

When he didn't reply she added, 'It's easier—I mean looking at something from a distance. Do you see?'

'Oh, yes, but surely that depends on how you are looking at it? Clearly and honestly or blinded by all the wrong feelings?'

'Feelings? Feelings?' Arabella wanted to know in a lamentably shrill voice. 'And you're the one who's blind.' She got to her feet, dislodging Percy who stalked to the door. 'I'm rather tired. Good-night, Titus.'

He was at the door before she could reach it. He was smiling a little and had kissed her before she could turn her head. 'Crosspatch,' he said, and actually laughed.

Which, naturally enough, caused her to burst into tears the moment she got into her room.

Feelings or no feelings, she woke on Christmas Eve knowing that they must be hidden. Besides the extra bustle in the house the carol singers would be coming in the early evening, she would be going to the church with an armful of flowers specially grown in the glasshouse and there was a Christmas lunch for the children in the village hall at noon. A busy day and she thanked heaven for it.

She dressed carefully, knowing that it was expected of her, and Titus nodded approval when they met at breakfast. 'I'll see you at the children's party,' he told her pleasantly, for all the world as though they had parted the best of friends. 'I've one or two things to attend to first while you're in church.' He added, 'We go to the midnight service, Arabella. Grandmother and Miss Welling come too, and so do the Butters.'

She thought she detected a warning note in his quiet voice. 'I shall enjoy that. Do we go to the morning service as well?'

'Yes. It makes a full morning so we usually exchange our gifts when we get back here around noon, before lunch. I dare say you've already seen Mrs Butter?'

'Yes, she's arranged everything beautifully.'

'She was the kitchenmaid here when Grandmother came here as a bride. She must have been very young—thirteen or fourteen, I suppose. She has been here every Christmas since then.'

'But she married Butter…'

'There was a butler in those days—servants were two a penny—Butter worked under him until he learned to drive and he's been driving ever since and running the place for me. He's more than a servant, he's an old friend—so is Mrs Butter. She used to give me slices of bread and dripping—I was always hungry and dripping in those days was delicious…'

Arabella looked down at her plate, picturing a

small hungry boy wolfing bread and dripping. 'You were happy here?' she asked.

'Yes. And I shall be again.' He added silkily, 'I cannot say that at the moment I am happy.'

'Well, nor am I,' said Arabella in what she hoped was a reasonable voice. Perhaps this was the right moment to talk—over a prosaic breakfast table in the cold light of the morning.

It seemed that it wasn't; Butter came in to say that the flowers had been brought up from the glasshouse and perhaps she would care to approve them when she had breakfasted.

'I'll come now. I've finished,' said Arabella, all of a sudden anxious to escape from Titus, sitting so close to her and yet so far away.

The flowers were beautiful and she was lavish in her praise. 'I'll take them with me now. I'm going to church early—they'll need to be arranged.'

She put on the new winter coat and added the hat she had bought in a fit of extravagance. It was of the softest felt with a narrow brim which curved around her face and tilted very slightly sideways. It matched the coat exactly and she was well pleased with it. She was pleased with her boots too—of the very latest style, making the most of her small feet—and since it was Christmas she tucked a green scarf patterned with holly into the neck of the coat. Surveying her person in the pier glass, she thought that she didn't look too bad—not that Titus would notice, she reflected, and went downstairs.

He was in the hall, huge in his overcoat, waiting for her.

'Shall we walk down?' he asked her.

Since Butter was hovering, ready to open the door, she said at once, 'Oh, yes, I should like that. Will you take the dogs?'

'Of course. We'll part company at the church—I dare say you'll be some time there. We're expected for coffee at the rectory at eleven o'clock; we'll meet there.'

They went out together and Butter watched them go and thought what a splendid couple they made. Trust the doctor to get himself such a perfect little lady...

Arabella, walking beside Titus out of the gates and into the lane leading to the village, was surprised to find that despite their quarrel she felt quite at ease with him, listening to his easy flow of casual talk. And he, used to putting patients at their ease, watched her expressive face and was satisfied.

He left her at the church after a brief talk—his arm around her shoulder—with the rector, and she was led away to see about the flowers while the rector enlarged upon the doctor's splendid character. 'Takes after his father,' he told her. 'Does a great deal for the village, you know, and very much dislikes anyone finding out about it.' He beamed at Arabella.

'But of course he has no secrets from you, my dear Mrs Tavener.'

She and Titus met again at the rectory where they had coffee, surrounded by the rector's son and daughter-in-law and their children, all talking at once and plying them with mince pies.

Arabella, led away to tidy herself before going to the village hall, remembered that Titus's various aunts and uncles would arrive at teatime and wondered if they'd be as much fun as the rector's household. She adjusted the hat, powdered her nose and accompanied Titus through the village once more.

The children's lunch was noisy; the little boys tended to fight among themselves and the little girls, in their best dresses, were shy to start with and then noisier than the boys. They ate everything on the long table and drank enormous quantities of lemonade before pulling the crackers, putting on paper hats and crowding round the Christmas tree to receive the parcels Arabella was to hand to each of them.

She was enjoying herself mightily; she had taken off her coat, put a paper hat on top of her own elegant headgear and was singing along with the children in a small clear voice.

Titus was enchanted. The world was a wonderful place in which to be and only he and Arabella were in it. He smiled a little—he was a little too old to have such romantic thoughts. If only she would let him explain about Geraldine—but he would have to wait for the right moment to do that. In the meantime they must hide their differences for a couple of days, and perhaps her idea of staying at the manor for a few days was a good one…

They went back home presently, with the dogs running free around them, and had sherry with Mrs Tavener and Miss Welling. They ate their lunch with a good appetite and much cheerful small-talk then separated to go their own ways—Mrs Tavener to rest, with Miss Welling to read aloud to her, Titus to his study and Arabella to tour the guest-rooms to make sure that everything was just as it should be. There would be six guests staying over Christmas and eight more coming to lunch on Boxing Day.

She went to look out of the window of the largest room overlooking the grounds at the back of the house and saw Titus strolling around with the dogs. He looked very much at home in elderly, beautifully tailored tweeds, his hands in his pockets. He was whistling too. The wish to join him was very great. If she did, she reflected, he would greet her with apparent pleasure and set himself out to entertain her with a gentle flow of talk. He would probably wish her at Jericho. She went down to the kitchen and spent the next half-hour conferring with Mrs Butter.

The guests arrived for tea—first Mrs Tavener's son, a very upright grey-haired man with a reserved manner, who shook Arabella's hand and begged her to call him Uncle Tom, and his wife, Aunt Mary, who peered at her through thick lenses and murmured softly that it was a great pity that Jeremy Titus and Rosa weren't there to see their daughter-in-law.

'My father and mother,' said Titus briskly. 'Uncle Tom is the younger son. Come and meet the cousins.' They were three young men and a girl of her own age. 'Josephine, Bill, Thomas and Mark.' She shook hands with them in turn, aware of their interested gaze.

It was Thomas who spoke, a serious-looking young man who looked as though smiling was an effort. 'We were beginning to think that Titus would never marry...'

'Head of the family and all that,' explained Mark. 'Wish I'd seen you first.' He was a cheerful young man with an engaging grin. 'I'm a medical man too—haven't had time to get married, let alone find a girl to love as yet.' He nodded towards Thomas. 'He's just got engaged and Josephine is on the brink. Before we know where we are the family gatherings will be littered with babies.'

Everyone laughed, even Thomas, and after that the talk became general over tea round the fire. Presently Arabella went away to help Mrs Butter with the dinner table; they had discussed the menu over the phone some time ago and had decided on smoked salmon, rack of lamb with several vegetables and sauté potatoes, and a trifle for dessert. The table looked charming with a starched linen cloth, the family silver, a centrepiece of holly, ringed around by red candles in silver candlesticks, and sparkling crystal glasses. She went away to change her dress, feeling well pleased.

It was after one o'clock by the time she was in bed. The church had been full and no one had hurried away afterwards but had stayed, exchanging good wishes, and old Mrs Tavener had had to be coaxed away and driven back. Arabella had accompanied her and Miss Welling to her own rooms and seen her safely settled with a warm drink.

'You're a dear child,' the old lady had declared. 'Titus is a lucky man.'

He might not agree with that, reflected Arabella in the morning, accepting a cup of hot chocolate from him and sitting down beside Aunt Mary, but he was behaving exactly as he should—the smiling glance, the hand on her shoulder—almost as if he meant it.

Breakfast was leisurely before church and it was only when they got back that the family, with the Butters, gathered round the Christmas tree. Arabella and Titus handed out the presents together and since everyone had brought a gift for everyone else the drawing-room was soon knee-deep in coloured paper. It wasn't until the last of the presents had been handed out that Arabella sat down to open her own pile.

'Move over,' said Titus and sat down beside her on one of the sofas while Butter went round with a tray of champagne. 'I wonder why one has such pleasure in opening parcels?'

'Natural curiosity.' Arabella was admiring a rose-pink silk scarf from Josephine. 'Exactly what I would like best,' she told her new cousin. They were going to get on well together, she and Josephine. They smiled at each other across the room and she picked up the next gift. She had seen quickly enough the little box with its label written in Titus's hand and deliberately left it until the last. There had been presents from the dogs and from Percy of course—chocolates, perfume, a little evening bag—and of course he had bought those, just as she had given him a Victorian ink-blotter for his desk from the four of them. Everyone else was still opening gifts and no one was watching them. She felt his hand on hers for a moment. 'How did you know,' he asked her quietly, 'that I collect rare books?'

'I looked round the library here and at Little Venice. I hope you'll like it.'

'I am delighted with it, Arabella. Thank you, my dear.'

She opened the little box then. There were earrings inside, diamonds set in gold, miniature replicas of the necklace.

She held them up. 'They're beautiful, and they match the necklace—' She looked a question.

'I had them made...'

'But you gave me the necklace only a week or two ago.'

He said patiently, 'I knew I would give you the necklace—oh, before we married—and it seemed that the earrings would go very well with it.'

'You did that before—' she paused and went on softly '—before you—before we went to Holland?'

She choked back tears and Mark called across the room, 'You two—what are you whispering about? Arabella, what has Titus given you? It must be something marvellous to make you look so bright-eyed.'

She got up and went to sit by him, taking the earrings with her, and everyone crowded round to see them. 'You must wear them,' cried Aunt Mary. So Arabella went to the Florentine mirror between the windows and put them on and someone cried, 'Aren't you going to thank him for them? Go on, it's Christmas.'

There was nothing for it but to go over to the sofa. Titus had got to his feet and she stretched up to kiss his cheek. At least, that had been her intention. Instead she found herself swept into his arms and kissed in a manner which took her breath away.

'Oh,' squeaked Arabella, and stared up into his face. His eyes were very blue and the gleam in them was no longer hidden.

'A pity we aren't alone,' he said softly, and let her go amid an outburst of cheerful teasing and laughter.

The rest of the day didn't seem quite real to

Arabella. Lunch had been a buffet with everyone milling around—talking about their presents, recalling other Christmases, discussing the rest of the family who would arrive in time for tea. Tea had gone off well too, with a host of new faces and names to remember and the cake to cut, and then a brief peace while those staying in the house went upstairs to change for dinner. She had worn the brown dress with the diamond necklace and the earrings and there had been a lot more talk while they had drunk champagne cocktails and then gathered round the table to eat turkey with all the trimmings and one of Mrs Butter's Christmas puddings. She had sat opposite Titus at the oval table and tried not to look at him, something which she found very difficult.

Boxing Day, with a house overflowing with guests and several people from the village coming in for drinks, kept her so busy that she had no time to talk to Titus—which was a good thing. She was still feeling shy about his kiss and puzzled too, although perhaps he had kissed her like that because the family was watching. When they were alone again she would ask him—they still had to talk about Geraldine…

He went back to Little Venice after dinner on Boxing Day, leaving her there until he came to fetch her at the weekend. She went with him to the door after he had said goodbye to his family in the drawing-room.

'Well, we buried the hatchet very well, didn't we?' he observed, standing close to her, looking down on to the top of her head, smiling a little.

'Well, I think…' began Arabella, to be stilled by the ringing of the phone on the side table.

Titus picked it up. 'Mrs Turner? Is something wrong?' He listened a moment. 'From Leiden? You said I would be back later tonight—good.' He glanced at his watch. 'I should be with you in two or three hours.'

He hung up and Arabella said, 'That was Geraldine…'

He gave her a cold stare, his face expressionless. 'If you say so, Arabella…'

He went out to his car without a word, not looking at her, and because she loved him so much she knew instinctively that he was in a white-hot rage. 'Take care, Titus, oh, do take care…!'

He drove away without a glance and she stood shivering on the step until the tail-lights had disappeared. It was a good thing that when she returned to her guests her white face was attributed to her having to part with Titus. She was surrounded by people intent on cheering her up, plying her with drink and the suggestion that she should go to bed and have a good night's rest.

'All the excitement,' said Aunt Mary. 'You must be worn out. And you've made such a success of it, my dear. We all understand how you feel, it's hard to be parted, but doctors' wives…'

Everyone went home after lunch the following day and Mrs Tavener and Miss Welling retired to their own part of the house, which left Arabella with the three dogs and Percy for company. She had phoned Little Venice early that morning and Mrs Turner had told her that the doctor had left for the hospital not half an hour since. 'Looked worn out, he did,' Mrs Turner had said. 'A good thing when it's the weekend and he can fetch you back. And all that telephoning just when he should have been going to his bed…'

'Oh, yes,' Arabella had said, 'the call from Leiden…'

'That's right, madam. Went on and on, it did. Must have been about a patient, I suppose, because I heard him say he'd ring later.'

It was a phone call Arabella wished she hadn't made, for it only made the day harder to get through. A long walk with the dogs made her feel better. She had tea by the fire in the little sitting-room with Percy on her lap and the dogs hugging the fire and, since the Butters were going to the village for an evening with friends there, she had undertaken to see to her own dinner.

She busied herself presently in the kitchen—making a salad, cooking scrambled eggs and making a pot of coffee. She ate at the kitchen table, tidied everything away and went back to watch TV, but after a while she switched off and, suddenly making up her mind, phoned Little Venice. Mrs Turner answered again.

She sounded puzzled when Arabella asked to speak to the doctor. 'He's gone to Holland, madam—in a terrible rush, he was. Expects to be back tomorrow some time. I expect he'll phone you from there.'

Her voice held a faint question, so that Arabella said at once, 'I'm sure that he will—if he had a plane to catch he wouldn't have had the time to do a lot of explaining. I shall hear all about it when he gets back and I'm sure he'll phone here once he has the chance. It might be something urgent.'

It was a good thing she was on her own, she reflected, for there was time to think. How he must have disliked having to spend Christmas here, being the perfect host and the perfect husband, she thought. I dare say he made the excuse of work at the hospital so that he could get back as soon as possible. I wonder what she said that made him to go Leiden in such a hurry?

Arabella picked up the magazine lying on the table beside her and began to tear it into ribbons. The exercise gave her a certain amount of satisfaction although she would have much preferred the magazine to have been Geraldine. It relieved her feelings a little, although a few good screams would have been a great relief.

There were two days to get through before Titus would come. She filled them with almost unceasing activity—grooming the pony and the donkey, going for long walks with the dogs, visiting the rectory to say what a delightful Christmas it had been, entertaining various ladies from the village anxious to enrol her in the WI, the first-aid classes, the committee for the annual church bazaar…

Friday came at last and no news from Titus. All the same she had a long session with Mrs Butter about meals for the weekend, saying lightly that she thought he would probably be home late that evening and arranging a light supper for him. She was filled with excitement at the thought of seeing him again even though a quarrel seemed inevitable and her heart, already badly cracked, would be broken completely. A good thing to get it over, she told herself, and took the dogs for yet another walk.

It was late afternoon when she suddenly decided that she couldn't face him. She would go out and walk up the lane behind the house from where she would be able to see the lights of the car. Only when he was in the house would she return. The Butters were in the dining-room so she went to the kitchen and through its doors to a passage lined with small rooms—the pantry, the old-fashioned still-room, the larder, the boot-room. At the end of the passage was another door, leading to the kitchen gardens, behind which were a variety of elderly coats, old hats and, ranged beneath them, a selection of wellies. She got into a jacket with a hood, pushed her feet into Mrs Butter's wellies and went outside.

It was still light although there was a bank of cloud beyond the hills. For a moment she wondered if she should fetch a torch, but supposing Titus was to arrive early and meet her? She buttoned the jacket tightly and set off.

The lane up the hill beyond the kitchen garden was a stiff climb, and she marched to it via the stables so that she might offer carrots pulled from the garden to Bess and Jerry. By the time she was almost at the top, with the thick crown of trees which topped the hill only a few yards away, it was dusk, the distant clouds suddenly overhead and the first few drops of rain falling. As she stood looking down the hill towards the village there was a sudden gust of wind and the trees behind her swayed and creaked as it soughed through them. Though not a nervous girl, she wanted to be home—secure by the fireside.

There was a shortcut down the hill, a narrow path which she and Titus had once taken; it would mean going a little way up into the trees but she thought that she could find it even in the gathering gloom. Somewhere on the right of her, she decided, as the first of the trees closed over her. The rain was coming down in earnest now and turning to sleet as the wind freshened. She took the path and at the fork a few yards further turned to the left, towards the village, took a step forward and rolled into a deep gully—right to the bottom.

It was filled with dead leaves and an inch or so of water. She lay where she was for a moment, too surprised to do anything, and then got slowly to her feet, brushed herself down and looked for a way to climb out. It wasn't a very deep gully but its sides were slippery with wet bracken and earth and when she took hold of a tuft of coarse grass it came away in her hand and landed her in a puddle of water. She would have to climb out before it got really dark so she went carefully all round it, feeling for a foothold in its sides, and came to the conclusion that there weren't any—nor were there any large stones which she could pile against its steep sides.

'How very unfortunate,' said Arabella. Not a panicky person by nature, she felt a nasty little pang of fear at the idea of spending the night there. Not that she would have to do that, she told herself robustly. They would miss her at the manor. A pity she hadn't brought a torch. If the wind would die down she could shout, but at the moment it would be a waste of breath. It just needs a rat or two, she thought gloomily.

The doctor stopped before his home with a sigh of satisfaction. Whether she liked it or not, Arabella and he were going to have that talk—but first of all he would wring her darling little neck and kiss her silent…

He was welcomed by the three dogs with delight and by Percy with dignity and then by the Butters in their turn, beaming at him, deploring the sudden onslaught of bad weather and at the same time offering tea, drinks and saying madam was in the drawing-room.

Only she wasn't. 'Well,' said Mrs Butter, 'she had a cup of tea here earlier, after she took the dogs out. She'll be upstairs. I'll call her.'

'Don't bother, I'll go,' said Titus and went up the staircase two at a time, knocked on the door and went in. Arabella wasn't there, of course; he went from room to room and then downstairs again. She wasn't there either.

'She wouldn't go out,' declared Mrs Butter. 'She took the dogs like I said, and I'd have heard the front door for we were both in the dining-room and you can hear it close from there.'

The doctor said, 'Ah, the back door,' and went to look, the Butters close behind. 'Is there anything missing?' he wanted to know, turning over the coats and capes hanging there.

'My boots,' said Mrs Butter suddenly. 'I had them on this morning—they were here, under that old jacket—I wear when I go down to the kitchen garden.'

'Take a torch, Butter, and go down to the village.

See if anyone has seen Mrs Tavener. I'll go up the lane. Wave the torch if you find her—I'll do the same.'

He shrugged into an old mac, gave up the idea of boots since none of them were large enough for his feet, took the torch Mrs Butter had fetched, and opened the door. The wind took his breath as he stood there, the dogs crowding round, anxious to help. They all went up the lane at a great rate with frequent stops while Titus bellowed, 'Arabella,' in a voice to rival the wind.

Arabella heard it. She was numb with cold and her feet, despite the wellies, were blocks of ice although she hadn't stood still. Indeed she had been scrambling in a fruitless manner up the sides of the gully and slipping down to the bottom again. She was frightened now and her answering shout had been no more than a squeak, but she tried again and was cheered to hear his shout in answer. A long minute later she saw the torch shining above her and looked up to see four pairs of eyes looking down at her.

The dogs barked, delighted to have found her, and the doctor said, 'Oh, you silly girl,' in such a tender voice that she very nearly burst into tears. She gulped them back. 'Don't any of you fall in,' she said.

Titus was examining the gully by the light of the torch. He bade the dogs sit and then said, 'Now, listen carefully, Arabella. Go to the end—that's it, as far as you can go—it's a little lower. I'm going to lie flat and reach down to you. Lift your arms as high as you can and I'll lift you out.'

'You won't be able to—I'm too heavy.'

He laughed. 'One of your more ridiculous remarks,' he said cheerfully. He waved the torch in the air in the hope that Butter would see it and stretched his considerable bulk on to the soaking ground. It was raining very hard now but he hardly seemed to notice that. He put his great arms down into the gully and caught Arabella's cold hands in his.

She landed in an untidy heap beside him, covered in mud and bits of bracken and grass and very wet. He got up and lifted her to her feet and she said in a small polite voice, 'Thank you, Titus,' and burst into tears. He held her close while she sniffed and snuffled in a manner totally devoid of any glamour, then she blew her small nose, mopped her face and said, 'Sorry.'

'My dearest darling girl,' said Titus, in a voice which she had never heard before. He might have said a great deal more only Butter came puffing up to join them. As it was he contented himself with a kiss which took her breath before observing, 'Mrs Tavener had fallen in the gully, Butter—she's wet and cold. Would you go ahead and ask Mrs Butter to get a warm bath ready? We'll be right behind you.'

Butter hurried off and Titus picked Arabella up as

though she had been a feather duster and carried her back down the lane with the dogs trotting beside him.

'I can walk,' said Arabella. He had called her his dearest darling girl. Had that been to keep her spirits up? And what about that kiss? Something to remember lingeringly.

Mrs Butter was at the door and so was Butter, with glasses and a bottle of brandy. 'Ah,' said the doctor, putting Arabella down but not letting her go. 'Just what we all need.'

'I don't like brandy,' said Arabella.

A remark of which the doctor, quite rightly, took no notice. She drank it down under his impassive gaze before he picked her up again, this time without the jacket, and carried her upstairs.

Half an hour later, warm and dry and very clean, her still-damp hair hanging down her back, Arabella went downstairs. 'You're not to dress, madam,' Mrs Butter had said. 'Doctor says a warm dressing-gown and you're to go to bed early.' First, however, she had to face him across the dinner table.

Titus was waiting for her in the drawing-room. He looked as though he had never been near a gully in his life—the epitome of a well-heeled gentleman with time on his hands. She went slowly into the room. It would be hard to ask him about Geraldine but it had to be done. 'Titus…' she began.

He was across the room and she was in his arms

before she could say another word. 'And before you say anything, my darling heart, I love you. I think that I always have only it didn't occur to me sooner… And before you fling Geraldine in my teeth, I do not care a jot for her—never have. If you hadn't been such a busybody, flinging me at her head at all hours of the day, you would have seen that for yourself. And, yes, I went to Holland—because Aldrik's mother has had a stroke.' He looked down at her. 'Well, my darling?'

'Well,' began Arabella, 'I love you, you see and I think I must have a jealous nature.'

'There are ways of curing you of that,' said Titus.

Neither of them saw the faithful Butter come to announce dinner and slide away again.

Presently Titus said, 'I shall always remember this day, my love.'

'Me, too,' said Arabella and kissed him just once more.

She was remembering that just eighteen months later, sitting on the window-seat in the drawing-room, an open letter in one hand, a very small baby tucked under the other arm. 'He's coming home, my poppet—listen…'

She began to read the letter again, out loud this time so that their son could hear it too, even though it meant nothing to his very small ears…

Dearest love,

By the time you read this letter I shall be on my way home. I have missed you so—the week has seemed like a lifetime without you. I picture you and our son sitting in the drawing-room reading this—I wonder if I am right? I cannot wait to be with you again.

Why, I wonder, do VIP patients always choose to be ill in far-flung places? He is recovering; he will be flown home some time next week and I shall be able to treat him without having to leave you both.

I am not sure at what time we shall land but I shall be with you at the earliest possible moment.

Titus—who loves you.

Tender Romance™

Four brand new titles each month

...love affairs that last a lifetime.

Available at most branches of WH Smith, Tesco, Martins, Borders, Easons, Volume One/James Thin and most good paperback bookshops

GEN/02/RTL2

Medical Romance™

Six brand new titles each month

...medical drama on the pulse.

Available at most branches of WH Smith, Tesco, Martins, Borders, Easons, Volume One/James Thin and most good paperback bookshops

GEN/03/RTL2

D0682974

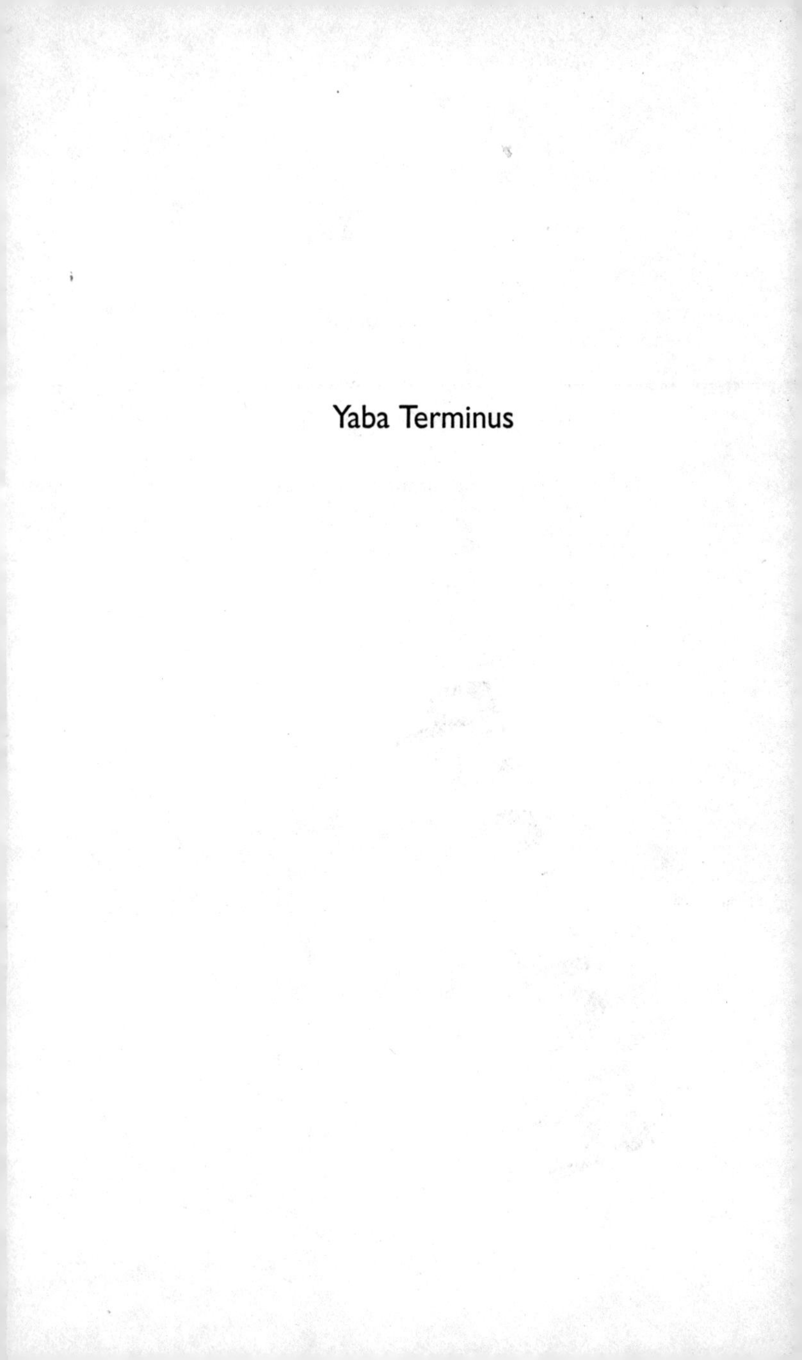

Yaba Terminus

Du même auteur

Kin-la-joie Kin-la-folie, L'Harmattan, 1993

Agence Black Bafoussa, Série Noire, 1996

Sorcellerie à bout portant, Série Noire, 1998

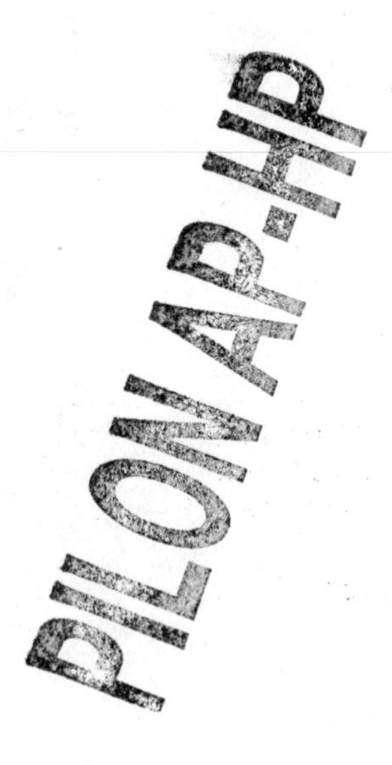

Achille N'Goye

Yaba Terminus

Nouvelles

Afrique
N
NGO

Hôpital Européen Georges Pompidou
Médiathèque
20, rue Leblanc - 75015 Paris
Tél. 01.56.09.22.90
Tél. 01.56.09.31.27

LE SERPENT A PLUMES

Collection Serpent Noir
dirigée par Tania Capron

© 1998 Le Serpent à Plumes

N° ISBN : 2-84261-098-9

Couverture réalisée par Alexandre Courtès

LE SERPENT A PLUMES
20, rue des Petits-Champs - 75002 Paris
http ://www.serpentaplumes.com

Yaba Terminus

I

DÈS LE COUP de sifflet, Midy se fia à son flair de femme et conclut à l'imminence du danger. L'instant d'après, une galopade tumultueuse, suivie de l'éclatement d'une porte, la paralysait. La gazelle revit aussitôt, comme dans un court-métrage, des scènes vulgarisées par la soldatesque de tous les pays, des scènes de viol et de tuerie souvent perpétrées en présence d'un témoin ou d'une caméra affichant, sur le coup, sa neutralité ; ruse de faux-derches destinée à procurer un max d'émotion aux oasis de paix.

Les structures du vieil hôtel craquèrent dans la foulée, plongeant la nana dans une terreur panique : des chaises qui crissent, basculent, trahissant des présences voulues discrètes ; des ombres qui surgissent dans les couloirs, s'interpellent, rameutent les proches, déboulent dans les escaliers, déménagent dans un désordre apocalyptique ; des mômes qui chialent d'un réveil nocturne aux taloches et braillent à tout casser, inconscients de compromettre une fuite embrayée en douce.

Dans sa terreur, Midy crut entendre quelqu'un lui crier de mettre les cannes : le groupe d'intervention de la Military Police (MP) cernait l'hôtel. La greluche se remua à la seconde. Les gestes fébriles, désordonnés, elle rejeta le drap et sauta hors du lit. Son pagne resserré autour du buffet, elle perdit un temps fou dans la recherche d'une blouse, finit par en dénicher une et l'enfiler, non sans râler au constat qu'il s'agissait d'une marinière, puis bondit, hors d'haleine, vers la fenêtre.

Chevelure défaite, frêle dans sa vareuse pour femmes fortes, Midy ressemblait à une poupée mal fagotée. Elle se dressa sur la pointe des pieds, se pencha à la fenêtre. La vue de la scène la pétrifia : la sortie de l'hôtel, d'ordinaire un trou à rats, s'illuminait sous deux projecteurs posés sur un camion de la terrifiante MP. Vingt, trente, peut-être bien une compagnie de gâchettes faciles, grouillaient autour. Les poulets ne faisaient aucun mystère quant à leur mission de nettoyer l'hôtel. Postés à l'entrée, certains d'entre eux cueillaient les bougres, déboussolés, qui voulaient décamper sous les feux de la rampe. Rudoyés, jetés par terre, les fuyards échouaient, sans trop savoir comment, sous la bâche d'un camion de ramassage. Pendant ce temps, un commando investissait l'hôtel. À entendre les cris et les supplications, la MP garnissait son tableau de chasse tambour battant.

Les assiégeants soulevèrent tout à coup les têtes, obligeant Midy à reculer de son perchoir. Trois, quatre, cinq clients du troisième étage passèrent en voltige, avant qu'elle n'ait conclu son mouvement, et s'écrasèrent au sol. Sinistre. Une clameur s'éleva parmi les badauds, tenus à distance hors de l'enceinte de l'hôtel, tandis que les flics accouraient.

Trois cascadeurs restèrent sur le carreau, désarticulés, le quatrième s'écroula après avoir tenté de se relever, le cinquième amortit sa chute sur son prédécesseur. Le veinard prit pied à la minute et, toute honte bue, traça dans la nuit. Un MP se lança à ses trousses. Mais la vue de la foule anéantit son ardeur : le zorro aurait vite fait de s'évanouir parmi la cinquantaines de migrants clandestins qui, chaque heure, s'infiltrent dans la ville.

Midy n'hésita pas. Son pagne replié sur les cuisses, elle se hissa sur le rebord de la fenêtre, prit la température au sol : des flics s'affairaient autour des blessés, après les avoir évacués vers les camions, laissant leur point de chute sans surveillance. La gazelle concentra son attention sur le carré, s'apprêta au saut périlleux. Une frousse indicible la figea au moment de passer aux actes. Les doigts accrochés à l'encadrement, elle s'accroupit afin de contenir sa frayeur. Sa porte fut fracassée à cet instant. L'assaut final. Midy se cramponna au cadre avec l'énergie du désespoir, tourna la carafe. Le temps de percer l'obscurité et d'y voir clair, un sentiment intense de sécurité la parcourut. Dieu ne l'avait pas abandonnée : Checain Tamba, son fiancé !

L'ange gardien lui susurra un chut ! en fusant dans la pièce. Il la rejoignit rapidement, la saisit à la taille et, réglo avec son épate sur sa bravoure, sauta dans le vide. La vue des uniformes, honnis sous toutes les latitudes pour leur choix délibéré dans le mauvais camp, arracha un cri pathétique à la greluche…

« Calme-toi, Midy ! marmonna une voix à son oreille. Encore un mauvais rêve… »

Midy, le visage en sueur, ouvrit ses clignotants et reconnut Mère Six, qui lui tamponnait le front avec une serviette. Elle poussa un soupir, referma les paupières et se retourna dans le lit. Deux minutes après, elle revenait à sa position initiale. Les yeux rouverts, braqués sur la femme, un sourire se dessina sur ses lèvres.

« T'as quelle heure ? s'enquit-elle dans un murmure.

– Deux heures trente-cinq. Tu délires pratiquement depuis que tu t'es couchée… »

La gazelle nota les traits tirés de sa colocataire. Taille moyenne, forte, Mère Six tournait le dos à la lumière, la poire à l'opposé de la fresque maltraitée par les pommades éclaircissantes.

Née à l'aube des années soixante, d'où son surnom de Mère Six, la matrone n'avait pas atteint l'âge de douze ans qu'elle boutiquait son corps. À ceux qui, aujourd'hui, jasent sur sa dérive précoce, la vieille gloire rétorque par une déclaration d'identité : comment déroger à sa tradition quand on est môme, partant, irresponsable ? Avait-elle seulement conscience du caractère prétendument dégradant de son petit biz, lequel restait après tout vital pour les siens ? Et d'arguer, convaincue de faire mouche, qu'il existe bien des tribus de toubibs, d'instits, de truands. Pourquoi pas des clans de matelas ambulants ?

Mère Six n'avait gardé aucune amertume de ses revers, repartant toujours de zéro, même quand une nouvelle impasse se profilait à l'horizon. Jusqu'à ce qu'elle réalise que son étoile pâlissait de jour en jour, ternie par une paupérisation lente, implacable, qui pénalisait sa clientèle autant que sa carrière. Avec le risque de la larguer sur une voie de garage, démunie, bien qu'elle se considérât toujours d'attaque. Elle avait alors tenté cette sortie ultime, hors du pays, pour conclure en beauté. Loin d'être enrayée, la machine carburait à plein rendement. L'approche de la quarantaine avait du reste moulé ses formes et les avait galbées, transformant son bifteck en étalon.

« T'as encore fait un cauchemar, lâcha Mère Six en brisant le silence. Et t'as de la fièvre.

– Passe-moi une aspirine, s'il te plaît…

– Faudra que t'en parles au pasteur. Le plus tôt sera le mieux. Les cauchemars à répétition couvent un mal sournois. Or tu les fais depuis ton arrivée… »

La vieille gloire se dirigea vers la kitchenette, dans un angle proche de la fenêtre. Elle puisa de l'eau dans une cruche, trifouilla dans une valise et y piocha une boîte d'aspirine. De retour auprès de la fille, elle attendit que celle-ci se relève pour lui tendre le verre. Midy s'en empara d'une main fébrile, avala le cachet. D'une brusque pression sur le coude, elle recula dans le lit, s'adossa au chevet. Elle resta un moment abrutie, la tête contre le mur et les yeux atones, tandis que ses épaules s'affaissaient dans un mouvement d'abandon.

À dix-neuf ans, Midy en affichait cinq de moins, séquelles d'une malnutrition infantile tenace. Malgré la finesse de ses traits, sa figure accusait les rigueurs d'une vie menée au pas de course, chose perceptible dans son regard hardi. Une gueule boudeuse déridait son minois pour le moins chafouin. Ses mandarines, telles des bananes naines, pointaient sur une poitrine rachitique. Sa voix chaude, quoique par moments acrimonieuse, signe évident d'un ras-le-bol des frustrations emmagasinées, restait cependant engageante.

Midy sortit subito de sa torpeur et surprit la matrone dans son observation. Elle s'empressa de lui remettre le verre, espérant ainsi la distraire. Remarquant sa poitrine exposée aux vents, elle la couvrit en vitesse et se glissa sous les draps.

« Confie-toi au pasteur, Midy. La malédiction jetée par tes vieux te poursuit. Y a pas de doute là-dessus. Les tiens ne vont pas aplatir le coup de sitôt. À mon avis, y a qu'une séance d'exorcisme pour t'en libérer…

– Tu m'vois raconter ces vacheries à quelqu'un ? J'en mourrais de honte…

– Nous vivons ici en famille. Personne, dans ce trou où nous avons sombré, n'est un ange. Cela vaut pour le pasteur aussi bien que pour le président. Au fait, tu pourrais, demain, te confesser au culte. Je peux arranger ça. Ça libère des obsessions.

– J'y arriverai jamais !

– Des crapules y parviennent et retrouvent la paix intérieure. Cette paix, t'en as grandement besoin. N'oublie pas qu'on est loin de chez nous et qu'il faut se secouer pour vivre. La vie d'ici est plus dure que là-bas. Sans un kobo[1] ni de quoi dasher[2], t'as aucune chance de crâner à Lagos.»

Tout en parlant, Mère Six avait contourné le paravent qui sépare les deux lits. Outre une armoire en tek massif, vestige de l'âge d'or de l'hôtel, placée contre le mur, la chambre comportait les plumards, un lavabo ainsi qu'une douche, tous deux hors service, la douche servant au finish de débarras. Les chaises avaient disparu, mais la table avait été convertie en meuble de cuisine.

La matrone souhaita une bonne nuit à Midy, puis s'arrêta net à la question inattendue :

« Dis-moi, Mère Six, t'es la maîtresse du pasteur ? »

L'interpellée resta un moment sans voix. Sa stupeur digérée, elle riposta avec le même argument.

« Pourquoi cette question ?

– J'ai vu ce baratineur entrer ici, l'autre nuit. J'ai tout entendu. Même quand il s'est approché de mon lit, dans le noir, pour s'assurer que je dormais… »

Un malaise, accentué par le silence de la nuit, plana sur la chambre. Il persista quelque temps, troublé par le bruit de fond des vagues du littoral et

1. Centième de naira, la monnaie nigeriane. (N.d.A.).
2. De dash, bakchich. (N.d.A.).

des véhicules. Mère Six revint lentement sur ses pas. Elle toisa la nana pendant une longue minute, mine de ne savoir quoi débiter, puis lâcha d'une voix désabusée :

« Écoute, Midy : je te considère comme une petite sœur, raison pour laquelle je t'ai prise avec moi à ton arrivée, il y a une semaine. Tout ce que je te demande, c'est de plonger dans le bain, même si l'eau est crade, afin de contribuer au paiement du loyer. À ce propos, je considère que tes vacances sont finies et qu'il est temps de bouger. Oublie ce que t'as vu ou entendu, et n'en parle à personne. »

Midy, qui ne s'attendait pas à cette douche, couva la matrone d'un regard hébété. Celle-ci regagna son coin en grommelant, se glissa sous une couverture. Quelques instants après, elle éteignait la lumière et, sans que rien le laisse prévoir, sortait de son mutisme.

« Au fait, pourquoi as-tu traité le pasteur de baratineur ? A-t-il essayé de te draguer ?

– Non ! réagit la gazelle, qui, à peine débarquée à l'hôtel, s'était vu pincer les totoches par le clergyman.

– Pourquoi alors le traiter de baratineur ?

– Ben… parce qu'il brode dans ses sermons…

– Tu mens, Midy ! T'as été qu'une fois au culte, et cela ne suffit pas pour porter un tel jugement ! »

Un bref silence s'ensuivit, après quoi la vieille gloire changea de registre :

« Qu'est-ce que tu fais demain ?

– On m'a demandé de passer un coup de balai

chez le malade du rez-de-chaussée. De quoi souffre-t-il, celui-là ?

– Un cas désespéré, ce pauvre Monteiro… »

Mère Six ne termina pas sa phrase, comme si l'évocation venait de lui rappeler la dure loi de l'existence. Mais le ton sec de sa reprise démonta la nana :

« Tu viens d'abord avec moi au culte pour tirer cette histoire au clair. Personne n'avale ici les kinoiseries. Tu passeras chez le malade après.

– Y a rien à remuer dans ce que j'ai dit, Mère Six. Et puis, le culte dure des heures et j'ai promis d'assurer dans l'avant-midi !

– Tu vas plutôt assurer au culte, compris ? »

II

Situé dans le quartier populaire de Yaba, bas-fonds de la métropole nigériane et paradis de sa population immigrée, le *Yaba Terminus* arborait ses trois étages décrépits, tel un monument ancien, dans un immense paysage de baraquements. L'entrée de l'hôtel s'ouvrait sur un réduit pourvu d'un comptoir, d'une télé et d'un réfrigérateur Westinghouse d'un modèle archaïque. Derrière le comptoir, accrochée au mur à hauteur d'homme, une étagère à trois montants alignait des verres, signe que le réduit servait également de bar, d'où les tables et chaises éparses sur l'espace opposé. Bien en vue sur le comptoir, un carton jauni affichait complet.

Deux couloirs perpendiculaires aboutissaient à la réception. Le premier, qui partait de l'accueil, menait aux chambres du rez-de-chaussée ; le deuxième passait devant l'escaliers conduisant aux étages, à droite du comptoir, et donnait sur l'arrière-cour. Les toilettes et douches communes logeaient dans cette partie de l'établissement.

Un Nigérian affable, inconnu de la plupart des clients, en assurait la gérance. Mais, par quelque curieux transfert de charges, le ménage et la police internes revenaient aux pensionnaires. Ceux-ci s'étaient regroupés dans une amicale des résidents, cadre, au départ destiné à dynamiser l'entraide et la fraternité entre les adhérents, qui, à la longue, coordonnait les activités d'intérêt général. Une équipe de six membres, tous éjectables et malléables à merci, veillait à sa pérennité sous la houlette d'un président-fondateur.

Deux ressortissants d'Afrique centrale avaient atterri au *Yaba*, il y a un lustre, pour un court séjour. Dix autres déboulèrent dans leur sillage en moins d'un an. Puis vingt, trente, quarante. Jusqu'à former un noyau dur de quelque soixante individus. Leur plus grand exploit fut d'éliminer du décor les nationaux et apparentés. La chambre étant payée au mois, ils en amortissaient le loyer en logeant à plusieurs, selon leurs affinités. Le doyen de la tribu dépassait la cinquantaine ; le vétéran, par ailleurs président de l'amicale et l'un des trois « Congomen » à rouler carrosse, revendiquait douze ans d'ancienneté. Quant aux dix-sept femmes, elles valsaient entre seize et quarante-deux ans, et certaines maternaient des mioches. Seize au total. Nés ici ou venus d'ailleurs. La tribu comptait trois couples légitimes, mais ceux-ci ne fournissaient que le tiers de ses babouins.

Les nationalités s'étaient également diversifiées au fil des ans. Angolais, Cabindais, ces derniers refusant obstinément d'être assimilés aux premiers, mais aussi Congolais et ex-Zaïrois composaient la communauté. Bien que provenant de zones linguistiques différentes, ils comprenaient tous le français ou le massacraient, et se targuaient de refléter leurs sociétés d'origine. Le club dénombrait effectivement deux ex-profs, sept déserteurs de l'armée, des étudiants désabusés, une pute déclarée, sans compter les chômeurs professionnels et les lascars qui considéraient leurs CV comme des secrets d'État.

La plupart des résidents étaient entrés clandestinement au Nigeria ou s'y étaient fondus avec un visa touristique. Ils se défendaient de vouloir s'y enraciner, alléguant, à cet effet, les expulsions massives qui revenaient de manière cyclique. Ils prétendaient en outre n'avoir rien à zyeuter, le mot « touristique » relevant de la pub mensongère. Fuyant une région sinistrée par la crise, l'incurie et les diktats du FMI, région en prime ravagée par des guerres et des épidémies, ils quêtaient des havres de paix, là où des gens apprennent à coexister après avoir longtemps croisé le fer. En transit pour le Nord, ils avaient échoué à Lagos afin de se remettre à flot. Leur viatique évaporé au cours d'une étape qui s'éternisait, ils vivaient d'expédients et consacraient leurs journées à peaufiner des magouilles. Pas de quoi nourrir un grand dessein. D'autant que l'ignorance du pidgin, la dureté de la mégalopole d'Afrique noire, la phobie des gangs nigérians ainsi que la peur du policeman les repliaient sur eux-mêmes.

III

Dès cinq heures du mat', le *Yaba* craquait sous les va-et-vient des lève-tôt. Vétérans, délurés, flemmards décidés à franchir le pas, se grouillaient en vue de monter au front. Trois quarts d'heure après, ils levaient l'ancre. Pour le port. Des bateaux mouillaient en rade pendant six mois, voire davantage, avant d'accéder aux quais et d'y être déchargés. Soustraites aux cargaisons par des matelots et des dockers sous-payés, des marchandises de toutes sortes s'y négociaient à prix cassés.

En possession de ces articles, les acheteurs rejoignaient des colonnes de mômes surnommés *chukwuemeka,* « Dieu a fait du bon boulot » en langue ibo. Grâce lui soit rendue ! Ces petits coquins hantaient les grandes artères de la ville, profitant des légendaires *go slow*, les embouteillages monstres de l'ancienne capitale du Nigeria, pour fourguer aux automobilistes des produits de contrebande : Tampax, réveils électroniques, montres, etc. Que la circulation soit fluide, chose impensable dans ce vivier du mal-développement, les diablotins pouvaient retourner la situation en leur faveur. Il suffisait, pour ce faire, de dégonfler le pneu d'un véhicule et provoquer fatalement un *go slow*. Bénéfique pour la classe ouvrière.

Pendant ce temps, les fainéants ronflaient dans leur lit. Réveillés à partir de neuf heures, ils se préparaient au culte quotidien qui, désœuvrement oblige, rassemble les expatriés dans une salle du voisinage de l'hôtel. Outre le prétexte offert aux meufs d'étrenner les super-wax, bazins et autres falbalas acquis sur place, ce culte dépêtrait les naufragés de la grisaille. Avec ses prêches, inspirés par les tribulations de ses ouailles, le pasteur, digne fils de la tribu et self-made-man en religion, opérait, chaque jour, le miracle de remonter le moral au peuple bloqué au terminus.

Sa toilette faite, pomponnée, Midy prévint Mère Six qu'elle allait l'attendre à la réception. Son sac en bandoulière, elle y surgit en cinq sec, tomba sur une salle vide. Les couloirs déserts déçurent son attente. Renonçant à son espoir de glaner des coups d'encensoir sur son maquillage, elle sortit de l'hôtel. Le soleil dardait ses rayons brûlants sur Lagos et la chaleur montait, de plus en plus étouffante, comme dans une chaudière. Midy rentra dans le local, s'accouda au comptoir. Dans un mouvement de tête, elle fonça à la chambre du malade.

La nana avait déjà veillé sur l'avarié. Le gars maigrissait à vue d'œil et son état fendait le cœur : sa poire, prématurément sénile, semblait servir au moulage de masques mortuaires. Clandestin, il n'avait pas voulu de l'hosto, laissant son mal le ronger à petit feu. Conscient de l'état désespéré de sa situation, il souffrait en silence, s'offrant parfois le luxe de sourire quand quelqu'un s'attardait près de lui. Il parlait alors par bribes, chaque mot semblant lui arracher le dernier soupir.

L'amicale avait tenté de le secourir. Son état s'aggravant et nécessitant un traitement conséquent, elle avait fini par jeter l'éponge. Avec des cotisants fauchés, la caisse d'entraide, au demeurant gérée par une trésorière douteuse, voyait ses ambitions à la baisse.

Dès son entrée dans la chambre, désertée par les autres locataires depuis des mois, Midy renifla une odeur familière. Son flair ne pouvait la tromper sur ce point : encore gosse, elle avait appris à guetter la mort autour d'elle, la reconnaître, la bluffer le cas échéant. Le rythme cardiaque irrégulier, le visage qui s'assombrit, l'âme qui décroche n'étaient plus un secret pour une gamine dont le milieu restait tributaire des épidémies.

La nana s'approcha du lit, constata le décès. L'espace d'un instant, elle parut désemparée et balaya la pièce d'un regard effaré. Elle se pencha à la fin sur la dépouille. Dans son combat ultime, le mourant avait glissé sur le côté. Midy bascula le corps au centre du lit. Après avoir fermé les yeux grands ouverts, elle essuya la bave, recouvrit le cadavre et disposa la tête sur l'oreiller, heurtant au passage un objet planqué dessous. Elle le tira : un passeport angolais au nom de Joâo Manteka, né à

Dolisie, République populaire du Congo. Mère Six, rumina la greluche, avait prêté un autre nom au moribond. Qu'est-ce que cela signifiait ? La photo était bien celle du défunt, alors pétant de santé, et le visa échu depuis un bail. D'un geste machinal, la nana glissa le document dans son blue jean. Elle sortit aussitôt, remonta au deuxième.

La vieille gloire n'avait pas encore fini sa métamorphose en putasse de luxe. Midy la mit au parfum et fut en retour soufflée de voir la caravelle, les yeux hors des orbites, perdre ses couleurs. D'une minute à l'autre, elle tournoya dans la pièce et se répandit en lamentations :

« On est fichus. Vraiment fichus. Qu'est-ce qu'on va faire ?

– C'est pour le rapatriement du corps que tu dis ça ? » questionna Midy ingénument.

La matrone fixa la nana de l'air désespéré d'une marmite dont la leçon pratique à une jeune mariée – comment secouer le popotin lors de la nuit nuptiale – dégénère en exhibition du twist again. Son dépit surmonté, elle accoucha d'une voix excédée.

« D'abord, t'avais pas à fouiner dans ce mouroir et je te l'ai dit. Qu'est-ce que ça te coûtait d'attendre après le culte ? Un connard serait tombé sur le macchab et t'aurais été peinarde. De plus, t'as pas cotisé pour lui payer le fret !

– Tu te mets en boule rien que pour ça ?

– C'est pas tout, fouille-merde : il faut un constat de toubib et d'un officier de police pour procéder à la levée du corps. Or, un flic voudrait aussi savoir qui et qui habitent l'hôtel, avec quels papiers... »

Les pendules ainsi remises à l'heure, Mère Six fonça vers la porte. Elle revint aussitôt sur ses pas. Pour fouiller dans son sac, chambouler la table de chevet avant de dénicher, évidemment dans le sac à main, l'objet de ses recherches : un vaporisateur. Les aisselles parfumées et la bouille soumise au verdict d'un petit miroir, elle sortit en crachant un ordre :

« Je monte prévenir le président. Il n'est sans doute pas au courant. Toi, tu restes là. Ne bouge surtout pas, sinon ça ne va pas être rigolo, mais alors pas du tout. »

Mère Six disparut dans le couloir en laissant la greluche dans le désarroi. La nana fit néanmoins montre de lucidité, puisqu'elle arracha la photo du document subtilisé et planqua celui-ci dans son sac. Une demi-heure après, sa colocataire rentrait dans la pièce, encore plus affolée, en compagnie de Ben Balewa.

Baraqué, le visage foncé et souriant, le présidentfondateur tenait un portable, son physique de malabar baignant dans une superbe djellaba. Le costume, de couleur mauve, lui prêtait l'air d'un authentique Nigérian, sa toison à la Wole Soyinka, digne fils du pays s'il en est, homologuant ce cousinage bidon.

Le mastard pénétra dans la chambre avec détachement, tandis que son accompagnatrice s'adossait à la porte après l'avoir fermée. La mise en scène détraqua la nana, toujours assise sur le lit, au point de regretter de n'avoir pas gardé sa découverte pour elle.

Midy avait déjà aperçu Ben Balewa à deux reprises. La première fois, elle ne l'avait pas flashé. Quelconque. La fois d'après, elle lui avait trouvé un look particulier, tant et si bien qu'elle s'était branchée sur lui. Le « présidium » (*sic*), lui avait soufflé son informateur, est un ponte. Nanti d'excellentes relations dans les sphères de la junte. Il s'est spécialisé dans la contrebande de pétrole, trafic auquel il cumule d'autres activités aussi douteuses qu'honnêtes. Personne ne connaît son vrai nom, Ben Balewa étant, selon des avis concordants, un nom d'emprunt destiné à s'accorder au ciel nigérian. Des histoires crapuleuses circulent sur son compte. Ses interlocuteurs craignent par-dessus tout ses coups de gueule, préludes à une explication musclée. Black Président, son pseudo depuis la disparition du fondateur de la dynastie, Fela Anikulapo Kuti pour ne pas le citer, passe alors sa fonction à la trappe.

Le président s'approcha de la gazelle comme un fauve en retard de collation. Ses yeux globuleux plantés dans le regard apeuré, il accoucha d'une voix faussement mielleuse :

« Petite, on ne se connaît pas, mais Mère Six m'a parlé de toi. En bien. Je constate qu'elle n'a pas brodé : t'es fraîche, suffisamment croquante pour qu'on sympathise. »

Déroutée par cette entrée en matière, Midy baissa les yeux devant le regard pénétrant, tandis que Ben se mettait à croupetons devant elle. Son haleine, polluée par un petit déj'à l'herbe, empesta l'espace de l'aparté. Le balèze laissa planer une minute de suspense. Le portable déposé sur le lit, il souleva sa main, mollo, mine de vouloir caresser le menton effilé. D'une pression subite de l'index, il redressa la boule baissée et bloqua le menton, obligeant la nénette à affronter son regard.

«Ce que t'as vu ne doit pas s'ébruiter dans l'hôtel. Entends-tu, ma petite chatte ? Personne ne doit le savoir. Il y va de ton intérêt, de celui de Mère Six, de tous ces cocos qui vivent ici. J'aurais souhaité que tu ne sois pas mêlée à cet aléa. Mais les choses étant ce qu'elles sont, je me sens obligé de t'enjoindre à la boucler.

– Z'avez pas à vous inquiéter, président, bafouilla la souris en tentant de se libérer. Je vais la boucler. De plus, je ne sais rien du défunt…

– Tu l'as touché ?

– J'aurais jamais osé, président.

– T'as rien piqué dans sa chambre ?

– C'est pas mon style : les trucs d'un mort sont vachement sacrés.

– Tu me rassures», conclut Ben en desserrant son étau, tandis que Mère Six roulait des yeux d'ahurissement.

Debout, sa grande taille dominant la gazelle, Ben Balewa trépigna d'indécision en dépit du quitus qu'il venait de donner. Conscientes que le plus dur se jouait à cet instant, les deux femelles se morfondaient dans une expectative angoissante, l'une conjurant le malabar dans son dos, l'autre ne sachant sur quel objet poser ses mirettes. Black President donna brusquement un coup de patte au parquet, dégelant l'atmosphère de manière imprévisible :

« J'ai ta parole, ma petite. Ne me déçois pas, car j'aime pas les entubages... Tu viens d'où ?

– De Kin.

– Ah ! s'écria Ben d'une voix amusée, c'est toi qui as floué tes vieux ! T'as pourtant une tronche à l'huile. Qu'est-ce que les apparences peuvent être trompeuses ! »

Midy ne réagit pas, jetant toutefois un regard de reproche à la matrone. Quelle salope !

« J'aime bien les petites dégourdies, reprit Ben Balewa, énigmatique. Mai-, fais gaffe : pas de crasses à la kinoise ici. Ça se paie très cher ! »

Après un bref silence, il vira aux actualités :

« Ça se passe comment, là-bas ?

– Toujours pareil : vie au ralenti, guerres alternées de pillages. J'ai rien connu d'autre.

– Normal quand les gens sont plongés dans un sommeil profond. On se croirait à l'époque précoloniale... Allez, les nanas, on se casse. Tous dans la Pidjott[1], sinon le pasteur va s'imaginer qu'on sabote sa séance de blabla. »

Midy se détacha du lit d'un seul élan et mit un peu d'ordre dans sa tenue. Entre-temps, Ben s'était approché de la vieille gloire et lui parlait à l'oreille, un œil malicieux sur la gazelle. Mère Six accueillit la confidence par un fou rire, puis ouvrit la porte.

1. Peugeot en pidgin (N.d.A.).

IV

La 504 parcourut rapidement la distance qui sépare le *Yaba Terminus* du lieu de culte. Ben surgit dans la salle, accompagné de sa suite, alors que le pasteur dopait ses ouailles avec l'espérance, son thème favori avec l'amour. Les amazones se faufilèrent dans la dernière rangée, tandis que le Black President piquait sur le prédicant. Parvenu à sa hauteur, il lui fit un signe du doigt, stoppant net sa tirade et le mettant en demeure de le rejoindre.

Trapu, le crâne endommagé par une calvitie corrosive, le pasteur ne payait pas de mine. Pur produit d'une désespérance qui engendrait des prophètes à la manque, Frère Jacob ne répondait à aucun modèle. Sa vocation, très tardive, reposait du reste sur une prétendue révélation, comme si le Dieu d'Abraham, faisant table rase d'un apartheid plurimillénaire, avait craqué pour un damné de la terre et l'avait élevé au rang de griot. L'étude en solo de la Bible, traduite par l'exploitation d'un terrain en jachère, creuset de toutes les détresses suscitées par des lendemains compromis, avait consolidé l'appel. Le denier du culte ainsi que des paumés lessivés de tout esprit critique l'avaient légitimé. Les voies du Seigneur restent insondables.

Le sermonnaire parut sidéré par ce qu'on lui rapportait. Les mains nouées sur l'embonpoint, il hocha la tête à plusieurs reprises et ne desserra pas les dents. Habituée aux intrusions du Black President, l'assistance mit la pause à profit pour cancaner. Au reste, le port du djellaba, en signe distinctif du muslim sous l'équateur, détonnait trop dans ce lieu voué à la Croix pour ne pas stimuler les commérages. Frère Jacob s'essuya le mufle au terme de l'aparté, retourna au perchoir. Quant à son compère, il regagna le fond de la salle, d'où il attendit que le prêcheur, ses esprits retrouvés, invite l'assistance à la prière avant de s'éclipser.

« Mes chers frères et sœurs, l'Éternel, dans Sa générosité sans bornes, nous donne la vie et en dispose selon Son gré, prouvant par là qu'Il reste le seul Maître de notre destin. Autant nous nous réjouissons d'une naissance ou d'un heureux événement, autant devrions-nous considérer le départ d'un des nôtres, aussi pénible et cruel soit-il, comme l'expression de Sa volonté et nous y soumettre avec humilité. Pour cette raison, prions pour les âmes de nos frères et sœurs qui nous ont précédés dans la maison du Seigneur… »

Alléluia ! Les fidèles fermèrent les yeux et soulevèrent les bras. Puis répétèrent l'oraison que Frère Jacob récitait pour le salut des disparus.

Midy espéra, tout au long de l'oraison, que celle-ci dérive sur le macchab de l'hôtel. Elle appela cette évocation de tous ses vœux, s'accrocha aux babines du prédicant. Entendre des cris étouffés, des reniflements ; voir des mouchoirs sortir des poches et des rivières de larmes couler ; frémir devant les pleurs ; jouir à la place du mort de la satisfaction de se sentir aimé. Mais la supplique s'acheva comme elle avait commencé. Vague.

La gazelle cogita sur les raisons de ce black-out. Selon les usages, des usages somme toute communs aux Bantous, peuple auquel appartiennent les expatriés, la survenance d'un décès devient le deuil de tout le monde. Impossible de s'y dérober ou de feindre l'ignorance. Quel crime avait donc commis le défunt pour être ainsi pénalisé ? Qui était-il et que faisait-il avant d'atterrir à Lagos ? Ces hommes et femmes réunis là acceptaient-ils de vivre, hors de leur univers, dans le mépris des règles qui les régissent ? Qu'adviendrait-il si quelqu'un, parmi eux, trépassait subitement ? Subirait-il un départ sans une prière sur mesure pour accompagner son âme dans l'au-delà ?

Aucun éclairage ne lui venant à l'esprit, Midy en conclut que son imagination la menait trop loin. Les choses devraient s'expliquer. Qui sait si, après le culte, quand tout le monde aurait regagné l'hôtel, celui-ci n'allait pas se transformer en chambre funéraire ?

La greluche battit tout à coup des paupières, se frotta les mirettes. Décor inchangé. Dans son trouble, elle se crut victime d'un mirage et redoubla ses cillements. Aucun élément ne bougea du tableau. Combien de temps s'était-elle absentée ? pensa-t-elle en roulant des yeux de panique. Qu'est-ce qui s'était raconté pendant sa rêverie ? Aurait-elle parlé comme dans ses cauchemars, à voix haute, ainsi que le lui rebâche sa colocataire ?

En même temps qu'elle se posait ces questions, Mère Six, qui se tenait à sa droite, raide dans sa posture de pénitente, lui donna un vigoureux coup de coude au flanc. Midy rouvrit les yeux, terrifiée au constat que la salle avait les regards braqués sur elle. Venait-on de dire quelque chose qui la concernait et qu'elle n'avait pas entendu ? Déphasée, elle crut s'être endormie debout, chose après tout impensable, vu que ses tentatives antérieures de pioncer sur une chaise, au cours d'une veillée funèbre, s'étaient soldées par un réveil brutal au sol. Un deuxième coup de coude la tira de son nuage. Midy s'ébroua la tête, lorgna la matrone et dirigea un regard angoissé sur le ministre du culte. Celui-ci, manifestement en attente de cette présence physique, embraya d'un ton coulant :

« Ma sœur, n'ayez crainte de rien. Nous sommes tous des enfants de Dieu, Ses pauvres créatures vouées au feu de la géhenne ou au salut éternel en fonction de notre attitude envers le Mal. Venez, sister, aux côtés de l'indigne serviteur du Seigneur. Forte de la bienveillance de cette assemblée de pêcheurs, venez solliciter le pardon pour vos péchés... »

Midy, pétrifiée, ne put cligner des yeux. À vrai dire, elle aurait voulu se terrer dans un lieu inaccessible. À défaut, voler hors de vue de cette meute friande de cachotteries d'autrui et prête à jouer les aficionados pour autant qu'elle se tienne, peinarde, loin de l'arène. Elle aurait souhaité s'évanouir tout de suite, laissant derrière elle une fumée opaque.

Mère Six la saisit par le bras et, sans qu'elle oppose de résistance, l'entraîna hors de la rangée. Elle la conduisit vers le prédicant, ses hauts talons martelant la travée dans un tac-tac lugubre. Frère Jacob les accueillit à bras ouverts, déclenchant illico un vibrant Gloria, dont le contenu et l'harmonie consommaient la ruine du chant grégorien.

La suite releva d'un scénario rodé. Le pasteur se glissa entre les deux femmes, puis entonna un chant de pénitence. Les sons d'une guitare et le martèlement d'une caisse embrasèrent le temple. Alors que des voix s'éclaircissaient ici et là, le public reprit confusément le chant. Puis se mit à chalouper avec indécision, ensuite de manière effrénée, endiablée, les bras ballottés avec frénésie. Les voix devinrent vibrantes, hystériques, insufflant à la séance une ambiance telle que le Grand Dab, en baba cool de première, ne put résister à la tentation de verser une larme.

Le pasteur empoigna les mains de ses invitées et les agita fébrilement. Midy se laissa driver, bougeant à peine ses pattes. Ses origines remontèrent tout à coup à la surface et le miracle s'accomplit. Inouï. Subitement décoincée, elle imprima à ses pas une allure résolue, déchaînée, comme dans les bas-fonds de Kin, où la maîtrise de la danse distingue le plouc du citadin et constitue un palier du civilisé. Les yeux fermés et les tresses balancées à tous les azimuts, elle parut planer, mue par le feu sacré, et se tortilla comme une possédée. Elle machina la croupe avec impudence, pivota sur ses hauts talons, battit des mains, gambilla au point de déborder d'un dixième de seconde dans sa prestation. Communion parfaite. Alléluia !

« Ma sœur, intervint l'orateur lorsque les dernières notes se furent envolées, nous procédons à cette séance chaque fois qu'une âme perdue rejoint la communauté. Par cette pratique, nous voulons resserrer nos rangs et nous rapprocher de Yahvé. En ce jour béni, il vous revient de nous relater les circonstances qui vous ont conduite jusqu'ici. Point n'est besoin de souligner que votre venue ne relève pas du hasard. Elle est, au contraire, une manifestation de la bonté infinie du Créateur, qui vous a déléguée auprès des incrédules pour témoigner de Sa générosité… »

La gazelle, qui s'était crue dispensée de cette épreuve après sa démonstration, rouvrit les paupières et décocha un œil incendiaire au pasteur. Elle s'essuya le visage, consulta sa chaperonne. Celle-ci renfrognant son mufle huileux, preuve que son choix était fait entre le copinage et le spectacle, Midy survola le public avec hardiesse. La gorge raclée, elle visa le fond de la salle et ne le quitta plus. Sa relation coula de source.

« Midy est mon prénom, Sala-Nguluzaku mon nom… »

La nénette ignora les murmures et gloussements de la salle, continua sur sa lancée :

« Personne, dans ma famille, ne porte ce nom ridicule. Mon père, pris de court par ma naissance avant terme, ne savait à quelle porte frapper : son patron refusait de lui filer une avance sur salaire. Incapable de trompeter son septième bébé, il s'est rabattu sur le slogan des prolétaires : ne compter que sur ses propres forces, ce qui ne l'a guère avancé. D'où ce nom fantaisiste, destiné à marquer sa longue marche merdique d'un repère. »

La salle, finalement attendrie, ne ricanait plus…

Scolarité bâclée, favorisée par les grèves chroniques du corps enseignant. La nana avait toutefois compensé ce handicap par un cours de secrétariat. Mais, avoua-t-elle avec désinvolture, elle n'était pas douée pour ce genre de trucs. Absence de notions de base. En dépit de ces conditions défavorables, ingrédients d'une dérive inéluctable, elle dégote un prétendant en préservant son petit capital. Checain Tamba, l'heureux élu, traficote aussi, à l'instar des mecs de son âge. Déluré, il réussit néanmoins à s'envoler, il y a un peu plus d'un an, pour la Belgique. Petits jobs, ballottement d'une piaule à l'autre. Malgré ces traverses, il se saigne aux quatre veines afin d'expatrier sa dulcinée.

La première fois, Midy ne voit pas le convoyeur de fonds. Disparu en dépit de sa bonne réputation. La fois suivante, elle décolle, débarque à Zaventem et s'y bute à Schengen : des papiers en règle, mais la touriste ne dispose pas de moyens de subsistance pour la durée de son séjour. La nana a beau clamer qu'elle a toujours vécu au-dessous du seuil de pauvreté sans jamais mendier, rien n'y fait. Refoulée. Par le même avion. Sans avoir entrevu la silhouette du bien-aimé, ni savoir qui allait rembourser son billet. Merde alors, elle ne l'avait quand même pas payé pour se taper dix-sept heures de vol non-stop !

Checain soupçonne un coup fourré de sa belle et le lui écrit. Il sait, en effet, que les conditions de vie au pays se sont dégradées au point que même les proches, des gens de toute confiance, excellent également dans les entourloupes. Sa déception ruminée, il propose à Midy de se rendre à Lagos, à ses frais, lui-même devant intervenir de cette ville pour l'évacuer. Une filière crédible y opérait. Placée au bas du mur, la gazelle bazarde la parcelle familiale à l'insu des siens, obtient du nouveau proprio un délai d'occupation d'une semaine, se casse.

Deux jours après, elle rôde dans les rues de Yaoundé, à la recherche d'un transporteur routier pour Lagos. Tous les renseignements la dirigent sur Bamenda, localité située à la frontière avec le Nigeria. Le tarif équivaut aux risques d'une entrée clandestine dans ce pays. Elle raque en dollars, affronte la tirée d'enfer: Calabar, Onitsha, Benin City, Ibadan. Après moult péripéties, elle atteint Lagos au cours d'une affreuse nuit de pluie et de tension, descend dans un petit hôtel où elle est dévalisée. La nana soupçonne un employé du vol. Mais son anglais calamiteux risquant de la trahir, elle renonce à porter plainte et se tire. Errance. Jusqu'à cette matinée maussade où, traînant dans une gare routière, elle assiste à une scène extra: une Nigériane massive, qui vient d'être carottée, rattrape son arnaqueur et lui tire à boulets rouges. Non pas dans sa langue maternelle, mais dans une de ces formules canailles en lingala! La greluche n'en est toujours pas revenue. Bref, la mastodonte la branche sur le refuge des «Congomen», au *Yaba Terminus*, où elle débarque dans l'heure et tombe sur Mère Six. Le soulagement. Qui vire en angoisse: personne ne connaît Checain. Rien n'indique par ailleurs que l'hôtel constitue leur lieu de contact. Une semaine déjà...

Tandis que la salle scandait des alléluias, Midy, le regard toujours collé à son prompteur, perçut le bras qui, dans l'embrasure de la porte, s'agitait avec insistance depuis un moment. Reportant son attention sur le gus, elle surprit Ben Balewa en train de passer un message codé au Frère Jacob. Celui-ci n'avait pas encore remarqué sa présence. Mais, quand cela fut certain, il barytonna l'intro d'un cantique. La reprise assurée par l'assistance, il refila une corbeille à un quidam de la première rangée, puis se tient à l'écart, la mine absente mais les yeux fixés à la quête. Celle-ci faite et encaissée, il s'éclipsa. Midy se sentit délivrée après le départ de Frère Jacob: le quart d'heure d'explication voulu par Mère Six s'éloignait.

V

Un gospel interminable mit fin au culte. La vedette du jour fut entourée, félicitée pour son courage. D'une manière générale, les hommes comprenaient son geste, tandis que les femmes marmottaient ou lançaient des piques. Petit à petit, elles se regroupèrent autour d'une panthère en pantalon jaune tacheté de noir.

Bien roulée, snobinarde à vue d'œil, la frangine avait des tresses hautes, façon antenne de télé, ce qui lui donnait l'air d'une girafe. Sa bobine citron contrastait avec celle de Mère Six, de couleur papaye, produit d'un combat sauvage contre le teint bois d'ébène. Tirant parti de son ascendant sur le cercle, la fumelle ne mâcha pas ses mots à l'égard de l'intruse : Midy constituait une menace pour la communauté. Capable de jeter les siens, déjà mal lotis, dans la rue, que pouvait-elle ne pas torchonner aux tierces personnes ? Son roman de petit capital préservé sentait aussi le roussi. Par ce baratin, elle voulait s'offrir une tunique de vestale, histoire d'usiner en sous-marin à l'hôtel.

Son réquisitoire débité d'une voix éraillée, elle se tourna vers la gazelle et souleva sa poitrine avantageuse de manière à créer des complexes :

« Nous, pauvres conasses, on merde à Murtala Airport, sans espoir de décoller, et cette gourde mal sevrée prétend avoir été à Bruxelles ! Pour qui nous prend-elle ? »

L'assistance accueillit l'observation par un éclat de rire, auquel Mère Six ne put résister. Pas du tout démontée, Midy toisa l'effrontée de haut en bas, puis lança des regards féroces à la ronde. Encore môme, on lui avait appris à rendre la baffe reçue. Peu importe comment, le plus important étant que l'agresseur le paye cash : mordre, griffer, cracher, s'accrocher à ses nippes jusqu'à ce qu'elles partent en lambeaux. Mais la galerie lui semblait si hostile qu'une telle sortie se retournerait contre elle. Temporiser. Ménager sa présence à l'hôtel.

« T'es prévenue, ma cocotte, ajouta la panthère en grinçant des dents : tiens-toi hors de mes plates-bandes. Sache que t'es à Lagos et non au pays ! »

Le coup de semonce tiré, elle s'en alla avec avec ses groupies. Alors qu'ils venaient de se barrer, deux jeunots se détachèrent du cercle et revinrent sur leurs pas. La trentaine, bas du cul pour le plus tordu, l'autre, un grand timide, promenant son squelette dans le sillage du précédent, les pingouins abordèrent Midy avec un certain embarras : Shako venait de procéder à son baptême. Tout nouvel arrivant subissait ce rite intitiatique, les moins chanceux pouvant l'endurer à plusieurs reprises.

« Cela ne t'a pas empêché de te marrer comme un con, le reprit Midy.

– Je suis contre cette pratique à cause de son ton humiliant. Ces gens souffrent de voir leurs semblables fuir nos pays mis à feu et à sang, comme si cela les gênait. Ils préféreraient sans doute que tout le monde crève là-bas… »

Midy ne se contenta nullement de l'explication et se tourna vers sa chaperonne :

« C'est qui, cette Shako ? C'est la première fois que je la vois !

– La copine de Ben. Elle revient d'un voyage à Cotonou et Lomé. Bizarre qu'elle soit venue au culte : ça ne passe plus entre elle et le pasteur… »

Une lueur d'inquiétude apparut dans le regard de la jeune fille. Mère Six s'en rendit compte et, sans rien dire, la fixa d'un air interrogateur.

« Il se pourrait que Ben l'ait envoyée, spécula la gazelle.

– Qu'est-ce qui te le fait croire ?

– Tu lui as peut-être parlé, tout à l'heure, de ma confession publique. Comme il veut situer les gens qui débarquent ici, il l'aurait dépêchée à la séance pour en savoir plus.

– Je ne lui ai rien dit de pareil…

– Dans ce cas, il aurait appris la tenue de ma confession par le pasteur, puisque tu en parles depuis deux jours. Et puis, tu ne m'as pas dit que cette garce ne me supporte pas !

– Entre elle et moi, c'est pas non plus le grand amour : elle me traite de putasse alors qu'elle en est à son énième coco, qui, d'ailleurs, va la larguer… »

La matrone resta un moment silencieuse. Difficile de savoir ce qu'elle ruminait. Toujours est-il qu'elle reprit la parole sur un autre sujet :

« C'est quoi, cette histoire de voyage en Belgique ? Tu ne me l'as pas racontée !

– J'en avais pas vu l'importance. D'autant que personne, dans mon quartier, n'a avalé qu'on puisse l'effectuer en moins de quarante-huit heures. Je l'ai pourtant bel et bien fait.

– T'as donc été chez les toubabs ! Qui t'as vu là-bas ?

– J'ai vu des Blanchards partout, du moins dans la zone de quarantaine…

– Si tu veux mon avis, Midy, je vais te l'dire : t'es une sacrée mythomane. Même que, cet avant-midi, t'as prétendu n'avoir pas touché au… heuh !… au malade !

– …T'es trop, Mère Six ! »

Puis, prenant les garçons à témoin, elle corrigea :

« Est-ce qu'on ment quand on donne la réponse qu'on attend de vous ? J'aurais pu dire la vérité au président, mais il n'en voulait point… »

Les deux pingouins échangèrent des regards complices, puis escortèrent les meufs sur le chemin de retour. La 504 du Black President stationnnait devant l'entrée de l'hôtel, le coffre arrière grand ouvert. Sans explication aucune, Mère Six accéléra le pas, obligeant ses compagnons à suivre son rythme. Frère Jacob jaillit du *Yaba* en compagnie d'un zigoto. Une fois devant la tire, il lui indiqua le coffre et se tint à l'écart. Le zigoto se coltina des casiers de bière, rentra à l'hôtel avec son mentor.

« Tiens ! s'exclama Mick, le bas du cul, c'est pourtant pas le jour où ils chargent le frigo. On va quand même picoler !

– C'est toi qui payes ? questionna Mère Six sans diminuer son allure.

– Avec l'espoir que tu remettras, un jour ou l'autre, cette tournée que j'attends depuis deux ans !

– Ne compte pas sur moi, le gars. J'ai déjà donné ! Tu pissais alors dans les pagnes de ta mère !

– T'es qu'une raquedal, Mère Six. La preuve : depuis le temps que les Ouestafs font ta fortune, t'aurais pu t'offrir un aller-retour pour Jo'burg[1]. Or tu hantes toujours le *Yaba* !

---

1. Johannesburg (N.d.A.).

– Pourquoi veux-tu que j'aille dans ce trou-là ?

– Parce que Jo'burg est devenue notre Europe, vu que l'autre se barricade et ne veut pas de ta bouille jaunie ! »

À cinquante mètres de l'hôtel, la bande vit Frère Jacob et Ben Balewa ressortir en vitesse. Mère Six héla le pasteur d'une voix forte, mais celui-ci lui renvoya un signe de la main et s'engouffra dans la bagnole, qui démarra sur les chapeaux de roue.

La plupart des locataires avaient regagné leurs chambres et jouaient du soukouss, tandis qu'une dizaine d'entre eux campaient au bar, où ils consommaient des litrons de Guinness. La bande occupa une table en vue. Sous prétexte que celle-ci gênait les va-et-vient, Midy obtint de la déplacer dans un coin reculé, d'où elle disposait d'une vue extérieure. Alors que Mick se targuait d'une prochaine livraison de drogue, son copain, dénommé Tagar, ne cessant d'inviter les meufs à lever le coude, Midy gambergeait en reniflant : rien n'avait changé dans le train-train du *Yaba*. À croire qu'un mort ne gisait pas dans son lit.

Impatiente de clarifier la situation, la nana ouvrit les hostilités en fonçant aux vécés. À son retour, elle loucha sur la troisième porte à gauche et ne tiqua pas en la voyant fermée. Avec la chaleur, pensa-t-elle avec un pincement au cœur, le macchab devait entamer sa phase de décomposition.

Quelque temps après, Mick et Mère Six, soudés par la fortune imminente du premier, se rendirent à tour de rôle aux waters. Puis ce fut à

Tagar, bientôt relayé par la gazelle, de se plier à la visite non guidée. Midy n'y fit qu'un crochet, d'autant qu'elle ne ressentait aucune envie de pisser. Elle rentra dans l'hôtel en rasant le mur, précaution somme toute stérile, vu que le bar tututait allégrement. Elle se glissa dans le couloir, sentit une fois de plus la forte odeur qui planait dans le bar. Ne sachant à quoi l'attribuer, elle saisit la poignée, tourna et força la porte : le pêne s'incrustait dans la serrure. Elle força à nouveau sur la poignée. Aucun doute : la porte avait été fermée à clef. Après avoir refait le chemin inverse jusqu'aux vécés, elle regagna sa table encore plus intriguée.

Joâo aurait-il été transféré à la morgue ? Quand, comment, par qui ? Pourquoi ne parlait-on pas de sa mort ? Est-ce que Mick et Tagar le savaient ? Comment interpréter la sortie précipitée de Ben et de Frère Jacob du culte, ainsi que leur départ en cata du *Yaba* ?

Sans le vouloir, Midy décocha un regard torve à Mère Six, persuadée qu'elle faisait du recel d'information. Relevant la tête, la matrone intercepta le regard sournois et fronça les sourcils. Son visage brunit à la seconde, comme si elle avait deviné les pensées de la gazelle, puis s'illumina dans un sourire prêtant à équivoque :

« À quoi penses-tu, ma bichette ?

– On n'arrête pas de pomper sans rien mâchouiller, marmonna spontanément Midy. C'est comme au bled. Faudra peut-être penser à mastiquer quelque chose. J'ai une de ces fringales.

– Moi, je ne bouge pas d'ici tant que ce petit chéri offre à boire. Monte chauffer la marmite si cela te chante. Ne mange pas tout. »

Midy se leva sur-le-champ. Après une courte hésitation, elle retira ses chaussures, guigna à nouveau la vieille gloire, puis disparut dans l'escalier. Dix minutes après, absorbée par la préparation, elle n'entendit pas la porte s'ouvrir et sursauta à la voix de Mick. Le garçon, qui venait de proposer à Mère Six d'aller au resto, avait été chargé par celle-ci d'intéresser la Kinoise, qui, selon ses dires, avait un déficit de bouffe à rattraper. Midy regretta de ne pouvoir être des leurs, l'état de la cuisson exigeant sa présence.

« Mais alors, ça change tout, déplora le jeune homme. C'est pour toi que je sors mes cartouches...

– Comment ça ? T'es plus entiché de la vieille ?

– Simple tactique pour la coiffer. C'est toi que je vise. Le Checain ne va plus se manifester ! »

Midy encaissa sans sourciller. Elle n'en poursuivit pas moins sa besogne, ses petits doigts se révélant aussi agiles que ceux d'un cordon-bleu. Mick se désespérant de ne savoir comment annuler le plan resto, la gazelle pivota sur elle-même et, de but en blanc, lui demanda s'il savait que Mère Six cochonnait avec Frère Jacob.

« Ça ne m'étonnerait pas, répondit le freluquet : le mafflu a abusé de la plupart des frangines de l'hôtel, y compris cette snobinarde de Shako !

– Pas vrai !

– Plus grave, renchérit-il, il l'a culbutée dans la turne du président, et celui-ci, prévenu, les a surpris.

La dérouillée mémorable ! Mais comme Ben fricote avec le prêcheur, notamment dans l'approvisionnement du bar en bibines, c'est Shako qui a payé la trahison par la perte de son poste de "deuxième bureau". Elle continue cependant à bosser pour lui.

– Décidément, ce Ben est un holding à lui seul, ironisa la nana. Il semble que la vieille se défonce aussi pour lui. Que peut-elle bien fabriquer ?

– Le président lui trouve des clients prêts à casquer un max de nairas pour sauter des marchandises de l'équateur. On les considère ici comme des produits importés. Quand ces deux-là sortent ensemble, c'est que la vache va turbiner et palper des artiches. Dommage qu'elle soit si radine.

– Pourquoi ce pasteur vicelard n'emmène-t-il pas ses proies dans sa turne ? Il en a une, non ?

– On suppose que sa taule préfigure l'antichambre de l'enfer, raison pour laquelle personne n'y entre.

– Un faux-cul. L'autre soir, il a limé cette vieille vache en ma présence. Fallait voir ça ! Pire que des chiens… Dis donc, Mick, pourquoi le bar fonctionne un jour inhabituel ?

– Va savoir ! En tout cas, le pasteur multiplie sa recette par ce biais ! »

Entrée en douce, Mère Six, qui avait suivi une partie de la crucifixion, toussota pour y mettre le holà, puis s'en mêla.

« Toi, Mick, tu sors d'ici tout de suite. Et ne m'adresse plus la parole. Quant à toi, la pucelle, t'as deux jours pour dégager. Me traiter, moi, de chienne ! Quel poison, cette gueule d'avorton ! »

D'un geste impérieux du doigt, elle écarta la nana de la table-cuisine et passa aux commandes. Midy, la mine des plus désolées, s'accouda sur le rebord de la fenêtre, la tête dans une main et le regard fixé sur sa remplaçante. La matrone s'appliqua à la préparation, en plaignant par moments son hospitalité mal récompensée.

Une voiture s'arrêta peu après devant le *Yaba*. Un taxi jaune, nota la jeune fille en tournant la carafe. La seconde d'après, elle frissonnait à la vue du passager. Frère Jacob. Souffrant le martyre pour extraire son encombrante bedaine du tacot. Un œil à Mère Six la rassura : baignée dans des volutes de vapeur, elle ne voyait rien de son angle. Le temps de ruminer un coup vachard, les circonstances ne lui permettant pas une explication casse-cou, la nana s'apprêta à jouer sa carte maîtresse.

Tout en lorgnant le tas de lard qui accédait à l'hôtel, Midy évalua le temps qu'il lui faudrait pour tchatcher avec un de ses fidèles, anesthésier un autre avec un verset, distribuer des sourires, monter. À 40° à l'ombre, le bonimenteur n'allait pas se laisser cramer dans le réduit. L'alcool ne le branchait d'ailleurs pas.

Son scénario synchronisé, Midy quitta la chambre et s'engagea dans l'escalier. Juste au moment où un poids lourd l'empruntait dans l'autre sens. La greluche descendit les marches en prenant son temps. Parvenue sur la marche palière comprise entre le premier et le deuxième étage, elle feignit la surprise lorsqu'un quidam la repoussa dans l'encoignure et lui pinça les nichons, non sans prévenir toute dérobade en la coinçant avec son gros ventre. La nana opposa une résistance passive et gloussa de bon cœur, après quoi elle se fit prudente :

« Mère Six t'a vu revenir en taxi. Elle t'attend... »

Le rappel à l'ordre eut pour effet d'établir un no man's land entre le pervers et la gazelle. Le clergyman canonna une œillade tordue au deuxième, zyeuta la souris avec appétit et, bien qu'il fût conscient des risques encourus, Mère Six passant pour une furie avec ses jules, tenta une nouvelle fois de pétrir les nénés. La jeune fille, son mauvais tour joué, ne ménagea plus le sagouin et le rabroua.

Le mafflu reprit sa montée, alors que la greluche dévalait l'escalier et fonçait aux toilettes. Manque de pot, Shako sortait de la douche, drapée dans une grande serviette. Quelques secondes durant, les deux nanas se toisèrent en silence. La panthère se forgeant au finish un masque de cannibale, la gazelle dévia de sa trajectoire afin de s'épargner d'une balle perdue.

« Grande sœur, lança-t-elle dans une improvisation risquée.

– Je n'suis pas ta grande sœur, coupa Shako. On doit avoir le même carat, toi et moi. Sauf que t'es restée embryonnaire.

– C'est la faute à mes vieux. Y connaissaient pas le lait Guigoz ! Au fait, Mère Six veut te parler...

– Qu'est-ce qu'elle me veut, cette roulure ?

– Une raison de la voir. Elle est dans sa chambre. »

La gazelle s'enferma aux chiottes, tandis que Shako reprenait sa marche vers l'entrée. Parvenue devant la porte, elle hésita un instant, tourna sur elle-même, puis s'écria :

« Hé, l'embryon, passe me voir demain entre 7 et 8 heures : Ben m'a chargée d'une commission pour toi. Si tu me manques, il te faudra attendre dix à quinze jours ! »

Midy brusqua sa besogne afin de ne pas louper le sommet tripartite. Mordre, griffer, cracher, s'accrocher aux fripes de l'agresseur jusqu'à ce qu'elles tombent en lambeaux. Elle ricana devant l'image du trio infernal réuni, le minois déformé par l'effort qu'elle mettait dans son rire.

La nana déboula au bar, surexcitée, et fit signe à Mick de la suivre. Elle ne l'affranchit pas, mais l'entraîna d'autorité dans l'escalier. Ça pétait dans la chambre. L'Harmaguédon. Impossible de mettre un nom sur une voix fulminante ni de savoir qui menait la danse, tant les injures sifflaient et se succédaient dans une cacophonie homérique.

« Qu'est-ce qui se passe ? demanda Mick à la nénette, qui s'était arrêtée sur le palier du deuxième.

– Shako et le pasteur se sont donné rendez-vous chez Mère Six, et celle-ci ne semble pas apprécier...

– Quel fouteur de merde, ce tas de jambonneau ! »

Les voix furieuses montèrent d'un cran. L'instant d'après, une claque, suivie d'un cri déchirant, retentit en provoquant un chambardement monstrueux. Lits, paravents, vaisselle partirent dans tous les sens. Shako perdit sans doute son manteau, puisque la vieille gloire, la voyant à poil, se mit à hurler à la sorcière. Des gens sortirent dans le couloir. Midy, rassurée par cette présence curieuse, tira sur la manche de chemise du freluquet et lui dit :

« On ne se mêle pas de ça. Filons au resto : il y a du monde pour séparer ces échangistes. »

Le tandem regagna l'hôtel après la nuit tombée. Midy n'accorda aucune attention au camion-benne. En revanche, son compagnon suspecta un excès de zèle chez les hommes de la voirie. C'est que Lagos revendiquait, entre autres titres, la palme de métropole de la crasse. Des bennes collectaient certes les ordures, mais, leur capacité de ramassage restant inférieure aux besoins, les immondices se multipliaient, y compris dans les quartiers chics, si bien que des montagnes d'ordures intégraient le paysage. À Lagos Island, centre de rayonnement de la cité yoruba depuis le XVIIe siècle, qui, lors du boom pétrolier, avait accueilli une usine d'incinération, celle-ci n'avait pu tourner, donnant au contraire naissance au plus grand monument d'ordures, fumant et odorant, cadre de travail pour des milliers de déshérités.

Craignant les suites de sa farce, Midy squatta la chambre de Mick et Tagar. Ce dernier, décoincé par une biture d'enfer, leur apprit la bataille rangée entre Mère Six, Shako et Frère Jacob, les sirènes s'étant d'abord liguées pour faire ravaler ses psaumes au prêcheur, ensuite pour régler leur différend, à coups de griffes et d'invectives, chacune revendiquant le leadership sur l'autre.

Mick plongea auprès du bifteck couché par terre. Le copinage n'appelle pas forcément le carambolage, le raisonna la nana en serrant ses fesses et ses flûtes. Gonflé, le play-boy se colla à la chaudière, espérant que la nuit finirait par lui porter conseil.

Tagar sortit à trois reprises pour vider sa vessie. La fois d'après, un locataire le surprit dans le couloir, dressé sur la pointe des pieds, en train d'ouvrir les écluses par la petite fenêtre surélevée. Sommé de stopper son arrosage et de descendre aux chiottes, il s'y éternisa afin d'éviter les coups de gueule de l'étage.

« Tu le connais, toi, João ? sonda Midy à voix basse.

– Nib… Encore un de tes julots ?

– Déconne pas, grogna la nana en tirant la conclusion qui s'impose. João est un pote qui m'a refilé un passeport au visa nigérian périmé. Peux-tu me trouver un preneur ?

– Montre-le-moi ! »

Midy retira le passeport de son sac. Le document sous le nez, Mick le déclara négociable, d'autant plus qu'aucune photo ne le particularisait. Il avait un acheteur potentiel. La greluche l'invita à la discrétion, puis tourna le dos.

Réveillée de justesse à l'heure du rendez-vous, elle enfila ses babouches, monta aussitôt au troisième. La gazelle parvint à bas bruit devant la troisième porte à droite quand on vient de l'escalier.

Un pressentiment étrange la parcourut au moment de frapper à la porte. Sans raison aucune,

une forte envie de faire demi-tour la tenaillait. Midy pensa à l'empoignade de la veille. Et si les trois numéros avaient percé son jeu ? Impossible. Tagar en aurait parlé. Et puis, le trio aurait fait convoquer les états généraux de l'amicale et l'y aurait traduite, de gré ou de force, quitte à la houspiller et la mettre au ban de la tribu. Et si Shako lui tendait un piège ? Ne l'avait-elle pas prévenue de se méfier ?

Un premier toc-toc resta sans résultat. Le deuxième, plus décidé, n'occasionna également que dalle. Intriguée, la nana posa la main sur la poignée, tourna et entrebâilla la porte. Shako, se dit-elle en frappant doucement, était déjà debout et l'attendait. Elle frappa encore plus fort et, n'obtenant aucun signe de vie, poussa la lourde. La vue du tableau lui coupa le souffle : la panthère, tombée sur le ventre entre le plumard et l'entrée, nageait dans son sang. Surprise dans son lit, elle avait voulu atteindre la porte, sans doute pour appeler au secours, entraînant avec elle ses draps souillés de sang.

Sa stupeur contenue, Midy balaya la chambre d'un œil avisé, notant en passant que la snobinarde vivait dans le luxe. Une nantie. Comme ses pareils. D'un bond, elle s'introduisit dans la turne et fit main basse sur une montre dame. Posés sur la table de chevet, des bracelets en or éblouirent sa vue. Elle s'en approcha, mais l'alarme sonna illico dans sa tête : que quelqu'un la surprenne là, elle patouillerait dans une telle mélasse qu'elle ne saurait expliquer, encore moins justifier, cette visite matinale après la semonce publique de la veille. Elle fonça vers la porte, remit la main sur la poignée et tira. Juste au moment où un quidam l'interpellait dans son dos :

« Qu'est-ce que tu fous à cet étage, à pareille heure ? »

VI

La gazelle offrit à l'apparition sa meilleure gueule d'enterrement. En peignoir, une serviette autour du cou et des espadrilles aux pieds, le mastard sortait manifestement de la douche. D'abord amusée, sa bobine se durcit devant le visage chafouin. Il mata la greluche, ce qui eut pour effet d'accentuer le trouble de celle-ci, puis répéta sa question :

« Je t'ai demandé ce que tu faisais là ! »

Pour toute réponse, Midy montra la chambre en bafouillant :

« C'est pas moi, président. Je te le jure. Quelqu'un d'autre l'a tuée. »

Une clef tourna dans sa serrure. Réalisant la gravité de la situation, Ben repoussa la nana dans la chambre et la referma derrière lui. Brusquement mis en présence du cadavre, il perdit de sa morgue et resta sans voix pendant une éternité. Il hocha finalement la tête et, sans préavis, allongea une mandale à la greluche. Celle-ci partit comme un boulet, s'écrasa dans un meuble. Sans un cri.

« Pourquoi tu l'as butée ? questionna-t-il en gardant la voix basse. Elle m'a proposé, pas plus tard qu'hier, de t'initier à son boulot !

– Ce n'est pas moi, président. Regarde mes mains… »

Recroquevillée au tapis, Midy, le regard suppliant, tendit ses nageoires. Black President les examina sans saisir la raison de l'invite. Les devinettes n'étant pas son fort, il exigea un décodage.

« Qu'est-ce qu'elles ont, tes menottes ?

– Clean. Je n'ai pas de sang dessus. D'ailleurs, tu peux remarquer que le sang s'est coagulé, ce qui veut dire que Shako a été tuée cette nuit. »

Ben Balewa, qui ne s'était pas préoccupé de ce détail, dut se rendre à l'évidence. Il congratula la nana d'un œil reconnaissant et, chose qu'il ne se serait jamais permis en d'autres circonstances, la souleva et la pria de l'aider à transporter la défunte sur son lit.

Midy releva d'emblée l'insolite : dans sa tentative de joindre la porte, Shako, mortellement blessée, devait marcher à quatre pattes ou tituber. Qu'elle tombe à ce moment-là, ses jambes seraient restées écartées. Or elles étaient serrées, comme dans un effort de contrer un viol. C'est dire que le meurtrier n'a pas bougé de la pièce, preuve que la victime le connaissait.

Ben retourna le corps et sursauta au constat que Shako avait été lardée de coups. Le couteau, toujours plongé dans le thorax, s'était encore enfoncé dans sa chute.

« Dis-moi, président, émit la gazelle qui se tenait

aux pieds du cadavre: est-ce que Shako dormait nue?

– Pourquoi cette question idiote? Tu ne vois pas qu'elle porte sa robe de nuit?

– C'est qu'elle n'a pas de slip, ce qui pourrait expliquer la position des jambes. L'assassin le lui a retiré après sa chute.»

La défunte transportée dans son lit et recouverte, Ben convia Midy dans sa turne, deux portes plus loin. Il referma la chambre à clef. Sept heures trente à sa montre waterproof.

La gazelle pénétra dans une ambiance enfumée. Nul doute que Black President grillait un shit à son réveil. Un œil au cadre releva que la taule était plus luxueuse que celle de Shako. La poivrote s'écroula sur une chaise, tandis que Ben disparaissait dans une chambrette attenante. À son retour, il n'avait rien mis sur son torse velu et musclé, mais portait un jean. Le malabar s'assit en face de la nana. Droit au but.

«Mère Six t'a briefée sur le problème qui se pose ici: éviter que les flics ne se mêlent de nos affaires, faute de quoi des expulsions sont à craindre. Ceci pour te dire que la mort de Shako doit également rester secrète.»

Ben Balewa se lança dans une explication technique, inspirée par la lecture des journaux européens, sur le mystère qui plane sur certaines communautés asiatiques d'Europe. En dépit de leur réputation mafieuse ainsi que de l'existence, en leur sein, d'une population âgée, ces communautés bernent les statistiques: on ne leur prête ni morts violentes ni cas de décès. Et pourtant, ces gens claquent comme tout le monde. Ils ont donc un truc pour camoufler les crevaisons dérangeantes. Black President en a dégoté un. À la mesure de la population du *Yaba*.

« La disparition de Shako, enchaîna-t-il, ne peut surprendre outre mesure, vu qu'elle bouge pas mal dans les pays de la sous-région. Comme je me suis brouillé avec elle, les gens trouveront normal qu'elle disparaisse du paysage…

– Pour toujours ?

– Pourquoi pas si elle tombe sur un autre mec ?

– Comment va-t-on l'enterrer ?

– Je m'en occupe. Par contre, le gros problème reste celui du meurtrier : il faut le démasquer. »

La sonnerie du portable interrompit le tête-à-tête. Le temps de s'en emparer et de gueuler un allo, Ben se dirigea vers la fenêtre et parlota un moment. Il donna ensuite deux coups de fil en pidgin, puis rejoignit la nénette avec une solution : son marabout allait lui révéler l'identité du tueur. Affaire classée.

« J'ai une petite idée permettant d'identifier le tueur cet avant-midi, mieux, avant le culte…

– Accouche, ma petite ! »

Pour avoir laissé la porte de la victime ouverte, le tueur voudra s'assurer que le corps a été découvert. La retrouvant fermée, il va chercher à savoir si le corps a été enlevé. Glisser une feuille de papier dans le trou de la serrure, suggéra la greluche. Si l'assassin l'enlève, il va commettre l'erreur de signer son passage.

« Tes soupçons se portent sur qui ?

– Sur le seul individu du *Yaba* dont on ne peut fouiller la chambre pour retrouver le slip…

– Je le tuerai de mes mains, lâcha Ben en roulant ses yeux globuleux… T'es quand même perspicace pour une gamine apparemment godiche !

– Une gamine, président, qui, depuis sa naissance, n'a cessé de voir des gens tomber autour d'elle malgré leur volonté de tenir debout : une gamine dont l'univers est un paysage désolé ; une gamine – comment dire ? – sacrifiée pour des crimes qu'elle n'a pas commis. »

Ben fixa la nénette avec compassion. Il glissa une main dans sa poche, tira trois billets de cent nairas et les lui remit.

« Un dépannage. Rentre chez toi et pas un mot de tout cela à Mère Six.

– Elle ne peut plus me piffer.

– Je t'ai dit d'aller m'y attendre, le temps de fumer un joint et de machiner le piège… »

La vieille gloire ouvrit la porte dès le deuxième toc-toc. Midy, dans un mouvement instinctif, recula à la vue du portrait démoli. Avec un œil au beurre noir, une poire tuméfiée, fendue, la machine-outil réclamait une révision générale. Elle sourit néanmoins devant la réaction de la nana, prêtant à sa gueule une forme encore plus caricaturale.

« Tu sors du boulot, ma bichette ? dit-elle en s'effaçant de l'entrée. Tu rapportes combien ?

– Qu'est-ce qui t'est arrivé ? répondit Midy à contre-temps.

– Le pasteur et cette salope de Shako sont venus

m'agresser. Si t'étais restée là, cela ne se serait pas produit... »

Un cyclone avait balayé la chambre. Midy entreprit de la remettre en ordre, ramassant ici et là des débris d'assiettes et de verres, tandis que la matrone évaluait les dégâts corporels dans un miroir.

« Hé ! s'écria-t-elle tout à coup : en essayant d'arranger ton fourbi, hier, j'ai découvert deux cents dollars...

– ...

– T'as des sous, planqués dans l'oreiller, et tu me laisses te gaver comme si j'étais l'Armée du salut. T'avais prétendu avoir été volée !

– Je trimbale toujours mes sous dans le soutien-gorge...

– T'as pas d'balcon pour porter de soutif, sale menteuse ! »

Black President surprit la matrone jetant les billets verts sur la cocotte. Son attention flotta un moment entre le visage amoché et les dolluches éparpillés. Sans crier gare, il sauta sur la gazelle et lui enjoignit de vider ses poches. Midy, tourneboulée, lança des regards désespérés autour d'elle. Ben la saisit sans ménagement, la plaqua au lit et se mit à la palper, extrayant quelque chose d'une poche du blue jean.

« C'est quoi, ça ? tonna-t-il en brandissant sa trouvaille.

– La montre en or de Shako ! s'exclama Mère Six, ahurie. Comment est-elle arrivée dans sa poche ? Quelle calamité, cette fille ! »

Midy, tête baissée, resta muette. Ben la tira de son silence par une claque qui la catapulta au plumard.

« Pourquoi as-tu volé cette pauvre femme ?

– … C'est plus fort que moi, chevrota-t-elle devant la patte menaçante. Je ne peux m'empêcher de prendre ce qui est hors de ma portée… »

Ben et Mère Six échangèrent des regards surpris. S'adressant ensuite à la greluche, Black Président lui révéla que la montre était un cadeau de sa part, offert, il y a deux ans, à Shako.

« Elle est à toi et tu en fais ce que tu veux. Seulement, les amis de Shako ne vont pas comprendre que tu la détiennes. Débrouille-toi pour que cela ne fasse pas de vagues. »

Le mastard se brancha aussitôt sur la bouille amochée. Mère Six gazant dans une diatribe contre ses agresseurs, il lui coupa la parole :

« Je dois me rendre d'urgence à l'aéroport. Un visiteur nous vient d'Europe. Le même qu'il y a deux ans. Prépare-lui la chambre d'en bas ! »

VII

Mère Six s'est endormie, bourrée d'aspirine, alors que le *Yaba* s'est rendu à son show quotidien. Midy, qui contemplait la montre depuis trois bonnes heures, la planqua subito et tendit les loches : quelqu'un rôdait dans le couloir. La jeune fille quitta ses babouches, s'approcha de la porte et l'ouvrit doucement: le grand timide montait au troisième! Un éclair fusa dans sa boule: et si c'était Tagar, le meurtrier? Le zigoto s'était longuement absenté, la veille, après avoir été surpris en plein arrosage dans le couloir. Son absence avait été longue, suffisamment longue pour qu'il monte chez Shako, la saigne et lui pique sa culotte. La nana vacilla entre l'envie de pister le suspect et d'aller fouiner dans sa chambre. Puis, au souvenir que le piège parlerait de lui-même, fonça chez les garçons.

La fouille fut rapide, méthodique, infructueuse. La gazelle fondit aussitôt vers l'escalier et parvint, les tripes nouées, à la marche palière. Tagar revenait dans l'autre sens. Soudainement dégonflée, elle dévala les marches quatre à quatre et s'enferma dans sa chambre. Le suspect s'arrêta un moment devant la porte bouclée, puis passa son chemin.

Un quart d'heure après, Midy hasardait sa gueule dans le couloir: personne. Elle monta au troisième, se frotta les pinces devant le bon fonctionnement du piège: l'assassin avait dégagé la feuille introduite dans la serrure. La jeune fille rentra se barricader.

Le *Yaba* reprit son animation après le culte. Contrairement à la veille, le bar carburait avec une clientèle nombreuse et bruyante, certains *bana-bana*[1] ayant préféré claquer leur pécule plutôt que de courir après des guimbardes. Midy descendit plusieurs fois à la recherche de Mick. Celui-ci res-

1. Vendeurs à la sauvette.

tant introuvable, elle le crut parti régler son bizness. Le play-boy émergea au *Yaba*, tracassé, aux environs de vingt heures. Il embarqua la gazelle dans le même resto que la veille. Son deal marchait. Sauf qu'il lui fallait verser un acompte de cinq cents dollars, somme qu'il ne savait où trouver.

« Ben ne peut pas te les avancer ?

– Il est pire qu'un usurier. De même que le pasteur. Pour 500 dolluches, ils réclament des intérêts de 100 à 150 % ! Tuant. »

Midy lui prêta deux cents dollars. Le tandem, qui était parvenu à destination et avait passé commande, se tritura les méninges pour savoir comment dégoter les dollars restants. Seule solution, proposa la nana en engloutissant son plat : piquer des bijoux à Mère Six et les fourguer.

« C'est le moment d'agir ou jamais, argua-t-elle : dans l'état où elle se trouve, la vieille ne va pas se recueillir devant sa quincaille.

– Tu ferais ça pour moi ?

– À condition de m'associer à ton biz.

– Ça gaze ! »

Son plaisir à peine digéré, Mick roula des regards méchants dans le resto. Il introduisit une main dans sa veste, tira un petit poignard et l'exhiba ostensiblement. Midy, effarouchée, suivit le regard furibond et découvrit, pelotonnés autour d'une table, quatre pégriots. Les Nigérians détournèrent la tête à la vue du cure-dents et, sans rien dire, se débinèrent à la queue leu leu.

« Qu'est-ce qu'ils nous veulent ? paniqua la gazelle.

– Ils nous ont sans doute vus hier et croient qu'on est pourri de fric. Tout peut arriver quand on n'a pas les moyens de les raisonner.

– Mais elle sort d'où, cette lame ?

– Un cadeau de Tagar. Son poignard de commando. »

Midy resta hébétée devant l'arme du crime. Elle revit le même bijou plongé dans la poitrine de Shako. Comment était-il arrivé entre les mains de Mick, alors que Ben et elle-même l'avaient laissé dans le corps charcuté ?

« Qu'est-ce qui se passe ? demanda Mick devant le silence de la fille.

– On s'est servi de ce poignard pour "couteauner" Shako !

– Quoi ?

– Shako a été lardée cette nuit avec ce poignard. »

L'incrédulité de Mick fut telle que Midy se crut obligée de lui croquer un dessin. Le jeune homme, bouche bée, écouta la narration sans l'interrompre. Après quoi il commanda une Guinness, l'avala cul sec, puis surprit la greluche avec sa confidence.

Par sa discrétion, Tagar avait gagné la confiance de Ben et de Shako. Avec le premier, il s'enferme des heures durant, surtout le matin, pour une partie de fumette, tandis que la seconde lui a remis le double de la clef de sa chambre. Il peut ainsi la rejoindre à n'importe quelle heure. Dieu seul sait ce qu'ils fricotent, car le bonhomme reste muet sur le sujet. Déserteur d'une unité de choc de l'Unita, il se croit traqué par ses ex-frères d'armes et trimbale, jour et nuit, le double du même poignard. Autre problème avec lui : il devient imprévisible quand il a pompé. C'est lui qui avait surpris le pasteur chez Shako et prévenu Ben. Par jalousie.

« Comment peux-tu vivre avec ce malade ?

– Il a un côté positif : contrairement aux gens du *Yaba*, il n'occupe pas le terrain.

– Qu'a-t-il fait de la petite culotte ?

– Je parie qu'il l'utilise comme mouchoir de poche.

– Beurk ! Selon toi, aurait-il cherché à la violer ?

– Rien n'est à écarter : son passé l'a rendu sans états d'âme. »

Midy eut un sommeil agité, si bien qu'elle dormit comme une souche durant la matinée. La greluche aida la matrone à se laver et lui donna ses cachets, puis descendit prendre sa douche. Une heure après, elle surgissait au bar, vide à cette heure, et fit un petit tour dans le voisinage. À son retour, mue par une inspiration subite, elle pointa à la porte de João-Monteiro. Convaincue que la chambre était verrouillée, elle força la porte et fut surprise de la voir s'ouvrir. Un homme ronflait dans les draps du mort.

Midy recula à la seconde. Mais l'homme, tiré de sa sieste par l'intruse, stoppa sa retraite d'un signe de la main. La greluche eut un haut-le-corps en pénétrant dans la pièce : l'odeur ressentie la veille ! Le formol. La chambre en était imprégnée. Et ce bougre qui devait s'imaginer inhaler quelque fragrance ! La nana repéra la valise et les deux sacs posés par terre : le voyageur dont Ben avait parlé.

« Qu'est-ce que vous faites là ?

– Ne renversez pas les rôles, répondit l'homme en s'asseyant au bord du lit : c'est à moi de demander à cette belle fille ce qu'elle vient chercher dans la chambre d'un célibataire !

– Où est passé le corps de João ?

– Quel João ?

– Le macchab qui était là ! »

Le gars lança des regards effarés autour de lui, zyeuta la greluche et, preuve qu'il avait bien saisi, se détacha du plumard d'un saut et s'enquit de quoi retournait son roman. Midy l'affranchit. Quand elle eut fini, le voyageur, son regard valsant entre le lit et la nana, jura sur ses aïeux que Ben allait lui payer cher sa mauvaise blague. L'héberger dans une piaule non désinfectée, qui pis es, dans un lit mortuaire !

L'homme, subitement pensif, fixa la nana d'un air dubitatif. Il claqua ses doigts au bout d'un moment, sauta sur un sac d'où il tira des journaux. Il les feuilleta avec nervosité, se demandant dans lequel il avait lu un entrefilet insolite. Le *Daily Times* en mains, il découvrit l'info en question dans la rubrique des faits divers : le corps d'une personne de sexe masculin découvert, tronçonné et en voie de calcination, dans une décharge publique. L'homme, décharné, serait à première vue d'origine étrangère. Enquête en cours.

« S'il s'agit de João, releva la fille, comment son corps serait-il arrivé là-bas ?

– Je connais Ben comme le fond de ma poche : il est capable d'utiliser des employés de la voirie, à leur insu, pour évacuer le corps. Tu ne les aurais pas vus passer par ici hier ?

– Nix. Mais il y a un autre macchab là-haut. Une gonzesse. Très classe. Faut pas qu'elle crame, celle-là.

– … Aide-moi à transporter mes bagages dans un autre hôtel. Je m'occuperai de Ben après. »

Quelques heures plus tard, Midy ne comprit que dalle lorsque Mick débarqua au bar, hors de lui, et l'entraîna vers les vécés. Le freluquet lui dit son fait : elle lui avait menti au sujet du passeport, puisque le document appartient à Monteiro. Comment le sait-il ? Le marché conclu avec le preneur et le fric empoché, il avait fallu procéder à quelques retouches, coller une photo. Or, il n'y a que Ben, dont la spécialité d'origine réside dans la falsification des documents, pour réaliser ce travail d'orfèvre. D'entrée de jeu, le malabar, qui s'était déjà fait payer sa partition, avait découvert le pot aux roses et confisqué le doc.

« Arrange-toi pour ne pas le croiser : il fume contre toi.

– Qu'il aille s'en faire mettre ! Est-ce qu'il t'a dit que Monteiro a canné et que son corps, débité comme un poulet braisé, grille dans une décharge ? »

Mick tomba des nues. Des explications fournies, il apparut que João, de son vrai nom Monteiro, est un ancien collègue de Tagar dans l'armée de l'Unita. Que la dépouille ait été sciée à l'hôtel, il n'y a que Ben pour le faire : il dispose d'un passe-partout et de la panoplie du bricoleur. Le président aurait accompli ce forfait durant le culte. Cela étant, s'écria Mick, l'ouverture du bar trouve une explication : les relents d'alcool devaient atténuer, sinon supprimer, l'odeur particulière de la charcuterie. D'où le formol employé.

« Il faut faire quelque chose avant qu'on y passe tous, lâcha-t-il.

– J'ai alerté un copain à moi !

– Parfait. As-tu la joncaille ? »

Midy lui refila les bijoux. Le freluquet lui conseilla de se planquer dans sa chambre jusqu'à son retour. Ils iraient dans un autre hôtel et y attendraient que les choses se tassent. Que son business décolle, atterrissage forcé à Jo'burg. Rendez-vous à 18 heures au bar.

Au comptoir, où elle poireautait depuis deux heures, Midy apprit par hasard que Mick avait fait ses valises pour une destination inconnue. Devenue nerveuse, elle sortit du bar et se mit à arpenter l'hôtel de long en large. Envie furieuse de pleurer, d'évacuer la rage qui la tenaillait. Griffer. Mordre jusqu'au sang. Mais pas une larme ne coula de ses yeux. Elle s'écroula par terre, le dos contre le mur, les yeux au décor mais absents.

Branle-bas soudain au bar. Midy sursauta à la vue du malabar qui jaillissait de la 504 et se ruait dans l'hôtel, provoquant la débandade des siffleurs. La nana rejoignit le petit attroupement formé devant l'entrée : Ben Balewa, après avoir coincé Frère Jacob au comptoir, fouillait dans ses poches. La brute sortit une Bible, l'expédia au diable sous les regards stupéfiés de l'assistance. La paluche à nouveau plongée dans le fourre-tout, elle tira un trophée, le brandit et le ficha sous le nez épaté.

« Jésus-Christ ! s'exclama le révérend en se signant. Qu'est-ce que c'est ?

– C'est à moi que tu le demandes ? hurla Ben en lui balançant un coup. Il sort d'où, ce slibar ? »

Midy voulut s'élancer mais resta tétanisée : quelqu'un lui titillait le cou avec la pointe d'un couteau. Elle loucha autour d'elle, tressaillit à la vue du bras tendu : Tagar tenait son poignard, enfourné dans la manche de sa chemise ! Comment avait-il pu le récupérer ?

Les confidences de Mick lui revinrent à l'esprit : Tagar voyait le président, chaque matin, pour une partie de shit. Ignorant sans doute la vraie nature de son partenaire, Ben lui raconte le meurtre ainsi que les soupçons qui pèsent sur le pasteur. Ainsi affranchi, le salopard, qui dispose de la clef de Shako, récupère son poignard fétiche, s'arrange ensuite pour glisser le slip dans la poche du pasteur. Une victime providentielle.

Entre-temps, Black President cognait sur le clergyman. Un marteau-pilon. Le mufle baveux tourna en un clin d'œil au chiffon sanglant. Le pasteur beugla au fou et appela à l'aide, mais personne n'osa s'interposer entre les pontes. Dans un réflexe de survie, l'homme de Dieu expédia son genou dans le service trois-pièces du malabar. Celui-ci encaissa. Puis assena un coup de tête, suivi d'un uppercut sur le tas de graisse. Le corps flasque s'effondra sur le parquet.

Ben retourna à la voiture, tandis que Midy se glissait dans l'hôtel. Le mastard l'aperçut au dernier moment et la héla d'une voix de tonnerre. Mais la greluche monta en vitesse, s'enferma à double tour chez Mère Six.

Assise sur le lit, celle-ci inventoriait le contenu de son écrin et eut un regard de commisération sur la cocotte. La porte sauta dans la foulée, laissant pointer la masse fumante de Black President. Midy tourna autour du lit sans découvrir le moindre trou. La peur de se faire broyer la dérégla au point qu'elle se mit à trembler de tout son corps. L'issue de secours s'offrit à travers la fenêtre. Elle y sauta à la seconde. Un œil au sol la remit en confiance : le voyageur conduisait une escouade de MP vers l'entrée de l'hôtel. Tandis que Mère Six suppliait la nana de descendre, celle-ci, voyant le bulldozer s'avancer, lâcha prise et tomba dans le vide Comme dans son cauchemar.

DIVAGATIONS FŒTALES

ENCORE cette sorcière, râlé-je en voyant la vieille sortir de son trou et tournailler dans la pièce. Celle-là, je l'ai dans le nez depuis que je l'ai identifiée, dans une vision dantesque, parmi mes persécuteurs. Elle me prend pour un débile, mais je suis plus futé qu'elle. Je sais, par exemple, que papa, tonton, ma frangine, tous morts dans des conditions obscures, hantent sa conscience. Qu'elle veuille maintenant ma peau, je ne lui ferai pas le cadeau de s'en servir pour couvrir un tam-tam, ultime diablerie des sorciers, vampires et autres génies du mal après avoir croqué leur proie.

Sans qu'elle s'en doute, je surveille la charogne du coin de l'œil, épiant ses moindres gestes. Elle fouille par-ci, bluffe par-là avec la vaisselle, trifouille dans un coin et ne fout que dalle au butoir. Qu'a-t-elle donc à tournoyer de la sorte, jour et nuit, autour de ma pomme ? Je ne suis quand même pas un bébé. Ni une plaque tournante. Encore moins un rond-point autour duquel on peut toupiller mille millions de fois.

L'esprit du bien m'enjoint de m'éloigner de la teigne. Sa présence à mes côtés, surtout en ce moment où je pèche par ma fragilité, favorise le transfert des fluides maléfiques. Or je tiens à renouer avec mes habitudes. Si je ne me frotte pas aux gens, c'est parce qu'ils sont bizarres et infects, d'où la suspicion que je leur porte. Les méchants me tapent sur le système. Je les repère d'ailleurs au pif. C'est le cas de cette vieille marmite qui a liquidé trois des miens. J'ai découvert qu'elle les a bouffés, au cours de trois orgies sataniques, afin de s'approprier la parcelle, la brouette, le parc de pousse-pousse, tout le bataclan. La sorcière. Je l'ai à l'œil depuis que je l'ai dépistée dans un cauchemar.

« Où vas-tu, fiston ? crie la vache alors que je quitte son champ magnétique.

– …

– Tu ne devrais pas sortir. T'es malade et t'as l'air d'un zombie. »

Qu'est-ce qu'elle en sait, la harpie ? La malaria, ça se soigne. De même que la fièvre d'Ebola, la grippe asiatique ou sa jumelle espingouine. Il suffit d'avaler de la nivaquine. Ou de la quinine. Faut pas être alchimiste pour le savoir. Mais quand on voit des films que nul ne peut imaginer, on vit un état supérieur. La révélation. Qui vous place au-dessus des fourmis. Conseil gratuit : il ne faut jamais écraser ces pauvres insectes. Ils peuvent exploser et vous scratcher en mille millions de morceaux saignants, au grand plaisir des forces occultes.

Je marche comme un robot, à pas chronométrés, de peur de fouler des fétiches ou des trucs comme ça. Ces choses-là peuvent éclater comme des mines antipersonnel et faire très mal. Elles peuvent aussi occasionner l'éléphantiasis, ce qui donne à l'imprudent échalas, comme moi, l'impression de chausser des *goodyear*[1]. Des gosses me suivent en pouffant de rire. Des fions, qui me semblent familiers, m'évitent en me zyeutant de travers. Des suppôts de Satan.

Un éclair fuse dans ma tête. L'alerte. Je dégaine mon Awacs, un morceau de miroir qui ne me quitte jamais, et feins de me louquer. En fait, comme j'entre dans une zone à forte concentration des ondes maléfiques, le miroir, tenu de côté, me sert de rétro et permet d'intercepter le mauvais esprit collé à mon destin. D'habitude, je stoppe net quand un quidam s'y inscrit. Sinon j'enclenche la marche arrière, sans me retourner, afin de bien capter la cible. De la voix métallique d'un flipper, je lâche un message de détresse à mon double : « Attention ! attention ! les ennemis passent à l'attaque ! » Je peux alors suivre la progression du suspect, juger de ses intentions à mon égard. Que son mufle s'éternise dans le radar et s'avère aussi moche que les sept péchés capitaux, je lance la contre-offensive, car le Malin machine ma perte. Le raid se termine fatalement par la

---

1 Chaussures à semelle épaisse (N.d.A.).

fuite de la taupe. Celle-là, je ne la quitte pas des yeux.

Pourquoi j'emprunte toujours le même circuit? J'en sais que dalle. Peut-être serait-ce parce que les chiens aboient sur mon passage en restant à distance. J'exècre à mort ces cabots faméliques. Ils divaguent comme les esprits errants, raison pour laquelle je les fixe, les yeux dans les yeux, et grogne à mon tour. Grrr ! Terroriser les terroristes.

Je fais mon tour du propriétaire, assiège le haut-parleur du bar du quartier pour écouter de la musique. Quand je me sens bien dans ma peau, je dodeline parfois de la tête et mbalaxe[1] un tout petit peu, ce qui amuse les gamins. Me voir tourniquer le derrière les met à chaque fois aux anges. Allez savoir pourquoi ! À propos, j'ai jamais su pourquoi ces petits diables m'appellent Sandokan. Toto-m'en-fout ou Jo-le-jazzeur me vont pourtant à merveille. Bien entendu, cela dépend des jours. Et des nuits. Mais, dès que je les vois ramasser des cailloux et devenir agressifs, je détale à reculons afin de garder le contrôle de la situation. D'autant que je soupçonne la poissarde dans leurs rangs. Celle-là, je la guette au tournant.

Une vieille femme me salue. Je panique à l'idée de flirter avec une sibylle. On ne me le serinera jamais: les génies du mal se déguisent sous une forme humaine ou animale afin d'enfiler leurs victimes. Je tourne les talons, reviens à la case départ et campe dans mon coin. Toujours le même. Un pré

---

1 Danser le *mbalax* (N.d.A.).

carré. J'aimerais bien causer avec quelqu'un, un prof ou un savant, discuter avec lui des équations à mille millions d'inconnues ou des trucs appris au collège, où j'ai loupé mon bac avec brio. Mais personne ne s'approche de ma poire. Ainsi mis en quarantaine, je parlote seulingue. Et ne m'en plains pas.

Maman m'apporte à claper. Il s'agit là, si je ne m'abuse, de mon premier repas de la journée. Impossible d'en être sûr, vu que je ne consigne rien. Je devrais pourtant essayer. Ne fût-ce que pour savoir comment elle va me liquider. Par la croûte ou par la famine ? J'avale quelques bouffées. C'est bon. Que non ! Elle a encore assaisonné sa tambouille de pili-pili. Ça pique fort. J'en ai la bouche en feu. Et si elle m'empoisonnait ou tentait de me cramer les tripes ? Va-t-elle seulement penser à alerter les pompiers ? Une sorcière ne peut se prévaloir d'une once d'humanité. Je repousse les plats trafiqués, me renfrogne et reste sourd aux supplications. Grève de la faim illimitée. Celle-là, elle ne m'emmènera pas en enfer.

Je crains la nuit. Ses silences déstabilisent et rendent nerveux. Les esprits malveillants en profitent, de surcroît, pour rôder. Je n'aime pas non plus dormir. Parce que l'état d'absence rend vulnérable. Le toubib prétend que j'ai des hallucinations. Est-ce que cela signifie que je fabule quand je vois des têtes de mort et des monstres dans mon sommeil ? Réveillé, les yeux grands ouverts, je subis leur guérilla au point d'être en nage. Seul mon chapelet les met en débandade. Encore faut-il que j'y pense, chose qui n'est pas évidente à cause de ma grande tension. Je brûle alors du thuraï. Ça purifie l'air et dégage l'atmosphère des agents hostiles.

Au lieu de ronfler, je scrute les ténèbres afin de débusquer les présences insolites. Ma vigilance paie au bout du compte, puisque des masques hideux se pointent, munis de langues fourchues et de cornes. Quand ils passent à l'attaque, je me transforme en courant d'air, plane, vire à perpète. Mais les hordes d'intervention souterraine finissent par me rattraper. Je lance des SOS. Personne ne m'entend. Sauf mon père, tonton et ma frangine, qui, le temps d'une séquence infinitésimale, surgissent pour m'exhorter à ne pas baisser la garde.

D'aucuns affirment que je déjante. Pourtant, je reconnais la sorcière, tapie derrière les boules bâclées, en train de les inciter à me porter le coup fatal. Pourquoi est-elle toujours là quand les ennemis attaquent ? Terrassé, la bouche écumeuse et la carcasse fiévreuse, je ne perds pas pour autant le sens des réalités : sa silhouette se détache nettement dans le noir, s'approche de moi. Croyant que je suis mort, elle se penche sur ma frime, vocifère je ne sais quels sortilèges et m'essuie la sueur. Je la laisse branler pendant quelque temps. Ruse de guerre. Quand elle s'absente, à coup sûr pour aller consulter ses congénères, je cherche mon chapelet sous l'oreiller. Manque de pot, le fétiche a disparu. Encore un coup de la charogne. Elle sait, la vilenie personnifiée, que je peux la neutraliser avec ce gri-gri importé. Par bonheur, la hachette, que je planque sous le matelas, me permet de garder l'initiative. L'humanité est sauvée. Où qu'elle aille, la sorcière, je l'ai à l'œil.

Aux Deux Manguiers

RIEN QU'AVEC SES ANANAS, Marie-Thérèse m'avait d'emblée flashé. Ajoutez à cela ses bras empâtés, son postère phénoménal, fidèle aux canons de l'art, mes instincts cannibales avaient resurgi et ceux qualifiés de bas, sans doute parce qu'ils opèrent hors caméra, s'étaient éveillés. Deux mètres de pied en cap, quatre-vingt-dix kilos de chair et de gras, l'Himalaya avait rallumé mes fantasmes. Sa voix de fausset ouïe et son visage chagrin gravé, mon cœur, déjà sensible à ce qui détonne, s'était débridé devant le côté relax, un brin fada, de la sirène. Envoûté.

Autant l'avouer, j'adore les pièces rares, celles qui rebutent les bonnes âmes et les laissent indifférentes. Les « bourreaux », ces meufs divinement massives, trônent à mon palmarès. Sinon, je me toque des albinos, malbâties, impotentes. À vos stylos, mes salopes ! Vicelard, moi ? Ne déconnez pas. Tenant en horreur les scènes de jalousie et les MST, je fouine dans le rebut de la gent féminine. Parce que les quantités négligeables sont nickel, de surcroît soucieuses des visites prophylactiques. Elles vous fichent une paix royale et ne vous taxent pas, contrairement à ces beautés voraces qui, comble d'ironie, entretiennent la légende de Kin-la-belle. Croquer une de ces pièces équivaut, de mon point de vue, à lui rendre sa féminité, mieux, à la valoriser. Avec l'avantage de bénéficier d'une perpétuelle reconnaissance du ventre.

Mais voilà, cela fait un bail que je connais Marie-Thérèse sans l'avoir culbutée. Je n'ai pourtant pas l'âme d'un boy-scout et ne suis, pour elle, ni un sigisbée ni un griot. Pis, pas une seule fois je ne l'ai sortie sans qu'une tuile, mais alors un gros pépin, anéantisse mes projets ou nous pète à la figure. Je suis donc très loin de me l'imaginer quand je la lève, pour la première fois, aux *Deux Manguiers*. Et d'un. De deux : de même que les Marie-José, Marie-Léa, Marie-Louise et autres Marie-Pauline portent respectivement, à Kin, les petits noms de Méjé, Mélé, Malou et Mépé, les Marie-Thérèse friment, quel que soit leur calibre, avec un pseudo poétique : Méthé. Un cas troublant, ma muse.

Après deux heures d'attente sous une paillote, force m'est de reconnaître que l'indigène, qui m'avait rencardé dans ce bar de Barumbu, une des vieilles cités de Kin, m'a posé un lapin. Carburant aussi à l'heure africaine, je m'en fous, d'autant que j'essaie de me brancher sur une poupée gonflable,

Méthé, également assise sous une paillote. La Cadillac buvote avec une souris de petit format.

Le contact visuel pris, je leur expédie deux bières, histoire de poser des jalons. Sourires. Avantage dans mon camp. Quand elles éclusent la pisse, je réitère mon geste de bienfaisance publique. À haute voix. Pour éviter toute équivoque sur la provenance de la flotte. Alors que le garçon va les servir, je le dévie de sa trajectoire, fait déposer les bibines sur ma table et siffle le rassemblement. Les frangines accourent. La timbale décrochée.

On trinque aux misères passées et à venir de la piétaille. Méthé, qui a de gros yeux blancs ensorcelants, expose en prime des bras velus et des lèvres pulpeuses. Bandant. Je joue cartes sur table, provoquant le déplaisir, à peine voilé, de l'autre poulette.

À deux heures, Dety, ladite poulette, se casse. Bon débarras. On file peu après, ma conquête et moi, à la recherche d'un nid d'amour. Le tour du quartier effectué, nous prospectons au-delà: les hôtels (terme pudique – vous l'avez deviné – pour désigner les bordels) sont fermés ou complets. À croire que les forces vives de la nation jouent les prolongations à guichets fermés. De guerre lasse, Méthé me propose son toit. À la guerre comme à la guerre !

La sirène crèche sur la rue des *Deux Manguiers*, du côté où les pluies diluviennes ont agrandi la rigole, en rongeant la rue au point de la rétrécir comme peau de chagrin. J'avance à tâtons dans le noir, posant mes pieds dans le sillage de la Cadillac. Nous débouchons enfin sur une parcelle rongée par les érosions. Le taudis, en terre d'argile, date des années vingt, à l'époque où Kin n'avait pas encore gagné ses galons de capitale.

Méthé ouvre la porte, entre de plain-pied dans une chambre à coucher. Figé à l'entrée, j'examine le bocal sous l'éclairage d'une bougie. Débectant. Non pas que j'habite une supertaule, mais j'ai du mal à croire que la cochonne, qui n'avait pas arrêté, durant toute la soirée, de s'arroser les aisselles avec un vaporisateur Lancôme, niche dans ce foutoir. Et quel foutoir ! Un trou cracra. Quatre gamins pioncent à même le sol, des pagnes en lambeaux tirés jusqu'à la tête, trois autres ronflent dans un petit lit à l'évidence destiné à deux gniards.

« C'est quoi, ce plan ? demandai-je, estomaqué, à Méthé qui nous fait une place dans le pieu.

– Les mômes de ma frangine. Elle dort, elle, dans la pièce d'à-côté. »

Scrupuleux à mes heures perdues, je soulève les yeux : le mur de séparation des deux pièces, aussi haut qu'un pygmée pur jus, offre une superbe vue plongeante dans l'une ou l'autre turne. Je m'imagine aussitôt dans les bras de Morphée, déplumé, dans cette tanière. Déballonnant.

« Et nous, on se fait des câlins où ça ? »

Méthé montre le grabat en m'intimant le silence. Moi, grimper l'Himalaya dans ce berceau, qui pis est avec le risque de voir ces babouins, apparemment endormis, me faire des croche-pieds pendant l'escalade ? Pour qui donc me prend-elle, cette pouffiasse ? Je ne suis tout de même pas un sauvage. De la tête, je lui fais signe de me suivre. Puis lui refile, une fois dehors, de quoi engaver son poulailler et me tire.

Deux jours après, infichu de refouler mes pulsions, j'émerge aux *Deux-Manguiers*. Des gens crachent sur mon passage ou hochent la tête. Mon péché mignon va leur servir de plat de résistance. Je m'installe, flashe une gazelle en dépit des lumières tamisées. Dety. La poulette tient le crachoir à une table, le dos tourné à l'entrée, et ne m'a pas vu arriver. En même temps que je passe ma commande, je susurre au garçon de signaler discrètement ma présence à la fumelle. Je ne sais comment cet enfoiré s'y est pris. Toujours est-il que Dety, manifestement de mauvais poil, se retourne et scrute dans ma direction. Un bref instant, je crains le retour de manivelle. Mais la pépée, m'ayant reconnu, hurle au revenant, plaque sa bande et vient me bécoter. Elle s'écroule sur mes jambes, noue ses tentacules autour de mon cou. Ma légende de charmeur ne date pas d'hier.

« Comment ça s'est passé ? attaque-t-elle en plantant ses pruneaux dans les miens.

– Méthé est cachottière à ce point ? »

Nous nous dévorons du regard. Mais, au-delà du visage cendré, ce sont les flotteurs de Méthé que je revois. Sous la blouse transparente, leur volume m'obnubilait et leurs contours, nettement dessinés, déréglaient mes sens. Alors qu'ils s'exposaient là, ils m'avaient paru hors de portée, telles des bouées de sauvetage qui s'éloignent du naufragé. Plongé dans mon fantasme, je n'avais pas accordé l'attention voulue à Dety. Mignonne et de bonne compagnie, elle l'aurait pourtant mérité. Elle venait d'ailleurs, par son accueil, de corriger mon image de marque auprès des mollahs des *Deux-Manguiers*.

Soudainement grave, Dety descend du trône, tire une chaise et tombe dessus. Elle l'avance de telle sorte que nos haleines se croisent. La sienne pue l'alcool, ça dégage les gros haricots rouges chez mézig. Confidences. Méthé est secrète. Toutes ses aventures galantes se terminent mal. Ses vestes l'ont tellement marquée qu'elle affiche une gueule de faire-part. Nul n'a réussi à percer son passé ni ce qu'elle vit. On se réfère en conséquence aux on-dit selon lesquels elle appartiendrait aux meufs, généralement foutables, qui dégagent des ondes maléfiques.

« C'est avec raison que j'ai voulu savoir ce qui s'est passé entre vous, renchérit-elle. Je me suis fait du mourron pour toi, mais ta présence ici me rassure.

– À quoi attribuer ce maléfice ? Je n'ai rien perçu de tel l'autre soir…

– T'as couché avec elle ?

– Pourquoi cette question indiscrète ?

– T'as pas compris que Méthé est une meuf porte-malheur ? Fais gaffe avec elle ! »

Le sortilège, poursuit-elle avec l'autorité d'une guérisseuse en consultation, proviendrait soit de sa naissance, soit d'un autre événement majeur de sa vie. On le sait : un nouveau-né prend son premier bain dès sa délivrance. Hygiénique, certes, ce bain répond également à l'exigence, rituelle, de plonger le bébé dans la vie, l'eau constituant son symbole le plus manifeste. La vie n'existe pas là où il n'y a pas d'eau.

Cela dit, plusieurs hypothèses se posent sur Méthé : ou elle n'a pas pris ce bain, ce que rien ne peut justifier, ou l'on n'y a pas trempé les plantes revigorantes, ou encore, ce qui paraît fort probable, l'eau utilisée a été impure. Il se pourrait aussi que Méthé, mariée très jeune, ait perdu son porte-couilles sans que les siens la soumettent, comme cela arrive parfois, au rite de purification. Ce rite consiste à prendre un bain macéré de plantes ou de racines idoines. Pour ne l'avoir pas fait, elle peut rester à vie une source de diffusion de mal.

« Comment peux-tu la fréquenter en sachant cela ?

– Elle ne pose problème qu'à ses branques. »

Débilité par ces révélations, je revis le film de la soirée. Rien ne m'avait intrigué durant les quatre heures de bringue. Le flop du corps à corps m'était du reste imputable, car j'aurais dû dégoter une chambre à temps. Par ailleurs, si je l'avais voulu, j'aurais chevauché la mastodonte dans sa crèche. C'est dire que les confidences de Dety relèvent de la superstition ou de la mesquinerie.

« Où est-elle ?

– Dans un dispensaire. Elle veille sur un neveu malade. Sa maman n'est pas là. »

Après un long soupir, Dety pose sa pogne sur mon bras, une lueur de supplication dans le regard :

« Je l'aime bien, Méthé, mais elle n'est pas faite pour toi. Il y a de plus cette histoire… »

Classique. Je m'empresse de doubler les drinks. Puis, sur un ton coulant, plaisant à souhait, lâche à qui veut l'entendre que je m'en branle des petits formats. Spécialiste des Himalaya, par conséquent endurci aux grandes ascensions, je me sens dans mon élément dans les hauteurs, cadres où ma prestation relève des performances.

Le visage de Dety vire au noir goudron. Sa déconvenue contenue, elle me demande d'une voix craintive, si je ne roule pas pour la sorcellerie, ce à quoi je réagis par un geste blasé de la main. Ai-je, moi, la tronche d'un fétichiste ?

Trois ou quatre jours après, je renouvelle ma fidélité aux *Deux Manguiers*. Habitant l'autre bout de la ville, je ne peux me permettre des virées suivies à Barumbu. Le serveur me confie, dès mon arrivée, que Méthé me cherche jour et nuit, ce qui conforte ma position. De solliciteur, je deviens VIP. Une surprise attend la doudou d'amour quand elle amène son bifteck : je l'exporte dans mon fief, quasiment à Pétaouchnock, où des amis nous attendent. Plus question de reporter le combat singulier d'une journée. La crise a sensiblement abaissé notre espérance de vie.

Cinq braguettes nous accueillent avec des regards ahuris. La chaleur monte cependant à grande vitesse, la bibine coule à flots. Un pote débloque Méthé et l'entraîne sur la piste. Spectacle. Je ne croyais pas trimbaler une bête de scène. La zone se tord de rire devant la montagne déchaînée, l'adopte. Des bouteilles de bière lui sont offertes. Un triomphe.

Au bout de cinq heures, je déclare forfait. Les copains proposent de nous raccompagner, mais je repousse l'offre. Pas de gardes du corps. Balade sentimentale. On emprunte des passages non éclairés pour regagner ma piaule, dans un quartier voisin. Une décharge d'ordures s'inscrit dans mon champ de vision. Des toilettes strictement destinées à usage domestique. Touristes et rastaques s'abstenir. Tandis que je fais pleurer le colosse, trois lascars surgissent d'une rue adjacente et remontent le passage en beuglant le hit de la saison. Vu l'heure tardive, je n'ai aucune raison de gâcher mon plaisir. Les pochards atteignent notre niveau. Découvrant la noctambule et la croyant seule, perdue dans la forêt équatoriale, l'un d'eux l'aborde.

« Tiens, tiens ! La pouffiasse d'hier ! Qu'est-ce qu'elle fout ici ? »

Les deux autres reviennent sur leurs pas et examinent l'objet de l'interpellation. Ils tournent autour d'un monument aux morts, sifflotent, se rincent l'œil. Un mammouth ! Et pas en Sibérie ! Leur cirque terminé, ils rendent leurs impressions publiques :

« Tu crois vraiment qu'elle a pris du volume en une nuit ?

– Vous faites erreur, lance Méthé de sa voix de tête. J'suis pas d'ici.

– Sale menteuse ! crache le premier cuitard à bout portant. T'as même injurié ma mère. Voici sa réponse… »

Et clac ! La bêtasse recule au lieu de se transformer en bulldozer et de m'écraser les morpions.

Un instant, je flotte comme un con, ne sachant quelle attitude prendre. Mes scrupules ravalés, je sors de l'ombre en attirant l'attention sur ma présence. Je ne pipe mot, mais foudroie le provocateur d'un coup de tête. Tapis.

Le moment de surprise passé, les autres s'avancent, ce qui me caille le sang : des soûlards ordinaires auraient détalé après ma démonstration de force. Cette réflexion à peine ruminée, je bascule dans les immondices, trahi par le commando qui rampait par terre. Dix minutes durant, le trio se refait une forme tonique en me bourrant de coups de pied et de coups de poing, sans considération de l'endroit où ça cogne. Toutes mes tentatives de réagir échouent dans la gadoue.

Méthé siffle la fin des hostilités, bêle au secours. Des fenêtres s'ouvrent, des curieux sortent, mais se tiennent à bonne distance : un des matadores les met en garde contre toute interposition, force devant rester à la loi. Des gendarmes en vadrouille. Les faux jetons. Ils auraient dû s'annoncer !

La tête enfouie dans les ordures, je guette le moment de reprendre du poil de la bête et d'étaler, par surprise, un matamore au sol. Mais quand je veux me relever, les muscles lâchent et la couche nauséabonde m'honore de son hospitalité. Dans les abysses de ma honte, je n'entends plus la voix de Méthé. Les zouaves, qui paradent et narguent à présent le quartier, reviennent par moments se défouler sur l'idiot du village.

Le chef du quartier s'amène, tempère l'ardeur de la troupe. Il m'assoit sur les ordures et constate les dégâts. Désormais, j'ai intérêt à raser les murs.

Bruit soudain d'un marathon. Anormal. Les gens raisonnables ne courent pas dans ce Far West. Il suffit qu'un fêlé crie au voleur, surtout la nuit, pour transformer un footing pépère en chasse à l'homme. Quitte à flamber, en cas de capture, avec un pneu imbibé d'essence autour du colbac. L'arrivée de mes copains, alertés par Méthé, met fin au suspense. Ils sont épaulés par des forces d'appoint fournies par le bistrot. Les zouaves, qui tentent de déserter le champ de bataille, sont repris, bringuebalés, passés à tabac. Ils supplient, demandent la protection du peuple. Rien n'y fait. Les badauds s'en mêlent. Lynchage. Je regagne ma piaule, la tête bien basse et l'esprit à la mise en garde de Dety.

Moins d'une heure après, un camion de gendarmes s'immobilise sur le lieu de la rixe. Le quartier bouclé, un adjupète procède aux semonces d'usage: trois de ses tireurs d'élite ayant été tabassés par des voyous, il menace de sévir si les habitants ne livrent pas le chef du gang. Palabre. Le chef du quartier blablate, use de manœuvres dilatoires. En pure perte. Aux bruits de bottes, Méthé se glisse in extremis au-dessous du plumard, non sans lui imprimer une bosse visible de la station Mir. La porte est défoncée. Arraché du canapé comme une mangue pourrie, je suis traîné et jeté dans le camion, où je sers de marchepied à la soldatesque. Les gendarmes de garde jubilent en prenant livraison du caïd. Ratonnade. Six jours au gnouf. Avec des tentatives musclées de m'extorquer les noms de mes complices. L'ombre de moi-même échoue la semaine d'après à l'hosto. Seigneur, pourquoi m'avez-vous niqué ?

Combien de temps s'est-il écoulé après cette dérouillée ? Deux, trois ans ? Toujours est-il que j'hérite entre-temps d'une décapo. Problème : je ne sais pas conduire. Un ami, piéton de carrière mais en possession d'un permis, s'offre pour me driver. Nous débarquons aux *Deux-Manguiers*, qui font montre de longévité dans le domaine. Méthé, encore plus enveloppée, détraque mes neurones. Imposante, le balcon vachement rembourré, elle toise le tiers-monde et me presse d'aller au radada. Sa mine chiante évoque, dans ma boule, une fresque de Mater dolorosa trafiquée en noir et blanc. Nous sifflons comme pour un Mundial des arsouilles, reportant cent fois la der des ders, tant et si bien que le pilote, carrément down, pique du nez à l'heure du décollage. Je relève le défi, l'alcoolo-faible à ma droite et Méthé sur le siège arrière, et m'engage sur l'avenue Kabambare. Mon plan consiste à déposer d'abord le poids mort dans son paddock, quitte à m'occuper de la Cadillac. J'ai hâte de démonter l'horoscope de Dety. À propos, qu'est-elle devenue, cette souris ?

« Lentement, mon coco ! » supplie le moniteur hors jeu.

Fonçant sur une ligne droite, la ferraille déboule sur Kasaï et Bokassa sans tenir compte de la priorité de gauche. Idem au croisement avec l'avenue du Plateau. En fait, raide comme une momie égyptienne, je n'arrive pas à lever le pied du champignon. La vitesse de croisière atteinte, le copain râle, incapable d'émettre un son audible. Je tente de freiner en vue de l'avenue Kasa-Vubu, mais la bagnole s'emballe, se braque à gauche, zig-zague, traverse l'avenue, rate un poteau, percute l'enceinte de l'école Sainte-Thérèse. Éjectée du siège sous le choc, Méthé plane, bute contre le mur, tombe sur le pare-brise en le pulvérisant. Le copain est coincé dans les tôles. J'ai réussi à éventrer le mur.

La fois d'après, nous poireautons au comptoir d'un flamingo, dans l'attente d'une turne. Méthé, qui n'avait pas été chaude pour ce rencard diurne, attend le match amical avec fatalisme. Indif à sa pudibonderie, je déguste une bibine en mitonnant les étapes majeures de l'escalade. Je me vois déjà caracoler la cochonne, la trouducuter, l'embraser, lui faire pleurer sa doche, l'envoyer sur orbite, l'élever au rang prestigieux de « bureau ». Remue-ménage soudain dans l'abattoir : une poule vient d'être retrouvée dans une chambre, à loilpé, foudroyée. Son branque a fuité en la voyant claboter. Morte au combat. Sans la garantie de décrocher la médaille de bravoure à titre posthume. Je lance un regard torve à la Cadillac. Et si cette montagne diffusait effectivement la scoumoune ? Match annulé.

Deux lunes plus tard, nous frimons au *Kung-Fu*, un dancing-bar de Bandal. Assis dans la partie découverte du bar, nous creusons en mâchant des noix de cola. Ça dessoûle et sert de Viagra. Méthé est égale à elle-même avec sa gueule de faire-part. Bien qu'elle rechigne à danser, elle décolle de la chaise à mon geste et sollicite mon accord avant de gigoter avec tel tordu venu en solo, sans sa petite nana, comme s'il allait dansser le ndombolo avec une chaise.

Agitation habituelle à la grille d'entrée. Des resquilleurs qui, à l'approche de la fin du concert, veulent s'éclater alors que les portiers s'y opposent. Des injures fusent. Une bousculade s'ensuit. Nous en profitons, Méthé et moi, pour dégraisser sur la piste. La Cadillac, qui me dévore de ses yeux blancs ensorceleurs, m'enveloppe dans ses bras immenses. Le Nyiragongo couve en moi.

Deux longues chansons plus tard, le calme est revenu dans notre secteur. Nous constatons néanmoins que des clients se cassent alors que, d'ordinaire, ils campent dans le bar après le concert. Méthé veut partir. Pour toute réponse, je lui montre les deux bières non consommées. Tchin-tchin !

Les portiers détalent tout à coup, renversent tables et chaises sur leur passage et sautent, à l'extrême opposé de l'entrée, la cloison servant d'enceinte au *Kung-Fu*. Dans leur fuite, ils entraînent les couards assis autour de la grille. Le temps de ruminer comment des microbes peuvent franchir, en cas de danger, des obstacles de plus d'un mètre de haut, je me retourne. Pour constater la disparition de Méthé. Je ne l'ai pourtant pas entendue décarrer.

L'entrée forcée, des militaires en civil investissent le bar. Aucun doute quant à leur appartenance, vu qu'ils pavoisent avec des gourdins et des barres de fer. Armée de métier. Des mecs tirés à quatre épingles se planquent, tels des rats, derrière le matériel de musique ou aux waters. Impossible de prendre la tangente. On est cuit.

Comme une dizaine d'autres clients, je plonge mon pif dans le verre et n'ose jouer aux astronomes. La pétoche s'empare de ma frime, tandis que les mutins patrouillent dans le bar. Ça cogne ici et là, ça menace de mort violente. L'un d'eux s'approche de moi à pas de léopard. Comme je reste incliné, preuve par neuf de mauvaise conscience, il m'assène un coup de gourdin. Je sursaute, porte une main à la boule. Saignant.

« Tu étais aussi à la porte, aboie-t-il. Je t'ai reconnu à tes loupes.

– J'ai pas bougé d'ici, grand chef, soupirai-je sur un ton gnan-gnan des plus attendrissants. Le chef d'orchestre, qui est un ami personnel, peut en témoigner…

– Si t'as pas bougé, t'as donc vu les bandits qui ont éborgné notre collègue. Où sont-ils passés ? »

Première nouvelle. Impliqué dans une telle embrouille, on risque de payer les crimes d'autrui, dussent-ils dater de Kongo-di-Ntotila, l'ancêtre légendaire des Bakongo. Trois matamores m'assiègent à présent. Le connard qui me tyrannise est baraqué, façon forestier descendu la veille de son arbre. Seul, d'homme à homme, je lui rendrais son pareil, même de manière symbolique. Mais, entouré du bataillon, j'ai intérêt à faire profil bas. Je n'ose pas avouer mon job de crayonneux. Ils m'écharperaient. Ennemi public. Prenant soin de ne pas le fixer, je lui montre, du doigt, la direction prise par les fuyards.

Le salopard, profitant de sa position dominante, m'assène un autre coup, au même endroit, puis m'enjoint de tracer. Un coup de pied au cul m'oblige à passer les vitesses. Parvenu devant la grille, je me retourne afin de zoomer la tronche du zigoto. Mon regard tombe sur le bétail que les vaillants soldats viennent de débusquer dans le snack. Les mâles sont alignés d'un côté, les femelles de l'autre. Méthé domine le troupeau par sa stature de reine mère. Je me dis que les mecs vont être humiliés, puis relâchés après avoir contribué à l'ordinaire des défenseurs de la bananeraie. Quant aux poules, inutile de préjuger de leur fin de soirée. Viol. Pour un crevard qui n'aura plus à fermer un œil avant de canarder.

Trois autres virées avec Méthé se terminent en foirades. La plus désastreuse a lieu la fois où, à bord d'un taxi, nous plongeons dans un canal, heureusement à sec, après avoir provoqué un accident. Entre-temps, les *Deux Manguiers* ont fermé, ce qui m'oblige à sortir la Cadillac du garage. Quand j'y arrive, cette fois-là, muni d'un cadeau rapporté d'un voyage, des chaises dispersées dans la parcelle me titillent. Je hèle un gamin, lui demande d'aller me chercher la sirène.

« Vous voyez pas les chaises ? rétorque le garçon après un temps de silence. Elle est morte avant-hier.

– Malade ? »

Le bonhomme examine ma carcasse de criseur[1]. Puis ajoute, le regard vicieux, que Méthé avait pas

1. Victime de la crise, désargenté. (N.d.A.)

mal fondu ces derniers temps. La sale « bestiole »[1].
Dix ans de plantages pour parvenir à l'apothéose.
La cochonne.

---

1. Virus du sida. (N.d.A.)

Week-end de la Pentecôte

LES CRASSES DES PARENTS retombent sur leurs mouflets, dixit la Bible, jusqu'à la énième génération. Taratata ! Qu'ai-je, moi, à branler de cette compta bizarroïde dès lors que je trimbale une « pierre dans le ventre » : pierre – ne s'agirait-il pas d'un fibrome ? – que personne n'a vue mais dont on ressasse, dans mon dos, qu'elle m'assurerait d'une stérilité coriace ? En quoi cette prédiction peut-elle me concerner, vu que j'assume, depuis la mort de mes dabs, le rôle de tiroir-caisse de trois tintins-furax ? Du reste, la mer qui nous sépare est telle que j'ai toujours considéré ces faux jetons, pourtant issus des mêmes œuvres que ma poire, comme des frelots par accident.

De douze ans mon cadet, le jeunot de ce triste héritage, vingt piges imméritées, échoue souvent chez bibi, à une heure indue, parce qu'il ne peut regagner son bidonville. À chaque fois, ses prétextes dénotent la provoc : cuite carabinée, manque de transport, frime de disposer d'un point de chute. Que voulez-vous que j'y fasse ? Un frangin, aussi flambé soit-il, reste un frangin. Je suis donc loin de réaliser la nature de mon fardeau quand j'entends, cette nuit, frapper à la porte. Le réveil indique trois heures. Je me lève de mauvaise grâce et enfile un pagne, l'esprit au poison que je devine dehors.

Kulabitsh entre dans sa forme olympique, bourré comme une vache, et me lance un salut empesté d'alcool et de hasch. Son état me laisse doublement sur les rotules. D'une part, je ne l'ai jamais vu ramper si bas, ce qui blesse mon honneur, bien que souvent bafoué, de garante de la saga familiale ; d'autre part, il a toujours nié gazer au chanvre. Indifférent à ma rage sourde, le parasite s'affale sur le divan et, sûr de ses droits inaliénables, réclame une bibine. Pour étancher sa soif, ajoute-t-il dans le but évident de tester mes nerfs.

« Qu'est-ce que t'as fait à Beya ? » je réponds pour esquiver sa demande.

Un mois que je n'avais pas souffert le foutriquet. Etalé sur le divan, il m'apparaît encore plus paumé. Ses cheveux sales, ébouriffés, tirent de l'adepte d'une secte rasta récusant l'hygiène. Son regard est trouble, fuyant tout contact avec le mien. Que peut-il bien cacher alors qu'on le voit déplumé en dépit de ses nippes ? Dire que j'essaie, par mon job et mes relations, de sauver la face en casant de tels déchets de la société ! Surpris par ma question, Kulabitsh me braque ses yeux éteints en murmurant :

« La pétasse ! Elle n'a eu que ce qu'elle mérite.

– Elle t'aime beaucoup, la petite…

– Laisse tomber, la sœur. Je t'ai demandé une bière… »

Le regard effaré se pose à nouveau sur moi. Ma curiosité l'emporte au finish sur la fermeté, et je vais lui chercher son biberon. Un arbre courbé ne peut être redressé.

Kulabitsh avale deux rasades d'affilée, arrêtant net le hoquet qui le fragilise. Quand il s'apprête à siffler la troisième, je mets d'autorité le holà, forte de ma position de cheftaine. La suite relève du scénario connu : le numéro se met à renifler, puis à zerver, agrémentant son cinoche bidon de plaintes sur sa vie fichue. Loin d'être remuée, je le regarde chialer avec méfiance : ou le cas social mijote un coup tordu, question de me soutirer du fric, ou il surnage dans la phase critique où tout vide-bouteilles, fouinant dans son tréfonds, revit sa longue dérive. En somme, le début de la sagesse.

Sa crise digérée, le coco accroche les clignots au plafond. Des reniflements le privent encore un moment de sa tchatche, après quoi il dégoise. Mollo.

« Crois-moi, la sœur, j'aurais jamais voulu te mouiller dans ce merdier…

– De quoi s'agit-il ? » tonné-je, un brin sur la défensive, avec l'inflexion que me confère mon statut.

Sa copine en titre et lui-même se réveillent assez tôt, il y a quelque temps, pour ne pas louper le train. Les tourtereaux ont décidé de filer dans la ville portuaire, à 350 kilomètres de la capitale, pour y passer le week-end. Vicky, sa donzelle, prépare le sac de voyage dans la chambre; Kulabitsh s'affaire au salon. Soudain, des bruits de chaussures de dames éveillent son sixième sens. Il se lève, tombe sur Beya. Il n'avait pas rendez-vous avec la nana, qu'il appelle affectueusement baby. Tilt dans sa tête: éviter le clash dans son mini-harem. En effet, si Vicky pratique la jalousie de combat, Beya, une mineure délurée, n'a rien à apprendre de la vie. Le beau gosse fuse dehors, entraîne la morue dans le voisinage. La gonzesse, qui tenait à couler le week-end en sa compagnie, lui joue une partition digne d'une traînée. Kulabitsh parvient toutefois à l'embobiner, tant et si bien que la gamine, furieuse, se casse.

Au retour du week-end, le play-boy raccompagne Vicky à son domicile, puis regagne sa niche. La nuit est tombée. Sa logeuse, qui vit mal sa ménopause, lui refile une convocation en proférant des menaces: elle ne veut point de locataires à problèmes et s'oppose à ce qu'un bordel s'installe dans sa parcelle. Kulabitsh encaisse, prend connaissance de la convocation. Rien de précis n'y figure, hormis l'injonction de pointer d'urgence à la gendarmerie «pour une affaire vous concernant». N'ayant rien à se reprocher, il court au poste. Le permanent de nuit le félicite pour son esprit civique, puis le place en garde à vue. Explications le lendemain.

Le gogo tombe des nues quand deux gendarmes l'introduisent, le lendemain matin, dans le bureau du chef de poste: le père et le frangin de Beya encadrent la morue, qui garde la tête baissée. Durant une longue minute, Kulabitsh tente de percer le mystère de sa garde à vue et de ces retrouvailles insolites. Des hypothèses lui viennent à l'esprit mais, aucune ne l'affranchit. Beya, tête toujours baissée, n'ose le mater, tandis que son frère, en narzo médaillé pour son emprise sur sa cadette, lui lance des dards venimeux.

Au moment où il veut occuper une chaise, tout le monde étant assis autour du bureau, Kulabitsh est soulevé par deux poignes d'acier. En position fixe. Bras croisés. Il prête ses loches sous bonne garde.

« T'aurais dû me prévenir ! je l'interromps, ulcérée par ces pratiques arbitraires.

– Ils m'ont refusé tout contact avec l'extérieur. Personne n'a d'ailleurs su que j'avais été bouclé. »

D'emblée, le sous-lieute lui signifie qu'il est accusé de détournement de mineure, en la personne de Beya ci-présente, et qu'une plainte a été déposée contre lui par sa famille. Démonté par cette entrée en matière, Kulabitsh tourne la citrouille autour de lui : des regards hostiles le remettent en phase. Entre-temps, la gradaille poursuit l'interrogatoire en lui demandant où il s'était rendu en fin de semaine, avec qui, par quel moyen. Réponses sans ambiguïtés du touriste. Le sous-lieute pousse ensuite la nénette à confesse.

« La sœur, s'écrie Kulabitsh en s'agitant, ce fut la totale. À la question de savoir où elle avait passé le week-end, cette garce a marmonné, en me désignant du doigt, qu'on avait été ensemble en vadrouille ! »

Le play-boy, bouche bée, dévore la nana sans rien comprendre. Chercherait-elle un alibi après avoir fugué ? Dans ce cas, pourquoi veut-elle lui faire porter le chapeau ? Ne réalise-t-elle pas la gravité d'une telle affirmation devant cette association momentanée contre son étoile ? Au reste, comment peut-on mentir aussi froidement ? Sa logeuse, des amis l'avaient vu partir avec Vicky et peuvent en témoigner. Le jeune homme veut protester, mais un gendarme lui cloue le bec avant qu'il ne l'ait ouvert.

« Ce n'était là qu'un avant-goût, poursuit le frangin en fermant les poings. Car la salope, en réponse aux questions posées, a prétendu que notre relation, qui remonte à deux mois, date de six mois. Elle a même allégué que c'est moi qui l'ai décapsulée...

– Alors, ce n'est pas vrai ?

– Je te l'jure, la sœur : c'est dans un... tunnel que j'ai ramé la première fois. J'ai même pas recouru aux préliminaires. Une passoire. Mais cet off merdique n'a rien voulu savoir... »

Le chef de poste décide une expertise médicale. Beya ayant soutenu qu'elle n'avait pas été consentante, il faut prouver le viol et le dater afin de confondre le délinquant. Quant à la plainte pour détournement de faux poids, il la laisse en suspens, puisque l'intéressée avoue s'être déplacée de son plein gré. Vu la gravité des faits, le sous-lieute signifie à Kulabitsh la prolongation de sa garde à vue. Sa relaxe ou sa mise à la disposition du parquet interviendra au retour de l'expertise médicale.

Huit jours après, la réponse tombe sur le bureau du zorro. Hamdoullah ! Beya mouille depuis deux lunes, bien avant de subir l'assaut de son pseudo-violeur. Relâché avec les excuses de la République, Kulabitsh ne peut toutefois pas quitter les locaux de la gendarmerie : le clan ennemi assiège le poste, équipé de fléchettes empoisonnées, en vue de fêter sa sortie. Il appert que des ténors de la tribu sont venus du village pour la circonstance. Ne voyant pas leur fille revenir au bout de trois jours, ses dabs avaient appréhendé le pire, d'où l'alerte donnée aux leurs en perspective d'un deuil. Sa sécurité ne pouvant être assurée dans les couloirs, et encore moins dehors, le jeune homme savoure les bienfaits d'un hammam dans une cellule surpeuplée.

« Quelle embrouille ! ne puis-je m'empêcher de lâcher. Je parie que les parents de Beya, décidés à la caser coûte que coûte, l'avaient obligée à mentir…

– Dans quel but ?

– Te coincer. T'amener à choisir entre la taule, ce que tu as risqué au regard de l'accusation, ou le mariage avec leur fille, chose qui leur évitait de bercer un petit-fils de père inconnu. Comment ça s'est terminé ? »

Trois jours supplémentaires de régime carcéral. Des haricots mal cuits midi et soir. Claper ou crever la dalle. Chiasse. Les assiégeants, que les gendarmes n'osent déloger de peur d'un carnage, finissent par décamper d'eux-mêmes.

De retour chez soi, Kulabitsh essuie sa proprio. La damoche lui livre sa pensée unique sur les chauds lapins, viveurs et autres crapules de son espèce. Preuve qu'elle a subi des pressions, elle le somme de libérer sa piaule illico presto. Le contrat de bail ? Elle n'en a rien à secouer. Ne paie-t-il pas ses loyers en retard ? Le bonhomme loge dès lors chez un pote ou l'autre, picole, carbure au hasch. Viré de son boulot pour abandon de poste, il tente d'attendrir l'ayatollah de service sur son sort, mais celui-ci reste intransigeant. La traîtrise de Beya l'obsède à ses moments de lucidité. Percer la cabale, connaître la vérité.

Après plusieurs tentatives, il parvient à accrocher la nana, de nuit, dans les parages de chez elle. La morue, décidément pas nette, fait montre d'amnésie en voulant lui lécher les amygdales. Kulabitsh la repousse avec héroïsme, lui crache son fait. Le faux poids reconnaît tout de go l'avoir chargé, à l'instigation de ses dabs, pour ne pas le perdre. Qu'il ait été coffré, elle lui aurait prouvé son amour gros comme un pamplemousse en lui rendant visite lors de ses congés scolaires. Le cavaleur craque : la gonzesse est barjo. Baffe. Des hurlements.

« Quand est-ce que ça s'est passé ?

– Tout à l'heure, la sœur !

– Tu ne vas pas dire que tu sors, à l'instant, du cachot. Ta mésaventure, si j'ai bien compris, date !

– Tout à fait. Vicky et moi étions partis dans la ville portuaire au cours d'un long week-end…

– Le dernier long week-end remonte à la Pentecôte, il y a presque un mois. Beya avait débarqué ici vers dix heures. Je m'en souviens très bien : elle était en larmes et n'avait pas desserré les dents, sauf pour dire que tu venais de la plaquer, dans la rue, parce qu'une autre nana créchait dans ta piaule. Elle est restée ici pendant quatre jours…

– Quoi ? s'écrie le frangin d'une voix brisée. Tu veux dire que ma baby était ici pendant mon absence ?

– Elle s'est calfeutrée le premier jour et n'a même pas voulu manger. Puis elle m'a aidée, les jours suivants, aux travaux ménagers. Une perle, malgré ce que tu en penses… »

Le visage du fils de mon père se décompose, signe qu'il est profondément perturbé. Pendant une minute interminable, il ne bouge ni ne desserre les dents. Il se lève après, tourne autour de la table. Son abattement est tel que je ne sais à quoi penser.

« Qu'est-ce t'as, Kula ?

– La sœur, les flics vont débarquer ici tôt ou tard. Il faut que je quitte la ville. Pour très longtemps. Mais je n'ai pas un rond et ne sais où aller…

– Que s'est-il passé ?

– Son frangin, alerté par les cris, a surgi dans le noir en vociférant comme un cinglé. Il tenait un couteau à la main. J'ai eu vite fait de le désarmer et de l'envoyer valdinguer. Pendant ce temps, Beya criait à tue-tête que je n'avais pas à toucher un cheveu de son grand-frère, ce qui a ameuté les gens et m'a obligé de lui filer des mandales. Son frère, profitant de la diversion, a tenté de récupérer le couteau. Je l'en ai empêché, puis l'ai fait valser. Beya a encore pris son parti en me rouant de coups. Hors de moi, j'ai ramassé le couteau et ai frappé. Juste au moment où elle s'interposait entre moi et ce zonard. Impardonnable. »

Tornade tropicale

PANGA NE SAIT PLUS où donner de la tête. Cela fait quelques heures qu'il pleut sans discontinuer. Non pas la petite flotte rafraîchissante, somme toute souhaitée après des journées caniculaires, mais la tornade dévastatrice, accompagnée d'éclairs et de tonnerre. Elle s'abat sur son univers comme si, là-haut, sur une nappe nuageuse, un ancêtre haineux avait voulu le punir pour un sacrifice non accompli. Pendant plus de deux heures, voire trois heures d'affilée, ça gronde, ça vente, ça crache des trombes d'eau violentes. Puis ça diminue d'intensité et ça s'arrête. Trêve de courte durée. Car les éléments reviennent à la charge, se déchaînent, déversent toute la hargne du ciel pendant une autre éternité.

Dès le commencement de l'enfer, aux environs de minuit, Panga s'était réveillé en sursaut. Il avait jailli de sa chambre, un pagne noué autour des reins, et s'était décarcassé. Deux seaux et une bassine libérés de leur contenu, il les avait posés aux endroits où la toiture, un assemblage de tôles acquises de seconde main, laissait couler la sauce. Cela n'avait pas suffi, puisque ça giclait de partout comme mille chasses d'eau tirées simultanément. Des marmites, des gobelets, tous les récipients disponibles dans la maison ayant été posés çà et là, il avait fallu déménager les quatre gosses de leur chambrette, devenue marigot, et les caser dans un coin de la pièce centrale.

À peine étalés sur des nattes, les mômes avaient dû renoncer à dormir afin de participer à l'effort de guerre: vider les récipients au fur et à mesure qu'ils se remplissaient. Entre-temps, lui-même s'était attelé à boucher les tôles pourries avec de la pâte de manioc. Tâche absurde. Le temps de monter sur un tabouret et de s'attaquer à une brèche, celle qu'il venait de colmater avait éjecté le foufou délayé, renouant illico avec sa fonction de jet d'eau. Désespérant.

Accalmie soudaine, troublée par des coassements lugubres. Piège ridicule de Nzakumba le Barbu, grogne Panga en ouvrant la petite fenêtre en bois. Les yeux hagards, il scrute la coupole à la recherche d'un signe qui le démentirait. Aucune étoile au firmament. Ni l'arc-en-ciel. Pourquoi subir ce châtiment? se demande-t-il en suivant les mômes qui vidaient les derniers récipients avant de se recoucher.

Devant lui, à dix pas du seuil, la crevasse draine des eaux torrentielles d'un rouge argileux. Les eaux écumantes ont emporté la planche qui permet à sa famille de rejoindre la civilisation, à tout le moins le souk immonde niché au pied de la montagne. À chaque pluie, cette crevasse s'élargit en sapant les assises de sa piaule. Sa cour, naguère un terrain de jeux pour sa nichée, tient à la fin d'une tranche d'ananas aux trois quarts rongée.

Malgré le noir compact, Panga survole les parcelles qui s'étendent à l'horizon. Quelques voisins, dégonflés ou frappés dans leur chair, avaient fini par déserter le bled. Débarqués ici il y a trois décennies, ils avaient cru accéder à la propriété en achetant, à vil prix, ces lopins de terre de désolation. Rien n'y poussait, hormis des arbustes rabougris et des plantes vouées au coupe-coupe. Les occupants eurent vite fait de les extirper pour torcher qui un abri de fortune, qui une baraque, qui un nid prétendument en dur. Des myriades de cabanes jaillirent ainsi sur les flancs de la montagne, formant un bidonville que les bien-pensants baptisèrent « zone annexe ». Plus qu'un besoin de disposer d'un toit ou d'un titre cadastral, ce fichu document restant d'ailleurs sans valeur pour l'administration, une volonté de contrer la fatalité animait les pionniers. Au fil des ans, ils eurent cependant à payer, chacun à son tour, la folie de s'être installés sur ces terres snobées par les nantis : déboisé, le terrain se fendait comme un mur bâclé, offrant ses entrailles béantes en guise de tombes à une population déshéritée.

Un craquement tire Panga de sa rêverie. Et si ses craintes se justifiaient ? Prenant la lampe tempête, il déboule dans la chambrette des gosses, procède à un examen minutieux. Rien d'anormal dans la charpente, excepté les gouttelettes qui tombent sans relâche. Fidepute ! Putain-con ! Bordel de merde, cela va-t-il s'arrêter ou non ?

Sans s'en rendre compte, Panga baisse les bras dans un mouvement d'abattement. Il a conscience d'être l'acteur passif d'un drame inéluctable. Impuissance. Colère. Kesekça ? peste-t-il tout à coup devant la balafre qui s'imprime dans ses yeux. La lampe soulevée, il tombe, horrifié, sur la fente qui lézarde le mur extérieur. Sa famille se trouve en danger, rumine-t-il, affolé. Il faut l'évacuer au plus vite. Mais vers quelle destination, son plus proche parent habitant loin du paradis perdu ?

Panga s'approche du mur afin de vérifier l'importance de la fente. Aucun doute n'est plus permis : le palais de ses rêves va s'écrouler. Comme pour éviter qu'il ne lui tombe dessus, il recule, bute sur quelque chose. Plié en deux, il découvre, catastrophé, que le pavement est également fissuré. Un maçon confirmé, bénéficiant – il est vrai – de son concours de touche-à-tout, avait pourtant mis sa science dans la construction de la baraque ! Ne lui avait-il pas fait cracher la peau des fesses, sous prétexte de jeter des fondements aussi solides que ceux d'une salle des coffres ?

Après avoir examiné la cassure, Panga remonte le mur et constate que la fente a pris naissance au sol. Le désastre. La piaule de merde, sapée dans ses assises, n'est plus qu'un château de cartes. Et sa femme, alitée, qui ne peut bouger ! Dehors, la pluie martèle la toiture un cran plus fort.

« Zahina ! crie-t-il dès son retour dans la pièce principale, il faut déguerpir. La taule va s'effondrer.

– Je ne m'en sens pas capable, geint la malade.

– Rappelle-toi les Kilandamoko. C'était la dernière saison des pluies. On les a retrouvés ensevelis sous les gravats de leur maison. Allez, les enfants, magnez-vous ! »

Tandis que la maisonnée fourre dans un sac des effets de première nécessité, Panga resserre nerveusement son pagne, puis se glisse dehors. Marchant à l'aveuglette, il surgit derrière la baraque pour un examen ultime : la crevasse de derrière, qui a balayé le petit coin la saison précédente, s'est encore élargie. Les éclairs lui prêtent une affreuse gueule d'ogre. Provenant d'un point situé plus haut, elle forme, avec la crevasse de devant, deux bras tentaculaires qui enserrent la bicoque et vont l'engloutir. Son oasis est condamnée. Tant d'années de sacrifices pour essuyer cette douche ! Déprimant.

Le cœur en peine, Panga contourne son palais en rasant le mur, longe la crevasse de devant. Un moment, il tourne en rond sous la pluie, déboussolé. Puis récupère, à deux encablures de son logis, la planche de traversée. La pièce, qui est recourbée dans sa partie centrale, mesure plus de quatre mètres. Après avoir repéré un passage étroit, il jette son pont de fortune.

Zahina, sa femme, ne peut transporter sa dernière-née et l'a confiée à leur aîné de huit ans. Parfait, approuve le chef de famille en briefant son monde : une fois de l'autre côté, foncer chez Papa Mapassa, le père des jumeaux, et y attendre la fin du cauchemar. Quant à lui, il les rejoindra plus tard.

La maisonnée part en exil sous une pluie battante. La mère, un pagne sur la tête, traîne un bambin, suivie de deux marmots dont le plus grand transporte la cadette d'un an sur son dos. La terre boueuse se colle aux babouches en procurant aux fuyards l'impression d'avoir des semelles épaisses.

Panga teste la solidité du pont. La patte posée sur une extrémité de la planche, il exhorte les siens d'ignorer les eaux en furie et de fixer l'autre bout de la passerelle. Cela dit, il enjoint Zahina de traverser avec un gamin. Habitués à cet exercice, quoique troublé par le grondement des eaux, les fugitifs rejoignent l'autre rive sans encombre. Un autre gamin passe, l'aîné s'engage à son tour avec sa charge.

Un craquement paralyse subitement la tribu. La seconde d'après, un affaissement rompt la monotonie du mauvais temps. Entre deux éclairs, les sinistrés notent qu'une partie de la bicoque a disparu du paysage. Pour une raison inexplicable, le père veut s'élancer vers les ruines, se ravise. Libérée un instant de la pression, la passerelle plie sous le poids du gamin. Celui-ci, figé en pleine traversée pour graver l'image de l'effondrement dans sa mémoire, s'assure d'instinct de la présence de sa sœur, puis étend les bras en vue de rétablir son équilibre. Au même moment, le père repose son pied sur la planche, lui imprimant un mouvement contraire. Le petit sursaute avec sa charge, perd pied et plonge dans les eaux furieuses. La tornade reprend aussitôt de plus belle.

Destin tragique

« NOUS SOMMES la risée du quartier, Palmira, et ça, t'es pas foutue de le comprendre. Tu t'imagines : moi, deux fois papy à quarante ans ! Et je ne parle pas de toi. La honte. C'est avec ta complicité que ce Zaïrien – comment les appelle-t-on encore ? – est entré dans cette maison. Un faux-cul. Toujours en train de boire, de danser et de magouiller. Tu soutenais qu'il est le fils d'un pape – sans doute autoproclamé – d'une Église du Christ sur la terre par le prophète Truc-Machin, comme si cela pouvait m'impressionner… »

Planté au milieu de la pièce, Manuel fulmine en créole capverdien. Il gesticule, pointe un index accusateur sur sa compagne. Le corps décharné, d'une maigreur choquante pour un cordon-bleu, il secoue les puces et à sa femme et à sa progéniture. Ceux-ci avalaient, devant le petit écran, leur dose quotidienne de série américaine. Pelotonnée dans un fauteuil, éreintée par une dure journée de travail et par les facéties de ses mômes, Palmira pleure. Manuel n'en est pas à sa première scène sur le sujet.

Linda, leur bébé de quinze printemps, s'entiche, il y a deux ans, d'un Zaïrois de cinq piges son aîné. Le lascar fait montre d'outrecuidance au point de débarquer sous leur toit, en leur absence, et de s'y prélasser. Les mouflets subissent le coco, qui, à la longue, se conduit en grand frère. Pendant des mois, les parents ignorent ses descentes régulières dans la maison. Pourtant, le sans-gêne s'y restaure, y pique un somme, se sert au frigo, tient des séances « enfants non admis » avec sa copine. Jusqu'aux résultats scolaires de Linda. Médiocres. La vérité éclate alors au grand jour : les langues se délient, permettant, entre autres choses, la découverte du carnet de liaison jamais signé, les absences répétées de Linda à l'école, les convocations restées sans suite. La maman évente en prime l'état de sa fille : enceinte. Trop tard. Renvoyée du collège.

Le père entre dans une sainte colère, jure d'étrangler le trouble-fête de ses propres mains. N'a-t-il pas couvert sa famille de déshonneur ? Après avoir piégé le mauvais génie, il le surprend en flagrant délit de squatt, vautré dans un fauteuil, une jambe posée sur l'autre. Loin de se confondre en excuses, le produit du mobutisme se meut mollement, dégaine subito un cutter et menace de saigner le donneur de leçons. Manuel, qui n'a jamais vu ça, bat en retraite. Humilié. Dépassé. D'autant que Linda rejoint son béguin dans le foyer où il vit.

Elle y accouche par césarienne, rentre au bercail avec le bâtard. Bondia papy !

Les conseils prodigués à la fille mère entrent par une oreille et sortent par l'autre. Vous faites vieux jeu, lance-t-elle à ses vieux lorsqu'ils l'asticotent. Grande, elle a fait son choix. Les délices de la vie ? Elle ne s'imagine pas les croquer sans son boy-friend, qui sort quasiment de la clandestinité. Le quartier le connaît. Pour ses disputes en public avec sa chérie. Une brute. Doublée d'un malappris. Voilà qu'il remet ça, puisque Linda attend à nouveau famille…

« Tu ne la surveilles pas assez ! tonne Manuel à l'adresse de son épouse.

– Comme toi, je suis absente de la journée : huit heures de ménage, matin et soir, sans compter le temps passé dans les transports. Je ne peux savoir ce qu'elle fabrique. De plus, notre fille ment comme elle respire…

– Elle est exactement comme toi : sournoise. T'avais aussi le même âge à sa naissance !

– Que veux-tu insinuer par là ? rétorque Palmira, un ton plus fort. Que je l'ai eue seule, comme la madone ? Qu'est-ce que tu peux être ridicule !

– Moi, j'ai assumé. On était au pays. Et nous n'avons gêné personne, ce qui n'est pas leur cas. Nous trimons comme des bêtes de somme et, pendant ce temps, eux s'amusent à alourdir nos charges. À raison d'une bouche à nourrir tous les deux ans, notre retraite est compromise.

– Il faudra peut-être la soustraire à l'emprise de ce garçon, suggère Palmira, conciliante. La renvoyer, par exemple, à Mindelo…

– Tu crois que les assistantes sociales la laisseront partir ? Elle constitue leur gagne-pain. Ce qu'il lui faut, c'est crever. En pleines couches, sous les roues d'un train, par noyade… »

Manuel n'en peut plus. Le caniche sautillant à ses pieds, il jette un œil à la pendule : 21 heures. La promenade avec le toutou. Humer l'air frais du dehors, oublier sa honte. Deux fois papy à son âge ! Qu'allait-on raconter à São Vicente, son île natale ? Il s'empare de la laisse, attache le caniche et sort par la porte de devant.

Le temps est couvert. Bien qu'elle soit éclairée, la rue baigne dans une pénombre due à la présence d'une hêtraie. Celle-ci avait été repeuplée après la création de la ZAC, il y a une quinzaine d'années, et longeait la rue sur toute sa longueur, face au quartier pavillonnaire.

Manuel a aménagé son nid, construit avec ses économies, à force de patience. Un petit jardin fleurit dans la courette de devant, une serre et une lapinière occupent celle, un peu plus grande, de derrière. Situé à dix minutes de la gare de la SNCF, le pavillon se dresse à quelques encablures de la Seine, non loin du centre-ville d'une petite cité de l'Ouest francilien. Seul inconvénient : il avoisine un croisement. Nuisances assurées. On ne peut tout avoir.

Toujours assise sur le fauteuil, Palmira pleure en silence. Une mère accouche d'un enfant, dit un dicton, mais n'accouche jamais de son cœur. Comment faire comprendre à la petite qu'elle a embrassé un mauvais parti, que son idylle tournera court ? Se toquer d'un Zaïrois pur et dur ! Serait-elle sourde à ce qui se raconte sur cette tribu ?

Sans qu'elle y prête atention, ses oreilles perçoivent le vroum pétaradant d'une moto. L'instant d'après, un scratch, suivi d'une dislocation fracassante de pièces métalliques, la tire de son nuage. Encore un accident. Le énième d'une série non close. Carrefour de la mort. La perpète pour les chauffards.

Palmira fuse dehors, talonnée par ses mouflets. Le caniche, perturbé, se glisse en cata par la porte ouverte. La moto choit en travers de la route, à deux cents mètres du croisement. Tandis que le conducteur et sa passagère se relèvent péniblement, des voisins expertisent les dégâts à distance avant de jouer les SAMU.

« Où est passé votre père ? » demande Palmira, subitement inquiète, en roulant les yeux.

Des secondes passent. Un gosse beugle tout à coup en montrant une masse informe gisant sur le bord opposé de la chaussée. Le temps de zyeuter la chose et de saisir, Palmira voit le gamin, devenu hystérique, désigner un bras sanguinolent. Le membre, arraché du corps, tient dans une manche de chemise. Un concert de pleurs s'élève, alors qu'un autre gamin, flashant un morceau de jeans, découvre une jambe déchiquetée. Des lambeaux de chair apparaissent ici et là. Une tête décollée traîne dans le caniveau. Écrabouillée. Avec la chevelure épaisse de papy.

La Ripaille des ninjas

« VIEUX MUNDELE, votre drame, aussi débectant soit-il, n'offre aucune occasion de mastiquer ni de se renflouer. Un sacré P.A.S.[1] de la Banque mondiale. Bref, vous me demandez de pilonner, à mes risques et périls, des salopards de la pire espèce. Sans déconner, vous êtes déphasé jusqu'à l'os. Désolé de vous le dire malgré tout le respect que je vous dois... »

Le sexagénaire fixa le gringalet d'un air dépité. Mundele Ndombe de son nom, autrement dit le toubab à la peau noire, il méprisait les couilles molles. Bicause il avait roulé sa bosse dans la territoriale. Non pas aux postes de béni-oui-oui, ces strapontins anonymes, d'ordinaire réservés aux sous-merdes, commis auxiliaires et autres larbins polychiés par la brousse, mais au top niveau de

---

1. Programme d'ajustement structurel. (N.d.A.)

commandement. De la dernière fournée de chefs de centre extracoutumier – la municipalité indigène, selon le baragouin colonial –, il avait négocié sa retraite en qualité de secrétaire général de province et ce, après l'indépendance. C'est dire qu'il avait eu à prendre des décisions, à veiller à leur application. Jamais il n'avait cédé devant les groupes de pression, ni tergiversé sur son parti s'agissant de questions d'intérêt public. Il ne pouvait donc concevoir que rien ne soit tenté, sous prétexte que la racaille dictait sa loi. Au reste, les torche-culs locaux – toutes tendances confondues – avaient beau fustiger le règne de l'arbitraire, il n'en demeure pas moins qu'ils beuglaient l'existence d'un État de droit, partant, d'une justice.

Le retraité détourna son regard du journaliste, des larmes d'impuissance perlant dans ses yeux. Craignant d'exploser et de bidonner l'entretien, il battit des paupières, l'esprit au meilleur moyen de fléchir son vis-à-vis. Son scoop tenait pourtant la route, les faits parlaient d'eux-mêmes. Dire que le plumitif à la manque, non content d'appréhender des tuiles improbables, rêvassait en prime à sa graille, autrement dit au profit à tirer d'un chantage éventuel. À croire qu'il lui revenait, à lui, la victime, de pistonner des raclures de cet acabit.

Mundele Ndombe survola le bar, l'air de quêter un soutien parmi la clientèle : les cuitards poursuivaient allègrement leur communion avec Bacchus. Sa main droite fourrageant la tignasse poivrée, il grinça des dents, zyeuta à nouveau le résidu de fausse couche : le pisse-copie s'escrimait à préserver son équilibre sur une chaise amputée d'un pied. À des années-lumière de la table, il ingérait le drame avec désinvolture, sans états d'âme. Dépité par tant d'effronterie, le pensionné posa ses prunelles sur ses jumelles.

Mbo et Mpia étaient atterrées. Le temps de déguster la tasse imbuvable, elles s'étaient repliées sur elles-mêmes, soumises une nouvelle fois à l'outrage. Tresses défaites, traits ravagés par la nuit infernale et par les vaines démarches de la matinée, elles gardaient les bouilles baissées, humiliées.

Assise à sa gauche, Mbo, l'aînée, avait le dos tourné à l'entrée et les bras croisés sur la table. Alors que ses avant-bras exposaient des griffades dégueulasses, elle s'échinait à soustraire ses joues entaillées à la vue du reporter. Casée entre celui-ci et le père, sa sœur n'en menait pas large : son cou ressemblait à un tatouage bâclé, tant les griffures s'entrecroisaient dans tous les sens, comme dans une affreuse caricature. Des babouches bon marché aux pieds, les deux filles cachaient des robes souillées sous des pagnes noués autour de la taille. Les larmes taries, elles ruminaient à présent leur débine. Mais le coup vache du chieur d'encre, un coup à s'arracher les plumes, en pleurer de rage et tout chambouler, les anéantissait.

L'immense dancing-bar ressemblait à une porcherie abandonnée. Entrée et sortie par une porte en bois déglinguée. Les murs, défraîchis par une peinture laquée antédiluvienne, offraient ici et là des formes géométriques, tels des gribouillis de peintre naïf. Les grillages des fenêtres accumulaient les pollutions des années. Nul ne s'en approchait. La peur du tétanos. Certains malins les comparaient du reste, par dérision ou autoflagellation inconsciente, aux vitraux d'un sanctuaire profane. Le mobilier métallique avait vécu, la plupart des chaises tenaient sur trois pieds, des cratères dénivelaient le pavement. La piste de danse, constellée de trous béants, semblait vouée à des parties géantes d'*awélé*[1]. Pas un acrobate ne s'y hasardait, le moindre faux pas pouvant occasionner le plâtre. Pour tout couronner, la zizique crachotait des décibels. Les baffles pourris. À l'image de la cité poubelle.

Le crayonneux inclina la tête devant les masques chagrins. Il la releva au bout d'un moment, lorgna les nénettes. L'instant d'après, il soulevait son guindal. Mais l'attention convergée sur sa personne l'empêcha de conclure, l'obligeant à revivre le drame.

La soirée carburait depuis huit heures dans la vieille villa. Les invités, des gens du clan et des voisins, se frottaient les pinces à l'idée de réactiver les molaires cariées à force de mastiquer du vent. Certains squattaient les lieux depuis le matin, question de ne point louper une orgie sans quote-part préalable. L'hôte, le respecté Mundele Ndombe, monument vivant du quartier et son arbre à palabres, n'avait pas mégoté pour fêter ses filles revenues d'Europe, nanties de diplômes de coupe et couture.

---

1. Jeu de société africain. (N.d.A.)

Deux jours durant, il avait fouiné dans les arrière-cours du centre-ville, claquant ses allocs et raflant des victuailles généralement inaccessibles.

Mbo et Mpia brillaient dans des robes de soie en parfaite harmonie avec leur teint bois d'ébène. La vingtaine, bien carrossées, les frangines avaient passé l'avant-midi chez une tresseuse pro. Le résultat remuait le palpitant de plus d'un zigoto : des tresses emmêlées, sophistiquées, relevant du travail de fourmi et, n'en déplaise aux demeurés, piquées dans un publireportage du magazine *Amina.* D'une chaleur communicative, elles allaient d'un convive à l'autre, s'enquéraient de la santoche d'un chacun, déplorant par-ci un pote fauché par la sale bestiole, s'esclaffant par-là ou révélant leur projet d'ouvrir un atelier professionnel dans la parcelle familiale. Celle-ci se prêtait à souhait à une telle activité. Située à l'angle formé par deux rues donnant sur un rond-point, elle offrait maintes possibilités d'aménagement. Ses allures rétro, accentuées par une récente couche de chaux, en imposaient à l'environnement vétuste.

Deux couples du voisinage s'éclipsèrent à minuit. Ils furent bientôt suivis par d'autres couples. Gorgés, dopés gratis, les parasites déclinèrent les invites à poursuivre la bringue jusqu'à l'aube et à plus soif. Et décampèrent avec mouflets et accompagnateurs, créant un grand vide parmi les convives. Les adultes restants se retirèrent dans la villa, tandis que les jeunots gambillaient dans la cour. Les réverbères, qui s'allumaient par intermittence, leur donnaient l'illusion des spots de boîtes de nuit en filtrant la lumière à travers les branches d'arbre.

Un danseur cria tout à coup au sauve-qui-peut et mit les bouts. Les gens accoururent sans retard. Plantés devant la clôture, ils dévorèrent des yeux le camion de l'armée immobilisé devant la villa. Assis dans la cabine du camion, le chauffeur et un comparse observaient de même les curieux. Barbant. D'autant plus que la bâche du véhicule dégageait un silence pesant, chelou, preuve s'il en est d'une présence humaine.

L'arrivée d'une jeep confirma l'appréhension de l'assistance. La bâche s'ouvrit sur une dizaine de malabars excités, procurant des sueurs froides aux témoins: des desparados de l'armée accoutrés en civil. Les Ninjas. La poisse.

En deux temps trois mouvements, les sacripants, qui étaient sur le pied de guerre, bouclèrent le rond-point et dévièrent la circulation, sommant les noctambules de déguerpir et les riverains de se cloîtrer.

D'autres forbans sautèrent dans la foulée du camion. Ils se lancèrent aussitôt dans une sordide manœuvre d'encerclement d'un nid ennemi. Avec ramping, roulé-boulé, quadrillage et tout le cirque de rigueur. Les fêtards ne demandèrent pas leur reste et détalèrent à toute blinde. Une mémé crut son heure venue de passer à la postérité en sautant la clôture. Les records planétaires pulvérisés, elle s'empêtra dans ses pagnes après avoir franchi l'obstacle, s'étala par terre. Out. La troupe, qui s'attendait à cette désertion massive, investit la villa pour procéder au recensement. Pièces d'identité exigées afin de faciliter cette opération nocturne éminemment civique : la carte de membre du défunt parti unique, à défaut, un certificat de baptême !

Un béret vert sauta sur ces entrefaites de la jeep, flanqué de deux gaillards en treillis. Râblé, la bedaine lestée d'un pétard et d'un poignard, le zouave arborait les insignes de major. Alors que ses gorilles braquaient des pétards en l'air, comme pour prévenir un coup tordu du ciel, le foudre de guerre crapahutait sur le trottoir piétonnier, tel un casse-cou sur un champ de mines.

Dès son irruption dans la villa, le chef militaire décocha des dards vipérins à la tribu, puis toisa le proprio. Mundele Ndombe ne sut où se terrer en reconnaissant l'intrus. Le rapport des forces établi, la gradaille cracha l'ordre de servir à boire et à manger au corps franc. Vaine requête. Les fantassins, accoutumés au self-service, activaient déjà les mandibules.

« C'est pas vrai ! s'insurgea Mbo, à l'évidence déphasée. Il faut appeler les keufs. Ces mecs n'ont pas l'droit... »

La mère tenta de la lui boucler. Mais la rebelle la repoussa sans ménagement, puis s'élança sur le major. Elle ne fit qu'un bond. Les gorilles, plus alertes, l'avaient ceinturée. Pas en manque de ressources, la nana canonna un molard dont la puissance de projection sidéra l'assistance : le jet visqueux atterrit sur le portrait du stratège et se mit à filer. Des moustiques bourdonnèrent dans la pièce. Tension max.

Contre toute attente, le major éclata d'un rire sardonique, entraînant sa garde rapprochée dans sa bonne humeur suspecte. Le mufle désinfecté, durcit, il agrippa la fille sans crier gare, la fit valser dans un mouvement tourbillonnaire violent et la cloua devant lui. Graillon.

«Tu ne le sais peut-être pas, grenouille: c'est l'armée qui fait la police dans ce pays, et personne d'autre.»

Mbo tituba sans que nul n'ait vu la taloche partir. Elle s'ébroua la tête comme sous le coup d'une crise épileptique, souleva sa main, la porta au clapet. La louche sous les yeux, maculée de sang, elle fut traversée par un haut-le-corps, dégurgita sans préavis et recula parmi les siens. Rangée. La terreur pivota sur ses talons, s'écroula dans un fauteuil. Examen du cadre pendant que la tribu s'essayait au langage mimique.

Le séjour était vaste, équipé de fauteuils «Boeing» dont les larges accoudoirs rappelaient l'envergure des premiers Jumbo jets. Armoire-vitrine démodée face à l'entrée, sono d'époque dans un angle, téloche en noir et blanc dans un autre. Antiquailles. Accrochés face à face, deux diplômes du mérite civique pendaient au-dessus des portes donnant sur le salon. Poussiéreux. Témoignages du passé. Du kif pour le poster, tiré trente ou quarante ans plus tôt, représentant le mandarin, alors jeunot et tout de blanc vêtu, en compagnie de deux toubabs. Collabo. Fourrée à côté de la cuisine, la salle à manger, qui venait d'être convertie en cantine par ses bras, regroupait ceux-ci dans un banquet bordélique. Vachement décontractés, les combattants piochaient dans les casseroles et se léchaient les pinces, preuves éloquentes de leur capacité d'adaptation. Des plats et des verres non consommés abondaient dans les coins et recoins du séjour. Le major retourna à la maisonnée, une moue de dégoût sur les babines.

« Quel gâchis, ces mets et verres non avalés ! Vous festoyez alors que nous claquons du bec pour assurer votre sécurité. Décapsulez-moi ce Johnnie Walker. Et fissa ! »

Le retraité prit la bouteille de l'armoire-vitrine et la posa sur la table basse, oubliant de proposer un glass au maréchal en gestation. Qu'à cela ne tienne ! Le galonné s'empara d'un verre, dont il balança le contenu sur son hôte. L'ancêtre ne broncha pas, écarquillant toutefois des yeux de stupeur devant telle classe. Le major rinça le guindal avec du scotch, aspergea à nouveau le vieux. La passivité de celui-ci acquise, il remplit le verre et s'envoya une lampée. Vive la République !

« T'es vacciné contre la crise, n'est-ce pas ? » lâcha-t-il après avoir rôté.

La question demeura sans réponse. Loin de s'en offusquer, le major dévora les trois femmes avec une délectation cochonne. Son observation suscitant le trouble dans le camp ennemi, il crut utile de le dédouaner :

« Tu tringles en prime trois chèvres en pleine pandémie ! Quelle injustice sociale ! Viens trinquer avec moi, on finira par trouver un compromis.

– … Le toubib me déconseille les alcools, Monmajor.

– Que ceci soit dit une fois pour toutes : les ordres, c'est moi qui les donne ! »

Et pan ! sur l'accoudoir. Le meuble ancien se disloqua dans un craquement sinistre. La terreur remplit de scotch un verre à moitié plein de bière et le tendit à l'habitant. Celui-ci saisit son calice, le porta à la margoulette. Alors qu'il allait boire, ses globes oculaires, en vol plané sur la figuration, interceptèrent l'insolite, l'empêchant de siffler le cocktail indigeste.

Sur un signe d'un gorille, les troufions s'agitaient subito au coin resto. Les arquebuses récupérées, ils se mirent à tournoyer dans la pièce, comme à la recherche de quelques trophées. Panique des assiégés à l'idée de vivre un pillage en direct. Mais les mutins se ruèrent à la cuisine, où deux fouineurs venaient de dégoter une dame-jeanne de Nabão, un vin estampillé portigue. Santé ! Entre deux coups, ils plongèrent les pattes dans les casseroles et s'en donnèrent par les babines, certains glissant des brochettes et des morcifs de poulet dans les poches. Provisions de guerre. Les lippes pourléchées et les pattes essuyées aux rideaux, ils surgirent dehors, tandis que les piquets du rond-point entraient dans la maison. À table, les z'enfants !

« Tchin-tchin, brailla le major à l'adresse du vieux, à notre soif ! »

Mundele Ndombe approcha son verre de sa bouche. Profitant de l'irruption du bataillon de relève, il déversa son contenu dans sa veste, par petits coups discrets, et récidiva pendant que les crevures raclaient les marmites. Manque de pot, un artilleur éventa la supercherie :

« Monmajor, le civil est en train de t'entuber. Y

boit nisco. À mon avis, c'est un mazout qu'il lui faut : un verre de son pipi avec une larme de mister Johnnie Walker ! »

La harde rappliqua à la seconde en vue d'assister à la séance de dégustation. Pas né de la veille, Mundele Ndombe éclusa sa dose en cinq sec, espérant de la sorte s'épargner le cocktail infect. Sa calebasse se mit aussitôt à tourner, ses tripes à gargouiller. Envie soudaine de vomir. En même temps, l'idée de chicoter[1] un pingouin, comme à l'époque de sa splendeur, germa dans sa caboche. En finir avec le spectacle humiliant. Sauver la face. Mais son regard circulaire lui apprit que son fantasme tenait du casse-pipe. Instinctivement, il baissa les yeux sur son fendard. Son absence, quoique de courte durée, alerta un autre fer de lance de l'armée nationale :

« Chef, ça sert à rien de gâcher du scotch pour cet ancêtre gaga : y vient de mouiller son froc !

– C'est ce style de poules mouillées qui veulent prendre les rênes de ce pays ! s'indigna le pilier du régime. Débarrasse-toi de ce falzar… »

Mbo et Mpia, horrifiées, s'abritèrent derrière leur mère. Pas question de voir le paternel en petite tenue. Le vieux se déloqua rapidos, stimulé dans son déshabillage par des coups de crosse au derrière. Le pantalon à ses pieds, il croisa les bras sur le slibar. Le commandant décréta une autre épreuve d'endurance :

« Tu vas nous exhiber le twist ou le jerk. Ça doit te rappeler ta jeunesse… »

---

1. Fouetter. (N.d.A.)

Le cercle battit la mesure de *Twist à Léo* de Manu Dibango et du bien défunt *Immortel African-Jazz*. Mundele Ndombe, sa réserve émoussée par l'alcool, démarra son one-man-show par un déhanchement débile. Les flûtes et les manivelles agitées à contretemps, il roula des reins, expédia le valseur aux quatre vents. Sa cadence maximale atteinte, il tourniqua le popotin dans les deux sens, se déchaîna. La galerie se marra et en redemanda. Les claviers toujours occupés à claper, elle applaudit à tout rompre, beugla des « ouais ! » enthousiastes et prolongea l'ovation au-delà du spectacle. Dîner dansant. Dans sa retraite, le harem garda les têtes baissées.

« Je t'ai déjà proposé un deal équitable, reprit le major sur un ton ambigu, mais tu sembles n'avoir pas saisi la portée de mon geste. Pourtant, j'aurais pu te virer sans compensation. Comme tu ne veux pas profiter de ma largesse, je vais t'aider à la prendre... »

Puis, s'adressant au corps expéditionnaire, il barrit d'une voix tonitruante :

« Dérouillez-moi ces « ma-sœur »[1] à la traîne ! »

Un silence lourd tomba sur la pièce. La tribu, qui n'en croyait ses oreilles, couvrit le guerrier en chef de regards interrogateurs. Un geste non équivoque réitéra l'ordre. Des supplications fusèrent aussitôt, tandis que les crevards, tous volontaires, se disputaient les proies, mettant le caïd en demeure de procéder à un tirage au sort. À défaut d'une pièce

1. Religieuses. (N.d.A.)

de monnaie, des billets de banque à six zéros prévalant sur la mitraille au pays de faux millionnaires, une capsule de bière soumit les combattants à une règle de jeu. Pile ou face.

Les poulettes ne résistèrent pas à la charge. Traînées manu militari, elles échouèrent dans la chambre des parents. Maléfique. La mère voulut contrer la partouze, mais un membre du commando lui assena un coup fumant sur la nuque, l'expédiant illico chez les ancêtres. Entre-temps, le fier Mundele faisait du surplace, les pattes couvrant ses attributs esquintés par une targette.

« Va te plaindre où tu veux, tonna le chef militaire en vidant la bouteille de scotch. Je t'accorde dix jours pour me céder cette parcelle à mon prix. J'ai pas mal de travaux à y effectuer, en commençant par la destruction de cette baraque. Mon délai n'étant plus reconductible, la prochaine visite sera fatale pour les tiens…

– Monmajor, marmonna le vieux d'une voix péteuse, la réponse à votre offre ne dépend pas de moi. Cette parcelle appartient aux miens depuis trois générations. Acquise par mon aïeul pour services rendus, d'où notre patronyme, elle relève du patrimoine familial…

– J'ai rien à cirer de tes fricotages tribaux, tempêta le client. Mes conditions ne changent donc pas. Autre chose : où sont les cadeaux que ces chèvres m'ont ramenés d'Europe ? Tu ne vas pas dire qu'elles ont oublié leur tonton ! »

Le père s'emmêla les pédales, transformant la visite de courtoisie en un pillage conforme aux traditions de l'armée. Sacs et valises venus de l'étranger furent éventrés, allégés. Casse gratuite, saisie de trophées. Deux heures trente chrono du début à la fin. Et pas un témoin.

Dès les premières heures de la matinée, Mundele Ndombe promena son monde d'un bureau à l'autre. Ses interlocuteurs, compréhensifs, avouèrent toutefois leur impuissance face à la dérive de certains éléments de l'armée. Un conseil lui fut cependant prodigué : saisir une feuille de l'opposition de la descente punitive, avec l'espoir que d'autres allaient la relayer et bouffer du zouave. Peut-être que ces tirs croisés donneraient lieu à une opération de nettoyage…

Le journaleux siffla sa mousse, s'en resservit une autre vite pompée. Ses états d'âme noyés, il bredouilla :

« Je plains votre mélasse, vieux Mundele, mais je ne peux m'exposer sans contrepartie. Nous avons affaire à une bande d'indisciplinés notoires, encouragés par les séides du régime en vue d'accréditer l'idée d'un pays chaotique sans la pogne de fer du tyran. Combien me donnerez-vous si je balance l'info, avec le nom et l'unité de votre persécuteur, puisque vous les connaissez ?

– Je n'ai pas d'argent, mon fils. Mes allocations de retraite ont été englouties dans cette maudite fête. Aidez-nous, je vous en conjure, Dieu vous le rendra…

– Vous avez plus besoin de Lui que moi, répliqua le plumitif. Cela dit, je me casse, vu qu'on n'a plus rien à causer. J'aimerais toutefois savoir pourquoi on vous a drivés sur moi. Serait-ce pour me piéger ?

– On a un peu d'thunes, papa, glissa Mbo alors que le fion se levait. C'est dégueu ce que propose ce monsieur, mais il représente notre dernier recours. On peut lui refiler quelque chose sur le capital de l'atelier de couture. J'ai planqué cet argent, dès notre retour, dans un lieu sûr. Et personne, même pas ma frangine ici présente, ne connaît la cachette…

– Des devises ? s'écria le loufiat, les narines frémissantes, en se rasseyant. Mais alors, ça gaze pour le papier… »

Puis, se tournant vers le retraité, il ajouta avec un plaisir mal dissimulé :

« C'est OK pour la tartine, vieux à moi ! Banco pour l'article. Ton bourreau va être servi. J'vais le descendre en flammes. Mais combien me propose cette charmante de moi… »

Le griffonneur ravala sa question en avisant l'entrée. Cinq crevards venaient de surgir alors que les baffles déversaient leurs décidels un cran plus fort. Mines patibulaires, yeux rougis de hasch, gueules de traviole. Le balèze du commando désigna le groupe à l'écart et fonça dans le bar, suivi d'un comparse. Les autres bloquèrent la lourde. Mbo, qui venait de saisir le regard affolé du crayonneur, tourna la tête et embrassa la scène : les Ninjas s'arrêtaient au milieu du bar, puis viraient vers la table isolée. Des pétards apparurent dans leurs louches et, devant l'assistance tétanisée, crachèrent le feu. Mundele Ndombe, en vieux singe à qui l'on n'apprend pas à faire des grimaces, plongea sous la table en entraînant Mpia. Le gratte-papier, une main sur son gri-gri de protection, reçut la balle dans la poire. De même que Mbo.

African-Soul

SHAMBUY n'a pas le triomphe discret. Expansif, il abat ses puissantes mains sur les épaules du régisseur, le secoue avec chaleur, saute sur un musicien de passage, l'étreint, en embrasse un autre, puis un troisième. Heureux. Look à la Don King, son maître à penser dans le show-biz et mentor historique de Mohammed Ali, le «big-manager» de l'orchestre African Soul ne sait comment faire partager sa joie. En tournée dans l'arrière-pays, son groupe vient de cartonner à l'issue de sa première prestation dans la ville minière.

Superbes, ses gars ont créé l'événement, spécialement le jeune chanteur si bien dénommé Chantal. Il fallait voir ça. Inouï. Après un léger flottement, par bonheur circonscrit à la demi-heure suivant le lever de rideau, Chantal a retrouvé sa forme des meilleurs jours. De sa voix efféminée, un brin nasillarde, il a électrisé le public, remué la salle, enflammé le voisinage. Des couples se sont rués sur la piste et n'en ont plus bougé. Tandis que des groupies assiégeaient le podium, des dizaines et des dizaines d'enragés, chauffés à bloc, montaient sur le plateau pour traduire leur panard. Et comment ! À deux, à trois, à quatre, ils exhibaient, chacun à son tour, le contenu de leurs lasagnes à une salle en délire, récoltant en retour des ovations nourries. Dans une mise en scène du cru, ils exécutaient ensuite la danse à la mode, sans surcharger la scène. Puis s'avançaient à la queue leu leu, lentement, comme dans une cérémonie de présentation des offrandes. Les gestes théâtraux, réglés pour entretenir le suspense, ils collaient le plus de billets possible – en grosses coupures, siou plaît ! – sur le visage en sueur de la vedette. Un sacre. Prélude à d'autres performances.

La recette dépassant les espérances, le big manager embarque ses poulains dans une tournée des grands-ducs. La virée est doublement payante, jure-t-il sur son parcours de croco : elle permet à ses gars non seulement de se détendre, mais aussi et surtout de les mettre en contact avec les viveurs de la bourgade, ce qui peut se répercuter, en espèces sonnantes et trébuchantes, sur les productions suivantes.

Un select club, situé dans le périmètre du lieu de concert, accueille la troupe bruyante. Les astres se révèlent une fois de plus favorables à Shambuy, puisque des allumés raquent à sa place. Mieux, c'est à qui offrirait le plus de bières et de J & B à ses hommes sans jeter l'éponge. Pas en reste, le proprio de la boîte, flatté par la visite impromptue et, bizness oblige, escomptant déjà ses retombées sur son établissement, met celui-ci à l'heure du groupe: le DJ balance de l'African Soul non-stop. Ambiance torride. Les artistes, d'abord regroupés dans un coin, se mêlent aux flambeurs et remontent la température. Bien que sollicité de toutes parts, Chantal échoue sur un cercle encore plus zinzin. Non content de maîtriser son répertoire et de le brailler, ce cercle, composé de jeunes sapeurs et de nénettes du même style, achète des poulets non détaillés. Fiesta.

Le big manager se retire avec quelques musiciens, aux petites heures, en conseillant la modération à ceux qui restent. La tournée, leur dit-il, n'en est qu'à ses débuts. Il les prie également de ménager les groupies, en préservant leur force de frappe financière, au risque de compromettre la suite du programme.

Pro jusqu'au bout des ongles, Shambuy hésite avant de sortir. Sa poule aux œufs d'or! De son allure taurine, il traverse la boîte en diagonale, pique sur la table des gais lurons. Ceux-ci, irradiés par la compagnie de leur idole, ignorent sa présence et poursuivent leurs libations. Le big manager note cependant que Chantal, entouré de la bande qui, quelques heures auparavant, lui avait fait la fête, s'éclate plus que de coutume. Renonçant à sa petite idée, il sourit. Il faut que jeunesse se passe, semble-t-il dire en levant le bras, d'un geste paternel, avant de tourner les talons.

Le concert est tiède le jour suivant, marqué par l'absence du crooner. Comme personne ne sait comment il a terminé sa soirée, tout le monde suppose qu'il est sorti de la boîte défoncé, au bras d'une étoile filante, et qu'il cuve son vin. Le réveil est chaotique quand on n'a pas son BEP d'alcoolo. Shambuy impose à son équipe le black-out sur le fugueur. Pas question de nuire à la tournée à cause d'un inconscient, fut-il mégastar. Le big manager fouine parmi l'assistance éparse, espérant tomber sur les compagnons de nuit de sa vedette. En vain.

Relâche le lendemain. Et toujours pas de Chantal en vue. Affolement de l'imprésario en dépit des propos rassurants de son état-major : le jeune artiste, au demeurant originaire de la bourgade, serait tombé sur une queutarde insatiable. Il finirait par rappliquer, qui mieux est, défauché par sa ravisseuse. De nature sceptique, Shambuy fonce à l'antenne des services de sécurité. Ballon. Il parcourt la bourgade dans tous les sens, surgit dans la famille du cantador, enquête au marché. Tintin.

Bide cuisant lors de la troisième soirée : une centaine de gens campent devant la salle, comme pour un sit-in. Alors que l'orchestre joue les variétés depuis une heure, seulement une dizaine d'inconditionnels, parmi lesquels trois couples d'amis, lesquels, d'ailleurs, se casent dans un coin isolé, paient leur billet et franchissent l'entrée. Parcourir plus de 1 000 kilomètres pour s'époumoner devant des chaises !

Passant aux nouvelles, Shambuy apprend que des rumeurs folles circulent sur sa vedette et que son public, échaudé, boude l'orchestre. Sans la voix de Chantal, grogne un fan en le prenant à partie, l'African Soul ne vaut pas tripette. Shambuy constate également que les badauds, loin de tortiller des fesses et de gambiller, affichent des mines déconfites. Ses tentatives d'expliquer cette tiédeur se heurtent à un mur de silence. Un heureux hasard le met cependant en présence d'un notable. L'homme, surpris par la nouvelle de la disparition, soupçonne une bavure d'un service parallèle et lui conseille de voir le pacha de la bourgade, seule personne à même de le fixer.

Après une longue attente, le big manager entre enfin, le lendemain matin, dans le bureau du manitou. Rondouillet, le menton pareil à une caisse de résonance, le personnage est sans grâce, au verbe haut, fidèle à l'image qu'on lui avait faite. Intendant d'une localité stratégique, charge qui lui a valu le grade d'administrateur spécial, il échappe au contrôle de l'autorité régionale et relève, par quelque curieux artifice, de celui du Père de la nation. D'entrée de jeu, le nabab coupe le sifflet au visiteur :

« Comment faites-vous votre boulot ? C'est scandaleux. Je devrais vous expulser d'ici...

– Je ne comprends pas, Excellence...

– L'individu que vous cherchez a été arrêté, il y a trois jours, sans papiers, et c'est seulement maintenant que vous vous manifestez. Vous vous croyez où ? Dans la forêt ou dans une démocratie laxiste ?

– ...

– Savez-vous avec qui il s'était acoquiné, l'autre soir ? Des bandits recherchés. Votre concert – c'est le seul mérite dont vous pouvez vous targuer

– les a débuchés de leur repaire. Pincés en flagrant délit d'association de malfaiteurs. Ils ont reconnu leurs méfaits devant le tribunal d'exception, dont les arrêts sont sans appel.

– … C'est une méprise effroyable, Excellence. Comme vous le savez, Chantal n'habite pas ici.

– Mais il est chez lui. Deux de ses supporters, membres éminents du tribunal, étaient d'ailleurs présents, à titre strictement personnel, à votre premier concert…

– … Ils auraient pu plaider en sa faveur, établir son innocence !

– Vous déraillez comme votre tournée, cher monsieur : c'est à l'accusé de prouver son innocence et non aux comptables de la justice. Votre bonhomme a retrouvé de vieux complices en revenant à ses sources… »

Étourdi par cette révélation, l'imprésario clignote des yeux pour marquer le coup. Le manitou, conscient de l'effet foudroyant de son annonce, se lève pesamment et contourne le bureau. L'œil mauvais et l'index pointé sur le visiteur, il s'approche, courbe l'échine et, d'une voix étrangement basse, canonne :

« Les poches de votre créature débordaient, lors de son arrestation, de grosses coupures provenant de braquages ! Ce n'est quand même pas vous qui les lui avez refilées au titre de cachet !

– Ah, non ! Excellence, s'écrie Shambuy en repoussant sa chaise, on est clean dans l'orchestre. En plus, Chantal ne pouvait participer, matériellement parlant, à un quelconque braquage…

– Là n'est pas le problème…

– … Puisque nous sommes arrivés…

– Tout doux, tout doux ! rétorque le nabab en se redressant. La mauvaise graine a été repérée à votre concert. Pour entrer dans la salle, il lui a fallu payer… »

Le big manager, qui ne voit pas où le roitelet veut en venir, s'accroche à ses lèvres épaisses.

« Une fois dans la salle, la vermine s'est encore signalée en distribuant des grosses coupures à la clique. À toute la clique. Elle a encore récidivé au club, preuve supplémentaire qu'elle piochait dans un coffre inépuisable. Ce magot, comme ils ne cessaient de dire… »

Shambuy écarquille les yeux, craignant d'entendre ce qu'il redoute.

« Ces billets, disais-je, on peut les retrouver dans votre caisse, chez vos musiciens et – qui sait ? – peut-être dans vos poches. Cela s'appelle faire du recel. Et vous prétendez être clean ! »

Sonné, le big manager avale la tisane amère, puis pare au plus pressé.

« Je m'engage à restituer les billets provenant, comme vous dites, de braquages. Encore faudrait-il que Votre Excellence veuille bien m'en donner les caractéristiques. Mais que faire pour sortir Chantal de cette embrouille monstrueuse ?

– Vous n'avez toujours pas compris ? s'étonne le nabab, un tantinet sarcastique. La racaille ne va plus jamais troubler la quiétude des honnêtes gens.

– Je voudrais bien comprendre, Excellence…

– Décidément, la pilule ne passe qu'au forceps

avec ces satanés musiciens : votre homme et ses acolytes, jugés et condamnés, ont été passés par les armes. Dès le lendemain. »

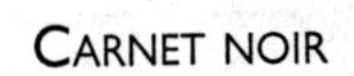

Carnet noir

PHILOMÈNE poussa un soupir au bas de l'escalier. Après un regard terrifié à la rampe, elle surmonta sa flemme et gravit les marches, les unes après les autres, l'air d'essuyer mille calvaires avec des sacs Monoprix. La bobonne n'avait pourtant rien d'une Nana-Benz, appellation des femmes d'affaires de Lomé, dont les formes opulentes, ajoutées au culte de la berline allemande, ont souvent dégonflé leurs consœurs d'Afrique centrale. Elancée et féline, partant, rompue aux danses acrobatiques usinées sous l'équateur, Philomène redoutait paradoxalement la montée depuis son emménagement, il y a sept ans, dans l'immeuble. Barbant.

Parvenue au premier étage, la flemmarde déposa ses achats sur le palier, souffla une bonne minute. Elle reprit sa montée au même rythme, sans forcer la note. Nouvel arrêt au deuxième, ensuite au troisième. Une fois devant sa porte, au quatrième étage, elle s'appuya d'une main contre le mur, totalement claquée, mais fournit encore l'effort surhumain de fouiller dans son sac à main, d'y piocher les clés, d'ouvrir. Onze heures pile. Stressant. Elle n'avait plus qu'à préparer le casse-croûte de ses deux mômes privés de la cantine. La nouvelle, débitée par son petit dernier, ne l'intrigua pas outre mesure.

« Maman, papa est mort ! »

Assis devant la télé, absorbé, Tony ne réagit pas à l'entrée de sa mère et ne réclame que tchi, pressant au contraire ses petits doigts sur la télécommande. À quatre ans, les jeux vidéo priment sur les flashes nécrologiques. Les sacs déposés sur le seuil, la mère balaya le séjour d'un regard anxieux, surfa sur le gamin, non sans refermer la porte d'un coup de patte brutal. Son œil à la téloche la mit sur le qui-vive : le gosse n'avait pas fauché son pater dans son jeu.

« Pourquoi tu dis ça, Tony ? rétorqua-t-elle, alarmée. Ton père est parti au travail.

– Ben ! reprit le mioche sans quitter des yeux le petit écran, y a un monsieur qui a téléphoné… »

La mère, qui venait de reprendre ses sacs de provisions, se figea à l'entrée de la cuisine. Elle déposa sa charge sur le parquet, relança le marmot.

« Quel monsieur a téléphoné et quand ?

– C'est un monsieur qui travaille à l'hôpital. Il a dit que papa est mort… »

Le cœur battant la chamade, Philomène fondit sur le gamin et lui arracha la télécommande, seul moyen de s'assurer de son attention. Qu'est-ce que c'était que cette histoire ? Romain, alias « le grand baobab », son mari, avait quitté l'appart, comme tous les jours ouvrables, à six heures du matin, pour rejoindre le chantier où il chinait. Ce chantier se déplaçait d'un coin à l'autre de la région parisienne, au gré des commandes arrachées par son patron, entrepreneur de bâtiment. Ouvrier spécialisé, Romain montait des échafaudages. Un métier à risques. Mais, après cinq ans d'équilibrisme au-dessus du sol, il excluait toute bourde de nature à l'envoyer dinguer sur la chaussée. Philomène ne savait pas exactement où il trimait, sauf qu'il pointait en grande banlieue. Deux correspondances en trois quarts d'heure de métro, une demi-heure de bus, Romain était censé débarquer à son travail entre sept heures trente et huit heures.

« Qu'a-t-il dit, ce monsieur ? insista la mère, de plus en plus affolée.

– Y'a demandé où t'étais, grognonna le bonhomme. J'ai dit que t'étais partie au Monoprix.

– Je t'ai déjà interdit de prendre le téléphone quand on n'est pas là ! T'es trop petit pour ça. Qu'est-ce qu'il a dit d'autre, le monsieur ? »

Un dring aux résonances de glas arracha la fumelle à ses certitudes. Appel annulé. Bizarre. Personne ne tube à pareille heure. Pétrifiée, ne sachant quel ancêtre invoquer, Philomène couva le poste de l'œil désespéré de celui qui attend une communication en PCV. Quand la sonnerie retentit peu après, elle fit un chut ! en tendant la télécommande à son fils. Mais celui-ci, ignorant le geste, vint se blottir dans ses pagnes. Toujours immobile, craignant d'écrouler son univers dès l'instant où elle décrocherait, Philomène fixa le turlu avec angoisse. Puis, à l'idée qu'une copine chercherait à la joindre, histoire de dire comment va-t-y ou de cancaner, elle sauta sur l'appareil. Le combiné soulevé d'une main nerveuse, l'autre serrant le gamin à l'épaule, elle s'entendit bredouiller :

« Allô !

– Bonjour, madame. Suis-je bien chez M. Makaya, Romain Makaya ? »

Les démarcheurs, rabatteurs et autres maniaques du biniou n'empruntent jamais ce ton macabre, pensa Philomène, démontée par la question et, du coup, désireuse d'en saisir le sens avant de réagir. Chauds, engageants, ils accrochent dès le premier abord. Le pigeon embobiné, infoutu de faire machine arrière ou de ruser, ça brode, entube, roule dans la semoule. Que voulait-il donc au grand baobab, ce blanc-bec ? Lui cloquer – sur l'air d'une oraison funèbre – qu'il avait gagné une salle de bains, une cuisine, un voyage aux Antilles ou un passage à *7 sur 7* ?

« Oui, finit-elle par lâcher d'une voix émue. Je suis sa femme. Qui est à l'appareil ?

– Monsieur Gravet, de l'hôpital Bichat. Service du légiste. C'est moi qui ai appelé tout à l'heure. Prenez votre courage, madame… »

Le visage de la jeune femme vira au noir cirage. Alors qu'un sentiment de malaise montait en elle, mille et une questions s'entrechoquaient dans sa tête, la mettant dans l'incapacité de poser la plus appropriée.

« Que voulez-vous ?

– … Avez-vous quelqu'un auprès de vous ? Un adulte, si possible. C'est important.

– De quoi s'agit-il ? lâcha-t-elle à bout de nerfs.

– Calmez-vous, madame. Vous comprendrez, j'en suis certain, la raison de cette insistance : votre mari est décédé ce matin. Son corps a été transféré à la morgue. Désolé de vous l'apprendre de manière aussi brutale… »

Le combiné s'échappa de la main de Philomène en même temps qu'elle hurlait. Elle tournoya dans la pièce, en battant désespérément l'air, se plongea les louches dans la crinière et s'arracha les cheveux.

Son seul soutien disparu, qu'allait-elle devenir avec trois mômes dans cette ville impitoyable ? Sans travail, comment allait-elle survivre, les prétendus amis, tontons, tantines et frères en Jésus-Christ s'avérant, par expérience, aussi étrangers que le quidam croisé dans la rue ? Comment prévenir les gens du village, là-bas en Afrique, de la catastrophe ? Avec quoi allait-elle rapatrier le corps, elle qui n'avait jamais rien mis de côté ?

Philomène s'écroula par terre en pleurant toutes ses larmes. Blotti dans ses bras, Tony vagissait par à-coups, non sans remâcher pourquoi sa maman chialait. Celle-ci demeurant sourde, le bout de chou chercha vainement son regard. Quand ses yeux finirent par intercepter ceux de sa mère, il lui sauta au cou et, de sa voix mielleuse de petit dernier, celle qui arrache sucreries et douceurs, lui marmonna à l'oreille :

« Dis, maman, si papa est mort, je pourrai jouer avec son mobile ? »

Philomène se remua à la minute. Le téléphone portable ! Romain en avait un, comme tous les mecs branchés de son style. Que n'y avait-elle pas pensé plus tôt ? Elle se rua sur le poste, composa le numéro. Aucune sonnerie. Mais le même bref passage dans le vide qui caractérise les appels lointains. Le disque s'enclencha aussitôt, la renvoyant à un répondeur vocal. Dépitée, elle ne laissa pas de message.

Peu après, elle recomposait le même numéro. Sans succès. Persuadée que son homme n'était plus joignable, parce qu'il gisait dans un tiroir frigorifique, le portable à ses côtés, déchargé, elle se résolut à se rendre à la morgue. En sortant sur le boulevard des Maréchaux, à deux pas de l'appartement, l'hôpital Bichat se dressait à quatre arrêts du PC. En temps normal, elle l'aurait gagné pedibus, pour ne pas lanterner à l'arrêt, mais les circonstances ne le permettaient pas.

Philomène arrangea vaille que vaille sa mise. Ses consignes dictées à Tony, elle se ravisa au moment de sortir : les deux écoliers allaient rappliquer. Tout en leur fricotant de quoi grailler, elle chercha son calepin afin d'alerter une cousine. Dans une situation comme la sienne, la présence d'un proche, outre son côté réconfortant, évite les actes de désespoir et permet d'ingérer le deuil. Sa recherche capota au bout de cinq minutes. Elle se tritura la cervelle pour retrouver le numéro de mémoire. Peine perdue. S'estimant victime d'une conjonction de faits inexplicables, peut-être bien d'un sortilège mijoté au pays, vu que sa dot n'avait pas été répartie entre tous les ayants-droit, ce qui avait mécontenté plus d'un, elle déboula en désespoir de cause dans l'escalier. Deux blocs plus loin, elle fusait dans un immeuble, fonçait vers l'arrière-cour et montait les marches deux à deux jusqu'au deuxième. Hésitation avant de frapper à une porte. Celle-ci ouverte, elle tomba en pleurs dans les bras d'une femme de forte corpulence et, entre deux sanglots, lui fit part de son infortune. Les deux ménesses se précipitèrent vers la petite ceinture.

Peu après, elles sillonnaient les couloirs, puis les allées du centre hospitalier, à la recherche du funérarium. Digne, Philomène digérait son deuil, tandis que Thété, son accompagnatrice, s'orientait dans le dédale et la guidait. Jusqu'à ce qu'elles surgissent sur une courette où des hommes et des femmes, tous blancs et de noir vêtus, allaient et venaient, en parlant à voix basse, signe qu'ils vivaient des moments pénibles. Un employé accueillit les deux paumées. L'objet de leur visite connu, il les pria d'attendre dans une pièce.

Cette pièce ne portait aucune décoration. La lumière pâle lui prêtait une ambiance impersonnelle par trop flippante. Posés aux quatre angles de la salle, des bacs de fleurs semblaient orner des tombes, procurant au visiteur l'impression désagréable de violer une sépulture. Un silence lourd, oppressant, confirmait cette affreuse impression de profanation.

Le regard embué de larmes, Philomène réalisa soudainement sa situation : elle était devenue veuve. À temps plein. Avec son lot de renoncement, de fragilisation, d'humiliations et d'obligations coutumières archaïques. Qu'avait-elle fait pour subir ce sort ?

Son estomac se contracta au fil de la longue attente. Sans qu'elle s'en rende compte, une boule s'insinuait en elle et se logeait dans sa gorge, la mettant à deux doigts d'exploser. En même temps, une frousse irrépressible l'envahissait. Elle allait voir le corps sans vie de son homme, le toucher, le couvrir de larmes. Dans quel état allait-elle le découvrir ? Intact, en bouillie, démantibulé, en décomposition ? Qu'est-ce qui avait pu causer la mort du grand baobab ? Aurait-il succombé à un arrêt cardiaque, à une hémorragie cérébrale ou des suites d'un accident de travail ? Comment peut-on mourir quand on pète de santé ? Tout en ruminant ces questions, Philomène sentit la froideur de la pièce la gagner et se mit à trembloter.

L'employé revint chercher les deux femmes et les conduisit dans une chambre funéraire. Alors que rien ne l'avait laissé présager, les ménesses, le seuil à peine franchi, braillèrent d'un seul coup et s'arrachèrent les cheveux, comme si, à la seule vue de la salle, quelque chose s'était détraqué dans leur organisme. Elles sautillèrent sur place, mine d'exécuter une danse rituelle, soulevèrent les pagnes et les blouses, pleurèrent à chaudes larmes. L'employé, qui avait pris soin de rester en retrait, détourna pudiquement le regard : les gens traduisent leur peine selon des gestes et des jérémiades propres à leur culture, mais la douleur, elle, reste la même. Les deux Africaines s'arrêtèrent net à deux pas du corps étendu et mirent un bémol à leurs plaintes. Souffle coupé et regard fixé sur le mort, elles se dévisagèrent un moment, n'osant en croire leurs yeux, puis, sans mot dire, reculèrent en cata.

« Ce n'est pas le grand baobab ! murmura Philomène en jaillissant dehors.

– C'est pas le père de Tony ! » renchérit Thété à l'adresse du croque-mort.

Brève mise au point sur le pas de porte. Les deuillants de la courette, intrigués par l'arrêt subit de la séance de pleurs, se muèrent en ethnologues, provoquant la gêne de la blouse blanche. Le croque-mort ruina leur vocation en entraînant ses clientes au bureau.

« L'identité du défunt ne fait pas de doute, argua-t-il en sondant les visiteuses. Il s'agit bien de Romain Makaya. Il ne peut y avoir de méprise, car c'est le seul Black décédé cette nuit...

– Si mon mari, qui s'appelle aussi Romain Makaya, est mort, montrez-moi sa dépouille... »

L'employé proposa illico une autre séance d'identification. Après avoir disparu par une porte, il réapparut derrière un guichet avec les effets personnels du mort. Philomène affirmant ne reconnaître aucun de ces effets, l'homme consulta un dossier. Son commentaire fut on ne peut plus clair :

« Le défunt s'appelle bien Romain Makaya. Et habite 356 *ter*, rue Championnet. Mon collègue a appelé, tout à l'heure, au numéro de téléphone qu'il avait donné lors de son admission à l'hôpital…

– Mon mari est parfois patraque, reprit Philomène, mais n'a jamais été hospitalisé. Nous habitons bien au numéro indiqué, malheureusement je ne connais pas ce cadavre-là !

– Eh bien, mesdames, déclara l'employé, confus, je ne sais comment interpréter cette situation. On va faire une enquête. Désolé de vous avoir dérangées… »

La fin de journée fut longue à venir. Dans son espoir de vivre le dénouement de la salade, Thété ne regagna pas son domicile et tint compagnie à sa copine, faisant montre de solidarité jusqu'à lui préparer le repas du soir. À deux reprises, Philomène avait tenté de joindre son mari. Son téléphone mobile restant muet, elle s'était résignée à attendre son retour, vers dix-huit heures. Nul doute qu'il ferait la lumière sur cette histoire de fous. Il était impensable qu'il ignore l'existence d'un homonyme qui, selon toute vraisemblance, proviendrait du même trou que lui. Quant à l'adresse présumée du macchab, elle préférait, du moins pour l'instant, ne pas y penser.

L'appartement reprit son animation habituelle, après dix-sept heures, avec le retour des deux écoliers. Thété se rappela à cet instant son devoir de mère et s'éclipsa. À son retour, elle rejoignit sa copine, toujours abattue, et s'appliqua à la rassurer. Les choses n'allaient pas tarder à s'expliquer. Qui sait si, le mystère élucidé, elles ne se reprocheraient pas de s'être fait du tintouin pour rien ? Le téléphone résonna à six heures pile, prenant tout le monde de court, sauf Tony :

« C'est mon papa ! »

Philomène fondit sur l'appareil. Le combiné à peine collé à l'oreille, elle se détendit sur-le-champ et, le visage radieux, affranchit la maisonnée avec sa question.

« Romain, c'est toi ? Où étais-tu passé ?

– Où veux-tu que je sois pendant la journée ? Je bosse, moi, ma belle. Pourquoi cette question ?

– J'ai essayé de te joindre, mais ton portable n'était pas accessible.

– T'es parfois une vraie cruche, Philo ! Je vais quand même pas tuber du boulot. Sinon le patron me vire pour concurrence déloyale. Qu'est-ce qu'il y avait de si urgent pour appeler ?

– Une embrouille indigeste. Très long à expliquer. Quand est-ce que tu rentres ?

– Dans une ou deux heures. J'ai un rencard... »

Philomène ne pouvait mariner. Et lui rapporta le film, selon l'ordre chronologique vécu. Son mari l'écouta en silence, manifestant de temps en temps sa présence par des « C'est pas possible ! » ou des « Non, pas ça ! ». Quand elle eut fini avec sa relation, il lâcha d'une voix désabusée :

« Mon rendez-vous est annulé. Je vais demander des comptes à ce salopard.

– Comment vas-tu demander des comptes à quelqu'un qui n'est plus ?

– Réfléchis un peu, Philo ! Je vais secouer son cousin qui m'a mis dans ces mauvais draps.

- Quel cousin ?

– Ce merdaillon, bon sang. Je vais te le secouer. Me faire ça, à moi ! À plus ! »

Romain était quelqu'un d'impulsif. Il réagissait à la minute, en paroles ou en actes, préférant regretter sa précipitation après coup plutôt que ronger son frein sur le coup. Maintes fois, il s'était mordu les doigts. Trop tardivement pour rectifier son tir.

Il reprit le métro dans le sens opposé, débarqua rapidement chez Flavien. Les deux gars ne se fréquentaient pas. Ils se connaissaient néanmoins depuis une éternité, pour s'être retrouvés, à plusieurs reprises, à des soirées de deuil ou de fête de leur communauté d'origine. Ils avaient en outre des amis communs.

Flavien créchait dans un squatt inhabité, dans une ruelle de l'Est parisien. De l'avis de ses compères, Flave, comme tout le monde l'appelait, était une référence. En quête d'un faux papier, d'un smoking, d'une nana, d'un contact, d'un coupon de transport ou de toute chose amère à acquérir, il fallait juste lui payer sa boutanche de Valstar, la méchante brune d'un litre, et le laisser agir. Flavien bénéficiait, pour ce faire, de deux atouts : sa petite taille et son bagou. Si sa petite taille lui permettait d'opérer sans attirer l'attention, en revanche, sa tchatche servait à entortiller. Les gonzesses, ploucs et traficoteurs de la tribu en savaient quelque chose. Au jour et à l'heure convenus, le microbe, sa tronche ingrate rayonnante, honorait son engagement, moyennant un pourboire proportionnel au coût de la chose commandée ou à son investissement.

Romain surprit le rase-bitume dans sa niche, lézardant devant la téloche, en train de se sculpter une gueule de bois. Sept bouteilles de Valstar jonchaient la moquette crasseuse, au-dessous de la table basse. Le visiteur en conclut que le filou devait en tenir cinq autres au frais, histoire de les écluser à l'heure H pour déclencher le coma éthylique.

« Ton cousin, qui est hospitalisé depuis trois semaines, a clamsé ce matin, attaqua Romain. Et t'es là à picoler, comme si tu craignais une rupture de stock !

– Cool, man, cool : j'aime pas cette musique-là. Déjà que tu rappliques sans rendève, comme les keufs, et sans t'asseoir. Où est ton problème si ce broussard se laisse crever ? C'est pas toi qui l'enterres, que je sache !

– Décidément, s'emporta Romain, tes neurones sont gâtés par la Val. Ton cousin est mort sous mon identité, parce que j'ai commis la gaffe de lui prêter, sur ton insistance, ma carte d'assuré social, et tu joues au finaud ! De plus, tu m'avais caché son état désespéré…

– Calmos, man. Où est le cactus s'il canne à l'hosto ? Y faut bien préserver leur boulot, aux croque-morts ! Tu crois pas qu'y a trop d'exclus ? »

Son credo affirmé, le rase-bitume tenta de se relever, puis retomba sur le canapé-lit avant de s'en extraire péniblement. Le visiteur suivant son mouvement, curieux de savoir ce qu'il allait inventer, Flavien se dirigea vers le frigo et chopa une autre bouteille. Son remontant à la main, il regagna sa place en grognant :

« Pourquoi en faire un plat, man ? T'as qu'à repriquer ta carte et basta !

– T'as pas l'air de piger, Flave. Je suis désormais considéré pour mort à la Sécu. Impossible donc de faire soigner mes mômes et ma meuf. Pis, étant donné que mon patron va continuer à raquer les cotisations, la Sécu finira par lui signaler, preuves à l'appui, que j'ai déjà lâché la rampe. Je vais perdre aussi mon job. Et c'est pas toi qui vas nourrir mon clan. Tu vois le topo ?

– Cinq sur cinq, man, cracha le trouduc en sifflant sa brune. On reparlera de cette chierie quand je serai remis du choc, okay ? En attendant, tu vas me faire le plaisir de dégager. »

Le microbe se remua du canapé avec l'intention de reconduire l'intrus. Trahi par la tournure du tête-à-tête, le grand baobab, qui considérait le bout d'homme de haut, cogita sur l'attitude à prendre. Il lui fallait négocier pour obtenir une solution buvable. Après tout, on ne traite pas avec les crapules de la même manière qu'avec les cols blancs. Au fait, se surprit-il à se demander, qu'espérait-il en venant voir le filou ? Qu'il lui rende sa carte ou lui en trouve une autre ? À quel nom ? Sa situation n'était-elle pas compromise ? Officiellement mort, il n'avait plus qu'à plonger dans la clandestinité.

Entre-temps, le rase-bitume essayait d'écarter ses pattes en vue de se donner une allure de Rambo. Il y parvint après moult tentatives foireuses et, malgré son équilibre précaire, pointa l'index sur le rabat-joie, mine de lui reprocher sa mauvaise foi...

« Dis donc, man, je les avais allongés pour ce carton merdique !

– Combien t'as payé et quand ? » fulmina le grand baobab, hors de lui.

Son gauche se détendit à l'instant, décochant deux crochets successifs. Le premier fracassa la face de rat, en provoquant une saignée nasale, tandis que le second projetait l'avorton parmi ses cadavres.

Ramolli par les marrons imprévisibles, Flavien resta un moment sans réaction. Le voyant à ses pieds, réduit à sa plus simple expression, Romain renonça à la branlée en hochant la tête. Sous-merde.

Le trouduc ricana tout à coup comme s'il venait de disjoncter, s'essuya le mufle. Il examina ses mains souillées, crachota une vacherie. Sans que Romain y prenne garde, il roula sur lui-même et sauta sur ses pattes. Le balèze exécuta un mouvement de côté. Mais le rase-bitume, plus véloce, plongeait à ses pieds, les happait et tirait, basculant le trouble-fête sur la moquette. Soufflé, infichu d'expliquer ce qu'il foutait sur le tapis cradingue, le grand baobab voulut se relever, offrant son crâne à la merci du microbe. Celui-ci saisit l'aubaine à la seconde. Il rafla un cadavre et le fracassa sur la citrouille en gardant le goulot dans sa paluche. Romain retomba en arrière, les mains sur la boule fendue, et beugla dans sa langue maternelle, lui qui bassine ses paincos avec la langue de Voltaire. Son challenger ne le laissa pas brailler le hit-parade des lamentations. Les yeux fous, injectés de sang, il revint à la charge, plus que jamais décidé à faire un carton. Ses petites jambes calées de part et d'autre du gaillard, il poussa un han ! féroce, perfora le bidon exposé à sa vue, arrachant un cri terrifiant à sa victime. Il enfonça une nouvelle fois son arme dans l'abdomen, récidiva. Un bêlement s'échappa du blessé alors que le microbe, sa revanche prise, retirait le goulot ensanglanté dans un rire démoniaque. Le visiteur porta les mains à son bas-ventre, recueillit les boyaux et les considéra d'un air incrédule. Après un regard suppliant au charcutier, il s'affala dans une mare de sang.

Black and White

COMME LES FOIS précédentes, Leta retrouve le même emplacement pour garer sa voiture. Il fait son créneau, arrête le moteur. Scrupuleux, avec un rituel de caméléon, il ne descend pas tout de suite mais observe les alentours. La cité reste fidèle à elle-même, calme, froide, comme le temps peut l'être par une nuit d'hiver. Lumières partout éteintes, rideaux fermés. Deux perrons, situés aux antipodes, sont cependant éclairés. Sans doute un oubli.

Cet examen fait, Leta consulta la montre de bord : 23 heures 17. Encore treize minutes à poireauter, songe-t-il en se voyant débouler à son rencard, comme d'habitude, à l'heure pile : une manie acquise durant sa jeunesse, après la lecture du *Comte de Monte-Cristo*. Singée par un quadra qui s'évertue à la rappeler, la ponctualité maniaque d'Edmond Dantès amusait la galerie. Leta le savait. Il en tirait même de la considération.

Cinq minutes avant le moment fatidique, il sort de la voiture et fonce, à grandes enjambées, vers sa destination, à quelque six cents mètres de son guet. Costaud, le corps athlétique, Leta porte un blouson de cuir et chausse des baskets. Pour ne pas réveiller les chats qui dorment, aime-t-il charrier. Le portillon n'est pas fermé, le seuil est arrosé par un réverbère. Après de petits coups discrets à la porte, celle-ci s'entr'ouvre. L'arrivant se glisse dans l'entrebâillement, referme la porte en notant que les rideaux sont fermés. Il enlace aussitôt la blonde dans une folle étreinte, l'entraîne en titubant vers le canapé, où ils s'écroulent. La nymphe roucoule, piaille, pouffe en sourdine et, ses doigts de fée mis en branle, entreprend de dégrafer le blouson du julot. Celui-ci, loin de rester inactif, bécote la joconde, la reluque, le re-bécote, éprouve son contentement sans mesure. Toute passion secrète reste volcanique. Sachant ce qui va se passer s'il n'écourte pas la séance, Leta se libère en douceur, retire son blouson et s'en va le déposer sur une chaise. Quand il se tourne vers la joconde, celle-ci s'est levée et tend l'ouïe.

« Qu'est-ce qu'il y a, Ginette ?

– T'as rien entendu ? Une voiture vient de s'arrêter ! »

Leta hausse les épaules et se dirige vers un meuble. Il y chope une bouteille et s'offre un double whisky, en alléguant la baisse des températures. Le verre sifflé, déposé sur une table, il constate que la méduse, encore plus raidie, fixe la porte. Au même moment, la portière d'une bagnole claque et celle-ci démarre.

Leta est troublé à son tour : il n'avait pas remarqué de circulation en arrivant. De plus, un square se dresse devant le pavillon, excluant toute descente nocturne à cet endroit. Par ailleurs, Ginette, divorcée de fraîche date, vit avec ses enfants. Ceux-ci sont partis la veille en vacances et ne vont pas rappliquer de sitôt. Son ex, un bonhomme excentrique, n'est pas non plus du genre à emmerder le monde. Qui pouvait donc venir troubler leur tête-à-tête ?

Fort de son physique de malabar, Leta s'avance vers la porte d'un pas décidé. Alors qu'il pose la main sur la poignée, son sixième sens l'en dissuade. Un bref instant, il flotte dans le coaltar. Puis percute le judas. Son œil à peine collé à l'ouverture, il recule en vitesse. Ginette, encore plus troublée, le fixe d'un regard interrogateur.

« La vache ! s'exclame le quadra, les yeux exorbités, en réduisant son volume vocal. Comment a-t-elle fait pour venir jusqu'ici ?

– C'est qui ?

– Brunette, ma femme. On a eu une dispute épouvantable. Elle a appris, je ne sais trop comment, notre liaison... »

Inconsciemment, Leta s'assure à nouveau que les rideaux sont fermés et les lumières extérieures éteintes. Il prend de même l'initiative d'éteindre le lustre, laissant la pièce baigner dans la lumière du couloir. La réaction ne se fait pas attendre. Brunette, voyant le couvre-feu décrété dans la maison, cogne à la porte en vitupérant.

« Inutile de faire ton malin là, Leta. Je t'ai vu entrer de mes propres yeux. Sors de là. Ta sale putain là, elle ne va pas jouir cette nuit. Je vais la mloumlou[1] pour lui apprendre à voler les maris d'autrui. Sors de là, Leta ! »

Ginette, déréglée, se retire dans le couloir. Le sordide de la situation est tel que, consciente de sa responsabilité, elle tremblote de rage et d'impuissance. Prise la main dans le sac, elle se sent ridicule, désarmée, dénudée. D'une voix inaudible, elle lance toutefois à son amant :

« Elle est complètement hystérique, ta femme. C'est Negrita qu'elle aurait dû s'appeler et non Brunette. Fais quelque chose, sinon elle va alerter le quartier ! »

Leta, piqué au vif, décoche à la méduse un œil réprobateur. Sa salive ravalée, il trépigne d'indécision, puis accouche d'une voix sans aménité :

« La meilleure chose à faire, à mon avis, c'est d'alerter les flics. Ma femme a une peur bleue des uniformes.

– Tu parles des flics ! Autant placarder nos ébats sur les murs de la cité. T'as pas encore compris que ce quartier est gagné à l'extrême-droite ? »

Leta, qui n'en peut plus de souffler le chaud et le froid, explose à cette réplique :

« Cela ne t'empêche pas de t'offrir de petits plaisirs, à huis clos, avec un immigré, black de surcroît !

– Commence par dresser ta femme au lieu de

---

1. Poignarder (en abidjanais). (N.d.A.)

chipoter, s'énerve la blonde sans hausser le ton. On ne se conduit pas de cette manière dans un pays d'accueil. Où se croit-elle, celle-là ?

– Tu me provoques, Ginette, grogne Leta en la rejoignant dans le couloir. L'hospitalité est une disposition d'accueil qui ne s'acquiert pas. N'est pas hospitalier qui s'en vante et qui, par ricochet, la dénature. Il n'y a plus d'hospitalité quand on ressasse son état à l'étranger, ce qui est une manière peu cavalière de l'inviter à débarrasser le plancher. Dans toutes les traditions, l'étranger décide lui-même du jour de son départ.

– Arrête cette logorrhée indigeste à l'abbé Pierre et ramène ta folle chez le psy ! »

Dehors, Brunette martèle la porte en vociférant contre la paire adultère. Leta rentre à pas feutrés au salon, où il récupère son blouson avant de rappliquer au PC de campagne. La voix grave, il confie à la nymphe que si, d'aventure, il pointait le nez à l'extérieur, il ne se retiendrait pas d'infliger une correction à sa meuf, bien qu'elle soit dans son droit, du moins dans la conception africaine du couple, ce qui risquerait d'ameuter le quartier. En revanche, si elle sortait, elle Ginette, sa présence dégonflerait la gendarme.

« Tu me vois affronter cette folle ? Avec son couteau, un malheur est vite arrivé. »

Leta glisse une main dans son blouson, en sort un pistolet automatique. Devant le regard ahuri de sa dulcinée, il lui avoue ne jamais s'en séparer. Une précision toutefois : les vigiles sont interdits de port d'arme. Mais, pour avoir contourné la réglementation en la matière, il peut trimbaler son arquebuse sous certaines conditions.

« Je connais bien Brunette. Comme beaucoup d'Africaines, elle croit que la femme blanche, physiquement molle, compense sa faiblesse par le recours à une arme à feu, notamment dans un cas comme celui-ci.

– Ça sort d'où, ce préjugé raciste ?

– Il est véhiculé par vos films, qui font l'apologie de la femme fatale : elle te flingue même pour une toux non programmée ! Mais revenons à nos moutons : il suffit que Brunette te voie avec le pistolet pour mettre les adjas.

– Mais, mon chéri, je ne sais pas tirer !

– Qui te demande de tirer ? Tirer d'ailleurs sur qui ? Pour que je me retrouve avec un macchab à rapatrier sur les bras ? Voici mon plan : tu sors, j'allume une minute pour qu'elle ne se fasse pas d'illusions et, tu peux me croire, elle va cavaler à la vue du pétard.

– Et si elle résiste ?

– Impossible. Grande gueule mais froussarde. Elle est même capable de te supplier de me prendre en location !

– Je suppose que tu plaisantes !

– Bien sûr. »

Leta montre à son amie comment utiliser l'arme en cas de légitime défense. Il ne l'affanchit pas, mais prend soin de caler le cran de sûreté. Ginette siffle un whisky, renonce après coup à la bagarre. Trop dangereux. Ses enfants à élever. Une réputation à sauvegarder. Le quartier à ménager coûte que coûte.

Dehors, Brunette menace de maintenir son siège tant qu'elle n'aura pas lardé la toubabesse.

« Culottée, celle-là, narre-t-elle à un auditoire invisible. Une vraie salope. Elle se permet d'appeler mon mari là à la maison. Et ce bon à rien, qui n'osait pas causer à une vraie femme chez nous là-bas, prétexte d'aller au travail pour venir ici. Moi, Brunette, fille de mama Ana et de papa Didier, je ne donne pas mon mari en cadeau de Noël. Sors de là, Leta ! Ça caille dehors et je finirai par geler ! »

Le Black fixe Ginette avec perplexité :

« Tu ne m'as pas dit que tu avais téléphoné chez moi.

– Comment as-tu alors su qu'on avait rendez-vous ?

– C'était chose convenue, il y a trois jours, lors de ton passage au supermarché où je bosse… C'est donc toi qui lui as mis la puce à l'oreille !

– Je lui ai demandé si tu étais là, en me présentant sous un faux nom, et l'ai priée de te rappeler notre rendez-vous. Y a pas de mal à ça. Elle m'avait paru coulante et digne de confiance…

– Pour mieux te tirer les vers du nez. T'as vu le résultat ?

– Après tout, on ne va pas continuer à se cacher, comme des voleurs…

– Et tes directeurs de conscience, as-tu pensé à eux ? Que vas-tu leur dire ? »

Puis, comme dans un monologue, le mastard poursuit :

« Après ton coup de fil, Brunette me fait sa crise, sans pour autant m'avouer que tu avais appelé. Dès qu'elle me voit sortir, elle se doute que les coïncidences n'existent pas, saute dans un taxi et me file le train. Quand je me gare à l'endroit habituel, elle fait arrêter son tac hors de vue, repère la piaule où j'entre et vient s'y faire déposer. Simple. Bête. Efficace. »

Ginette avale un autre verre de whisky. Retapée, elle prend son courage à deux mains, arrache le pistolet et sort. Dès qu'elle contourne le mur de derrière, elle tombe sur la meuf qui s'avance à sa rencontre, drapée dans des pagnes, et braque la seringue. Leta, qui gère la crise derrière un rideau, allume à ce moment précis, puis éteint, obtenant sur-le-champ l'effet escompté : à la vue du pétard pointé sur elle, Brunette fait machine arrière. Une détonation éclate dans la foulée, obligeant Leta à rallumer. Brunette, d'abord étourdie, esquisse une grimace de douleur, puis s'effondre d'une masse. Tourneboulée par la tournure de la promenade de santé, Ginette rentre en catastrophe. Pour se buter à Leta à l'entrée de la cuisine.

« C'est quoi, ce coup de feu ? braille le vigile en arrachant le pistolet. Tu ne me l'as pas butée ! »

Le Black hurle en fondant sur la morte, son arme à la main. Un deuxième coup de feu siffle à ses oreilles alors que, plié en deux, il chiale devant le corps sans vie de sa femme. Leta se jette à la seconde par terre, braque le pétard sur le pavillon d'à côté. Deux minutes passent. Soudain, il perçoit le reflet d'une fenêtre qui se referme à l'étage, localise le tireur fou, saute sur ses pieds et presse la détente. Tintin. Le temps de débloquer le cran de sûreté, il voit le feu craché et tombe, mortellement atteint. Crime passionnel, titre, le lendemain, une presse innommable.

TABLE